Index

Pizza Crow I

I have a bad habit of leaving my window open in the middle of the night. I suppose it comes from living in a hot room in the Florida suburbs for the first twenty years of my life. But now I'm an adult and I live in a bad area. I really should be more careful.

Luckily, I haven't had a break-in by an actual person, but I did wake up one morning to find a crow had found access to my room. He was pecking at my desk, trying to pick up the leftovers from a s'mores Pop-Tart I'd left out overnight. I don't eat the edges, they taste too dry.

I wasn't really scared of the crow, since it didn't seem agitated or diseased. I figured if I just ignored him, he'd run out of scraps and just leave on his own accord. I was right to an extent.

The crow left, but unexpectedly he would return several hours later. I thought perhaps he wanted more food, but to my surprise, he instead dropped a small gift on my windowsill before quickly departing. Upon closer inspection, it was a gold wedding band with the word "Irreplaceable" engraved along the side in an Olde English cursive. My first thought was that this bird was paying me for the meal and, as a struggling twenty-something, I immediately began to imagine how I could profit from this. If I kept pawning the rings the crow brought me, I could start a second income with just the parts of my breakfast without any frosting.

It seemed genius.

From then on, as long as I left out my Pop-Tart scraps, the crow would return every day, bringing with him some small shiny ring. Gold and silver. Thick and thin. Some plain, some engraved. None were ever truly worth anything, however. I was patiently waiting for the day one came with a diamond on its head, but that day would never come.

Once I switched his treats from Pop-Tarts to store-bought bird seed, I immediately noticed a change in my rewards. In exchange for the seeds, I was given trucker caps, the cheap kind with the netting in the back. They were, once again, nothing valuable, but I definitely picked-up on the fact that it seemed different foods were traded with different currencies. So I collected a few of the caps, just enough to hand out to my friends, and moved on to some other edible to see its effect.

Crackers got me bumper stickers. Berries got me spools of string. Shredded chicken got me McDonald's toys. I kept switching it up hoping that, eventually, I'd land on something valuable. But then, handing over a french fry bought me a seashell, and after that I decided to take things in a completely different direction.

You see, I shouldn't have gotten a seashell. I live in Peoria, Illinois. There's no beach from which this crow could be traveling to. Not with how fast I was receiving them. I realized then that something strange was going on. And it wasn't some get-rich-quick scheme. It was a paranormal phenomenon. Something worth recording.

Over the next two months, I started a meticulous experiment. Every three days exactly I would switch up the food and then write down the rewards. The results of my study are listed below.

DATES	FOOD	REWARD
6/12 - 6/14	Geckos from the yard	Thimbles
6/15 - 6/17	Apple sauce	Teeth bones [note: larger than human]
6/18 - 6/20	Rice	Old pennies
6/21 - 6/23	Worms	Brightly colored shoe strings
6/24 - 6/26	Spoonfuls of hot sauce	Arrow heads
6/27 - 6/29	Plain water	Cigarettes [note: unused]
6/30 - 7/02	Mushrooms	Skittles [note: one by one]
7/03 - 7/05	Peanuts [note: in shell]	Plastic jewels and sequins
7/06 - 7/08	Hot strip steak	Sewing needles
7/09 - 7/11	Tomatoes	Live hermit crabs
7/12 - 7/14	Crickets	Razor blades
7/15 - 7/17	Pizza	Pages

The last entry on this list was unintentional. The pizza was actually for me, I'd left out a dish of plain salt for the crow. It seems however the crow prefers Italian food to a mountain of spice. I'd left the box of pizza on my desk as I used the bathroom, and in just those short five minutes, the crow kicked over the bowl of salt, flew through my window, grabbed one of the razor blades he'd gifted me, and sawed through the top of the pizza box. When I came back from the bathroom, the crow had gone through at least three slices all by himself. Upon seeing me, he looked panicked then quickly flew off.

I was mad at first, and I had absolutely no intention of feeding the crow another slice. However, that changed the following morning, when I received my present. It wasn't nearly as dazzling as some of his earlier gifts. It was just a page of lined notebook paper rolled up in his claw. When the crow dropped it, I quickly unraveled it and read its contents. It fascinated me.

There were ten paragraphs, all written in blue pen. The language was English and the font was print, not cursive. There were several little typos scribbled out and replaced. And there was a title at the top, but it had no author. This was clearly the first page of a much larger story. And to get the next page all I had to do is continue to feed the bird the same type of pizza. It took a total of eighteen days before I reached the conclusion.

I present the story in its entirety, "Bedfellows", in the following chapter.

Bedfellows

Andrew left his office job shortly after he and his girlfriend Catherine broke up. Due to the unusual situation of their relationship, Andrew would have to take on a night shift in order to keep his and his ex's lives respectfully separated.

Andrew wanted to stay close to his friends and family in the Bay Area, but his job options were limited. Most were security guard positions which frightened poor Andrew who had experienced a home invasion firsthand when he was just a boy. Criminals, specifically burglars, terrified him ever since. This left Andrew with a handful of delivery driver openings to choose from. He went with the most interesting of which: NightCap. They deliver gourmet cappuccinos after dark.

Andrew wouldn't have to act as a barista, just the driver, which was great because he had a license to drive and a terrible culinary sense. If there's more than two ingredients involved, Andrew just can't get it to taste right. One of the many reasons his ex found their short time cohabitating to be a frustratingly one-sided experience.

The first week of his late-shift was rough, especially whilst transitioning between sleep schedules. Andrew kept awake by stealing a few sips of some of his customers' beverages. Just the extra-caffeinated ones that only require a small sip to get the buzz.

Majority of Andrew's deliveries went to the areas surrounding Stanford and Berkeley. A lot of researchers and start-ups pulled all-nighters analyzing their experiments and needed to stay sharp as to not nod off from exhaustion. Unsurprisingly, these clever minds were hard to fool and some became wise to the slightly diminished levels in their cups.

"There's only eighteen and a half ounces. There's usually twenty," griped a particularly observant scientist with an eye for minute differences. He measured the size of atoms for a living.

Despite his dreary head, Andrew was quick with a good excuse. "That's just so there's room for cream and sugar!"

"Well then..." droned the scientist. "Go ahead."

"Go ahead what?" shrugged Andrew.

"Add in the cream and sugar for me!" demanded the scientist.

Andrew gulped. Cream *and* sugar. Plus coffee. That's three ingredients total. One ingredient over his skill cap. He tried his best, but alas managed to screw up even such a rudimentary recipe.

"What the hell did you do?" griped the professor. "Now it tastes like burnt pistachios!"

Luckily this professor only asked for a refund instead of placing a direct complaint with Andrew's boss. After that ordeal, Andrew decided no more free drinks. Considering his sleep cycle should have conditioned by now, he worried something else may have been keeping him down during his shift. The obvious culprit was his recent break-up.

Andrew decided to use his newly acquired health insurance to visit a therapist, Dr. Azikiwe. He agreed Andrew's low energy wasn't just sleep related, he seemed to be suffering from depression. Dr. Azikiwe prescribed him a mood stabilizer.

"These should keep you from getting too low," explained the doctor. "Just take two of these at night and you'll be all set."

Dr. Azikiwe was still new to Andrew as a patient and didn't understand that his job was at night. Otherwise, he would have instructed him more specifically and more properly to "take two before bed."

Andrew followed his misinformation to a T and ended up swallowing his medicine minutes before picking up his first order. It was three flat whites and two long blacks, ordered to a marine conservatory in Moss Beach. That's only a twenty-minute drive from their kitchen in Daly City, as long as Andrew took the Pacific Coast Highway, a scenic stretch of road elevated just over the coast.

Many mood stabilizers are antipsychotics that induce a calming effect following the initial consumption. This effect can be noticeably dizzying, and its durations vary from person to person. But despite the low dose prescribed to Andrew, he seemed to be significantly more affected than the usual patient.

As he traversed the winding cliffs beside the ocean, his delivery began to spritz all over his car's center console, pooling at the bottom of his cup holders. Andrew's turns were becoming erratic and fidgety as he swerved all over the road, splashing the beverages' liquids side to side. Andrew's meds were blacking him out.

There weren't many drivers on that road after midnight, but luckily a security guard on his way to work was only a few meters behind Andrew. He witnessed Andrew's sedan lose control completely and crash into the shoulder of the road. It smashed right though the guard rail and hurdled over the side. It began to violently twist as it rolled down the cliffside towards the beach below.

The security guard stopped his car alongside the road and put on his blinkers. He tried his best to descend the steep cliffs beside the road, heroically darting to the wreckage of Andrew's car. When he finally reached the crumpled mess of steel, it was flipped over on its head. He saw a dark puddle spilling out from the cracked front side window.

The security guard stooped down and looked inside expecting to see the driver's head split open and bleeding. But instead, the driver was missing, and all that was left were five cups of coffee spilled on the overturned roof of the interior.

Andrew's body was luckily teleported far away from the accident as soon as he'd fully lost consciousness. At that moment, he was transported to a bedroom in Redwood City, long before his car even impacted the guard rail.

Andrew's pills had knocked him out cold to the degree where he could have slept another four or five hours if undisturbed. But the bedroom Andrew was in was not a part of his dingy junior-one in San Bruno. There were no crumbs on his back and the mattress was on top of an actual bed frame instead of lying directly on the floor a foot from the nearest television. The pillows had covers and there were multiple blankets and even sheets! These were not the conditions Andrew had grown accustomed to. These were the comfortable arrangements of his former relationship.

Andrew was sleeping beside his ex yet again. Returned magically to the apartment they used to share months ago. Neither of them was aware they were bedfellows once again. While Andrew slept under the spell of his medicine, Catherine was passed out from pure exhaustion. She'd been drawing for hours, trying to complete her latest contract as a graphic designer. When the muse hits, Catherine could be up for three days straight preparing a final draft. This workaholic lifestyle is one of the many reasons Andrew couldn't stand their brief period of cohabitation. There was never enough "us-time".

While Catherine *was* exhausted, she's always been a light sleeper as opposed to Andrew who, drugged or not, sleeps like a rock. So when Andrew's boss began calling for Andrew's whereabouts and the whereabouts of their customer's orders, the constant buzzing woke Catherine up from her deep slumber. Immediately, she knew what had happened. Andrew must have disregarded their careful arrangement and fell asleep at the same time as her.

Catherine and Andrew were cursed. If they ever fall asleep at the same time, they end up in the same bed together. The bed in this scenario is the chosen sleeping arrangement of whoever falls asleep first, whether that be a couch, a sleeping bag, or the traditional mattress. Luckily, it was Catherine who'd fallen asleep first in this case or else Catherine would have ended up on Andrew's passenger side and they both would have plummeted to their death.

Catherine, unaware of Andrew's innocence, disregarded this stroke of luck and unsparingly kicked Andrew in the ribs, launching him out of the bed and onto the floor. Immediately after realizing he'd been awakened, Andrew remembered he was last driving a car. He began swearing and screaming while attempting to find his buzzing phone. It'd fallen out of his pocket into the bedsheets. Andrew quickly tossed his body back onto the bed.

"No! No!" shouted Catherine as she delivered kick after kick to Andrew's face. He wasn't trying to join her again, he just wanted his phone. But it was hard to find it with his ex's toenails being thrust into his eyes.

"I'm just... trying to... quit it!" he demanded. With his sense of touch alone, Andrew managed to find the phone by following the vibrations. He grabbed the phone and escaped his ex's wrath. Running out into the privacy of her hallway, Andrew answered the phone and tried his best to excuse himself from his evening's responsibilities.

He immediately blamed the medication for the crash. His boss wanted to know why he walked away from the scene of the accident as the authorities had reported. He lied and explained that he wasn't sure how he survived but he flew out the car window during the crash. He woke up some distance away carried to safety by some unknown Samaritan. His boss believed his story citing that "he sure sounded like his face had taken quite the beating." This was true, but it wasn't from the accident. Catherine's kicks had swollen his lips.

His work world settled, Andrew still owed his ex-girlfriend an apology. She'd overheard his excuse to his boss but she still wasn't happy.

"You need to accept some responsibility," scolded Catherine. "I get that you were prescribed incorrectly, but the fact that you didn't even consider medicine could make you drowsy is not very adult. You need to look out for you!"

"I have been," sneered Andrew. "It's fucking depression medication, okay? You're the one who always told me to go get an official diagnosis. Well I did and I'm very lucky it didn't kill me."

"Look I'm glad you're okay... but you almost ruined something I've been working hard to maintain," griped Catherine pointing to the new pictures hanging on the wall. They were of her and a new man. A lot taller, a lot more built. "You wanna' talk about luck? This is the one week Yuki's gone on business."

Andrew looked at the spot where the photos of Yuki now hung. He frowned and sighed, "You replaced the old pictures..."

"We never had any pictures there?"

"I know. But there was a really cool picture of a shipwreck. It looked kind of old and elegant."

"Do you... want it?" sighed Catherine. "It's just down in storage."

Andrew nodded. He then asked Catherine if she could lend him a ride home, but she refused. "The last thing I want Yuki to hear is that someone spotted you in my car."

Times like this are why Andrew chose to move out into an apartment only twenty minutes away, a fairly priced Uber could remedy the situation. Andrew couldn't imagine how bad it would be if he'd moved to a new state. He'd be in massive debt every time an "accident" occurred.

Andrew's boss gave him the rest of the night off to recover, so when he got home he considered balling up on his mattress. But despite his meds almost killing him, they *were* having a positive effect on his mood. And for the first time in ages, he felt like he'd be wasting time if he didn't take advantage of this night off. He decided instead that he had the energy to go out to the bars. They wouldn't be closing for another two hours.

Andrew decided on a small pub within walking distance to his flat. He had to wait in a small line outside, which gave Andrew's mind ample time to reconsider his choice and book it back home. He decided to concentrate on the thought of those photos on the wall in Catherine's apartment. Naturally, seeing Catherine moving on urged him to do the same. And that wouldn't be possible if he didn't get outside and meet somebody new.

But as Andrew made his way into the pub, he found it hard to leave his stool at the bar and enter the crowd on the dance floor. He'd forgotten how kinetic this bar got and began to regret his selection. He considered pounding down a few more drinks to ease the tension but it wasn't that simple. It was nighttime, Catherine's sleeping time, if he drank too much and passed out, he could end up back in her bed once again. Begrudgingly, he had no choice but to pace himself.

For a moment, Andrew considered packing up and going home, where'd he use his drunken fuel to scream angrily at a video game. But just before giving up, a young lady by the name of Diane suddenly sat down beside him and introduced herself. She looked a year or two older than him and was absolutely stunning. She claimed she recognized him, but he assured her he would have remembered such a pretty face.

"I was probably wearing a hairnet and a face shield," she laughed. "I work for Marrisoft. I do materials testing."

"Wait," chuckled Andrew, "are you saying I delivered to you?"

Diane nodded excitedly. "Just last weekend! There's actually a 24-hour diner next to our lab, but they don't make anything like you guys do. You're the only place serving peppermint macchiato at 4AM."

Andrew shrugged. "Well don't get your hopes up if you think your gonna' get a free one off me. I don't actually make the drinks myself."

"Oh of course not! Trust me... I don't need any caffeine tonight!" she laughed loudly. She gave her nose a little flick.

Perfect. thought Andrew. *She's high off her ass on coke.* Normally, this would be a sarcastic statement. But in Andrew's case, he really did appreciate her commitment to hard drugs. One of the many troubles Andrew had while going out on the town was that once he got started he couldn't stop till six in the morning. Which sounds cooler than it is feasible. Only at 6AM would Catherine be waking up to start another round of drawing, making it safe for Andrew to doze off.

Andrew was happy that Diane's coke habit should keep her awake longer than the usual hookup. All that was left to do was fill in all that time they had together.

Jumping immediately into a sex scene would seem a bit misleading considering there was in fact a lot of deep conversation up until they finally made love between the hours of four and five. Before they boned, they shared their respective struggles with chronic illness. And before they banged, they

13

discussed their mutual fear of firearms and explosives. And before they humped, Diane went into greater detail on her work with quantum tunneling. And before they sucked, Andrew discussed the numerous details about our society he considered largely subpar.

They're conversation only transitioned into foreplay when they were done geeking out about their childhood experiences with Hot Shots Golf. An hour of tiring fornication passed by before the two laid satisfied and exhausted on Andrew's floor-bound mattress. After an hour longer of dizzying pillow talk, Andrew shut himself up and allowed them both to get some rest when it was safely six o'clock.

Andrew slept peacefully with Diane in his arms till about noon. At this point, he was awoken to the sound of something wet spilling followed by Diane's shrill voice shrieking at the top of her lungs.

"Are you fucking serious?!" shouted Diane. "Who the fuck are you?" Diane shot off the mattress and stood at its bottom edge. Andrew shot up out of his sleep and saw Diane's naked body was now covered in yellow, chunky fluid. He turned to his right to see the same thick slime around the rim of his ex's mouth.

"Catherine?" shouted Andrew.

Catherine didn't respond. She just laid there beside him, looking dazed. Her eyes fluttered. She looked around the room, turning her neck slowly. She looked completely baffled. She kept rubbing the top of her head.

"I didn't consent to any threeway you fucking perverts!" shrieked Diane.

"No! No!" shouted Andrew. "God no, she's sick! Can't you tell?"

"Who the fuck is she, Andrew?" griped Diane, sliding the vomit off of her chest onto the floor.

Andrew thought fast and came up with a good lie. "She's my roommate," he explained. "She gets sick drunk then blacks out. Sometimes she falls asleep in the wrong bed."

Diane huffed angrily. "God, what the fuck was I thinking coming home with the delivery guy," she steamed. "You don't even have a fucking bedframe!" Diane began throwing on her clothes overtop of the remnants of sick still dripping off of her.

"Please, I insist you use my shower, then I can call you a ride home," pleaded Andrew, but Diane wasn't having it. She shook her head, grabbed her purse from Andrew's couch, and ran for the exit.

Left alone, Andrew turned to Catherine and grabbed onto her shoulder. "Hey!" he shouted, while shaking her violently. "Heyyy!" He shook a little harder. "Catherine, why the fuck are you drunk at this hour?"

Catherine's eyes began darting about to all sides of the room as she suddenly snapped back into full consciousness. Her face looked surprised as she wiped her mouth and look around at her whereabouts. "J-Jesus Christ," she stuttered, in amazement. "He knocked me out..."

"What?" exclaimed Andrew. *"Did you get mugged?"*

"Yuki..." she gasped. "That bastard Yuki. I knew he had a temper but now I see it's serious."

"Oh my god," exclaimed Andrew softly. "You're dating a fucking wife beater!"

"Oh calm down," hushed Catherine, sitting herself up onto her elbows. She began feeling around the top of her skull for a lump and or a bruise. "There's nothing noticeable on me is there?"

"Are you trying to cover up your fucking assault?" growled Andrew. "Cathy, you've got to..."

"Catherine. We're not dating anymore. You will call me Catherine."

Andrew sighed aggravatingly. "*Catherine*... you've got to go to the authorities."

Catherine shook her head with a sly smile. "Trust me, neither of us want that."

"I don't like you, yeah, but I don't want *this* either."

"Yes... you do." Catherine rolled her eyes. "This is worth it, if it solves all our problems."

"How on Earth..."

"His parents own Sato, Andrew," she explained. "That's *the* Sato Saki. They're a big brand in Japan. And he has the connections that can get me a job with them."

"No..." said Andrew. "Please. This isn't worth it. Just let me stick with my night job. It's really not that bad."

Catherine held out her arms, gesturing to Andrew's squalid living conditions. "You should be working as an engineer! Or a lab tech! Look what this curse has done to you! You're fucking struggling to get by. You can't survive in San Francisco delivering coffee for a living," pleaded Catherine. "I'm going to get a job on the other side of the world. It's happening just like I said it would. I'll draw the art for their labels and once they're a hit, I break-up with the brat and they'll need to keep me on board to keep using my designs."

Andrew stared down at the stains and holes in the bare fabric of his mattress. If he could just afford a fitted sheet, his room would look so much nicer. "If you live in Japan, and we still fuck up, it's going to be quite the expensive mistake to fix. The ticket back home would be a thousand dollars."

"That's a negative way of looking at it," sighed Catherine. "After all, it's basically a half-price ticket to the East. The trip there is free. You only have to afford the return flight."

Catherine stood up off of the mattress and checked her phone. She opened her Uber app and considered calling herself a ride.

"Wait. Wait," called out Andrew. "Just let *me* give you a ride."

"Oh god no!" scoffed Catherine. "Are you fucking serious? He can't see me get out of *your* car. Why do you think he flipped at me?"

"He found out I was over..." said Andrew with a look of guilt. "Oh god... am I the reason you got beat up?"

"Oh, don't blame yourself. That fucking sociopath had my neighbors spying on me. They saw you leave and spilled the beans."

"Are you serious?"

Catherine nodded. "He's a major drug addict. Paranoid as shit all the time. Luckily, he was on smack when he socked me, which makes it a Hell of a lot easier to explain how I just disappeared into thin air. I'll just say he blacked out." Catherine walked over to exit Andrew's bedroom, but froze when she stood just under the doorway. "I'm sorry I ruined whatever it was you had going on in here by the way..." she said referring to Andrew's fling with Diane. "I hope its salvageable."

Andrew sat up on his mattress and shook his head. "It's not your fault," he replied. "I got her number. Maybe I can see if she'd agree to a cup of coffee, so I can have a chance to apologize."

Catherine smiled. "You were always good at apologies."

"Yeah well, it's hard to be sincere though, when I know I'm telling a lie..."

Catherine shrugged. "Uh... then don't lie? Your situation isn't the same as mine. Why don't you try and tell her the truth?"

Andrew went silent. He'd never considered it before.

After Catherine left, Andrew sent a long thoughtful message to Diane. He told her the truth was complicated and that it was best explained in person. Diane agreed to see him again as long as they could meet somewhere in public. For convenience, they decided on the diner Diane had mentioned that's beside her lab: The Yellow Plate Cafe.

"I know it sounds crazy," said Andrew, trying his best to explain it all slowly, "we draw together like a pair of magnets. And we have no choice in the matter. It'd be easier to explain if we had some sort of origin story, but our relationship was... rather plain. We had no contact with dangerous chemicals or cutting-edge devices, it just started happening one day."

"Exactly when did it start?" asked Diane with a look of genuine curiosity.

"One month since we'd met. We'd just had a fight and I drove off to sleep at my parents' place. She called me before I got in bed saying she couldn't sleep without me beside her. I told her I'd gotten too drunk and I couldn't drive back over. But miraculously, by the morning, I'd suddenly appeared by her side, tucked in her bed. After that, we noticed we couldn't sleep apart. At first it was romantic, but as our relationship fell apart after the honeymoon phase, it just became... a nightmare."

"I can imagine," replied Diane. "I had to share custody over a pet rabbit with one of my ex's after we broke it off. Any contact your forced to have with them becomes baggage you have to carry into the future. I know that it can suck. And yours certainly sucks."

"Wait, so you believe me?" asked Andrew with a look of disbelief.

"Well yeah," said Diane with a grin. "I mean it's certainly more acceptable than that you let some alcoholic roommate sleep with you on occasion."

Andrew nodded. "I guess that's true. I was just thinking on my feet."

Diane nodded. "You know I had a friend who couldn't get a boy out of her head that she'd never met before. She dreamed of him every night, until one morning... *they met for real on a cable car to work.*"

"Weird," replied Andrew.

"And my dad, he guessed my mother's name before she even introduced herself. It just popped up behind his eyes."

"...Are you saying you think this is all related somehow?"

"No. I just think it's important we realize what we're dealing with. Romance."

"There's nothing romantic between me and her. Not anymore."

"But there *was?*" asked Diane.

Andrew sighed. He reluctantly nodded. "There were moments where... it worked really well, yeah. But if you're suggesting our disease is a sign that were fated to be together, I'm gonna' have to shut you down right now. We've already considered it and now we're *far* past it. If this curse is the universe shipping us together, neither of us are willing to concede, even if its destiny we save the world together."

Diane nodded. "Look I'm all for fucking over predeterminism, but I'm just saying, if it's the universe that wants you two stuck together, it's gonna' be harder to fight this. You're better off trying to adapt."

Andrew bowed his head. "We're both trying to. Desperately."

"It might help if you had a partner who... believed you?"

Andrew gave Diane a sour glance. "I thought you regretted sleeping with 'the delivery guy' who 'doesn't own a bed frame'."

Diane rolled her eyes. "Get a bed frame! It would make you so much more attractive!"

"Fine geez!" snarled Andrew. "Well would you wanna' come pick one out with me?"

Two hours later and Andrew's once bare mattress was decked out with all the amenities of a functional adult lifestyle. There were layers of sheets tucked under the covers. Soft white cases slipped over the pillows. A headboard, some bed posts, and four wooden legs hoisting it all a foot off the ground.

Diane and Andrew immediately put these accessories to the test, applying a pounding force to the center of the bed frame over and over for hours at a time. This testing would then continue for the next few weeks with time in between for romantic dinners, movie dates, and serious conversations about their future.

Diane and Andrew were quickly falling in love.

Every now and then, Diane would surprise Andrew by ordering coffees from NightCap, prompting a visit from her man while he was on the job. She'd often borrow him for a quickie while he looked good in his dorky little uniform and when she was done she'd hand her order right back to him. "I bought these for you," she'd tell him. A little treat to help him through his late-night shifts.

Reciprocating the thought, Andrew would surprise Diane with treats as well. In the form of hard drugs.

"Now, I know we talked about my hang ups with coke, but I got my hands on a drug we could both enjoy..."

Andrew unscrewed the lid to a thermos and pulled out a small sandwich bag stuffed at the bottom. He pried open the plastic lips and held out the two small squares of paper stowed inside.

He held one out for Diane to stick on her tongue. Then Andrew did the same to himself. An hour later, Diane was making up theme songs to fit specific episodes of Golden Girls and Andrew was interviewing an imaginary version of JK Simmons he formed out of his own shadow on the wall.

"Come on girls don't be nervous... Rose just looooves a little person."

"Where did you draw the line with being Vernon Schillinger?"

"Dorothy's getting mighty cocky, even though her friend's a Nazi."

"Were you and Miles Teller capable of a friendship off set?"

Knock. Knock. Knock. Both of their hallucinations were suddenly interrupted by a loud rapping at the front door.

"Oh shit, the police," exclaimed Diane.

"Fuck no. Is it really?" followed Andrew with a look of terror.

"It's me, Andrew! Please open up!" hollered a young woman's voice from behind the door.

"Who the fuck is she?" barked Diane, paranoid from her drug.

"It just sounds like Catherine..." said Andrew picking himself up out of his squat. He walked over to the door and confirmed it was her by checking through the peephole. Under the spell of the drug, she looked a bit odd in Andrew's eyes.

Andrew opened the door, then began rubbing his pupils trying to get her to return to normal. "I apologize for what must be glaringly obvious sign that I'm impaired, but I can't stop imagining you as a pirate."

"I'm, uh, wearing an eyepatch, Andrew," she said with a grim expression.

"Uh... oh! That's real?" Andrew reached out and tried to touch it. Catherine swatted his hand away before he could reach.

"Please... don't," she said. "Just... I want you to know that it worked. So now you can quit that awful job of yours and get a career started."

"It worked?" Andrew could barely believe what Catherine was inferring. "Your leaving?"

"Do you need me to write this down?" sighed Catherine with a look of aggravation. "Cause it's important you don't forget this."

"I won't! I won't!"

"Then you need to quit your job, okay?" explained Catherine. "Cause I'm gonna' be in Yokohama in twenty-four hours. Starting then, you've got to start going to bed at night again."

Andrew stared with his mouth jarring. "You're gone for good?"

Catherine nodded. "My advice, sleep with a passport on you for the first couple of weeks. If there is an accident that'll be your only way back home..."

"I, uh, I appreciate this. You coming to see me, I mean." Andrew paused and stood awkwardly for a moment. "Should we... hug?"

"No," sneered Catherine. "Your girlfriend is right there."

"What? Why would she ca-"

"Goodbye, Andrew... goodbye." Catherine picked up her bags and quickly hurried down the hall.

"Well good riddance..." whispered a voice from behind Andrew. He slowly shut the door and turned around. He saw Diane staring at him from her place on the couch. In his mind, the glowing t.v. screen behind her cast a bright white aura around her body. "Aren't you happy?"

"Should I be?"

"Of course! The drug must be making this hard to comprehend. You're free now, kid. There's nothing left holding you back!" exclaimed Diane. "Plus, think about it. I can get you a job at Marrisoft.... now, we can be on the same schedule!"

Andrew broke into a smile and nodded.

"We can do dinners together, and breakfasts together; it'll be great!"

Six weeks later, and things were not great.

It turns out one of the defining characteristics of their relationship was an unrecognized healthy distance. Andrew used to work 8PM to 4AM and Diane worked noon to 8PM plus overtime. Their love only existed in a small space between the hours of 4AM and 12PM, five hours of which were devoted to Andrew's sleep. Within that remainder were three hours of sex, food, and relaxation every day that made their relationship into a breathtaking game of touch and go. But now, they were completely overlapped.

"Why are you trying to control my whole life?" shouted Diane throwing a beaded pillow into Andrew's chin. "I'm allowed to put whatever I want in *my* body."

"It's not healthy to snort a line of caffeine before a day of work. It's weird! Just drink coffee like a normal person!"

"It saves time!" Diane picked up the baggie of caffeine and swung it around in the air. A white measuring cup stuck inside clanged around within the powder. "It saves money, I don't have to order out, and I don't have to brew anything."

"It makes you look like a huge drug addict!"

"So that's what's come up again?" roared Diane. "You're terrified your dating a fucking crackhead?"

"I never said crackhead. I just want you to cool it sometimes."

"It's not your choice! Your choice is staying or leaving whilst I do it. And that's the full extent."

Andrew shook his head and flared his nostrils. "If we're partners, why doesn't my opinion matter in any of this? I'm trying to start something serious with you and your acting like a freshman in college."

"I didn't do drugs freshman year!" sneered Diane. "I've never experienced sleep deprivation till I worked in the fucking start-up culture. This shit is a requirement if you want to advance!"

"That's weird, cause I'm currently working the same shitty overtime as you, and I'm not breaking under the pressure..."

"Our minds aren't the same!" Diane grabbed her baggie of purified caffeine and brought it into her kitchen area. She plopped it onto the counter, grabbed a plastic straw out of the cabinet and stuck it deep into the powder.

"Deal with me, now!" she screamed, as she deeply inhaled. "If you're my god damn lover, you'll god damn fucking deal with this shit."

"Fuck you!" Andrew ran for Diane's bedroom and shut the door behind him. He flicked the lock on the doorknob then laid down in her bed. He immediately coiled a pillow around his head and tried to block out the sounds of her shouting and rapping at the door.

In the silence, Andrew finally felt some peace. They'd been fighting like this for over a month. It's been so exhausting. Sometimes it was drugs. Sometimes it was unfaithfulness. Diane had a problem using vices to deal with work stress, but that's not what bothered Andrew the most. It was the fact that she had no willingness to start cutting back. All she wanted was for Andrew to mirror her flaws, so there'd be no argument over who was the better partner.

For a moment, tucked under the pillowcase, Andrew thought about his time with Catherine and whether there was a pattern to his behavior. Was he really as controlling as Diane said he was? Either way, his frustration was clear, and he wanted to be anywhere else but there. He held his breath for long durations, forcing himself to hyperventilate. He used the dizziness that ensued to latch on to that tired feeling and trick himself into a state of sleep.

Andrew woke up two-hours later to the sound of an explosion and a plume of smoke filling the room. *Yuki!* was his immediate thought. He imagined the psychopath barging into the room with an armed militia of Yakuza prepared to cut off his head. But as the smoke cleared, Andrew realized the explosion had come from a small home-made bomb made by an amateur chemist tripping on caffeine.

"These are the things that make me mentally label you... *drug addict*!" shouted Andrew as he threw his face up from the pillow.

"What kind of drug addict knows how to assemble a working petard?" griped Diane.

"...The ones that scare me the most."

"Holy shit!" shouted Diane, pointing to a wet spot that had formed on her pillow. It was a stain from Andrew's droll. A habit he repeats only whilst dreaming in an exceptionally deep state. "Were you, were you... you son of a bitch, you tried to leave me for her!"

"What?" exclaimed Andrew with a look of confusion.

"You fell asleep, I'm not fucking stupid, I know what that means!" growled Diane.

"I got frustrated, but I wasn't trying to cheat on you. I was trying to rage quit. I wanted to teleport as far away from this shit as possible."

"To Japan?"

"Yes, to Japan! I need a good, long break from this constant fighting..." whined Andrew, "but I guess... *but I guess*... it didn't work."

"What's that mean?" asked Diane, kicking the debris from the door frame into a neat little pile. "She's not sleeping? Didn't you say she has a habit of staying up for days at a time?"

"But the chances of catching her on one of those off days... I don't know. Something feels wrong."

"Why's it any of your concern?"

"She put herself in a fair amount of danger just to benefit *me*... if that danger killed her, I feel responsible."

"There's no saying she's dead just because it didn't work one time."

"Fine then." Andrew threw himself out of bed and cracked his back as he stood up tall. "Most people can't stay awake after the third night without sleep. I'll give it till then. But if I don't end up on the other side of the world, you need to take this seriously with me."

"Go ahead and try," sighed Diane, scowling at Andrew, "but I'll leave it like this. If you're wrong, and you end up in her bed. We're over."

Andrew shook his head and looked down at the floorboards. He left the room without another word.

For the next three days, Andrew altered his habits to nap overtop of when Catherine should be asleep at night. To no surprise, Andrew woke each time still stuck in the States. The ominous feeling floating around his head became more certain with each passing attempt. If there was a cosmic connection between he and Catherine, it was certainly sending a message. Catherine wasn't sleeping anymore. Cause Catherine wasn't with us anymore.

"He fucking killed her," snarled Andrew, pounding lightly on a table mat at the Yellow Plate Cafe. He was trying his best to keep in control of his emotions as he explained the situation to Diane. "I feel so responsible."

"She had a stupid get-rich-quick scheme that blew up in her face."

"It wasn't just to boost her career. I was in mind when she did it. It was practically selfless."

Diane rolled her eyes. "Fine then, it's not her fault either. Blame the curse! That's ultimately the culprit here."

"I guess so... but it sucks the authorities won't acknowledge my curse as a real thing. It's the only evidence I have that she's gone and so they won't listen to me. I don't know what kind of connections Yuki has in Japan, but they don't even report her as missing."

"So you need hard evidence if you're gonna' prove something's up?"

Andrew nodded. "Maybe I'll hire a PI..."

"It'll be cheaper and more effective... if you just do it yourself," suggested Diane.

"How so? I'm no detective."

"Think about it, for a second," replied Diane. "What if there's levels to this curse, Andrew?"

"What exactly are you suggesting?"

"Fate wants you two to end up together," explained Diane. "In life, that's your bed. But perhaps if it wants you together eternally, it wants your *final* resting place to be shared as well."

"Are you suggesting I kill myself... to find the body?" smirked Andrew.

"All the evidence is gonna' come from that cadaver," replied Diane, with a dead serious look. "The months of abuse will all be recorded in her tissues if you recover her fast enough. That should at least raise suspicions as to who done it."

"But killing myself... that's not like falling asleep. I can't wake up once I'm displaced."

"I'm sure you can," said Diane with a short grin. "What comes with you when you teleport? Your clothes?"

Andrew nodded. "I always wake up in my pajamas from the night before."

"Then we rig them with electronics," suggested Diane. "Something that can start your heart after we flatline you."

Andrew sighed. "Be honest with me, dear. Are you on drugs right now? Or are you saying you can seriously build this device?"

Diane shrugged. "I'm on drugs right now *so* I can build you this device."

Diane chose to work overtime that night, waiting after hours until she was the only left in her lab space. Once the coast was clear, she opened her backpack and took out a wet suit they'd bought earlier that day that would fit Andrew's measurements. This suit is where she'd build the electronics. The wetsuit should act as a proper shell just in case Catherine was discarded underwater as many stiffs often are.

A timed activator was built directly into the pocket that would constantly read from sensors passing over Andrew's chest. Once he flatlined, the device would wait ten seconds for him to teleport to Catherine's grave, then release the proper concentration of epinephrine into his bloodstream to restart his heart.

Once the suit was finished, Andrew snuck into Marrisoft in order to try it on. He slid on the pants, zipped up the back, then slid the needle built into the sleeve deep into his wrist.

"Woah! Woah!" exclaimed Diane. "There's no need to prick yourself, yet. Not till it's go time."

Andrew nodded and pulled up the hood of the wetsuit over his brow. "Then maybe it *is* go time."

"Tonight?" asked Diane with a look of worry. "But there's still too much to decide, isn't there?"

"Like what? What's stopping us?"

"Let's start with the killing method..."

Andrew looked around the equipment in the room, then shrugged. "Just shock me with a pair of wires. Doesn't have to be fancy..."

"Fine. I guess that makes sense... but have you considered the afterwards yet? In case you find the body, what to do you proceed to do?"

"It's complicated, but I have it hashed out," explained Andrew, taking a seat in front of a chalkboard. "To avoid any suspicion pointing towards myself by mistake, I'm not going to reveal myself to the authorities at all. I'm simply going to leave her body at the nearest police station and dip."

"And then you get home by..."

"I wait it out. They'll mail the body back to America after the investigation closes so her family can have it. Then, I repeat what we did here tonight."

"So then you'll be needing a second syringe of epinephrine... I wish you would have told me it needed to be multi-use. But I suppose I can just show you how to reset it yourself."

While Diane prepared a second unit of epinephrine to hide in the pocket, Andrew procured a pair of wires and stripped the plastic off the ends with a pair of pliers. Andrew then attached the wires to the output on a pulse generator and tested the murder-machine at a high voltage. Sticking the tips of the wires together, heat and sparks flew from their contact.

"You know," smiled Andrew staring at the arc of lights he'd made. "You're gonna' have a fun time killing me."

Diane finished her work with the epinephrine and looked up at Andrew. "You're kidding, right?"

"I'm dragging you into a plot to avenge my ex... I figured killing me is the only joy you can get out of any of this."

"Or... I just enjoy helping you because we're dating," sneered Diane, "and unlike you, I support your less than ideal characteristics... no matter how stupid and self-destructive I think they are."

"Are you saying that your cooperation in my murder... makes you the better partner?"

Diane nodded, then grabbed the wires from Andrew's hands. "Lie down on the bench, here."

Andrew did as instructed, taking deep breaths to try and calm his nerves before they're inevitably barbequed.

"Are you ready, then?" questioned Diane, holding the wires close to a bare spot of flesh on Andrew's abdomen.

"Hold on," interrupted Andrew. "I know we've been mad at each other lately... but just in case I don't come back. I want you to know I've appreciated the time we've spent together."

Diane nodded and gave a long sigh. "If I do this for you, can you please just agree to let me do the drugs I want."

Andrew rolled his eyes. "Fine, yes, just do the thing!"

Diane stuck the wires to Andrew's flesh and watched as he began to convulse around the waist. His feet curled up and his legs began flailing, almost kicking Diane in the face. She waited patiently holding the wires steady until the device in Andrew's wet suit let out a loud muffled beep. That meant it had sensed a flatline and started its timer.

Not many people have actually witnessed Andrew's disappearing when it happens. Any partners he's been with have been fast asleep when he teleported away from them. But Diane, watching from right above, got to see the full transition and it wasn't like anything she was expecting. It was sudden and rapid. She watched his body implode like it were made of sand, all of his matter mashing together at once into an infinitesimal point in the center of his heart.

A week went by and Diane began to worry.

Diane had been expecting some sort of long distance phone call, something cryptic but telling, but nothing of the sort came her way. There was never any sign Andrew had made it there safely. Diane gained an obsessive interest in Japanese news, specifically sources covering the Yokohama area. She looked for any information regarding murders or missing persons, but it never related to an Andrew Williamson or a Catherine Gilbert. If a body was suddenly found in front of a police station she was sure it'd make the headlines.

Without Andrew by her side, Diane's time spent with drugs became more regular. Diane leaned into decompressing with coke and molly and soon found herself enjoying the high at any minute of the day not spent at work. With her drug-fueled energy, her search for Andrew peeked into an almost obsessive venture. Finally, after three months of disappearance, Diane's efforts were eventually rewarded. Her questions were answered in an unlikely news bulletin regarding strange seismic activity at a bottling plant.

"Workers are complaining... they say it's too unsafe work," spoke the new anchor, he was holding a microphone up to the lips of the plant's manager.

"It's like an animal dug its way inside the cement," said the manager. "Something's down there, putting a lot of pressure on the material." The manager pointed to a crack between his feet. It stretched far along the surface of the factory's floor. Swelling along the sides of the cracking proved to be a hazard for employees to trip over and so they got they day-off. It seems the floor was being forced upward by some unknown pressure building beneath the foundation.

"The workers will be on paid leave until we get to the bottom of this..."

Two weeks later, an excavation occurred to fix the issue, which would unknowingly cause an international uproar. Early-on, x-rays showed the pressure point wasn't shaped like a nest, but like the size and shape of a single human body. But upon cracking open the cast and peering inside, they discovered two.

The visceral imagery of the uncovered anomaly is what made the headlines. It seemed like an archaeological mystery. A pair of bodies were squeezed together, face-to-face, palm-to-palm, in a mold that could only fit one. The bodies had flattened against one another, each of their heads looked like half of a pistachio.

Their rows of ribs had aligned like the teeth of a zipper and penetrated into one another.

"They're investigating several leads," explained the anchor. "Oddly enough, evidence shows some link between the killers and a small US company Marrisoft. Several electronic devices were found on the victims matching components patented by said company."

Diane threw her laptop off of her legs and quickly ran to her bathroom. She began flushing her drugs bag by bag in a manic attempt at preparing for the investigation that would surely be coming her way.

She thought about the image of the two mashed together like that. It filled her, and certainly most viewers, with pure disgust. *But perhaps,* she thought, *perhaps whatever did this, whatever sick voyeur needed these two together, is sufficiently satisfied. And maybe, maybe even a little aroused.*

Oh, we are, Diane. Trust me, we've been waiting for them to make-up for quite some time.

It's nice that we finally got the big kiss scene we've been waiting for.

Pizza Crow II

Upon continuing with the same style of pizza, large, thick-crust, pepperoni and mushroom toppings, I noticed the pages began to loop. Everything was identical to the first set. The handwriting was, most surprisingly, completely unchanged. It looked like it had gone through a copier, every word was placed and shaped exactly the same. It couldn't be just a photo though, there were clear indentations in the paper from the strokes of a pen.

I kept repeating the loop over and over, waiting for some screw up, but it never came. Then, one day, my usual pizza parlor Monte Carlos' was closed. So I bought the same style, same toppings, same size from another restaurant. Mary's. They don't deliver, so they're far less convenient. But I'm happy I made the trip. This little difference changed everything.

The story changed. Pages from "Bedfellows" no longer came. They were suddenly replaced by a new tale. "Belligamy".

Belligamy

Having five kids by the age of 30, Stozi was used
to waking up to the sounds of shouting coming from one of their
bedrooms. Kids wake up early. And when they do, they seek out
attention. First from their siblings, creating an army of high-
pitched lungs attached to cranky attitudes. Then from the adults,
to whom these lungs fire their gripes like grapeshot. But on this
one particular morning, Stozi's kids did not wake him with a
deafening scream or a harrowing cry. Instead Stozi was woken up
by the sounds of beach waves gurgling out of an alarm clock he
had not set the night before.

Confused, Stozi reached over to his night stand and pressed the
large grey rectangle atop the digital clock. The alarm shutoff.
Stozi stared at the time. 5:00 AM. He looked out the window. It
was still dark out. This was a strange time to have set for the
weekend.

Stozi wondered if Aaron, his wife of five years, had set the alarm.
Maybe she had to work overtime on Saturday. Maybe she had a
doctor's appointment. Maybe the kids had some red-eye soccer
scrimmage planned by obnoxious coaches. Stozi turned toward
Aaron's side of the bed and reached over to shake her awake,
but instead he received a cold prick on his fingers. It jolted
Stozi's eyes open.

"Aaron?" grumbled Stozi, still half-asleep. He focused his blurry
morning vision where his wife would normally be laying. But the
covers were flattened, and there was nobody there. Stozi saw
something shiny resting on her pillow, its bottom half was tucked
beneath the sheets. Stozi grabbed the metal tool and held it up
close to his face. It was a scalpel. It was shiny, and either brand
new or well-maintained to the point where it looked brand new.
It looked rather mundane, a standard operating device, except

for the material it was made from. It seemed to have been forged out of pink-colored steel.

While analyzing the tool in his hand, Aaron noticed he fell asleep with his wedding band on. He normally took it off before he took his evening shower. "Did... somebody put this on me?".

Stozi was answered by a strange noise coming from downstairs. It sounded like someone swinging a bat into the front door to his house. Aaron's heart didn't skip a beat. He immediately assumed it was one of his offspring using a hard toy to beat on something expensive.

Stozi sat up out of his bed and rubbed his eyes. He then sighed a good sigh and prepared himself to herd the flock. He marched out of his room and descended the stairs in nothing but a pair of thin pajama bottoms. Stozi knew that his chubby, topless form embarrassed his kids. He counted on it as a defensive measure to encourage docile behavior in exchange for his decency.

Stozi reached the hallway at the bottom of his steps and turned the corner to face his kitchen. Inside, he noticed his front door had a strip of its wood carved out down the center. A huge splinter had been cut out, leaving a hole large enough to fit a hand through.

"Uh... kids?" Stozi's heart sank, he began to worry his offspring may have been taken. He hurried forward into the center of his kitchen and was greeted to the sight of the possible intruder. "ehm, Mr. Bacon?" exclaimed Stozi. "Why are you in my kitchen?"

Mr. William Bacon was a neighbor of Stozi's with by far the largest home on their block, an eight-room McMansion at the top of the street. Mr. Bacon traveled a lot and rarely interacted with the rest of the neighborhood, but his wife was a sweet old woman in her 60s who happened to be the first face to introduce itself after Stozi and his wife moved from Brooklyn to their boulevard in suburban PA. Mr. Bacon's wife always spoke fondly of him, but the crazed look in his eyes had Stozi second guessing her opinion.

Mr. Bacon lifted his arms over his head. A pair of beautiful, shimmering katanas were clutched, one in each hand. Mr. Bacon charged at Stozi and swung the blades downwards at his chest. Stozi screamed and lunged out of the way, falling backwards onto the granite tiles of his kitchen floor. "Stop!" shouted Stozi. "What are you doing? What did you do with my kids?"

"It's not what you think," growled Mr. Bacon. "They're all safe. You'll survive. Just let me kill you!" Mr. Bacon's swords had slashed against the solid floor, leaving two long black streaks in the finish. Stozi could see the blades were made from the same pink metal as his scalpel.

Mr. Bacon lifted the swords from the floor and prepared for another swing. Stozi took the opportunity to scurry along the floor into his adjacent living room. He grabbed some heavy clay coasters from the end table and began chucking them like frisbees into the face of Mr. Bacon. He raised his swords up to his head in the shape of an X, making an effective shield.

Mr. Bacon slowly approached Stozi with his left sword outstretched. He had the point directed at the soft spot beneath Stozi's Adam's apple. Stozi quickly pushed himself off the floor back onto his feet. He dashed to the back wall of his living room and turned to face the bookcase behind him. Stozi thought he may be able to climb it. From his perch on top, Mr. Bacon may not be able to reach him.

Stozi tried to scale the bookcase like a ladder, treating each shelf like a rung. He was able to climb four feet off the ground when his hands reached the top of the bookcase. He pulled upwards, trying to lift his body on top, but he inadvertently threw the whole bookcase off balance.

Mr. Bacon saw the impending fall and took a few steps backward to remain uninjured. Stozi, on the other hand, saw his life flash before his eyes. He felt the weight of the last year's fifty bestsellers crush down on his chest. The bookshelf clamped onto his torso and pushed all his organs up against his sternum. Lucky for him, the excruciating pain lasted only fifteen seconds before Stozi felt the pressure on his body magically vanish. It was replaced with the sensation of a heavy blanket tossed over his shoulders.

Stozi lifted up his head, exhaling rapidly. As he panicked, he swiveled his head back and forth, scanning the room. He was suddenly back in his bedroom. Tucked back in his bed. Stozi quickly tore the blankets off of him. No bruising. No blood. All his organs felt like they'd been return to their proper bedding. Stozi sighed. For a moment, he wondered if it had all been a dream. But looking to his left, he still received the sight of a pink scalpel in his wife's place.

Stozi heard loud banging stomping around on his first floor. The footsteps ran over to his staircase and began to ascend. *Fuck.* thought Stozi. *He didn't leave.* Stozi had a small amount of time to plan for Mr. Bacon's second assault. The man would have to guess correctly as to which bedroom was the parents'. In the meantime, Stozi tried his best to remain silent as he crept out of his bed. He tried to keep the springs from creaking as he stood up and tiptoed to the area right beside his bedroom door. Stozi held his breath and made his back flush with the wall.

He heard Mr. Bacon rummaging through the bedrooms on the second floor. He'd kick open each door, see it contained children's toys and swear in some foreign language under his breath. He just about guessed every other bedroom wrong before finally coming to the correct door where Mr. Bacon delivered one final kick.

This time Mr. Bacon caught sight of the adult-sized bed in the center of the room and knew he chose correctly. He charged forward into Stozi's bedroom but only made it two steps in before his neck was impaled on the tip of Stozi's scalpel. As soon the door had swung open, Stozi had swung the blade from his hidden spot beside the door frame. It landed in a vital artery, splashing blood from Mr. Bacon's throat onto his clothes.

Mr. Bacon's outfit was very similar to Stozi's. It looked like he'd just gotten out of his bed. Beneath a gingerbread brown zip-up he'd clearly thrown on before going outside, was a plain white tee, now dyed red from the leaking wound at its collar. Below the tee, was a pair of felt, grey sweatpants. And on his feet were bear-skin slippers. Stozi couldn't resist taking this footwear and sliding it over his own toes. They were expensive slippers and Stozi felt he'd earned them as penance. He'd tell the police they were always his.

Speaking of which, Stozi ran over to his phone charger plugged into the outlet behind his bedpost. He wanted to call the authorities to come collect his attacker. But as he ran over to the chord there was no cell phone connected. He searched under his sheets just in case it got dragged under the covers in his slumber, but no dice.

Stozi had a house phone downstairs in his kitchen. He hurried down as fast as he could, while simultaneously yelling for his kids and wife. Despite dispatching his murderer, they were still missing. As Stozi reached the kitchen, he stared into his living room. He was shocked to see that the bookshelf had in fact fallen over. *That was no dream.* thought Stozi. But then why was his body no longer crushed under its shelves?

Stozi looked for his house phone, but that too was missing. A lot was missing. And a lot made no sense. Slowly, it was becoming clear this would not be an ordinary morning.

Stozi realized if Mr. Bacon was still here, so must be the other neighbors. He ran outside and ventured out into the dark early morning. The sky was indigo, the stars and moon were still showing, and the street lights were still on.

Stozi began yelling for help, scuffling along the sidewalk. He tried to call near the houses right beside his own. His block sat on an incline, with most of the smaller houses on the flat plane at the bottom. Four or five larger properties were then crowded at the top of the hill. Most of these higher-mortgage residents were generally less intimate with the community.

Stozi wandered up onto his friend Veronica's porch and began knocking on the door. She lived right next door with her wife and child. None of them answered Stozi's wrapping. He wondered if they were scared of intruders. Stozi stepped back off their porch and cupped his hands around his mouth. "Veronica! Beth! It's me, Stoz!" he shouted at their bedroom windows. They wouldn't answer.

"Mr. Krantz." came a voice from behind him. Stozi jumped in surprise and quickly spun around with his scalpel drawn. "Mr. Krantz, no!" shouted the low, raspy voice. It didn't match the spritely young face emitting the sound. It was the twenty something boy from the garage-mahals at the top of the block. Stozi couldn't place a name.

"Borky?" Stozi guessed.

The boy nodded. "Josh Borky. But just Josh works."

Stozi shook his head. "Your Borky, now."

The boy nodded. "Eh... okay?"

"Sorry, there's already two Josh's on this block and I can't remember a third," explained Stozi. "Mr. Agne's first name is Josh. And so is Veronica's kid. Have you seen either of them?"

Borky shook his head. "I haven't really been looking for them. I don't really know them. I'm really trying to find my wife."

"You're married?" asked Stozi.

Borky gave a little nod.

"Kids?"

"No."

"Good, smart." said Stozi, staring at the ground. "They don't come recommended. They just have you worrying all the time..."

"I'm still plenty worried without 'em," replied Borky through a pair of sad eyes. "I can't find my wife, Mr. Krantz. Or my dad. All three of my brothers are gone too. Nathan's only six years old. He's got me terrified."

Stozi looked up from the grass and stared at Borky. He was dressed in a thick black bathrobe with his initials embroidered on his left chest. On his feet were a pair of grey-blue Sperry's without any socks. There was loose wet grass around his ankles.

Sticking out the most among his bedroom attire was a belt around his waist with a gun tucked into its holster.

"You open carry?" asked Stozi.

Borky shook his head and pulled out the weapon. "I mean I do. But this isn't it. All my guns were gone when I woke up. Thought maybe my dad took them. This was the only weapon I could find. Even my kitchen knives had been stolen."

"Well where did you find that, then?" asked Stozi staring at the pink metal comprising every part of the pistol.

"It was tucked into my wife's bed."

"You mean you don't sleep in the same bed as your wife?"

Borky rolled his eyes. "We're intimate, Mr. Krantz. But she needs good sleep on account of her job. And I, unfortunately, wake her up with my snoring."

"I found my weapon in place of my wife, too," said Stozi. "Are any of your brothers married?"

"None of em'."

"What about your father?'

Borky shook his head. "Divorced."

"I thought so," Stozi remembered overhearing some gossip on that matter. "Well then, kid, it seems that everyone left here is straight and actively monogamous." Stozi thought about his attacker, Mr. Bacon, he also fit those criteria. Stozi also recalled what Mr. Bacon had said before he slashed at him. *They're all safe. You'll survive. Just let me kill you.*

"I think some of us are more aware of what's going on here than others." Stozi froze to consider his options. Unfortunately, Borky's family, the Borkys, were next door neighbors to Mr. Bacon. If there was anyone responsible for all this, Stozi was most suspicious of the rich-folk atop the hill. Specifically, anyone particularly close to Mr. Bacon. "To be honest, I'm not sure if I can trust you're not a part of this. And don't take offense to that if you really *are* being honest with me. I'm just pointing out that we can't team up without adding a third to our posse that I can trust. That way you're outnumbered."

"I... guess I understand that. Do you have someone in mind that falls into our demographic?" asked Borky.

Stozi nodded. "It's Jackie Heim." Although Stozi was better friends with Veronica, he saw more of Jackie on a day to day basis. They've been carpooling together since Jackie had changed jobs to an office building next to Stozi's. They also belong to the same church. Stozi considers Jackie a friend, but he's far from his best friend. He can't talk about the same things he does with Veronica. Jackie is a bit older than them. Part of a different generation that's a little bit more conservative.

Stozi told Borky they were going to walk over to Jackie's house, but that the condition was Borky would have to walk in front with his hands up in the air and his gun holstered. "Just till I have more eyes and ears." Borky was fine obliging. He'd do anything to get an ally on this strange, strange morning.

The two walked single file up the boulevard till they came to the last modest house on the west side of the block. Anything further came with a pool and a basement kitchen. This was Jackie's home, an angular bungalow made of beige bricks.

Before even approaching the front door, both Stozi and Borky were too distracted by an odd site coming from the manor beside it. The side of the house facing Jackie's was completely blown out with a gaping hole in the wall about the size of a garage door. Stozi allowed Borky to go investigate and report his findings.

Stepping through the hole, Borky found himself inside a lavish bedroom with vintage furniture and priceless artwork on the walls. All of these expensive pieces were untouched, but the king-sized bed against the back wall was heavily damaged. While half of it looked immaculate, the other half was crushed completely flat. Borky peeled the tattered blanket off the destroyed portion and brought it outside for Stozi to see. There were black tread marks left on the sheets. Borky pointed down at the ground, directing Stozi's attention to two lanes of matching tread marks. They were dug deep into the carpet, debris, and dirt leading out from the bedroom down the alley between the houses and into the backyards in the center of the block.

"What kind of truck is that?" asked Stozi. He'd only driven one vehicle his entire life, a 2003 Volkswagen Passat, and he could barely remember which was the make and which was the model.

The Borkys, on the other hand, had four cars. All exotic. With an additional motorcycle added to the collection shortly after the divorce.

Borky examined the marks closely and shook his head. "Mr. Krantz this isn't from a car..." Borky motioned for Stozi to follow as they walked the path left by the vehicle. The two of them followed it into Jackie Heim's backyard and stood in awe at the path of destruction that led off into the distance. The vehicle had mowed down the hardwood fences and arborvitae that kept the borders of the backyards clear.

Borky fearlessly began to traverse the emptied path, but he'd only crossed through one garden when he stopped at one Mr. Milton's yard. Here he yelled for Stozi to come see.

Mr. Milton's backyard had an extra fraction of land added on, purchased from his poorer neighbors. He wanted an extra-large backyard, so his dogs could have a big space to play in. It was always a relatively empty space as any decoration usually became his largest Leonberger's chew toy. So, it was absolutely jarring that a priceless stone sculpture had suddenly appeared at the very back of his property.

The statue was definitely new and untouched by canine teeth. Stozi could immediately tell it was a clue to all the weirdness as it was clearly made from the same pink metal as their weapons, crafted into the shape of a bride in a large frilly dress. She wore a long wedding veil and held one hand over her mouth as her eyes held back tears. The other hand was held outwards with its fingers spread, as though ready to accept a suitor's ring.

"I miss my Molly," frowned Borky. "She wore a dress like that. Really big and stupid looking."

"Wow. That was almost romantic," scoffed Stozi. "Tell me kid, does this statue look familiar to you at all?"

Borky shook his head. "Why would it?"

"No offense kid, but your parents are kind of shady folk. Especially your dad. Have they been discussing any plans like this? Do they have any powerful enemies who could turn a whole block into a battle royale without notice? Anyone with access to massive amounts of sleeping agents?"

"Powerful enemies? ...Sleeping agents? Mr. Krantz, my dad's just a trust-fund baby. He doesn't fund a private militia. He's quite dim..." explained Borky. "Although, there was something going on with some of the other folks on our side of the block. But my dad wasn't included... and that made him all pissy. His friends were having these events, but he wasn't invited."

A series of metal bangs suddenly echoed over Mr. Milton's backyard. It sounded like heavy machinery had been booted up inside Mr. Milton's house. Over the churning noise, Stozi could make out a softer sound. Like drywall cracking. "Let's go!" shouted Stozi.

Suddenly, a tank busted through the back wall of Mr. Milton's house. It had sprung out of a bottom floor dining room where it had been hiding patiently. As it tore out of the building, the roof collapsed inwards, and all three stories of the house imploded. The debris spilled down the incline of the backyard like an avalanche. The tank rolled along with it at the leading edge of the smoke and rubble.

Stozi had gotten a head start, predicting the noise would spell disaster. He began running for the nearest alleyway out of the backyards. Borky, on the other hand, was caught off guard, stuck in the revelry of his tender moment.

Borky panicked and thought he could perhaps take out the driver inside. He whipped out his pistol and took the proper stance to fire. He shot six well-placed bullets, aiming for the front panel of the vehicle that barricades the control center. But the material of the tank was the now familiar pink metal. It was a hard surface that could not be scratched by the incoming fire. The bullets ricocheted and left Borky with no choice but to try and outrun the tank. After running a few feet, he was relieved to see it wasn't chasing him. But that look of relief was short lived, as Borky's face twisted into terror.

The tank's cannon dipped down and twisted slightly left, targeting the patch of earth just behind Borky's heels. It fired.

Stozi heard the shot and picked up his pace. He was trying to get as far as he could from the blast. The street was only a few feet before him. He galloped over to the sidewalk and into the grass beside it. He leapt from the stone lip along the side of the road and immediately felt his chest receive a sharp pinch.

At first, he thought it was just the exhilaration giving him a near heart attack. Or perhaps shrapnel had just shot straight through him. But staring down at his shirtless chest, he saw his body had suffered no new wounds. He reached a hand over his heart and was surprised to find his heart wasn't palpitating out of control but had stopped beating entirely. The feeling left him dizzy. He quickly lost his balance. As he gripped his chest, he felt his body tumble backwards. His head landed in the soft grass, but he banged his spine on the lip of the street. Right at the moment of impact, he couldn't hear the sound of his own fall as a blast occurred behind him.

The explosion wafted a warm breeze overtop of Stozi's fallen form. He watched as the dark sky hanging above him was covered in a cloud of soot.

Stozi felt his heart start up again. He took a second to catch his breath, before making his way up to his feet. Stozi covered his mouth with his hands as to not choke on the dirt floating in the air. When it cleared enough to breathe, Stozi began to call for his partner. "Borky!" he shouted. "Where did you get to?"

As the dust settled, Stozi got his answer. Staring down the alley into the backyards, Stozi could make out splashes of gore sprayed across the grass like morning dew. Some of the larger chunks identified Borky as the victim. Half of his head was stuck on the side of a nearby fence. The other half was smeared on the plastic window sill to a forest green playhouse.

One particularly long string of Borky had a bend in the middle and was sticking out of a pile of dirt like a flag. At first Stozi thought it was a leg. But a man suddenly appeared beside it and plucked it out of its burial, revealing a hand at its end.

The man in question ran by so fast it was tough to get a look at his face, but Stozi recognized the yellow gym shorts and bright green tank. It was Jackie Heim; dashing about in his jogging gear.

Stozi sprinted off at the same vector as Jackie but sticking to the front yards where he was safe from the tank's fire. "Jackie!" called Stozi trying to get his attention. Every time they both passed by the space between houses, Stozi yelped. When they were both four or five houses ahead of the tank, Jackie finally turned his stride toward Stozi and held a finger to his lips signaling for Stozi to remain quiet. He motioned for Stozi to follow him inside the nearest house. It was the block's smallest estate, a stone cottage that's been vacant and advertised for over two years. It used to be occupied by one Ms. Harriot Hamm, till she mysteriously vanished one month after last being seen. Her kids rarely spoke with her and her disappearance was only realized after neighbors became concerned that her garage door had been left slightly ajar for over a week.

Jackie grabbed the handle at the bottom of this same garage door and yanked it upwards forcing it to open against the damaged gears and pulleys on the inside. These systems had remained broken since whatever home invasion had stolen away Ms. Hamm all those years ago. Jackie managed to pull the door up just enough to slide their bodies under. Jackie slipped in with only a view grease stains smeared on his back. But Stozie had a little more trouble. His belly was pudgy and unclothed causing it to chafe painfully against the metal lip at the bottom of the garage door.

Jackie shook his head and helped his friend squeeze through the gap by tugging on his legs. Once he got through, Jackie helped Stozie off the floor of the garage as he cringed in pain.

"I'm not saying you need to lose weight," sighed Jackie. "But you need to at least put on a shirt if you're gonna' look like that."

"What the fuck is going on, Jackie?! Please tell me you know what's going on?"

Jackie told Stozi to wait a minute and disappeared from the garage. Stozi heard his footsteps going down the stairs into the basement of the abandoned home. Stozi heard boxes getting thrown around in the back of the cellar, then footsteps ascended back up to the first floor. Jackie appeared and tossed a black shirt into Stozi's hands. "Tell me if this fits."

It did, but barely. It was a long sleeve, crew neck that squeezed every inch of his body. The material was elastic, but it still choked him around his neck and wrists, since it was definitely two sizes too small. "It'll do, for now," said Stozi. "How did you know this would be down there?"

"Ms. Hamm's kids are a bunch of hippies on the West Coast and they're not coming any time soon. They aren't taking care of this place and they're not hiring someone to sell it for them. They just have that stupid posting outside," griped Jackie. "So I've been using it for storage."

"That's pretty illegal. Doesn't sound like you," scolded Stozi. He'd always known Jackie as the boy-scout of the neighborhood. Literally, he taught boy scouts. And read to kids at Bible School. He's the kind of white bread you always see at the store but can't understand whom would buy it because you tried it once and it was so sweet and so grainless that it might as well have been coffee cake.

"I've been taking a lot more risks," shrugged Jackie. "Like grabbing this." He held up Borky's arm and wiggled the hand in Stozi's face.

"Please stop!" shouted Stozi smacking the thing away. The wedding band on the ring finger fell to the floor. Jackie reached down and grabbed it; he then stuffed it in the pocket of his shorts. It clinked as it fell inside.

"Unless we all wanna' end up like this poor boy, we're going to have to work together to take out that tank," commanded Jackie with a general's draw. "Have you discovered we're locked into this block?"

Stozi nodded. "My heart just stopped as soon as I tried to leave... I think we can guess that whoever made this happen lives on the block," guessed Stozi.

"Well I think I, at least, know who's behind the tank," said Jackie. "You know Larry Stein?"

"Oh, isn't he one of your snobby friends from up the street?" sneered Stozi.

"They're not my friends..."

"No, they're not. You just suck up to them cause their rich and you want to feel like your home is a part of their hill."

Jackie hung his head and sighed heavily towards the ground. He knew he had this coming. He and Stozie had been in a bit of a rough patch, lately. Ever since Jackie had to miss Stozie's birthday barbeque and duck fry. Jackie claimed it was work related, but Stozie was suspicious he'd skipped the celebration for a wine & cheese party inconveniently timed on the same day, same afternoon.

Stozie decided to drop his aggravation. This wasn't a good time to bring tension into their team up, "How do you know it's Larry?" he huffed.

"Larry's ex-military. He's had tank training."

"Oh wow. Good to hear you know him so well..." groaned Stozi.

"Fo. cus. please." enunciated Jackie. *Bang.* The sound of ricocheting gunfire ripped through an adjacent room in the cottage. It was followed by the sound of a window's glass shattering to the floor.

"Somebody's trying to break in," said Stozie. He kept unseen and moved quickly into the kitchen connecting to the garage. He then turned the corner and entered the dining room, where he saw a man hesitating to enter the window he'd broken open. He was an old man that Stozie didn't recognize. He looked too scared to set any part of his body on the borders of the window he'd broken in. He didn't want to cut himself.

The old man was well into his eighties and was shaking and whimpering like a small child. He looked too pathetic to consider as a threat. Stozie decided to come out from his cover and help the defenseless elder inside.

"Stop right there, schvartze!" The old man stopped his attempt to climb over the glass and pulled up his gun. It was a pink-metal hunting rifle. It trembled in his hand, shaking the end of the barrel far off of its intended target.

"schvartze?..." muttered Stozie as he raised his hands over his head. "That's... some real ancient evil right there."

"Where the fuck is Crazy Jack?" whined the old man. "I thought I saw Crazy Jack come in here."

The old man began to scream. "Jack! Crazy Jack! Did he kill you?!"

"Mr. Milton you senile fool," growled Jackie as he stomped angrily into the dining room. "You just brought attention to our fucking hiding spot!"

"Jack, please. I take it back. I can't do this," cried the old man. "This is too real. I don't want to die. I saw a man get his head lopped off by William. There was *real* pain in his eyes. I'm scared!"

"Stop being a coward and find your own place to hide!" hollered Jackie,

"Protect me! I can't do this!"

For a split second Stozie was able to witness Mr. Milton get carried away like a rabbit in the talons of a bird. When the missile hit him in the side of his ribs, streams of snot launched from his nostrils and his jaw flew open like all his nightmares had come true. Mr. Milton flew out of sight leaving a white streak of smoke that had burned from the back of the rocket. As soon as the explosion went off, Stozie felt Jackie's hand latch onto his shoulder and yank him. He was being dashed out the door of the cottage out into its front yard. "He's expecting us at our own homes!" shouted Jackie as he pulled them along. "And he's flattening as many hiding spots as possible! His manor will probably be the last home he'll destroy."

Jackie led them to the shelter of Larry Stein's bear den. A big blue house on the polar opposite side of the block to Stozie's.

"Do you think he left it unlocked?" asked Stozie as they ran right up to the front door.

"No," said Jackie bluntly as he reached into his pocket. He pulled out his own wedding band and slipped it on. A lightweight axe, twice the size of a hatchet, appeared in his hand. He reached it over his head and swung down at the door, wedging it into the wood. He repeated these strokes till the door was chopped down the center. Jackie then charged forward with his shoulder out and tore the door to pieces rushing right through it. Stozie followed in his wake of destruction.

"So... you woke with an axe?" questioned Stozie as he followed Jackie through a home theatre.

Jackie nodded.

"All I got was a fucking scalpel," griped Stozie holding out the little pink blade.

"That's... sweet."

"Sweet?" questioned Stozie.

"Well you know, it's cute. That your lie is so small."

"My lie? What are you talking about, Jackie?"

"You're supposed to be sharp. Don't do you do Analytics for Boeing?"

"Jackie, please!" begged Stozie for answers.

"It's... your lie. All of these weapons represent some lie we've told our wives. The bigger the weapon, the bigger the lie," explained Jackie.

"And you've put this all together, how?"

Jackie raised up his axe for Stozie to see clearly. "I guess mines pretty obvious, so I put it together for my own case. And earlier on when I came across Mr. Agne, I found his choice of weapon rather on the nose as well. I put two and two together... and perhaps you could substantiate my conclusion, if you're not too ashamed of what must be a... little white lie."

"I... can see what this *could* mean, if what you're saying is true," said Stozie. He stared at the medical tool in his hand and recognized that it was the primary tool used in a recent surgery. "I don't know why I hid it from my wife. But I got a vasectomy without discussing with her first. She still has no idea."

"Well you've got five kids... it makes sense you'd want to stop there."

"Yeah well, Aaron really likes kids. Her parents had a dozen. But I can't handle anymore, yet I was too chicken shit to tell her. In case it disappointed her."

Jackie shook his head with a smirk. "It's good that you feel guilty about it, it really is, but take the size of your tool for what it means... it's not that big a lie. She must not feel as strongly about it as you fear."

"Well then, what about you? Your axe is a lot bigger than my weapon... what have you been hiding from Abby?"

Jackie didn't reply at first, so Stozie started to examine the evidence. The type of axe Jackie was holding was a familiar tool. Back before his office job, Jackie was a fireman. He'd show all his friends his favorite toys that came with the job. Stozie had a sudden realization and started scanning the fabric of the shirt Jackie had given him earlier. "Oh my god," said Stozie reading the manufacturer's label on the inside of the collar. It was CarbonX. "Do you still have your old equipment stashed in that house?" guessed Stozie. "Oh no! You're still working fires somehow!"

Jackie groaned. "Volunteers don't get locker space."

"You fucking asshole."

"It's only when they're down a man!"

"How are you going to support Abby if you get cancer too-"

"I already do!" barked Jackie. "What's done is done, I don't know why I have to stop doing what I love at this point. As long as I keep fit, I'll survive. And I'll keep Abby safe too."

"Come the fuck on," snarled Stozie. "You've changed, boy scout. I wish you'd go back to being the stuffy old Republican I knew you as. The one that's supposed to be aggravatingly pure and responsible."

"Help me, survive this," begged Jackie. He grabbed Stozie's arm tightly. "And I'll tell her... we'll make a plan. We'll raise money. We'll make sure she'd have the support if I died."

Stozie pulled away from him. "I'll tell my wife too... if we get through this that is. But do you think all these lies are the reason we're being put through this. Is this godly vengeance?"

Jackie shook his head. "It's not god, Stoz. It's man. With magic. The boys up on the hill. From my time spent with them, I've seen their collection. They've got halls and attics and secret chambers in their basements. Their filled with talismans and animal heads; blessed artifacts to fortify their luck."

"So far I've seen Mr. Bacon get his throat stabbed and Mr. Milton fly away on a rocket. I wouldn't call that good luck."

Jackie nodded. "They've cursed themselves. It was one thing when it was just greed. You can achieve funds through bright white spells and holy water. But lust. Lust comes with a price. You have to dip into dark magic. Mr. Milton bought a very old statue that could rewrite history and give its user a new wife. All the old boys up on the hill conspired to perform the ritual over and over until each of them got to wife swap with the youngins in the boonies. Tight, youthful wives with no cost to their fortunes. After seeing Mr. Borky lose half his estate to his old crone, the statue became instantly more attractive than the thought of divorce."

"So they win this battle and then... take one of our wives?"

Jackie nodded. "At the end, after only one us is left standing, they put the wedding ring of their choice on the statue's finger and get that man's bride."

"Ah fuck," growled Stozie, stomping his foot. "Do you know who it is this time around? If it's Mr. Harlton, then he's coming for me. That pricks always flirting with my Aaron. Honking his fucking Benz every time he passes by while she's working in the garden. He's particularly silent when I'm right beside her..."

"Some of them had hang-ups about trading their loved ones for fresher models. They're not sociopaths, you know, they just have tempting options other men don't. But they all knew where Mr. Milton stored his statue, I think only one of them pulled the trigger. I'm guessing the man behind the tank. The biggest sin must belong to the biggest sinner."

Stozie agreed. "A big lie means not a lot of love in their marriage. He's probably just fine giving her up. We need a plan in order to take him out, but I'm not sure what can stop a tank. I can't pierce armor with a fucking scalpel. And I don't think your axe is gonna' do it either."

"You're right." Jackie pulled off his ring, making the axe disappear into thin air. Jackie put his ring away and pulled out a new one, belonging to someone else. "What we need is someone else's lie. A bigger, badder lie."

Jackie handed the ring to Stozie to try on. Stozie stared strangely at it. It felt weird putting on someone else's personal jewelry. The meaning could be seen in the very engraving around the circumference. The pattern looked like vines, connecting to pedals that blossomed around the diamond on top.

Stozie slipped on the ring. It was a tight fit. All at once, a four-foot shovel appeared in his hand. The weight caught him off guard and tugged on his arm, sending half his body towards the floor. He grabbed the back end of the shovel's wooden shaft and hoisted it up like a barbell.

"This is... who'd you get this off of?" cringed Stozie. "I can only imagine what secret they have buried..."

"Whoever it was, it couldn't win against my axe," boasted Jackie with a smug grin. "Whatever douchebag lives right between you and me."

"Mr. Agne? The guy who moved here from Athens? Jackie, you axed the guy who setup the blood drive for your wife."

"He wanted blood. I gave him blood," snickered Jackie. "Look it doesn't matter. The dude attacked me first and we need his weapon to take out the tank. I'm fast. So I'll be supplying you with a distraction. Zig-zagging serpentine right towards his front side. He'll fire. I'll dodge."

"Jackie... that's stupid. He might hit you."

"I can dodge one shot, I mean it'll send me flying but it won't kill me... I'm counting on you to pry open the hatch on top of the tank with the shovel. From the inside give him a good stab with your scoopula."

"...it's a scalpel."

"It's a science shank. Who cares? You know what I'm talking about."

Stozi was far from confident in their strategy but it was tough to refuse. After all, Stozi technically had the easy part, at least up until he got inside. Then, he wasn't sure what in store for him.

Stozi prepared for his run from his house's backyard, while Jackie remained on the opposite end of the block in the gazebo in the corner of Larry Stein's yard. Jackie made himself clear and visible to attract the tank's attention. Currently, its whereabouts were surprisingly unknown, keeping still since they've emerged from their hiding. At some point, it must have cut through Stozi's home whilst searching for the remaining contenders, as Stozi was now hiding in the remaining wreckage, ducking behind the remains of his wife's home office. She sold homemade earrings online for a living. It would have been great if some of her soldering tools were available to melt through the tank's latch. But they were gone. Unfortunately, it seemed any other deadly weapons besides the ones they woke up were taken away like their families.

Stozi and Jackie decided to wait for the tank to make the first move and then they'd catch it while in transition whether it went after Jackie or not. Stozi waited, his back against a steel tool drawer, for what felt like over an hour, although it was tough to tell. Time was no longer passing like it usually did. The sky was stuck at the first hour of dawn. Halted in continuous purple.

Stozi was waiting for the erupting sounds of the tank to signal their attack. He was caught off guard when he instead heard the loud cracks of a gun break the nerve-wracking silence. Stozi peered out over his cover and saw his friend being chased away from the open ground of the patio. Not by a large vehicle, but instead by a red thread extending down to Jackie's footprints. It shined downward onto the backyard from the upstairs window of the conjoined Stein estate.

Stozi groaned in frustration. Their plan had backfired entirely. Stein must have ditched his war machine and switched out for Mr. Milton's rifle. Stein must have snuck upstairs back at his home nice and quiet, while they were expecting a terrifying calamity to reveal.

Stozi witnessed the laser sight atop the rifle following Jackie's tail all the way into a row of bushes beside the gazebo. As soon as Jackie disappeared into the brush, the rifle fired again. This time it was followed by a horrid shout.

Jackie didn't reemerge. Stozi was worried he'd lost the game.

Alone now, Stozi realized the best weapon he had left was the element of surprise. He could perhaps perform a sneak attack on the less armored Stein from inside his residence. Stozi was careful to keep well-hidden as he traveled around the perimeter of the block until he reached the front yard of Stein's estate. He crept around the animals and shapes carved into the topiary garden out front, keeping behind them and out of sight of the manor's front windows.

Stozi slipped inside the manor's front door still destroyed from Jackie's axing. He quietly approached the nearest pathway up to the manor's second and third floors. Stozi avoided the glass elevator and decided on the spiral staircase instead. He got to the first step and began to ascend.

He kept his steps quiet as he reached the halfway point at the first floor's ceiling, but apparently his sneak attack had not gone unnoticed. Stozi could hear Larry Stein creep out of his bedroom and walk to the top of the steps above him. He heard a soft jingling noise, as Larry fooled around with the content of his front pocket.

He was reaching for the proper ring.

"Shit!" shouted Stozi. He leapt for his life over the railing of the staircase. Just in time for Larry's original ring to activate and send a tank slamming downwards. It crushed the entire staircase and anything beneath it. Which, fortunately, did not include Stozi, who had dodged the clever attack and now swung from a nearby chandelier. With a bit of heroism, Stozi heard horns of triumph play in his head as he swung from the rafter down onto the top of the tank. He slid on Mr. Ange's ring and wedged the shovel into place, prying open the hatch with surprising ease.

"Prepare to die rich boy!" shouted Stozi with fatherly lameness. He charged forward through the tight confines of the vehicle and hooked his arm around the neck of Larry Stein. "Are you the bastard that started this war?"

Stozi squeezed harder around Mr. Stein's throat, till Stein reached his hands up and tried to pull the grip off his neck.

"I wanna' know why you did it!"

Mr. Stein tried to speak, but the clamp around his throat was too tight. He managed to swivel his head just enough to convey a 'no'.

"Just tell me the truth!"

"I... didn't start... I'm..." Mr. Stein couldn't muster the last sound. But his lips clearly mouthed a surprising choice of words. 'Gay'.

Stozie let up on Mr. Stein's neck, enough to let the man speak.

"I have another family. And another lover," said Mr. Stein. "I went along with the charade, but I really didn't have any interest in Milton's statue."

"Where? ...what?!"

"He lives in Rhode Island. We served together. Made love for the first time in a tank just like this. I'm scared to leave behind my beard, though. My sisters and brothers are all still very much alive and well... and we're a very Catholic family. I need a wife if I'm to stay an active part of the Stein business."

Stozie sighed. "Then what are you attacking everyone for?"

"Same reason as you. I don't want to lose Debbie. She's dull enough to believe anything. It's so easy to sneak around with Joey."

"No offense," frowned Stozie. "But if Deb's your age, I don't think anyone's trying to steal her away."

"If it's Milton or Bacon who started this then your right... but of course there's somebody else who knew about all this," explained Stein. "There's always our Crazy Jack."

"Why the fuck do you all call him that?!"

"He's our pet wild man! He's so desperate to fit in that he'll do whatever crazy shit we ask. Drink this piss. Fight that guy. Punch yourself in the face. He's fucking desperate... he thinks if he buddies up to us, we'll pay for his wife's surgery."

"But you won't?" asked Stozie.

"I mean we will, now," continued Stein. "He's gonna' make us. He'll take one of our wife's and the statue will make his wife ours in exchange. Once she's the wife of a millionaire, she'll get better healthcare than anything Crazy Jack can afford."

"Oh my god," exclaimed Stozie. "But Jackie's dead, now, right?"

"Negative moron," groaned Stein. "He's right outside waiting for you." Stein pointed to the periscope's lenses hanging in front of his face.

"Waiting for..." Stozie leaned forward and took a look for himself through the periscope. "... he's waiting for me," whimpered Stozie, gazing at the image before him: Jackie holding Borky's pistol, pointing it directly at the top of the tank's hatch.

"He'll shoot you as soon as you pop out of this cockpit... but there's a way you can escape." Stein brought his hands up to Stozie's throat. "Did you know you can only die in this game at the hands of a pink weapon?" Stozie nodded. He's received a reset before after being killed by something otherwise. "Then let me do the pleasure. My hands certainly don't count, and you'll end up back at your house."

"Maybe I should just let him win?" said Stozie. "Right? I mean, it won't affect me, and he gets what he wants. You brought this statue right to him. You and your bougie friends all had a part in this."

"What can I say? He's your friend. I'm not. Why listen to me? But truth is, I'm gonna' lose my Joey and that fucking sucks cause he doesn't deserve that. And my friends had some power mad ideas, but they never followed through and that says *something* about their relationships with their wives. They mean *something* to them."

Stozi sighed. Perhaps his friend really was making a mistake. It was most certainly the stress of their desperate situation. A low-income household with both parts of the couple needing extensive medical care. That's a tough spot, but perhaps messing with reality itself wasn't a good means of solving it.

"I just wish I could trust you," cringed Stozi.

"You don't have to," shrugged Stein. "This isn't a final decision. You're just buying more time to make a choice. Neither you nor I have to die right this second."

The end of Stein's sentence was followed by the sounds of footsteps clunking from up above. Impatient and growing suspicious, Jackie, or Crazy Jack as some call him, decided to climb on top of the tank himself to investigate Stozi's drawn out attack.

Stozi still hesitated to take the offer. In fact, he slipped on his original wedding band and activated his scalpel. He held its thin tip to Stein's throat. "Jackie's not a bad guy. After all, he's doing this for Molly, not himself. And, I'm sorry, but you're just not going to get me to care for you rich fucks and your gold digger brides and your secret boyfriends."

Jackie suddenly leapt down from the open hatch above, adding a third to an already dense cockpit. He held out his gun to the two other men inside. "I really appreciate that," said Jackie, aiming the tip of the pistol at Stein's forehead. "The tank echoes like a tin can. I heard what you said, Stoz. And I appreciate you understanding my difficult situation."

Jackie closed one of his eyes and prepared his kill shot. "Allow me to get what I want."

Stein quickly leapt forward onto Stozi and spun them both around, switching their respective places in the confines of the vehicle. While Stozi struggled to breath pressed against the controls to the tank, Stein was now wedged between Stozi and Jackie. Jackie began to fire round after round into Stein's back. Stein used his body like a human shield to protect Stozi from any of the blows.

Stein worked fast to transport Stozi back to his bed. As blood poured fast out of his wounds, Stein had to stay conscious long enough to choke the life out of Stozi's lungs. Stein squeezed hard on Stozi's neck till his face turned blue. He held on tightly, even as Stozi swung his scalpel into the back of Stein's hands, plucking out bits of tendons and nerves.

"Well consider this," coughed Stein with his final breaths. "You may not believe it, but your wife is just as much at risk. You're not rich, but your middle class rich and that's good enough to afford one spouse with cancer. And while my wife, and the wives of all my friends are old and decrepit, I'm sure Crazy Jack would find your wife quite doable..."

Jackie unloaded another barrage of bullets into Stein; this time pressing the barrel of the gun right up against the back of Stein's head. The lead pierced Stein's skull and sent brain matter splashing onto the controls of the tank, blinking and buzzing in the empty space left beneath Stein. Giving in to the pressure around his neck, Stozi had disappeared into thin air.

The suffocation itself was no worse than having been crushed by a bookcase. In fact, it was far less painful. There was no feeling of internal redecoration; only a slight sting in his throat and a growing shadow that enveloped over his eyes

When he finally gave into his unconscious state, he was greeted with a sudden surge of energy that bolted him back awake. There he was. Back in his bedroom. Or what was left of it at least. Stozi's return was less comfortable this iteration. His bed had been flipped over whilst Stein pulverized the surrounding walls. Stozi felt the bed crushing against his back and the cold floor pressed against his face. Stozi squeezed out of the uncomfortable position and crawled around on his knees searching for his scalpel. Frustrated that he couldn't find it in the rubble, he simply pulled his ring off and put it back on, resetting the scalpel back to his hand conveniently.

Stozi crept out of the crumbles of his bedroom and took a seat on the bottom side of his overturned bed. He took a moment to consider the dying ramblings of Stein that had begun slipping in and out of his head like the final words of a dream. It was hard to shake them off. Could there be any truth to it? He accepted that Jackie was responsible for the tournament. But would Jackie, his long-time friend, be considering *his* wife as the prize?

Stozi was jolted out his thoughts when the silence of his bedroom was interrupted by the familiar machinery of the pink tank as it reactivated from far off in the distance. Stozi heard the vehicle speedily trekking across the backyards. The tank was fast approaching the ruins that were Stozi's abode.

Stozi's bedroom now lied on the first floor of his house, collapsed and dispersed into the bathroom beneath it. Stozi searched for a broken shard of the mirror hidden amongst wreckage. But though he found the frame, it seemed all the pieces had been removed or had completely vanished. Perhaps they fell into the category of unapproved weapons and had therefore been banned from the battle in real-time.

Stozi's option to continuously kill himself before anyone else could get him with their weapon seemed not to be as feasible as he first thought. As the tank quickly approached him, Stozi considered a backup plan, perhaps he could talk plainly with his friend.

When the tank pulled up to Stozi's fallen temple, it stopped and shut off its engines immediately. The latch on top popped open and Jackie crawled onto the top of his vehicle. "Sorry," he said jumping down from the tank. "Didn't mean to intimidate you... I just never rode in a tank before. This might be my only opportunity."

"It's a shame that when this over you won't remember it," laughed Stozi.

"Oh... no. I'll remember it. From what I understand, after reality is changed by the statue. The winner is the only one who keeps his memories of what things were before and the competition itself."

"Well," shrugged Stozi with a grin. "Then maybe you won't be the winner."

Jackie nodded while his smile faded. "You won't make this easy for an old friend, huh?"

"You've not been honest with me... again," griped Stozi. "Our friendship is becoming strained by quite the string of lies. Perhaps, you could just tell the harsh truth now considering I won't possibly remember when you win."

"Stozi I've lied about being busy during some of your parties ... which is what I think you're referring to. But it wasn't to join the boys at the top of the block. I skipped their festivities as well. It was all just missed so I could work at the firehouse without my wife accounting for my lost time. I'd tell her I was at *your* BBQ. Or *their* imported ham tasting."

"I figured that much, Jackie, but what's your intentions with this game. I feel like if they didn't involve me, you would have just been honest about your doing from the very beginning."

Jackie swore that wasn't the case. "I didn't tell you because I didn't know how you'd react. And I'm clearly desperate for this ritual to work."

Stozi sighed and held up his scalpel. "We're all liars I suppose... I just wonder. Is my wife safe from your deception? Or should I be afraid you'll take her away from me, if I allow you to kill me?"

Jackie pointed to the tank parked behind him. "I have Stein's ring, Stozi. It's the one I was going after. And the one I wanted most. Stein doesn't want his wife for anything but keeping his family's wealth. I'm targeting the least loved women of the lot. It's fair. I'll treat her like a real woman, and Stein will give my wife the wealth she needs."

"Wealth and no love. He loves a man, you know?"

"Yes... I'm fully aware. What's your point?"

"Maybe you really want someone with not just the money to help your wife. But someone that actually loves her. It's almost flattering, but maybe you know I could give her that. And maybe, you know, you naturally don't want a fossil out of this for yourself. You could give your wife good health and wealth, and my wife could rock your world. Perhaps I'm more willing to accept that than you'd think."

"..." Jackie stared at Stozi like an oddity. "Quite frankly, you're beginning to worry me. These ideas are... deranged. I feel bad. I think this experience has worn on you."

"Right," Stozi sighed staring at a fallen towel rack at his feet. It clearly hadn't met the games standards as a clear, obvious weapon. Not that it mattered. Stozi wasn't sure if he felt like fighting any longer. He realized there wasn't much of a chance at winning. Jackie was a boy scout. A lying, mischievous boy scout. Who'd spent the game gathering the right resources for survival.

Jackie had a tank, a sniper rifle, a pistol, an axe, and perhaps even more rings ransacked off the fingers of fallen fathers and DINKs. Stozi had a scalpel and nothing else. Even the shovel he'd been gifted had disappeared. It must be a slight punishment of resetting. You continue playing, but you lose all the rings you acquired.

Jackie made the kill shot as clean as possible as to avoid causing his friend too much pain. He used the sniper rifle to empty Stozi's skull in a quick blast. Stozi barely had time to process that he was being shot. His last second of thought was the image of the rifle's scope appearing out of thin air and being pressed to Jackie's eye. This memory, along with all others associated with the battle royale, would disappear instantaneously as Jackie became the winner. Stozi's memories of the past decade would quickly be replaced by a whole new timeline where he hooked up with a much older woman. Her name was Abby.

Abby was never interest in kids and so they were able to stockpile their money. When they decided to move into the suburbs, Stozi was able to afford a much larger house at the top of the hill. Stozi wouldn't know it, but he smiled a lot more than in his previous life. As did Abby. In fact, Abby was so less stressed the smoking habit she'd kept hidden from Jackie had never developed. She never had to worry about her husband dying from occupational hazard. Stozi had always worked behind a desk. And so, Abby never got cancer, and these funds were instead allocated toward luxurious cruises and block party soirees.

On the other hand, Jackie now found himself married to a woman half his age. And with a full memory of his past life, he was at first ecstatic to have such a hot, new wife. But he hadn't realized just how different being married to Aaron would be. She had a lot more energy than his former wife, which had its pros and cons. She was far more optimistic about Jackie's dangerous work as a fireman, but she also had a much stronger need for offspring.

Jackie quickly realized he was never cut out to be a father, as the sleepless nights and constant crying drove him to the edge. He eventually had to quit the job he loved as a fireman, as the energy required to raise half a dozen rugrats drained him too much for such an athletic career. Jackie found himself once again trapped behind a desk bored out of his skull. And worst of all, there was something not quite right about his youngest girl. As her face developed and matured, it began to seem more and more familiar. It was like Jackie had met her before.

One night as Jackie lied in his bed unable to rest, the memory of Stozi's kids from the former timeline appeared before him. Why did their kids look exactly the same?

Pizza Crow III

The only difference I could find between Carlos' and Mary's pepperoni and mushroom pizza seemed to be the taste of the sauce. Mary's was far less sweet, and far spicier. This little difference seemed to change the story I received from "Bedfellows" to "Belligamy". I began to theorize that further changes to the pizza's formula could allow me to tune my gifts to different tales. Like turning the knob on a radio.

I noticed the two stories I had so far both dealt with the theme of love, which I believe to be the result of keeping some of the pizza's elements the same. The theme is either determined by the toppings or the crust. I've decided to change each of the aspects one at a time, to see the differences I could create.

I follow this entry with "Captured by Animals" and "Red Constellation". The earlier caused by switching to thin crust, the later caused by switching to onions and peppers.

Captured by Animals

I've found that the best dialogue comes from characters who think they're alone. So I hide in the bushes and listen to couples as they camp in what they think is an isolated part of the woods. Although risky, and admittedly intrusive, it rewards me with the best material I've ever written.

The campers are most often seen on the weekend, especially at the beginning and end of the school year. Anytime really when the neighboring Colorado State has off. This gives students free time to shirk their homework responsibilities and seek adventure with a mate in the nearby woods of Rocky Mountain National Park.

Because of the proximity to the school, most of my subjects are students. But I always know I hit the jackpot when a teacher tags along. The mentor-mentee relationship budding into secret romance is immoral and complex, which makes for excellent drama.

My book series *Camp-biguous* was capable of topping the Romance category on Kindle due to one of these awkward relationships. I was proud of the accomplishment and I'll never forget the couple responsible. Their names have been changed for the purpose of anonymity.

I call the male Rover due to the dark grey Land Rover Discovery he takes to the edge of the woods before camping. Usually it's him and his girlfriend that pop out of the front seats; the latter being a twenty-year old girl who volunteers in Rover's lab. I call this young woman Spot, due to the patterns on her dresses.

The first few times I spied on them were relatively uneventful. They acted just like any regular couple. Making food by the fire. Staying up late and telling old stories. Intercourse. It was all accompanied by painfully dry dialogue that I could find between any two subjects on an outing. I wanted something more dramatic.

Little did I know, my patience would pay off when one weekend the same Land Rover would appear at the forest's edge. But instead, Rover would pop-out with a different woman by his side. And she was the same age. Roughly fifty-five. Due to the regal look of her eccentric jewelry, I'll be calling this older woman Duchess.

Duchess and Rover did things differently than Rover and Spot. Duchess led their treks through the woods. Duchess chose the camp grounds. Duchess setup the tent and blankets. And Rover just brought the snacks. These responsibilities were usually reversed between Rover and Spot.

And when the two made love, Rover stuck to the bottom of the pile and had little opinion as to when they started or stopped. He seemed much more relaxed through the experience, if not a tad mindless.

When the fornification was over, they wrapped a pair of beach towels around their waists and took a seat around the fire. They took a moment to catch their breaths. In the silence, I could hear rustling in the bushes. As it got closer, it became distinct. It was a pair of footsteps approaching from just up the hill.

Suddenly, Spot came out of the trees. She was dressed in a long white maxi covered in polychromatic polka-dots. In her left-hand was a cell-phone turned into a flashlight with the proper settings. In her right hand was a pine-cone. She quickly hurled the latter item into the back of Rover's head. He shouted in pain and hopped out of his seat.

"I'm sorry to intrude but..." Spot wiped a tear from her eye. "You're making me sick."

Duchess turned towards Spot and screamed. She covered the top of her body with her forearm and crossed her legs under her towel.

"My god, she's here to kill us..." exclaimed Duchess.

At this point, I got nervous my romance might turn into true crime. But luckily, instead of an outburst, Spot simply put away her phone and took a seat around the campfire with equal spacing between the other two campers.

"This sucks," sighed Spot, staring into the fire. "I suppose it's hard for you to go any younger than me without crossing a legal boundary, but I never would have imagined you cheating with a woman more than twice my age!" Spot picked up a twisted branch lying at her feet and threw it angrily into the fire. "You're making me feel horribly unattractive."

"Age isn't everything, dear," proclaimed Duchess.

Spot sneered. "You need to stay out of this, homewrecker."

"I don't think so," replied Duchess. She stood up and repositioned herself beside Rover. "You're interrupting the first weekend I've had away from the office in six months. If you're not here to kill us then whatever you have to say can wait till Monday. Then he's all yours again."

"God she's not even sweet!" griped Spot pointing an open hand towards Duchess. "Is this all just because you can bring her around your friends and your kids without them calling you an old perv?"

"Trust me, no... it's not that," replied Rover, finally getting a word in. "I assure you my relationship with Duchess is no less clandestine than ours was. And it will have to remain that way."

Spot didn't understand. She shook her head in confusion.

"You don't recognize the Dean of Biology?" asked Rover.

"Wait. Oh my god," Spot adjusted her place in her seat. "Rover... is this your boss?"

"It's sort of like when you got bi-curious," explained Rover. "I let you to sleep with a chick to see if you liked it. Well, it's no secret I'm turned on by power imbalances in relationships, and *I got curious* as to what it was like on the other side of said imbalance."

"To supplement his many shortcomings as a teacher, he earns his way through pleasing me sexually," said Duchess with a long smile.

Spot shrugged. "What's wrong with him as a teacher?"

"Well for one, he sleeps with his students..." said Duchess with an eye-roll.

"So you were just *curious*?" asked Spot. "So then... I'll ask you what you asked me. How does it compare?"

"I kind of like the guilt in her eyes when she knows she's in over her head," smirked Rover. "I could ruin her career with a few choice words and she knows it. So she works hard to make me feel special."

"Creepy," sneered Spot.

"Hypocrite," scoffed Rover. "Don't pretend you don't find it appealing too."

"You've got it all wrong," argued Spot. "I've never appreciated our relationship *because* of the power imbalance. I just liked *you*. It was about you, *regardless* of the age difference. *Regardless* of your teaching status. *Regardless* to the point where if we were born the same year, we'd still be together."

"Bullshit." Rover shook his head. "I know firsthand now how alluring it is."

"Well then what's your decision?" asked Spot, clearing her eyes of a second pass of tears. "Is it so alluring you don't want to go back? Cause I'll still have you... even after all this. As long as you promise it was just experimenting."

I began clutching tightly to my notepad. I knew his final decision would be the climax of what would become my most popular tale. All I had to do at this point was stay absolutely quiet, and yet, my baser instincts suddenly betrayed me at the worst possible moment. Much like a man sweats when he's nervous, my body handles tensity and agitation with a primal growl. I felt it rise uncontrollably from the space beneath my chest. This low buzz began to flow out of my mouth like a yawn. I couldn't hold it back.

"What was that?" called out Rover looking around the campgrounds. Both the women went on high alert and began scanning the nearby bushes with their eyes.

I quickly threw my notepad over my shoulder and got down on all fours. If they were to spot me, I would prefer it while down on my paws where I don't seem too out of sync with the rest of nature.

"Bear!" shouted Duchess, launching out of her seat. She must have spotted my eyes twinkling in the bushes. Despite their wariness, I couldn't look away and risk missing something juicy. "Grab your things and run!"

Within a few brief moments, I witnessed one of the greatest love triangles of the century disappear before my very eyes just because I couldn't control a grrr. It unfortunately left me with the burden of deciding for myself how their story should end. Which, I know, I shouldn't have to complain about. The job of a writer *is* to be creative after all.

I ended up giving it to Spot in case you're curious. And it's not because I honestly think those two should end up together. I decided upon what I thought would simply have more dubious implications. After all, it raises more questions for the reader. Can a couple appreciate a relationship in two completely different lights, yet still make it work? One enjoys the dirtiness of it all. And one enjoys the genuine company. It made for a provocative fictional ending, but I always doubted it was better than the real thing. We may never know how it was really resolved, but I made sure missing out on that would never happen again. If I wanted to be the number one New York Time's best-seller, I needed the utmost authenticity and that meant learning to control my instincts no matter the cost.

I've idolized the NYT best-sellers since I first gained the consciousness level of a human being. Before that, I had the simpler life goals of your average ursus americanus. I wanted food. Living right outside of Fort Collins my best choice for sustenance was to walk onto the nearby campus and raid the dumpsters and garbage cans for scraps.

At first, I was gaining most of my nutrition from pizza crusts and chicken bones outside of a local dollar-slice pizzeria. But over time, I found better options. The key was to go where the rich kids were. Fraternity row.

The selection here was far more vast. Sammy had discarded latkes and brisket. NAK had half-eaten pastels and chivitos. And Adelphikos had just boat loads of bouje mac and cheese. I was surprised no one ever called the cops on me that whole brief period of culinary delight. In hindsight, I believe any witnesses to my trespassing were most likely turned off by the idea of cops snooping around their frat houses. Especially given the selection of drugs I found on their premises.

It was not uncommon that I'd find myself high or drunk after ingesting the frat trash. Their foods were often laced with hallucinogens, uppers, and downers. At first it just made me dizzy, remedied by a quick nap in a shady spot in the bushes, but eventually my curiosity had permanent effects.

I was munching on brownies at the bottom of a compost heap outside of AGR when I noticed the usual effects of ingesting stimulants. I felt a numbness in my nose, followed by sparkles in my cheeks. I expected to feel my heart rate go up, but instead the sensation in my chest was focused around my lungs. I was breathing rapidly, consuming massive amounts of oxygen to support some change brewing in my anatomy. It was extra support for a growing brain.

Whatever cocktail of drugs was in those brownies had an unusual reaction with the neurological chemistry of an American black bear. I found myself slowly breaking apart my thin stream of consciousness into various aspects. Setting, climate, time of day all became recognizable from the usual pinhole of light and sound I used to follow. Fresh food suddenly became distinct from garbage and I felt utterly sickened by my previous behavior. I suddenly realized how stupid I was acting, trotting around, a wild animal, in the middle of the human domain. I had levels of self-consciousness for the first time and it was urging me to flee back into the safety of the woods.

From then on, my ever-growing intelligence commandeered my body for obtaining massive amounts of information. I felt compelled to spy on humans that came into my forest in order to better understand how to use this big curvy brain of mine. The notes I took were originally just for learning purposes, but eventually the idea to publish came to mind after several encounters with a man I call Peanut.

Peanut is Peanut due to the handfuls of trail mix he chews incessantly while painting. Peanut paints almost every day in different corners of my domain, finding interesting little landscapes that I never appreciated even when I was a part of the picture. I learned from watching him the importance of not just creating, but also the joy of sharing said creations. I tried this pleasure for myself by stealing various cell phones from sleeping campers and posting my notes as novellas online. It's been the most thrilling use of my newfound intelligence I've yet to discover.

I know it must sound a little creepy, but my appreciation for writing has become so great that I've developed strategies to get the most out of my spying. There are algorithms I've created solely for judging the potential of a campout for writing material. Newcomers are always best; frequent visitors treat the woods as a second home and are too mundane. Those who treat camping like a special occasion tend to do more special things. Party size is key too. One is too small as there's no one to talk to. And four is too big for the conversation to get deep. Two or three are therefore the perfect sizes. You've already seen the beauty I got out of a love triangle, but there's something to be said about a simple one-on-one.

Stella and Bailey were, by far, my favorite one-on-one. Stella was Stella because of the Stella Artoise in her mouth when I first saw her. And Bailey was Bailey because of the bottle of Bailey's he was gulping down. Stella and Bailey were both older. I could tell from their mannerisms they were happily and faithfully married for quite some time. They were parents visiting their child for CSU's official Parent's Weekend. At the end of the day, most parents checked-in to hotels to sleep before grabbing Sunday breakfast with their kids the following morning. But Stella and Bailey were different. They decided to go camping.

At first it was relatively boring. A lot of chit-chat worrying about their child's future. But once Stella finished her fifth Stella, and Bailey finished an entire fifth of Bailey's, the two were both feeling a vibe that quickly evolved into a juicy, middle-aged make out sesh. Stella paused the action for a brief moment to pick something out her sleeping bag. She came back with a wooden paddle and a sly expression on her face.

"I want you to use this on me."

Bailey, who had seemed all gung-ho just a moment prior, suddenly seemed shy. He began looking all around the nearby trees, as though he were paranoid they were being watched.

"But it's sort of loud isn't it... won't that attract too much attention?"

Stella gave Bailey a strange look. "We're in the middle of the woods, who could possibly hear it?"

"I just..." Bailey looked nervous. He grabbed the paddle from out of his wife's hands, then set it down gently by the fire. "I really don't wanna'. It's too familiar."

"Familiar, how?"

"I feel like..." Bailey sighed and took a seat in the grass. "I feel as though you're purposely overwriting a lot of my memories with other women."

"Overwriting? In what way?"

"We redo them," said Bailey with a shrug. "Scene by scene. We act them out. You and I. And then that takes some of the charm away from the original."

"Oh come on!" scoffed Stella. "When have I..."

"Halloween three years ago."

Stella looked shocked. "...I don't remember that?"

"Well you had us do it in the bathroom during the costume party. At the time, it seemed like a bit of harmless fun, but later on, I remembered telling you about an almost identical situation I had with my first girlfriend in college."

Stella shrugged. "Well I'm sure we weren't dressed the same?"

"My girlfriend and I went as Garfield and Jon. We went as Shaggy and Scoob. It's not identical but the pet-play concept is still there." Bailey took a deep breath to relax himself, then pointed at the paddle. "And now you're encouraging me to use a paddle on you, which sounds an awful lot like the quirky little tale of how I lost my virginity to a school-girl fetishist..."

Stella remained silent.

"So honey, are you doing it on purpose?"

Stella didn't respond.

Bailey pressed harder. "Are you intentionally replacing my memories?"

"Maybe," Stella looked away and gulped. "Yes, okay! Yes. But it's your fault for telling me!"

"Telling you what?"

"About your past endeavors..." Stella launched up out of her seat. "Why would I want to *know* those things?"

"I wasn't bragging. They were all perfectly reasonable responses at the time," responded Bailey. "You asked me why I wasn't welcome in Jack's home anymore *and it's because* I fucked Deborah in his bathroom!"

"Fine! But I still don't see anything wrong with wanting to relive those things with you!"

"Let's just make *new* memories; that's less weird."

"To be honest, I don't know why it makes me so upset," whimpered Stella. "It's just the thought of you with anyone else breaks my heart."

"We've raised babies together, yet you still feel insecure?"

Stella nodded.

Bailey sighed. "Even if we did do it together tonight, it would be impossible for you to repeat every sexual encounter I've had before you."

Stella gave Bailey a stern look and shook her head. "You told me you've had sex with only four women. It can't be too long a list."

"But that list includes a threeway. Are *you* really going to do a threeway?"

"I'll just replace the second girl with a sex toy," replied Stella. "I can make it feel the same way."

Bailey smiled. "I don't doubt it... but I still don't like the idea of you replacing my experiences. You don't have the right to erase my past."

Stella sighed. "I understand."

"But maybe instead of redoing everything, a better way to do it would be to improve upon them."

"Improve?"

"Yeah. That way it stays fresh in my mind. Let's make it better!"

"I'm forty-five years old," laughed Stella. "I don't think it's feasible for me to improve upon what a twenty-something did to your body."

"That's impossibly mean to yourself, honey," scolded Bailey. He kicked off his shorts and threw off his shirt. "Here, get naked with me."

"Right away? Right now?" laughed Stella.

"Yes, you see, we are *improving* on how it was," explained Bailey. "You see she wanted to do a bunch of over the clothes stuff to start out, and I'm far too A.D.D. to admit to liking that."

Stella nodded. "Yeah?... Okay!" Stella tore her top off and joined Bailey in his nudity. "While we're at it, let's just skip the oral, nix the face-to-face stuff, and you can just do me from behind."

Bailey nodded excitedly and got into position. "Exactly! You see we're fixing all the annoying little nuances from last time. Including the condom."

"Uh... you don't have a condom?"

"I do but I thought... okay never mind, we'll still wear the condom."

Bailey and Stella proceeded to put on a masterful performance. To keep my excitement from producing another growl, I was sure to bring along a tiny bottle of whiskey to keep myself calm this time. I stole it out of a backyard on frat row.

By the time Bailey and Stella were complete, I was feeling rather drunk. I managed to keep clandestine up till now, but I still needed to get my notes online. I stowed my pen and tablet in a nearby hollow and rested in the bushes until dark. It was at that point that I snuck back into Bailey and Stella's campsite. I crept quietly into their tent and grabbed their cell phones. Bailey's was locked, but Stella left hers on, still opened-up on a sleep-sounds app.

I opened her browser, logged into my email, and got to typing as fast I could. I was reading off of shorthand, so I had to fill in the blanks as I scrambled to write it all down before they woke. I tried my best to keep a consistent tone I've been using in my other work. It's a bit cold and detached. Which, I know, sounds nothing like me. But acting frigid means less writing for me, which is kind of the goal in these situations. It's a lot faster to say,

"He looked insulted" than let's say "Bailey had a look of distrust that he's mastered from years of parental neglect."

The story of Stella and Bailey would end up attracting the attention of an agent who's been searching for a hot, new romance artist to tackle a project geared toward Gen-Z and younger millennials. I'll call my agent Buddy, cause he's the first human friend I ever made. And no, he has no idea I'm a bear and I don't see that changing anytime soon. Lots of writers prefer to be kept anonymous even to their publishers, so it never seemed strange to Buddy that I'd never wanted to interact in person.

The project I would end up making for Buddy had to be something special. This would be my first step outside of independent publishing, so I knew I needed something eventful. The problem with my writing is its reliance on others. Autumn had just passed when I got my assignment. I rarely found campers during the winter months, but if I didn't get material to my agent quick enough he'd drop me as a writer.

I worked hard to make it happen. It felt unnatural for me to be working so hard. Not in the winter. In the winter, bears are supposed to be asleep. But there I was, trudging around in the cold, moving to each of the usual hideouts, trying to find some signs of life.

I finally lucked out after the first full week of February. It was a Friday night when a bright beam of light penetrated through the dark; it was followed by a loud engine. There was a snow bike weaving through the trees. On top was a female rider dressed in puffy pink snow gear. She looked a bit too heavy for the bike she was riding on, but she managed to steer it well regardless. She seemed to be following a path laid out on the screen of her phone, wedged into a cup holder built into the left handlebar.

Normally, my algorithm wouldn't permit me to follow a single. There'd be no dialogue and that's my bread and butter. But my desperation to find a subject was so severe, I decided to follow regardless, perhaps out of sheer boredom. I wedged my notebook in my jaw and got down on all fours. I followed along close behind her, using my animal stamina to keep up.

She led me to the top of a hill where the trees grew too close for her to continue on bike. She hopped off her vehicle, locked it to a tree, and grabbed her cell phone from the cup holder. She trudged forward into the thicket until she reached a tall tree with a nest in its branches. I glimpsed over her shoulder and could make out a tracking app on her screen. The type used by ecologists to find the animals they chipped. I expected the girl was looking for whoever made that nest above her, and when she held her mitten to her lips I thought she'd let out a series of bird calls. But instead, it was entirely English.

"Hello?" called out the ecologist. I've named her Lady, due to the bright, pretty colors on her coat. "Is there time for you to talk?"

A white flash came out of the snowfall and landed on a nearby branch. "I've always got time," came a low, raspy voice from the bright yellow beak of an owl. "The life of an animal can be quite uneventful considering we aren't capable of event planning."

"Have you made any progress with Alecia?"

The owl shook his head.

"Are you trying very hard?"

The owl frowned. "It feels too wrong."

Seeing a talking owl might concern most witnesses but being a composite of Yogi Bear and Thoreau myself, I was used to such weirdness. My best guess was that one of the rats I share my dumpster food with ingested the same drug as myself and must have been promptly eaten by this aerial predator.

"If you don't mate with her, that's it for the Colorado Lemon-beaked Snow Owl," scowled Lady.

This owl shrugged his wings. "Is it worth perpetuating my species, if it means having to mate with an animal?"

"*You're* an animal?" griped Lady.

"But with human intelligence. Regardless of our phenotype, our minds aren't equal. How would you feel if you could only propagate the human race by fucking somebody mentally handicapped?"

"I suppose... there would be some moral issues..." Lady sighed and peeled a pair of silver goggles off of her face, revealing a pair of deep blue eyes. "But I'm afraid your hesitation isn't entirely motivated by right and wrong. I think your still confused about... us?"

"I'm not confused."

"I'm the first human you interacted with in your enhanced state. It must have been extremely emotional to make your first connection. But you can't say you love me if you haven't met very many people."

"But I want only you, darling. You've won my heart with your mastery confections."

"It's just a pinecone with some bird seed and peanut butter. I keep telling you, we can all do that. Specifically, children."

The owl frowned. "But before you, I felt so empty."

"That's because it's like you said, the life of an animal fails to entertain the complex mind of an adult human. Our relationship is just an attempt to fill that hole."

"Then tell me, girl with far more experience thinking human than I, what is the proper way to fill the void?"

Writing. I thought. *Creating. The arts.* But none of these answers left Lady's lips. Instead, she closed her eyes and shrugged. "I think for most people it never closes up. It's just a part of you. A part of your brain. A very human organ that helps with your direction."

I dropped my notepad and cringed. Not because I disagreed with what Lady had to say, but I always assumed the cure for the emptiness was obvious. And now, I wasn't sure. I considered whether I'd made the same mistake as the owl. Finding the utmost importance in the first thing to present itself.

"Then what do you suggest I do?" asked the owl, glaring hazily at his talons.

Lady sighed. She took out a thick pink notebook from the lining of her jacket, opened to a specific page near its center, and crossed out something inside. "Well for starters, don't have kids. Or else you're revoking all your rights to explore this feeling any further."

The owl perked up. He nodded.

"Second of all, don't just limit yourself to your hometown." She shut her notebook, then slid back on her goggles. "If you follow me back to my lab, I'd like to show you some pictures from around the world. It's good that you can fly. There's plenty of places you can end up."

I threw down my notepad and stomped it into the snow. I suddenly experienced a new feeling. It was like panic but not the life or death kind. It was a horrible realization that I was unsure of myself. That I was stuck.

I got back down on all fours and charged away, leaving my work behind me. I didn't want it. I didn't want anything else but to escape where I was. But what horrified me is that, I couldn't just go. I *wasn't* an owl. I couldn't fly over top of everybody and settle down where it's safe. I realized I was stuck in this forest till the day I die.

I felt claustrophobic for the first time. And just when I thought I had it all figured out. I knew I needed help sorting this all out, but Buddy wasn't going to be much help. I couldn't even get the concept of being trapped here made clear without first explaining I'm a bear.

I was lucky enough to run into Peanut during my existential jog through the woods. There he was at the top of a cliff near the center of the forest. He was painting with deep purples trying to capture the sunset over the clearing below.

I'd never formally introduced myself to the man, but given my desperation for guidance, I decided to give it a chance and open communication with my muse. I tried to make it clear I was his admirer from afar. I think not being human made it a little less creepy.

I stood up straight on my back legs and walked forward out behind his easel. I just stood there till he saw me. And when he finally did, he put down his paintbrush and reached down into the snow at his ankles. He picked up a can of legumes between his heels and brought it up to his mouth. He then put a couple in his palm and reached out over top of his painting. He was trying to feed me.

"I, uh," I stuttered. "I... er. No thanks."

"Suit yourself," sighed Peanut. He pulled his hand backwards and dumped the snacks down his own throat.

"Do you need an explanation?" I asked. I wasn't used to showing my true self to humans, so I expected a drawn-out origin story would be required.

"No, I don't think so. I don't really see what good it would do," frowned Peanut. "It's probably scientific, to which I am lost."

"Well if you have nothing to ask me... I have a lot to ask you."

Peanut wiped flakes of peanut skin from his mustache. "Proceed."

"Are you happy?"

Peanut nodded. "Compared to my former youth."

"Are you *trapped* here?"

"Like under house arrest? No. I can come and go as I please. But, to be honest, I've never really thought about leaving. Not since I got here." Peanut turned his easel around and showed me his latest work. "There's a lot of good material around here. And you don't have to go too far from civilization to find it."

I agreed with him. I told him about my goals of becoming a well-known writer. I told him I've been spying on people. I told him how much it meant to me.

"I thought that making things is... all there is," I sighed. "Is there really more to it?"

"Well not everyone's an artist, or an inventor, so there's certainly other skills that keep people feeling alive."

"I don't have many options for work here in the forest, so I guess I was hoping there wasn't much more to life than creating."

"Well then just leave the forest," suggested Peanut.

"A talking bear can't just walk around from place to place. I'd get tranquilized and put in a zoo."

Peanut thought about it and reluctantly agreed. "You wouldn't make it very far without ending up in a lab here at the university, that's for sure."

"So then... I'm actually trapped here."

"I wouldn't say trapped, cause this isn't really a trap. An office space or a jail cell, that's a trap. You're just *bound* here. Which isn't as bad. Things move around, here. They shift and they change. How can you feel trapped when the world is constantly rearranging itself?" Peanut turned around and reached for a backpack he laid against a tree. He pulled out a painting he'd drawn far earlier in the springtime. "It's the same spot three months prior," explained Peanut, pointing out over the cliff. "You see how you can barely tell they're one in the same? The sunset's bright orange in this, but now it's deep shades of blue."

"So you're saying as long as I keep finding new subjects to write about, I'm not really trapped, it's just the world is coming to me, instead of me coming to the world."

Peanut nodded. "It sounds like you're starting to get it... you ever write about me, just out of curiosity?"

"Nah... you come alone. It doesn't make for interesting dialogue."

Peanut laughed. "I know some real characters I could convince to come out here, if you need some more subjects."

"Could always use more work."

"Great. I just hope they don't make you uncomfortable..." sighed Peanut, "a few of them are swingers."

I shook my head. I smiled. "In my line of work, that's just the type of behavior I'm looking for."

The Red Constellation

By the age of fifteen, Serena was already a savvy and wary young woman. She'd been warned of the terrifying monsters who took the form of ordinary men. They'll take advantage of her if ever given the opportunity. These lessons were drilled into her head by the terrifying life experiences shared by both her mother and her grandmother. Neither thought it was appropriate to sugar coat the world for even an adolescent, and so Serena's childhood naivety was early-on replaced with the awareness of a managing adult.

One of the perks of such an awareness was knowing when an adult was being inappropriate to minors. While her less vigilant classmates were too careless to notice the continuous ogling by some of their teachers, Serena was quick to report these perverts before they snowballed into an even larger problem for their public school.

Serena's extra-sensory powers were always on high alert, especially when she was out in public, particularly downtown. The neighboring city beside their suburb was not known for its safety or warmth and has nationally high-rates of assault and sexual violence. Serena's mother never took her into the city and Serena herself refused to follow her friends when they went in looking for ethnic food, clothing, or an otherwise exciting adventure.

The only times Serena had visited the city were when it was absolutely required, circumstances like those involving the hospital or when her class went on field trips. One such field trip of particular notoriety was to the city's science museum. Her ninth-grade class was let loose to enjoy the day playing with the exhibits unchaperoned, with their only requirement being to meetup back at the ticket booth at 3PM.

Serena wanted to just hang out with her friends, but they'd all decided to ditch the museum and head into the mall across the street as soon as the teachers weren't paying attention. Serena didn't feel comfortable going with, so she ended up miserably alone. All the strangers around her had her on edge the entire time. She thought she might be able to satiate her agoraphobia by seeking out an exhibit so boing it'd be completely empty. Such an opportunity quickly presented itself in the form of a planetarium in the astronomy wing, where no one was waiting in line for the next showing.

Serena ran on in and was pleased to see the theatre was entirely empty. She was able to enjoy the dark, isolated experience in peace. The first fifteen minutes of the show were a relaxing projection on the ceiling detailing the origins of the most notable aspects of our night sky. And then a thirty-minute light show followed, where the celestial objects strobed and changed color in sync with pop-hits from the early 2000s. It seemed the show had not received any sort of update for over a decade.

When the forty-five-minute show finally concluded, all the lights came back on and the viewers were instructed to exit. Turning her attention off of the ceiling, Serena leaned forward in her chair and stood up. After giving a big yawn to accompany a stretch, she noticed someone was staring at her from across the room.

While Serena was staring at the lights on the ceiling, a second person had joined the audience. It was an old man of his sixties who wouldn't take his eyes off of her. Serena didn't mind at first, but when she moved toward the exit, she noticed the old man had stopped in the doorway. It looked like he was waiting for her to leave. Serena held her breath and looked down at the floor as she was forced to pass him to get through the exit.

"The stars are jealous of you," gurgled the old man as Serena passed by.

Serena shuddered. She spun around and snarled at the creep. "You really shouldn't say that to a girl at my age."

The old man snarled back, "It's not to be taken flirtatiously."

"Oh of course not!" replied Serena rolling her eyes sarcastically. "Soon as I tell my teacher, you'll say it was to be taken sweetly, not romantically. I just remind you of your daughter or something."

The old man bowed his head and pointed to a patch on his old blue hat. It was the vintage insignia for NASA with the white lettering and the red chevron. "I used to work for them," frowned the old man, "till I became employed by larger powers."

"A children's museum?"

"I don't work here!" griped the old man. "I pay for admission. Every day. I communicate with the idols on the ceiling. They speak to me like the real thing. Today, they told me about you."

"And what did they say?" asked Serena, reaching her hand slowly into her little pink crossbody. She wrapped her hand around a canister of pepper gel hidden inside.

"Sirius says you should die, but Vega thinks there's another way," shrugged the old man. "But some way or another your lineage has to end."

"Alright star child, if you're not crazy exactly what lineage is that?" snarked Serena.

"Bethany and Barbra. Katherine and Ruth."

"Yeah well... none of those are my last name, so..." Serena took out the pepper gel and aimed it right under the brim of the man's hat. "Move along, now."

"But that's your mother's name," said the old man, slowly backing away. "And your mother's mother's name. And her mother's. And her mother's," explained the old man. "It's the only lineage you should ever be concerned about. That's the trail of your family curse."

Serena had heard enough to know she needed to get real help. This stranger was beginning to sound a lot like the monsters she was warned about. The same ones that once kidnapped her grandmother in the middle of broad daylight and the same ones that attacked her mother her freshman year of college.

Serena ran. She ran and she ran until she reached the nearest adult. It was a young museum curator with a little black V-neck and a pair of formal khakis. Serena informed the employee that the old man was skeezing on children. But they didn't seem to care.

"He's just senile," she laughed. "An old rocket scientist from before you were born. His ramblings sound alien but it's all just outdated space jargon."

"It didn't strike me as alien, miss," pleaded Serena. "It struck me as rapey."

The curator gave Serena a look of shock. "Look, I'm not the only girl on this staff. He's never done anything like that to any of us. He's just a tad boring."

"Well maybe he doesn't *like* girls your age..." sneered Serena.

The curator rolled her eyes. "Look kid, your class is packing up to go," she pointed to a line forming at the buses outside the window. "You should really catch up and I'll inform the manager for you."

Serena was wise enough to know there would be no conversation with her manager. She'd received similar replies from her school when she first started reporting their teachers' misconduct. She figured this museum would repeat the same mistakes. They'd ignore the problem till it's too late.

Serena was lucky she'd gotten away unscathed, but while *she* would never have to return to the museum again, leaving the problem unsolved meant leaving a great danger for other little girls to fall victim to. And that thought made Serena sick to her stomach.

But when your young, there's so much more emphasis on self-defense rather than altruism. It's not necessarily that youth have a particularly strong ego or carelessness, but when you're so little and have so little power and so little connection, there's just as little you can do to change the world.

That day at the museum would have some unfortunate effects on Serena's sense of security. After these events, Serena's agoraphobia would grow into paranoid territory. After all, the legends her mother and grandmother warned her about had become undeniably real and had walked right up to her. And so, like the matriarchs before her, her agoraphobic behaviors began to consume her. She limited her social space to her personal property and any necessary time spent in a classroom.

During her first two years of college, Serena avoided many of the same risky environments her new friends couldn't wait to invade. Keeping her mother's attack in mind, Serena avoided all the house parties she received offer to and kept her drinking contained to her dorm room or that of a close friend. She gained a reputation as the sort of mom of her friend group, keeping her various friends company when they were too sick or too depressed to go out on the town with the rest of the crew.

"You're always there for us," they'd tell her.

"Cause I don't go anywhere else!" she'd reply.

Her friends were well-aware she was a bit of a shut-in. She missed out on so many lasting memories and possible suitors due to her introverted lifestyle. Her friends would prod her all the time to get some sunlight. Most of them were honestly concerned with her habits. But when drunk and frustrated with her behavior, sometimes meaner things slipped out. She'd hear her title as mom quickly turn to hermit. And asking her to go out would change into desperate begging with added snideness. They'd tell her she's lonely. They'd tell her she needs therapy. They'd make it clear, "You need to go out and blow off some steam, Serena. We're afraid you're gonna' go mad..."

Serena questioned her own decisions more than her friends would ever have guessed. Every celebration she skipped to satisfy her own fears weighed on her. She couldn't even seek comfort in the shows streaming on her laptop. Every female character she could relate to eventually conquered their social awkwardness for at least one night and then ended up with some life changing story. A lover. A job. Or some other dream come true.

Serena's doubts culminated in an ultimate decision to step outside and enjoy some public intoxication on a very specific night. One that she could not bare to leave indifferent. It was her 21st birthday and she informed her friend group that she would very much like to go to a bar. She tried her best to make it clear though, this would be a difficult step for her and she'd need a fair amount of help. Her friends, absolutely ecstatic about her choice, promised to make her feel comfortable throughout the entirety of the expedition.

Serena's friends began their accommodations with providing her with the perfect pregame to ease her anxiety. They filled her body with green tea margaritas to level her mood then downed a few shots of chamomile brandy. Then they adorned her with birthdays gifts in the form of sweaters, jackets, and knitted hats. All the necessary gear for her to keep warm as they traveled about the winter weather. Serena was born at the end of January.

With a literal jacket layered over her liquor jacket, Serena's friends were confident she may be ready for stage two. It was time for them get a taxi and head off campus to the downtown part of the city. As they sat in the cab, Serena's friends grabbed the aux cable and decided against any dance music or high tempo beats, instead they played relaxing orchestral songs, the type Serena used to mellow out before exams.

When they left the cab, Serena's anxiety was still at bay, but it began to fight back hard as she looked up and down the main street. The crowds of rowdy youths flooding the sidewalks filled Serena's head with terrifying scenarios. She immediately informed her friends and they decided their best option was to get away from these riotous gangs and to head to the closest bar possible. They settled on Snowy's, a more mature venue with an even mix of generations.

Here, Serena had her first public drink bought with a valid ID. She wedged herself into a booth as close to the wall as possible and created a barrier out of her friends between her and the strangers surrounding her. The bar had live music that kept her feeling light and cheery and overall the night out was going as well as it could. She admittedly wasn't doing much talking amongst the crowd she came with, but even in her silence she was enjoying herself. She was just proud to be out and about for once. She even began to wonder if this was something she could muster on perhaps a monthly basis. And maybe even more if increased gradually.

After the live band finished their covers and the music was replaced with a mix of pop-beats the girls began to finish their drinks quickly to make their move to the next bar. Serena explained to them that she was hesitant to travel outside for too long and asked if they could go to a bar on at least the same block. They compromised on The Twisted Tutu, a college bar on the other side of the street. It was a lot more packed and had nowhere to sit, but Serena had worked enough momentum to give it an honest shot.

Serena paid her tab and walked outside to join the rest of her friends as they waited for traffic to slow down, so they could cross. But as the rest of the girls hollered, screeched, and laughed, Serena stood in silence. Not out of comfort such as in the bar, but quiet like how frightened animals pause when danger seems to be closing in.

Serena thought she was seeing things. There was a star in the sky that just didn't look natural. It was ruby red and it looked as though it was closer to Earth than any other light in the sky. The star hung right over top of The Twisted Tutu like a waypoint on a map and cast a pillar of crimson light overtop of the establishment. The glow was so bright it stung at Serena's eyes, even when she looked away it completely enveloped the top half of her vision.

Serena didn't have to ask if her friends saw the light as well. If that were the case, their eyes would be squinting just like hers. Serena began to worry.

Serena's mother and her grandmother both had deep psychological issues that sometimes manifested as visual hallucinations. But these two saw attackers where there were none and mistook shadows as men sneaking up behind them. They'd never mentioned seeing flashes of color or lights in the sky. But still, perhaps it was all the same. Serena was seeing things that no one else could and that alone was scary enough to ruin the confidence she was slowly building. Suddenly, the need for retreat became inescapable.

Serena panicked. She tried so hard to make this night work and look good in front of her friends. She needed to make it look as though she wasn't surrendering to her troubled mind. She wanted it to seem like she had no choice but to leave. She used the numbness forming in her extremities to ignore the pain and shoved two fingers hard down her throat. As she popped them back out they were followed by the sound of rushing water splattering onto the street. A torrent of pale green alcohol was ejected from her throat right into the center of her friend group. At first, they were horrified and scattered in all directions. After checking to be sure Serena hadn't touched their shoes with her bile, they all began to laugh.

"It's official... she's an extrovert now," joked one of the girls. "Puking in public... she's growing up so fast."

"Can somebody else get her home, though?" asked another. "I'm not ready to quit yet."

"I'll take care of her," replied a third. It was Kassie, a short blonde girl who Serena had provided with indoor company on multiple occasions. Kassie had MS and so she tired out fast when she was having off days. Feeling her illness beginning to weaken her, Kassie was more than happy to surrender alongside Serena.

Kassie put out a call for a Lyft and helped Serena back to her apartment. "You poor thing," said Kassie sliding a comforting arm over Serena's shoulders. "Did you at least have fun tonight?" Kassie stared at a string of green spittle streaking down the front of Serena's new coat. "It certainly looks like it."

Serena smiled. Then she nodded. Up until the strange red light, Serena really was enjoying herself. In fact, it was a shame her surreal visions drove her away or she felt she could have made it till closing time. But with these new symptoms flaring up out of nowhere, Serena's soaring confidence had been shot down. She wasn't sure if she'd ever go out again. In fact, after this night, she didn't even want to drink anymore. She was convinced her heavy consumption had somehow exasperated a latent symptom of her mental illness she had not witnessed before. She was afraid to activate it again and hoped that if she quit drinking perhaps it would be a one-time thing.

Three months would pass before Serena would ever have to consider downtown again. At this point, the summer was fast approaching and the race to acquire internships had begun.

Serena was looking for a spot at a top Chemical Engineering company. The interview process usually only required two steps: first was a phone call with the head of HR, then second was an in-person interview with the hiring manager. But Serena's top choice for the summer was with Kastle-Rye and they had a special third stage. A night out with her future coworkers. A requirement to tell if she'd fit in socially with the rest of the staff.

Serena tried her best to look fun. Since people rarely saw her, her wardrobe mainly consisted of loose shirts and soft pants. But to impress the others, she decided to order a nice dress online. She stared in the mirror and was satisfied with the results. She chose an all-black top on purpose. Her nerves would be impossible to shut down, so she wanted dark clothes to mask the pit stains that would surely develop. Antiperspirant works for the casual user, but her panic attacks flooded her sleeves like a crack in the side of a dam.

Serena tried all she could to calm herself as she arrived for dinner at Twice Mountain Brew. She didn't want to seem unpleasant being the only one not drinking, so she kept her orders quiet and ordered virgin daiquiris that could pass visually as the real thing. As the dinner went on, she kept her breaths deep and long, trying hard to focus on the conversations around her. If she couldn't manage to strike a conversation with the other employees she was in danger of not getting the job.

Serena forced herself to talk about whatever topics were being passed around. She talked music with the HR head sitting beside her. She shared her thoughts on top tier fast food chains with the sales strategist across from her. And she even managed to get in a nice discussion on her latest true crime obsession, Daughters Who Kill, with her would-be boss.

By the time the bill came for the table, Serena's confidence had caught its second wind. But just as quickly, it dropped from mid-air, as a member of marketing having finished his third glass of sangria made a loud, convincing shriek. "Waddon' we go to uh' dance floor?" he mumbled quickly. "There's one just two blocks away!"

Serena was so sure somebody was going to laugh off his comment and offer to drive him home, but to her surprise everyone around her was taking the man deathly seriously.

"We've got room in the budget!" laughed a young treasurer.

"I've haven't been to Tortoise Shell since I was in college," shouted a thirty-something staff trainer, excited to relive her youth.

"Well then what are we waiting for?" said her future boss.

Their party came rushing out onto the street, while Serena tried desperately to keep up. She tried to mentally prepare herself for the uncomfortable situation awaiting her, but the rush was making it difficult to calm down. And when she got outside, her anxiety only heightened.

A red pillar of light was once again protruding downwards from the night sky. It pierced straight through a thick cover of storm clouds, originating from some hidden star in the sky. It touched down behind a row of buildings they were shambling towards. The chances of seeing this crimson beacon again were incremental, she had no doubt it would certainly be illuminating their next destination. And upon their arrival, she was unfortunately validated.

The circumference of the beam managed to encapsulate the entire perimeter of the dance club. Tortoise Shell was a three-floor techno lounge that was no more appealing to Serena even without the crimson spotlight hanging overhead. If it wasn't for her desperation to remain employable, she would have kept her hands to her sides, but she reached out and ran her fingers through the light beam. It didn't feel warm like a heat lamp. The air felt no different at all. All the more convincing that this was all in her head. There was nothing that seemed real about it.

Serena saw the last of her future workmates get carded at the door. She had to decide fast or she'd lose them in the large crowd waiting inside. She forked over her card with a shaky hand to the bouncer out front. He asked her if she was feeling alright before he could let her in.

"You look like you're gonna' be sick, we can't serve you if you've had too much already."

Serena shook her head. "I haven't even started drinking," she explained through a dry, quivering mouth. "I'm just nervous."

The bouncer's stern look broke and let a smile appear on his face. "Not much of an extrovert?"

"It's... to get a job."

The bouncer gave a small laugh and handed the license back to Serena. "Best of luck, then."

Serena reached out her shaky hand and retrieved her license. She slid it back into her purse before taking a long breath and heading into the wild crowd shambling inside. There was a path carved out through the mess by the rest of her party, so she hurried along before the opening closed. She quickly found herself following the marketing rep that had suggested this club in the first place. He was at the back of a long line of familiar faces heading up the stairs to the least crowded bar all the way up on the top floor.

Serena felt a small amount of relief as the density of people slightly diminished around her. Although her biceps were still pinned to her sides, she was capable of lifting her forearms to accept a drink passed down from some lucrative member of the staff in front of her.

The entire environment around her was off-color, it was like she was wearing a pair of sunglasses with deep red lenses. She couldn't tell what the drink in her hand was, whether a coke and rum or vodka sprite, it looked to her like a Shirley Temple. And with taste being heavily influenced by visual perception, it tasted like cherries.

Serena slurped down her drink fast attempting to get a nice buzz going. She figured that staying sober didn't seem to work in getting rid of the red glow, so why not try the opposite. Perhaps she could deaden the overactive neurons causing the hallucination and make the red tint inevitably vanish. But as the night went on, her fantasies only seemed to grow worse.

Serena, taking advantage of her hellscape, had decided to flirt with the bouncer from earlier. He'd come onto the dance floor to escort a rowdy pair of young ladies slowly transitioning into a physical altercation. He shut them down before it could result in anything more than hair pulling and demanded that they leave before he forced them too. He watched them from beside the first-floor bar as the girls followed his conditions and left peacefully. That's when Serena stepped in.

"fucking bitches, right?"

"Fucking bitches?" laughed the bouncer with his hands on his hips. "What the fuck? They're just drunk."

Serena wasn't sure why she'd said that. For some reason it seemed like a good way to start a conversation, but on second thought it was a little jarring. She panicked and couldn't come up with a follow up. She tried to shrug, but it came out as an awkward lean to the left that almost threw her off balance.

"You said you don't get out much," chuckled the bouncer, "like how bad are we talking here? Cause you seem to be lacking basic social skills."

"I have the basics!" grumbled Serena. "I can be basic... *Do you like your job? Do you go to school nearby?*"

"Yes. And no. I do this full time," the bouncer kept checking over Serena's shoulder to make sure his underling was handling the door okay. "How's your job prospects going?"

"I'm proud of myself for making it this far... but I can't do this regularly. If I get the job I'm just gonna' have to be skilled as shit, cause they won't keep me around for being a social butterfly."

"You don't need to worry about that. I skip every Christmas Party and Corporate Tailgate, but I'm still the one getting the raises. At the end of the day, bosses are greedy and skills make money. Being friendly is for people with nothing else to contribute."

"For some reason, that comes across as shocking coming from someone in such a social atmosphere."

"Maybe if I were a bartender... but as a doorman, I'm pretty much paid to hate fun. Speaking of which, there seems to be some kind of trouble at the door. I've got to do my job."

"Can I follow along?"

The bouncer shrugged. "Sure. Just don't get in the way if it gets physical."

At this point, the alcohol was foaming up dopamine throughout her skull and so while the red aura enveloping the bar hadn't made any sort of regression, Serena was still able to ignore it. She managed to focus on the positives. Even basked in the same shade of crimson used in disaster movies whenever the power fails and the monsters get out, the bouncer still managed to look surprisingly cute.

As Serena hobbled after the luscious doorman, she expected she'd get lucky enough to see him in action, flexing his muscles to barricade the entrance from some overly-drunk brute refuting his denial of service. But instead of a drunken junior-year nubile screaming "lemme' inside!", the voice arguing with the bouncers was soft and pathetic. It seemed almost sad.

"I just need inside for fifteen minutes!"

"Sir our dance floor is not wheelchair accessible, I'm afraid you're going to have to go to another bar."

"Five minutes! Just five minutes!" pleaded the old man. "I just need to wave to an old friend."

"Text him that he's got to meet you out front."

"No!" whined the old man. "It's not like that." He tried to roll the wheels of his chair forward, but the bouncer had his foot stuck in the spokes to prevent him from moving any further.

"Back up!" shouted Serena's crush. She was certain he was about to get physical and so she rushed forward to catch a good glimpse, but as she saw him shove the old man backwards, she was instead filled with horror. Not at the insensitive action against an elderly man, but at the face of the elderly man himself.

This man was no stranger.

"Y-yeh!" Serena couldn't keep her fright inside of her head. She drunkenly stammered and dropped her drink from the sheer shock. It was the old man from when she was just a girl. He was wearing that same NASA cap, only now he was bound to a glossy wheelchair with jet black upholstery.

As Serena's drink fell to the ground, the plastic cracked and the fluid inside splashed overtop of the legs of every doorman guarding the front entrance. They all turned to face her, including her crush.

"She's too drunk to hold her drink!" shouted one of the doormen. Serena turned to face her crush, but he sided with the other bouncer.

"Ma'am please step outside or we'll be forced to remove you," said her crush.

"You're an asshole!" she screeched. "Don't make me go out there you fucking jerk!" The alcohol in her system made it hard to explain the situation calmly. She felt a feeling of legitimate betrayal seeing her object of affection acting against her.

"Ma'am please... we can talk about this outside, but you've got to go."

Serena wouldn't budge. She wasn't going anywhere near that old man.

"Serena, please..." pleaded her crush. He was trying his hardest to be polite but keep consistent with his job's standards.

"Fuck you!" Serena's fear was translating into rage, as her crush began treating her like human garbage. Her man valued his job responsibilities more than human interaction, so he grabbed onto Serena's elbow and shoulder and yanked her outside where she tripped in her heels and flew forward. She was expecting to feel a sharp pain in her face as the pavement outside collided with her nose, but instead she felt something soft catch her fall. It felt like she landed in a cushioned armchair.

"Hello Serena," whispered a raspy voice in her right ear. Serena screeched in terror. She'd just been flung directly into the lap of the old man.

The old man's chest deflated and his face winced into a tight point as Serena slammed her hands down into the old man's lap to help herself up. She crushed his crotch under her weight. She quickly threw herself up onto her feet and jumped out of her heels. She had no time to be hindered. She sped off down the street leaving the expensive shoes in front of the bar for some stranger to later stuff in their purse and carry away. Not that Serena cared, she was far more concerned for her safety.

Serena was too freaked out to go home where she'd be all by herself. She decided it'd be safer to stay with a friend.

"I don't know how he found me!" cried Serena into the arms of Karissa, the girl who'd helped her home all those months ago. Karissa sat Serena on her guest bed and gave her ample time to let out all her feelings. Serena explained her past at the science museum and what the man had tried to do to her as a child. "How did he know my name?" asked Serena. "I can't remember everything from that day, but I wouldn't have told him my name! I was terrified of him!"

"If he's a real creep, maybe he got your name from the museum somehow," suggested Karissa. "Maybe they had a list of all the kids visiting that day, then he looked you each up online till he found a matching face."

"That's fucking horrifying!" shrieked Serena. "I wonder if he's been stalking me all this time. It's been years."

"I bet so," validated Kassie. "So are you gonna' call the cops?" Kassie held out Serena's phone. Serena reached out but didn't latch on. She was interrupted by a sound at the apartment's front door. The sound left Serena shaking in fear. It wasn't like a normal knock. They were bumps. Low pitched with no reverberation. They weren't being sounded at the usual height of a human hand but instead, these spaced out beats were emanating near the bottom of the door.

Kassie got up and checked through her peep hole. These weren't knocks at all. It was a wheelchair repeatedly and softly ramming into her door. "What did... what did that guy at the club look like?"

"No." whimpered Serena. "No! That's not possible..."

"Come on, I'm in a fucking wheelchair!" shouted the old man from the other side of the door. His voice was soft but audible. "I can't hurt you!"

Serena, still intoxicated, felt her emotions suddenly sway left again, and her sadness quickly flowed into an outburst of rage. She charged up to the door and pushed Kassie aside. She undid the locks on the door and threw it open. She cocked her fist and laid it over and over into the old man's wrinkled mug.

Serena was not a physically fit specimen, but her anger alone escalated her untrained punches into a formidable assault on the old man's face. Each punch left a thick welt in its place. The man's left eye was blackened. His forehead was cut open. And his mouth was covered in strings of blood-laced dribble.

Once the old man looked as though he were about to lose consciousness, Serena stopped her beating.

The old man struggled to open his eyes. "*Are you dern?*" he mumbled through a swollen lip. He gasped for air and bent his chest over his left wheel. He was reaching down towards the ground trying desperately to reach a denture she knocked straight out of his mouth. After pawing at it, he brushed it on his shirt, wiping off the blood that smeared along the fake enamel. He stuck it back into his upper jaw.

"How the fuck did you find me!" snarled Serena. "And who the fuck *are* you?"

"The lights," grumbled the old man. "I need to explain the lights."

"The lights?" questioned Kassie. She'd witnessed all of Serena's assault from close behind. "What the fuck is he talking about?"

"*She knows...*" snarled the old man. "I know she sees them."

"You're the reason for those fucking lights!" shouted Serena. "I thought I was going insane! Have you been fucking drugging me?"

"They're not *my* lights," explained the old man. "They're coming from the stars. It's a message and you're not getting it. So they sent me to help explain."

"You're still rambling about stars," sighed Serena. "Maybe you're not just a child predator. Maybe you're that *and* you're senile."

"I'm just here to deliver the message in person. The stars have guided heroes for millennia, but in your special case, they're trying to tell you *no*!"

"No what?"

"If it's highlighted, don't go in there!" growled the old man. "They thought a big red light would be enough to get that point across. Especially for someone with massive anxiety. Humans naturally avoid red. It's an omnicultural symbol for danger. But you just walked right in anyways."

"Only... only the second time," shrugged Serena. "I had obligations in there."

"Well whatever they are they shouldn't come before your safety," scolded the old man. "There was a fucking rapist in there. Your rapist."

"My rapist?" scoffed Serena. "Is it you?"

"No! I don't know who it is! It was somebody in that club. It's destiny that they hurt you."

"Destiny?" questioned Serena.

"You know you were the product of rape, correct?"

Serena hesitated, but she ultimately nodded. She was sadly very aware. Her mother needed her to know the truth, so she wouldn't be naive. She knew her father was a rapist, as well as her grandfather. But she'd only ever thought of that as a bleak coincidence. Or perhaps an all too common phenomena kept in the dark by many others.

"It's no coincidence. Your bloodline is cursed. Every child your bloodline fosters is to be born out of rape."

Serena, having seen some impossible feats, was open to the old man's rambling. "Where does the curse come from?"

The old man shrugged. "It's ancient. Centuries old. There were tons of curses back then, the products of bitter gods with reckless power. Your ancestor probably did something slightly catty to someone with a short temper who could bend reality... and so your lineage's fate was sealed."

"So the stars... they're trying to protect me from this curse?"

The old man nodded.

"The stars... care for me?"

The old man shook his head. "Don't misunderstand. The stars themselves are just more bitter gods. They don't care about your protection. They care about their pride. They cringe every time a human calls themselves a star. It's not even our kings... it's our lowly, our bards, jesters, and sex workers. Movie stars, rock stars, pop stars, and porn stars..."

"So the stars hate that we compare ourselves to them?" asked Serena.

The old man nodded. "In their eyes, humans can't be anything close to a star; you are doomed from conception. Pain makes gain and there is nowhere near enough pain in childbirth to result in anything meaningful. But look at a star and you see how its luster is purchased. When a star is born, the magnitude of pain is incomprehensible. Massive red giants reach their peak and betray their orbiting planets rich with life; evaporating tens of billions of sentient lives, tens of trillions of primitive beasts, and trillions upon trillions of single-cell organisms. The more demise the greater the star conceived, or at least that's how *they* consider it."

"That's sick..." exclaimed Serena.

The old man shrugged. "The culture of celestials is savage and alien. While all other humans shy in comparison to their great conceptions, your family is the closest thing to have ever come close. You've infringed on their sacred life cycle. Your family is a cycle of agony continuing farther back than recorded history, each generation born out of excruciating pain and lasting paranoia and misery. The stars don't like that you've treaded on their turf and so they want you snuffed out."

The old man reached up to his face swiped at a bead of blood dripping down from his left nostril onto his silvery mustache. He wiped the dirty knuckle onto his pant leg then latched onto the wheels of his chair. He pushed backwards on the tops of his rims and let his chair slowly reverse away from Kassie's door.

"My advice," said the old man, whilst rotating his chair to face down the hall, "don't focus on the why. Just accept the help and follow their warnings exactly as they appear."

The old man pushed forward and began to wheel away.

"Aren't you going to stop him?" shouted Kassie from behind Serena. Serena didn't reply, she just stepped backwards into the apartment and locked the door behind her.

Serena sighed then hopped back onto the guest room mattress. She laid down her head to rest. Kassie lobbed Serena's cell phone at her, arcing it just over her head without hitting her.

"He's not going to stop coming after you," scolded Kassie. "Call the cops before he gets too far."

"I can't do that," frowned Serena. "

"Nobody is fated to get raped! Just listen to how that sounds. It sounds an awful lot like something a rapist would say to justify his crime!"

"It sounds psychotic, I know. But you don't see the lights. They're these massive spires that pull down from the stars. If you saw these things, you'd be convinced of nonsense as well. It's better than thinking you've gone insane."

"I guess it doesn't hurt to believe what he's saying, if all he's saying is don't go into a handful of bars. It's not a life changing requirement."

"The thing is Kassie, I'm not sure if I'm gonna' follow the rules even if I believe it. There could be another option for me," Serena sat up on the bed and pointed to Kassie's front door. "Did you see what I did back there when I lost control?"

"You beat up an old man."

"And I solved the matter. There's something very progressive about violence. It's tough to muster up but when it comes it gets things done and over with."

"I'm sorry, Serena, but what are you suggesting here?"

The very first time Serena came across the old man in the NASA cap all those years ago, he changed her mind about ever leaving her apartment after dark. But this time, his resurgence had prompted an opposite response. Serena now planned on going out every night of the week. And contrary to the old man's warnings, she planned on heading right into the heart of each red light.

She made a ritual of it. She would first pregame with a cheap six pack of Natty Bo. She wanted to relive the confidence she felt when she pummeled the old man at Karissa's apartment. The drinks she had beforehand certainly helped fuel that aggression.

Once she was nice and loose, she would head to whatever club was marked by the red pillar in the sky. She'd always go alone, convinced that a group of friends would only put more innocent women in danger. Plus, she didn't want her to bore them. She wasn't going to dance and drink. On the contrary, she would immediately find a nice isolated part of the bar with a good view of the crowd. She'd steal a seat from the bar and sit cross-legged with a notebook in her lap. Then, she would begin to write.

She made note of the people within her immediate vicinity. Basked in the red light, all their faces looked capable of being sinister, so nobody ever stood out in any ominous way. Instead, it was less about finding somebody suspicious and more about finding somebody twice. It would be helpful if they had some defining feature to help them stand out.

Within the first week she had her suspicions focused on a man with a dark blue fedora. She wasn't trying to stereotype, but the man had appeared under the red light two bars in a row. He was drinking beside her at Flying Yonkers, then just happened to be playing skeeball all by himself at Daniel Booster's. But the city was small and there were only so many places one could drink. So she gave it a third spot before making any drastic measures. And thank god she did, because no matter how long she waited, she didn't catch sight of that hat anywhere near her at The Grainery.

"What were you planning to do if it was him?" questioned Kassie. Morbidly curious about friend group's mom going on a quest for vengeance, Kassie had been arranging for them to meet and chat quite frequent. "Are you going to kill the guy?"

Serena nodded. "I listen to a lot of podcasts on my commute to work. I like the true crime ones. Especially the ones on serial killers." Serena pulled a pink plastic spray bottle from her purse, the kind that usually stores a moisturizing solution for on-the-go needs. "I read about the Iceman, who took people out with little spritzes of cyanide. It makes it look like a heart attack."

"That little bottle is full of cyanide?" questioned Kassie. "Where did you get cyanide from? You're probably on a fucking list."

Serena shook her head. "I purchase a regular amount of produce. No more than you'd find in the apartment of any girl in her twenties on that fruitarian fad. I just kept the pits and seeds overtime till I had enough to extract a lethal dose."

Kassie rocked back and forth in her chair with a look of shock. "Is it too late to convince you to go back to being a homebody?"

Serena smiled. "I haven't decided yet what I'm gonna' do when he's long gone. Maybe I will go back to keeping indoors. After all, even with the danger gone, it's what I'm accustomed to."

"That seems like a waste, right?" sneered Kassie. "I mean to put it in all that work not to reap the benefits... it seems you earned the right to live your life outside like the rest of us."

"But that's not what this is about!" argued Serena. "This is about doing what I couldn't as a little girl. It's about solving the problem, not just for me, but for everyone! Avoiding these bars protects me, but it doesn't get a rapist off the street does it? I bet yourself has wandered into these red bars without ever knowing it. You don't get the knowledge I have, so I've got to use it to benefit us all."

As noble as her mission sounded, Kassie couldn't see that with each go at finding her predestined assailant the nights grew darker and darker for brave Serena. Her habit of spiking herself before heading out at night was growing in severity. In order to keep the same effects, she had to counteract the inescapable tolerance she was building. After only a month of investigation she'd evolved from her Natty Bos unto a whole bottle of Olde English. Unable to guess the exact amount she needed to add to remain at a constant level of drunk, she often overdid it, leaving her too intoxicated to remain vigilant. Her work was getting sloppy and she knew it, but her sick mind was justifying it as a means to appear more "vulnerable". She figured the drunker she looked, the closer her predator would venture.

"Hi."

"Hello."

"Howdy."

"Privet."

Whilst perhaps not her predator, it was immediately apparent her clear intoxication definitely lured in more talkers to her vantage point. Despite whatever dark corner she hid at in the bar, there was now always some man in nice clothes trying his luck with her. She used this to her advantage, hoping that by flirting back, her future assailant would witness a man stepping in on his target and interfere. And while at first all her strategy produced was a useless list of phone numbers, eventually she found what she was looking for.

Serena was talking with a sharp-dressed graduate student from Saint Petersburg, when an incoming flashing object distracted her. It appeared in the corner of her eye and caused her to abandon her conversation mid-sentence to investigate. It was a light-up t-shirt, a Wi-Fi symbol expanding and retracting to the beat of the club's music.

Serena had to tell the graduate student she was speaking with to get lost. Her suspicions had been aroused unlike they'd ever been before. This man in the light-up article wasn't just an ordinary display of peacocking. It was so exaggerated and attention seeking, it was practically predatory. Like an anglerfish casting its glowing head piece to lure in its gullible prey.

As she approached the man in the light up shirt, she looked up into his face only to have her suspicions heightened even further.

"I thought I recognized you," came a familiar voice. "Do you remember me?"

Serena held a hand under her eyes to shield them from the blinding aura emitting from the man's chest. His face suddenly became apparent. She couldn't believe it. It was the bouncer from the Tortoise Shell. It had been what felt like forever ago, which only added to her suspicion

"Serena, right?" he asked with a crooked smile.

Dressed in casual clothes Serena could barely recognize the bouncer, she couldn't even remember his first name. But he spotted her, and knew her name exactly, almost as if he'd been thinking about her a lot.

Serena was curious. She took the drink from the bouncer's hand and held it to her lips. There was no way she was going to actually ingest any of it. She took it in her mouth as she tipped the glass up, but as she tipped it back down she let the fluid fall out from between her teeth. She swallowed nothing but air.

As the drink slipped in and out across her tongue, Serena thought it was odd the drink tasted like red Gatorade. It wasn't just the lights this time, it had the faint salty flavor of electrolytes. Only it was more likely GHB.

Serena had a test if she were to ever get this far in her suspicions. It was a simple morality check that required only a small bit of acting on her part. All she needed to do was feign illness and see the bouncer's reaction.

Mid-way through a conversation on how her job prospects had turned out that first night they'd met, Serena shut her eyes for a few seconds more than a casual blink. She opened them with a flicker of her eyelids then gave her head a shake as though she was fighting off the will to sleep.

Her gestures were noticeable enough to conjure up a question about how she was feeling, but the bouncer just kept on talking as though he'd seen nothing. This was a good sign.

Serena egged it on a little harder, taking a sudden step backwards as though she were losing balance. As she positioned herself back up straight with the help of a nearby barstool she rubbed her palm down the side of her face.

Still, the bouncer showed no concern. Perhaps the copious amount of alcohol she'd consumed had made her overconfident, but she decided to just go for it. She repeated her routine to look like she'd lost balance, only this time she fell forward.

The bouncer caught her instantly. Like a catcher waiting patiently for the pitch.

"They're asking you to leave," whispered the bouncer in Serena's ear. "They say you're too drunk to stand-up." No one was saying anything of the sort. In fact, the bouncer was using his massive frame to completely cover-up Serena's limp stature from any good Samaritans who would try to stop the next step of his plan. "Don't worry... I'll help you home."

Serena let her body go limp and leaned onto the bouncer's chest allowing him the opportunity to carry her away. Wherever he shoved she allowed her body to follow. She didn't want to show too much resistance as to arouse suspicion from the rest of the bar-goers.

The bouncer never even pretended to ask for her address and stayed quiet the entire Uber ride. They, of course, arrived at the bouncer's apartment where he quickly shoved Serena inside. Once his door was shut, he played no more games. He picked her up and flung her over his shoulder and carried her into his room. He shoved her body onto his bed and planted a kiss on her lips.

Serena worried she may have let it go too long, but luckily for her, he didn't go any further. The bouncer jumped off of his bed, grabbed something from his closet, and ran into his bathroom. He shut the door behind him.

Serena knew this was her chance. She quietly slid off the bed without disturbing its noisy springs. She reached into her purse crudely thrown into the corner of the room and found her spray bottle. She tip-toed up to the bathroom door and waited there with her arms outstretched.

When the bouncer opened the door, he immediately froze in shock. He wasn't expecting to see Serena standing up straight and wary, aiming the nozzle of a spray bottle at his face.

Serena took a moment to take in the strange outfit the bouncer had emerged in. It seemed he had a ceremony planned for his assault. He hadn't just lost his clothes, he'd replaced them with a fetish she'd never seen before. It was a full body spandex suit like you'd find on a fanatic at a sporting event. Only it was made entirely out of fishnet.

Serena shook her head, then pressed down on the head of her spray bottle. A single string of liquid shot through the air and landed on the bouncer's face. It soaked through the spade-shaped perforations in his outfit and wetted his eyes and lips.

Immediately, the bouncer winced in pain and tried to wipe the fluids off his face.

In her drunken stupor, her inhibitions were dulled, and so Serena suddenly felt exhilarated. She began to fire more shots, over and over, in rapid succession. With each press on the top of her bottle, she imagined herself in the corner of her bedroom, cowering at a safe distance from a spider building a web on her wall. She'd grab a bottle of carpet cleaner from under her sink and spray the toxic chemical onto the web till the spider curled up into a ball and fell to the floor, drowning in a wet spot of noxious fumes.

The bouncer did very much the same. His limbs first tried to cover his face, but unable to prevent the inhalation of the cyanide, they were soon curling inwards over his chest. He fell to the floor onto his ass, as his legs pulled inwards as well. Soon he was on his side in a fetal position and his coughing slowly became replaced by the sound of soft wheezes. His face was turning blue and his whole body was shaking. It looked as though his head was about to erupt, but instead, it just went stiff.

Serena thought about her next moves carefully. She didn't want to hide the body. She didn't even want to touch it. If things played out like her murderer podcasts, the authorities should just think the boy had a heart attack. Although he was a bit young for that. Perhaps, instead, they'd chalk it up to an overdose.

Even if it was deemed a murder, Serena felt she was safe. There was nothing linking her to the bouncer besides the account of some sleep deprived Uber driver. He surely wouldn't have much to say. Plus, the fact that he died in his fishnet suit would probably tie the murder to whatever fetish communities he belongs to online for which Serena would have no association.

Serena left her phone off to make sure her location could never be tracked to the bouncer's home and she didn't plan on turning it back on till she got back to her own place. This would make it hard to get home, however, as she had no idea where she currently was. She decided to leave the bouncer's apartment and look for a familiar landmark outside.

She saw mainly suburbs surrounding the apartment complex on its left and right. And on the other side of the street was a strip mall. And behind that, way off in the distance, was a bright red light towering up into the night sky.

Serena clenched her fists and knelt down on the ground trying to hold in her screams. She pounded at the dirt as tears rolled down from her eyes.

It didn't make any sense. She only struck when there was no doubt left. That bouncer was her rapist. Where was the evidence to the contrary? His brand of evil was far from subtle. The man emerged from his bathroom in a fucking full body stocking.

Serena needed answers. She knew who'd have them, but she wasn't sure where he'd be. The children's museum was certainly closed at such a late hour, but the old man might not be in bed. He'd told her he only used the planetarium to talk to the stars in the day. At night, he could talk to them far easier. He'd certainly go where the sky was clearest. Somewhere close by where the cities light pollution fell just enough to make contact with the bodies above. And it's got to be wheelchair accessible.

Serena knew just the place. There was a street on the southside of town surrounding the capital building, where they'd updated the street lights for the very purpose of eliminating the sky glow in a "progressive" part of their town. The streetlights on the road have been replaced with low-cost, energy efficient sodium lights.

It was significantly improved compared to the rest of the town. With all the shops closed, this street was mainly abandoned except for a single soul. A man in a wheelchair parked in an alleyway between a darkened pizza place and a locked-down parking garage. As she approached, she could make out his face pointed up towards the sky. His mouth hung open and his tongue kept prodding at the roof of his mouth. He was making a noise that sounded like the crackling of a fire over the groan of a far-off explosion.

Upon seeing Serena approach, the old man shut his mouth, ending the violent ambience abruptly. The old man pushed his chin down and stared at Serena. Unbeknownst to Serena, he could see a thin blue beacon encompassing the perimeter of her body. With that glow always pointing towards her, the old man always knew where she was. He saw her coming from miles away.

"The stars were just passing their grievances onto me. I hope you realize when you mess up, I mess up."

Serena jumped forward and laid a fist into the old man's stomach. His dentures were vomited into his lap along with a wad of half-digested bread. "How do you call that messing up?" growled Serena.

"You're not following directions!" shot back the old man, wiping his lips with his sleeve. "You were supposed to stay away!"

"Tell me what's going on. Did I kill the wrong guy?"

"No..." sneered the old man. "You sure as Hell got him."

"Then why are the lights still there!?"

"Because your still cursed, idiot!" snarled the old man. "You killed the rapist, but you didn't break the curse. So the responsibility for raping you just moves on to somebody new."

Serena threw her arms down to her side and gaped her mouth. "There's another rapist, now?"

"There always will be!" shouted the old man. "You can't just get rid of him. That's why you're supposed to be avoiding these places."

"So what if I do it again?" asked Serena. "What if I just kept killing till there's nobody left in the city that could do that to me?"

The old man snickered. "Then you'd have to kill every fertile man on the face of the earth."

"Come on... that can't be true."

"When the duty of your assailant passes on from one man to the next, it's not targeting someone with a certain gene or specific temperament. The only thing qualifying them is their dick and two working testes. In other words, you're not just passing it on, you're literally creating *more* rapists, which, by the way, they weren't destined to be till after you interfered. Way to ruin somebody's life."

Serena jumped forward with a look spite. The old man winced, predicting she'd fire another shot into his stomach, but she was able to contain herself. She was more confused than angry. "I'm not gonna' spend the rest of my life hiding and running, I want to do something about this..."

"Well then go ahead and just keep killing," exclaimed the old man, "the cops will gun you down eventually and the stars will have your bloodline ended all the same."

Serena shook her head. "Can't I just kill the demon that cursed me? Couldn't *that* break the spell?"

The old man sighed. Despite all the pain she'd made him endure, he honestly felt pity for the girl. She was just a victim of a cosmic horror, hopelessly flailing about for some sudden relief. "The stars have already considered this approach. The being is immortal. There's no killing it."

"What if I try anyways?"

"There's no point!"

"Then let me die!" argued Serena. "If it all this ancient god will do is kill me then the stars get their wish all the same. Just let me go out the way I want to. I want to face the author of my pain before I leave this plane. Please. Show me."

The old man slowly turned his face upwards towards the sky. He opened jaw as wide as it could go and began to wiggle about his tongue once again. The sound of a raging inferno echoed along the walls of the alley. Although alien sounding to Serena, this was the language of the stars. The same ominous tone that drones along the surface of every star as their gases rise and fall over top of one another.

"Fine." The old man snapped his head back forward. "The lights have agreed to guide you."

Checking behind herself she could see a new pillar made of bright white light touching down far off in the city.

"Are they... *in town*?" asked Serena. "How are they so close by?"

The old man shrugged. "Gods can have many heads and they tend to sprout up in major populations like our city, here."

"Is there anything I should bring to defend myself?" asked Serena, naively.

The old man scoffed. "Do you own a space suit?"

Serena shook her head. Of course not.

"Then no. Nothing can help you."

Serena followed the light in the sky to the westside of town where rows of apartment buildings have dilapidated past the point of legal occupation. By the time the sun had begun to rise, Serena had reached the building in which the light intruded from above. The front door was boarded up, but she managed to knock it open with a few strong kicks. She began to ascend the staircase running through the center of the building, popping into each floor along the way. When she reached the third floor, she found the end point of the white light beam shooting straight through the ceiling and ending on a red piece of felt just outside a door marked 312.

Serena came up close to where the waypoint ended and saw that the red felt in its center was a cheap substitute for a welcome mat left there by some tenant long ago. Serena reached forward and turned the door knob. She was lucky enough to not have to kick the door down this time. It was already left unlocked.

Serena opened the door and slipped on in. Immediately, Serena began to choke. Not on a noxious gas inside, but by an apparent absence of any gas at all. The oxygen inside this apartment was gone. Serena had to quickly pedal backwards and make her way back out into the hall. As she inhaled deeply to refill her lungs, she looked up into the apartment she crawled away from. It was pitch black inside.

"So we meet." A strange voice emanated from inside the apartment. It spoke slowly, syllable by syllable, and each syllable was pronounced whilst the voice took in air. And it never seemed to need to exhale. "Do you know me?"

"No," said Serena, "but I know you've cursed my family. And I'm here to ask you to take it back. And I'll make amends for whatever my ancestor did to deserve it."

"There's no amends," wheezed the voice. "We have no feud. Only a partnership."

"Who benefits from this partnership? Cause I certainly don't."

"Your ancestor did. A masochist. She chose her fate."

"No one would choose this fate," argued Serena. "It's indescribably wrong."

"Would you believe she'd commit to anything in order to get her revenge on the stars?" replied the voice. "They aided the pagans that slaughtered your ancestor's village. They came from the cold North and should have been hindered by the heat waves of your region, but when your village needed the Sun the most, it vanished for twelve days. Cooling the air of your village enough for the pagans to enter and slaughter freely. When the sun disappeared, / crept in. I am a void. An absence of light and thing. I offered my help to the last surviving villager, your ancestor. The carnage she'd witnessed had made her a masochist and so she accepted her fate willingly with the promise that it would put the stars in their place."

"Well I'm not my ancestor. And I'm not willing to sacrifice my body for vengeance. I'm begging you to take this fate away."

"...I cannot. Doing so would restore the stars' pride which would greatly cost me. Especially now, when I am weaker than ever. There's barely a corner of the universe left where stars have not bored into my darkness."

"Please, I'm begging you. Can't you be reasoned with?" pleaded Serena. "Perhaps if the curse can't be removed... it could be replaced?"

"What could better scorn the stars than to be usurped by carbon life?"

"Something better. Something more direct." Serena had an excellent idea in mind. "Perhaps, I could kill their acolyte."

"...go on."

"I've met a puppet. The stars use him to enact their plans on Earth. He may be the only worshipper they have left on this planet. I could kill him. It would certainly be a nuisance."

"*All* of their acolytes."

"What? There's more?"

"There will be. They communicate with stargazers and ufologists, astronomers and astrologists. Anyone they can contact that will suit their ultimate goals. If you kill this acolyte, they will find more. But as long as you commit your life to killing them hereafter, I will lift your curse."

Serena agreed. Killing a few folks obsessed with their telescopes seemed a lot more reasonable than killing every last man on the face of the Earth.

"The curse will be lifted upon your first kill. From then on, it will not be reinstated unless your new responsibilities are clearly and intentionally ignored."

Serena would get right to work.

Across town, the children's museum had just opened its doors. And so, the old man arrived right at the crack of dawn just as he did every morning. He liked to go extra early during the summer before the tourists would inevitably crowd the place.

When the old man wheeled into the planetarium's handicap entrance he was expecting to be the only one there. And so, he was absolutely surprised to see a stranger sitting in the front row. They were dressed unusually warm for the summer, covered in thick baggy clothes that masked their face and body shape. The stranger's identity would have been otherwise clandestine if it weren't for the bright blue pillar of light the stars projected overtop of her body.

This stranger was Serena. Although Serena couldn't see the glow, the stars always had her marked in the old man's vision. The old man found it awfully concerning that Serena was attempting to sneak up on him. Before she could make her way to the planetarium's handicapped seating, the old man quickly wheeled away out of the dark to a more public area.

"Why are you following me?" he barked at Serena as she came following after, out of the planetarium and into the neighboring Pluto exhibit.

"It's me," whispered Serena. She held up her finger and beckoned for him to come back into the planetarium. "I just want to talk in private."

The old man shook his head. "You're acting weird and I don't like it." He rolled his seat backwards past a model of Charon and Nix. "Why are you wearing a disguise?" he called out from a safe distance.

Serena followed after him. "Like I said, we need to be private for this conversation."

The old man frowned and looked around trying to find somebody to act as a witness. He cursed out loud as he realized he'd wheeled himself back into a room just as dark and isolated as the planetarium. A morbid display simulating how little light the surface of Pluto would receive from the Sun. It would seem to an Earthling that it was stuck in a perpetual dusk.

Serena charged.

"No! No -- No!" cried out the old man, as he pushed against his wheels with all his might. Serena easily chased him down and got her hands onto the back of his chair. She held on tightly to the back handles and pulled him in closer.

The old man began to plead. "After all I've done to guide you through the worst days of your life, you're going to kill me?"

Serena shook her head in disappointment as she pulled her spray bottle out from her purse. "I think you've severely over-valued yourself."

"I'm the good guy in all this," begged the old man as Serena positioned her bottle up to his mouth. "The stars may have acted out of pride, but it was in your best interest. How can you justify this?"

Serena held her spray bottle up to the old man's lips. "I appreciate your help so far. But if you really want to benefit me, you'll be better off dead. In return for killing anyone following the stars' orders, I'll have my curse lifted."

"And what does that solve?" begged the old man. He slithered out of his own chair and flopped onto the floor. He flipped himself onto his back and tried to row his body away shoving with his elbows. "You're just replacing one predator with another!" he shouted pointing up at Serena.

Serena gave a shrug. She wasn't ignorant. She could clearly see the roles were reversed as they were the first time they'd met. But the difference was she wouldn't let the old man get away.

Serena sprayed her cyanide into the air creating a heavy mist above the old man. It slowly rained onto his body from above before he could crawl away. As it absorbed into his lungs, he immediately began to choke.

"You don't want this," he wheezed. "Your just making things worse..."

Serena knelt down beside the old man and shoved the tip of her bottle up his right nostril like an inhaler. She gave two big sprays directly into his sinuses, forcing the old man's face into a look of terror. His head shook with horrible pain as the poison burned the innards of his skull. The tremors only lasted a few seconds however, before the top half of his body came to an abrupt stop.

This was the first of what would be a long string of murders at the hands of Serena. From that day forth, every week, she'd hunt down a new affiliate of the stars. She'd go out after midnight with rags drenched in poison and curl them around the lips of unexpected stargazers completely unaware that they'd just entered into a very dangerous war between the literal forces of darkness and light.

Every now and then Serena would feel a bit of guilt when staring into the eyes of one of these suffocating astro-geeks. But after enough drinks she'd always find a way to let it go. I mean, after all, how innocent were these guys really? They were colluding with alien forces, so they were clearly asking for it. Don't put on space talismans and sacred robes if you're not looking to fight. And if they were really so innocent, they never would have been searching through space to begin with.

Pizza Crow IV

While "Captured by Animals" once again centers around the theme of love, "The Red Constellation" is completely distinct. It centers around sexual violence which I would say is as far from love as you can imagine. I'm concluding that our theme is determined by the toppings.

So then what of the crust? I need to run more experiments but I'm certain "Captured by Animals" is the first of the stories to be told from the first person. So then it seems the perspective of the narrator is determined by the type of crust. Thin, crispy crust, or St. Louis style, brings out the first-person perspective. Thick and doughy, like a Sicilian, brings out the third person perspective. So then if my calculations are correct, something in between, thin but still soft, should bring out the second person perspective.

I ordered a NY-style pizza from a joint called Piez and got the following.

Young Adult Series Simulator

You enter the Barnes & Noble terribly confused as you were certain bookstores had gone extinct years ago. Somehow good old B&N was hanging in there and had apparently become a popular marker in the world of Tinder dating. You've had your last three dates, here. Three different girls requesting you get a frozen coffee drink together at the conjoined Starbucks.

You always get there early, trying way too hard to beat your old habit of always being late. With time to spare, you immediately go through the magazine section like when your parents would take you there as a kid. But unfortunately, the gaming magazines have all gone digital and the remaining publications on the Men's wrack are geared towards stock advice and health & fitness. You walk past the coffee shop to make sure your date isn't there yet, but no one matching her profile picture seems to be present. So instead, you head towards the back of the store.

You wonder what trash would be heavily advertised at the entrance to the kids and teens section. You see a specialized cardboard wrack holding the latest book from the At Most Fear series. You've vaguely heard about it. Your friends who read for fun have mentioned it to you as an addicting young adult series with a terrible premise but great characterization. You read about a movie adaption of the first book coming out next Summer.

With fifteen minutes to spare, you decided to crack open At Most Fear: Book 3: Gust Stories and try to get a feeling for what the youth are into nowadays.

~

Ceero and Elto Stratus were hurtling down a highway through the Great Plains. Their father, the one and only Senior Airmen Nim Stratus, was incapacitated in the back seat. Their family pet, Thunderbird, had betrayed them, sending a bolt of electricity through their father's chest. The burn looks bad and it may have cooked some of his internal organs.

Elto had to drive being the oldest of the brothers. Elto was sixteen. They were driving in the GMC Syclone they "borrowed" while fighting off Category 6 hurricanes down in Tampa. After that summer in Florida, the boys decided to never set foot in the South again. They hoped maybe they could find some peace in the heart of the country. Oklahoma City was their next destination.

"Dad, did you need anything?" asked Ceero. His father had been in a state of partial consciousness for the last week and a half. He breathed heavily all the time and he napped all day. His eyes opened for a split second to tell Ceero he just needed rest.

"Ceero can you come give me a hand?" asked Elto, as he gripped the steering wheel tensely. "I'm too scared to let go of the wheel. Can you fiddle with the radio, please?" Elto was so inexperienced driving because his father never had the free-time to teach him. All three of their lives had been completely dedicated for the last two years trying to finally put an end to the curse on their bloodline. The Bane of the Tempestarii leaves every generation of the Stratus family escaping an onslaught of storms and otherwise incumbent weather. Given supernatural origins, this weather can become sentient and chaotic, attacking more like a monster than a puff of precipitation.

"I can't believe my childhood pet may have just murdered our father," sulked Ceero. His eyes were welling up with tears. "I had Thunderbird since he was just a thunder chick. He was always so well behaved. He used to charge my cell phone!"

Elto's eyes sunk remembering all the good that bird had done over the years. "He defibrillated me once..."

"I think he's being mind-controlled by Oya," explained Ceero. "When she absorbed Zeus, she gained control over all forms of lightning. That must include thunderbirds as well!"

"Then we have to stop her," growled Elto, swallowing his nerves and picking up speed. "If we can't kill her, we can at least separate Zeus from her body."

Ceero didn't respond. He had become distracted again and turned around to face the back seat. It was hard for Ceero to take his eyes off his father's wounds

"You know watching him all day isn't gonna' make him any better," griped Elto. Out of the corner of his eye, he saw Ceero shaking his head.

"It's not just dad..." stuttered Ceero, "there's a twister building up behind us!" Elto was too nervous to take his eyes off the road, but for a split second he peered into his rearview mirror. Over his dad's shoulder, Elto could make out a tornado about to touch ground right behind their tailpipe.

"Use the hammer!" shouted Elto, he took a deep breath and let his hand off the wheel long enough to press the moonroof button. Ceero stuck his head and arm out the top of their car and aimed a Craftsmen brand claw hammer at the bottom of the funnel cloud. A blast of sound energy erupted from its metal crest and caused an explosion that boomed like a bass note. It scrambled the flat soil beneath the tornado. The heat and pressure disrupted the tornado's careful structure and caused it to disintegrate into rocks and dust.

The boys were lucky to have their magic hammer. Unknown to Oya, this hammer hides the body and soul of Thor himself and makes him imperceivably to other gods and supernatural beings.

By wielding the hammer correctly, any mortal can use an ordinary woodworking tool to harness the power of a thunder-god.

"How much longer till we're off these plains?" asked Ceero, watching Oya prepare a new twister to replace the last. This one was taking longer to form but was three times the size. A blast from their hammer might not be enough.

"Fifteen more miles till OKC!" shouted Elto looking at the map he had unfolded on the dashboard. They couldn't use their phones ever since Oya controlled the weather above them. She made it, so they never had service. Their paper map wasn't the most updated sheet and so it didn't recognize that OKC had long ago expanded in size. They arrived in the city ten minutes ahead of schedule before the massive funnel cloud could fully form. The budding F5 was forced to disband. It couldn't form on such a dynamic surface as a cityscape.

"She'll find something else," warned Elto. "Let's use her time scheming to stay put in the city. We need to get dad to his old friend." This friend was none other than Sergeant First Class Manfried Mammatus. Or as they used to call him in the air force, Dr. Mama.

"He's got two, three days max," explained Dr. Mama, examining the wounds on Nim's abdomen. "There's nothing I can do. There's not enough time or resources for an organ transplant."

The boys reluctantly understood. Dr. Mama was right. They couldn't stay in one place long enough for surgery. "Regardless, your father has requested I keep him here till he dies. He needs me to guide him into the proper light."

"...what is the light?" asked Ceero, looking confused.

Elto excused himself so that he may have an important talk with his little brother in private. "Dad's not well enough to go on," explained Elto. "So, you know what that's leading into correct?"

Ceero nodded. "He's dying, yeah?"

"When you die," replied Elto, "there's a lot of different places you can go. Dad wants to go to a place called Heaven where the Christians go when they die. Well, most at least. The point is, Dad knows Oya is gonna' try and knab his soul before he reaches Heaven's gates. It's a very real fear and I believe it's why father hasn't passed on yet. He's hung on long enough, so Dr. Mama can help him make it to Heaven."

Dr. Mama had it all planned out. Before he was a medic in the Air Force, he was an ordained minister. He learned to keep his complicated and often morally ambiguous friends and comrades out of Hell. Dr. Mama believed warding off Oya's presence would be a similar feat.

That night, Dr. Mama set up a room for the brothers to sleep in. There was a comfy bunk bed in the guest room. Elto took to the top bunk, while Ceero took the bottom. Ceero had always had trouble sleeping since he first realized at the age of seven how dangerous the rest of their lives would be. The thought of constant struggle sometimes left him feeling hopeless. This weight on his head made it hard to get comfy, especially when it was never *his* bed. Ceero had no real home. Neither did Elto, but for some reason, he could only sleep just fine. Ceero and Elto were never far from one another, even when they slept. Ceero would always hear Elto pass out after fifteen minutes. He'd know he was asleep cause Elto snored like Thor's thunder.

Elto didn't know his little brother had trouble sleeping. He always thought his little brother's red eyes were just Oya's doing. Keeping the air dry and uncomfortable wherever they went. Because he didn't know Ceero was an insomniac, Elto made little effort to sneak out of their bedroom. He simply jumped off the top of the bunks and hurried to the living room. He thought Ceero would be fast asleep, but he was completely aware his brother had just snuck out. What for, Ceero didn't know. But after ten minutes of silence, Dr. Mama's living room was suddenly filled with the sounds of loud choking. Ceero ran out of the guest bedroom and caught Elto in the act of suffocating their father with a pillow. "Stop!" shouted Ceero. He charged at Elto and knocked him off of Nim right before his oxygen ran out.

"No," grumbled Nim. "Let him do it," he begged softly.

"Dad knew you'd try to stop us," explained Elto shoving Ceero off of him. "But dad wants to die! Right now! So we can get back on the road. He fears we're sitting ducks."

"But dad!" wept Ceero. He leapt on top of his father and asked him how they should carry on without him. He'd kept them safe for so long.

"I've taught you well," smiled his dad. "You've learned the secret long ago. To survive a disaster, you must always stay... likable."

"What?" exclaimed Ceero. He didn't understand. Frustrated, he just held tightly onto his father and gave him a tight squeeze. He didn't want to let him go.

Nim patted his son on the back and tried to comfort him. In the meantime, Elto ran to get Dr. Mama and asked him if he could help put his father down peacefully. Dr. Mama agreed. "I know what must be done," he explained. "Your father had this planned out for a while."

Ceero let go of his father only to investigate a foreboding noise picking up outside. It sounded like strong winds were closing in. Ceero ran to the window of Dr. Mama's third floor apartment and peered outside. The night sky had quickly changed from clear to cloudy as the stars all suddenly vanished. Lit by the glow of street lamps Ceero could see the lumpy underside of the clouds rolling-in overhead. "She's brewing up something..." droned Ceero. He kept watch on the weather while Elto volunteered to be Dr. Mama's assistant.

Dr. Mama and Elto first injected Nim with a dose of poison that would slowly put him down peacefully. They then set up a projector to shine above Nim. "When your father's soul ascends," explained Dr. Mama, "he'll be able to follow the map we project onto the ceiling."

The projected image became crisp revealing the image of our solar system. Dr. Mama then handed Elto a metal cross and two nails. "You're taller than me. Reach up there and pin this in on Heaven." Elto wasn't sure where that was in the solar system. Dr. Mama directed him to the moons of Jupiter. "Just stick it right there on Europa."

Dr. Mama then handed Elto a roll of thin red tape. "Star of David," he instructed. "Right overtop of Mercury." This mark would block Nim's view of Oya's realm, making it harder for her to lure his soul.

When Elto was finished marking-up the map he ran over to help his little brother. Together they nailed boards overtop of the windows. "What did you see out there?" asked Elto as he used the hammer of Thor for ordinary crafting purposes.

Thor called out from the inside of the tool. "Don't just use me to hang up wood. Point me at whatever it is and fire!"

"I'm not sure if that's going to work this time," explained Ceero. "It's no tornado. It's a dust storm." Ceero pointed out the window at the plumes of sand approaching from far off the in distance. It wouldn't be long till the particles would try and force their way into the building.

"She knows we're in the city, but she doesn't know where," explained Ceero. "I think I can use Thor as a distraction. I'll create thunder somewhere far away off in the city and she'll think we're hiding wherever it came from."

"A decoy!" shouted Elto. "Great idea."

"I'll make it seem like we're firing her from an entirely different building," replied Ceero. "She'll keep invading the buildings I chose instead of this one."

"Hopefully this works..." grimaced Elto. "If she gets her sand in here, she'll use it to get dad's soul!"

"I'm not gonna' give her a chance," called out Dr. Mama. "Elto I need you back here!"

Elto hurried over to his father's bedside and saw his eyes shut closed. Elto reached out to his father's wrist and felt for a pulse. It was cold and lifeless.

"The package has shipped, boy," sighed Dr. Mama. "Now let's make sure it reaches the right address."

Elto nodded. There was no time to mourn. "What needs to be done?"

Dr. Mama shoved a Bible in Elto's hands and told him to read any passage on any page. "I'm gonna' put on some recordings of a choir section while you preach. That should simulate the sound of Heaven and block out the noise of any siren calls Oya emits from Mercury."

Elto did as he was instructed and opened the book at random. He read from the top of the page on the left. Psalm 148. How convenient. It seemed fate had a small part in everything no matter how insignificant. "*You know how to interpret the appearance of the sky,*" read aloud Elto, "*but you cannot interpret the signs of the times...*"

Ceero tried to tune out Elto and the gospel music so he could concentrate. He was looking over another paper map, unfolded on the floor in front of the window. This was map of OKC made over a decade ago. Ceero touched Thor's hammer to a point in the city and slid it across the page like a stylus.

Far from their hiding space, a sonic blast shot out the window of a distant hotel. Ceero looked out the cracks between the boards on the window. He saw the coming sandstorm squeeze through the buildings of the city like a wave of water. It suddenly descended upon the hotel he'd selected. The wind picked up and the sand particles began to swarm like angry bees. They eroded the outer layers of the hotel's walls, leaving its foundation brown and exposed. The sand slipped through the cracks and entered the inside of the building. Ceero watched in horror as sand coated the inside of all the hotel's windows leaving it impossible to tell the fate of the guests left inside.

It wouldn't be long till Oya found out the Stratus family wasn't there. Ceero had to choose a new point on the map to fire from. But, little did he know, this map was just as outdated as the last. He accidentally chose to fire from a building that no longer existed. The thunder shot from an empty point up in the air. Oya suddenly put together that Stratus' were firing remotely.

"Shitstorm, I screwed up," called out Ceero. "I think she's onto us!" Ceero watched through the cracks as flashes of lightning erupted in the dust clouds overhead. Upon closer inspection, these were static charges released by the flapping of thunderbird wings. "Thunderbird is checking through the windows of every building," relayed Ceero to the others. "We don't have much time before his finds us."

Elto couldn't focus on what his brother was saying. He was trying his hardest to keep reading from the Bible despite the terrifying visuals he was receiving. Elto had become an integral part of the ritual and so he was gifted with temporary supernatural witness. He could see his father's soul rising from his body. It was made of a shimmering blue light and reached out toward where they'd marked Heaven.

"Once he's phased through the ceiling, his choice will be sealed!" explained Dr. Mama.

Ceero watched Thunderbird suddenly swoop down and pass by Dr. Mama's apartment. He fluttered by once. Then twice. Then, it decided to examine the suspiciously boarded up window more closely. Thunderbird landed on the apartment's window sill and stuck its eye to the cracks between the boards. Ceero ducked out of its view but Thunderbird could still see Nim's death ritual taking place in the background.

Thunderbird suddenly began shrieking out in rage and discharged onto the window, superheating the glass and shattering it. The boards behind it caught fire, making a smoke signal to mark the location of the Stratus family. The sandstorm quickly closed-in on the coordinates.

"We're out of time!" shrieked Ceero. "Elto, please. What do I do?"

Elto stopped his incantation and let Dr. Mama handle the rest. Elto plucked Thor's hammer out of his front pocket and ran off to protect his little brother. He directed the hammer at the burning window and blew out the fire with a quick, cool blast of sound. But it was too little, too late.

Tendrils of sand sought out the signal and reached through the ashes of the window. Elto concentrated and quickly created a wall of sound in front of him and Ceero. It isolated the sand to the window side of the room and kept it from reaching their father. At first it seemed the shield might be enough, but slowly the sand began to condense before them. The particles combined tightly into solid matter and took the shapely form of Oya herself. Her sandstone avatar walked forward marching with the strength of a god through the opposing force of the sound wall. She was cutting right through and would soon have Thor's hammer clutched in her outstretched hand.

But Elto wasn't going to lose their last magical ally to Oya. It was time to turn the tides and return an ally from Oya's control.

Elto dissolved the sound shield willingly and swung the hammer over his shoulder. Free to move, Oya lunged at Elto. Elto flipped the hammer around in his grip and swung its claw deep into the eye socket of Oya's golem-form. She cried out in pain as Elto levered the hammer till Oya's face split in two. He wedged a healthy portion of sandstone off of her avatar. The lump glowed as it flew through the air. It then disappeared into a flash of light before it could touch the ground. Zeus suddenly took its place. Hovering beside them, he held out his hand and commanded Oya to back off. He shot out a bolt of lightning that froze Oya's golem into unmoving glass.

"He's out of here!" shouted Dr. Mama as he witnessed Nim make the last few feet of his ascent into Heaven. "She can't touch him now."

Zeus tossed more lightning bolts out the burnt window, up towards the clouds above OKC. Shards of glass began to fall to the streets below. Piece by piece Oya's sandstorm was being reduced into recyclable waste product. Oya realized she was losing the battle and quickly retreated. She took the remains of her sandstorm with her to recover on the dusty plains outside the city.

"It's time for you two to get moving," boomed the voice of almighty Zeus. "When I was one with Oya I saw her plans to kill the oracle of Punxsutawney, Pennsylvania. You need to get there before her. It's powers to predict weather give it the foresight to know how to defeat Oya. Ask him to see your fortunes and you'll learn how you've already defeated Oya in the future!"

"You won't be coming with?" questioned Ceero, concerned their old friend wouldn't be joining them in their adventures again.

"While you two escape the city, I'll stay here and hide. Oya won't leave Oklahoma till I'm back inside of her. I'll put up a long enough fight that should buy you plenty of time to explore Pennsylvania without her interference," explained Zeus.

"Please... you don't have to go back!" pleaded Ceero. He had missed his old card game buddy for far too long. But it seemed Zeus had already made up his mind.

"Carry on boy," replied Zeus, bidding his young friend goodbye. "You must get the oracle down South, so far down South that Oya can't freeze it to death with a blizzard."

"See yah later, Z," called out Elto. He yanked Ceero away and ran the two of them out of Dr. Mama's apartment. They took the staircase down to the ground floor in order to avoid a Tower of Terror-like scenario.

When they hit the bottom floor, they fled out into the street and piled into their GMC Syclone. They revved the engine and sped off down the street. Ceero peered into the back seat once again, but this time his father wouldn't be there. Instead, he saw Dr. Mama's apartment building out the back window. Ceero watched as Zeus rose out the top of the building and began taunting Oya to come win him back.

"It was just a lover's quarrel!" jested Zeus. "Don't you want to reignite the flame?!"

A blanket of sand quickly closed in on Zeus's floating body. He delivered zaps of electricity to the swirling cloud, paralyzing each coming tendril. Zeus smiled as he looked behind the dust and saw his friends escaping into the distance.

"How many hours to Punxsutawney?" asked Elto as he drove them northeast, up towards Missouri.

Ceero checked out the key in the corner of the map and compared it to the space between OK and PA. He estimated they'd arrive in about twenty hours.

"Then maybe it's about time I start teaching *you* how to drive," suggested Elto. "It would give me a chance to sleep while you take the wheel. It's safer for me to be rested."

"A cop's gonna' pull me over if he sees my young-ass face behind the wheel," griped Ceero. "I'm more than willing to try, but I probably should only drive at night when it's too dark to see a driver's age through the windshield."

Elto agreed but suggested Ceero practice right now. In the middle of nowhere Oklahoma, he was just as unlikely to be seen.

As Ceero carefully switched seats with his brother, he took control nice and easy. Ceero was a fast learner and had already demonstrated his knack for operating heavy machinery when they stopped those mudslides in Washington with the front of a bulldozer. "This is a breeze comparatively," said Ceero confidently. "It's so much easier to keep steady without the side of a mountain falling against you."

~

Sorry to tear you away from the moment, but your date has arrived. You quickly set down your book and smile. They look just like their profile picture. You introduce yourself and offer to buy the two of you seasonally flavored frappuccinos. Your date accepts and after a brief wait in line you deliver the drinks to your table. While you both periodically slurp the hard slush through your straws, you take turns summarizing your lives. As the caffeine starts stimulating your inquisitive side, you ask their opinion on top tier vegetables, but they're more interested in the book you were reading when they arrived.

"At Most Fear?" they say with a genuine interest. They want to read the summary on the back; they ask if you'd mind. You don't at all as long as they don't lose track of the page you were on. Your date recognizes the premise. They've, in fact, been hearing about the series incessantly from their friends. But your date seems less than impressed with the theme of the stories. "Don't they just keep getting attacked by different weather?"

You nod but go on to defend the book's better aspects. You particularly enjoy one of the brothers and have an intriguing theory regarding one of the gods. Your date tries to remain interested but reminds you they haven't actually read any of the series, so they don't know what you're talking about.

You adapt to the criticism and change the subject. You ask your date what series they prefer. They tell you about a few books they were forced to read for their English elective. They preferred non-fiction accounts by young women of pre-1900s America. You zone in and out of the proceeding rambling until the end of the date.

Before your date leaves, you hug them goodbye and exchange phone numbers. You then head back to your seat and pick back up your copy of At Most Fear. Your mind goes over the events of your date trying to answer the big questions. Did they like you? Do you like them? And are you too distracted to keep reading?

You consider buying the book, so you can finish it later in your own home. But the price is jacked up since it's a big release. You decide it'd be cheaper to just buy a second coffee to reattain your focus.

You manage to start reading again. You skip a few pages of fluff to speed things up a little, after all you don't want to be there all afternoon. You skim through a side quest in Chicago that *introduces the main love interest. You've got to cut corners somewhere and it might as well be Bechdel violations. You tune-in again when the boys finally reach Pennsylvania.*

~

Ceero, Elto, and their new pal Thrud decided to get a good night's sleep before their heist in the morning. They slept at a traditional Mennonite bed and breakfast just outside of Punxsutawney. The boys and girls were not required to sleep in separate rooms, so Ceero was selected to share a bunk bed with Thrud. When particularly exhausted, Elto snored like the thunder out of Thor's hammer, which was hard for the rest of the party to sleep through. Elto was decidedly isolated to a rise in the stables out back.

Despite being isolated from his noisy brother, Ceero still struggled with his insomnia. And Thrud's endless yammering didn't help.

"Your brother is strange and magnificent," swooned Thrud. "I might just be grateful he rescued me from that bird, but sometimes it feels like something more, you know?"

"That bird was my best friend," replied Ceero, sullenly. "I'm disappointed we had to kill him."

"Does your brother save girls all the time? Or am I his one and only?" asked Thrud leaning over the side of her bunk.

"We've done heroic things before," shrugged Ceero," but I guess it's all been to save ourselves or our family. I guess you'd be the first innocent bystander he's rescued."

"Oh... that's good enough," smiled Thrud. "Now do you think having a goddess as his arch enemy has left him wary of other goddesses... or strangely curious?"

"Oya has left my entire family with grief and irreparable trust issues," grimaced Ceero. "However, my brother is a sixteen-year-old boy, so yes, I'm sure you've peaked his curiosity."

Ceero didn't mean to sound so glum, but the weight of losing so many loved ones so fast had left him irritable. He wasn't sure how his brother was taking all the death so well. It was like as long as their old allies were replaced with fresh blood, Elto was only vaguely remorseful. He only seemed to care more about setting up exciting new character pairings and reaching descriptive new settings. There was never any time for him to focus on the past.

Ceero sat up in his bed and stared out the window towards the stables. He imagined his brother inside the loft in the attic, snorting like a boar and sleeping soundly.

"I just rescued her, man!" groaned Elto. "Please don't take it the wrong way." Despite being less perturbed than his brother, Elto was as wide awake as Ceero. He was unable to sleep while Thor scolded him from the confines of his hammer.

"You're both the same age and that concerns me!" shouted Thor. "People of the same age tend to date when placed in these scenarios."

"Wait, how is your daughter sixteen?" questioned Elto. "I mean if you're a Norse god, you've got to be at least a thousand years old. Why is she so young?"

"I don't cave to societal pressure as easily as the other gods. I waited to have kids when I felt mature enough to handle the responsibility. For some that age is twenty, for others it's one-thousand, for others it may be never!" explained Thor. "For you, it better be never."

"Wh- now why is that?"

"Don't touch my daughter boy!" shouted Thor.

By the time morning came, none of our adventurers had managed to gather much sleep at all. The gods in their party never really needed sleep and, so it seemed, they never seemed to need to shut up.

But despite their outwards appearance being tired and dreadful, Ceero and Elto were both confident in their coming mission. Mainly because the treasure they were thieving was not a highly regarded artifact. They were stealing a fat squirrel.

Punxsutawney Phil was the mysterious oracle they'd been sent to collect. With very little value on the head of a psychic marmot, he was not kept behind lock and key. Instead, he was kept on display in a flimsy glass terrarium built into the corner of the local library. There were glass windows, so tourists could see inside the terrarium from outside the library; this was their point of attack.

Thrud would be the first one in. Thrud has the power to shapeshift into various black birds including crows, ravens, rooks, and the daurian jackdaw. To keep the brothers out of legal trouble, the party had decided to make the abduction look like the work of a hungry predator bird instead of human thieves.

To allow Thrud entrance into the exhibit, the boys sniped the windows from afar with a sonic blast from Thor's hammer. Once glass shattered to the ground, Thrud swooped in through the opening with her talons drawn. But while the exhibit was easy to penetrate, they hadn't planned for Punxsutawney Phil to be much of a threat.

Phil stood up straight and put a finger to each side of his temple. He then shut his eyes and used telekinetic powers to grasp onto Thrud before she could strike. She was frozen in mid-air by Phil's amazing level of psychic strength.

Elto and Ceero had been watching the heist from the safety of their Syclone. Elto dropped his binoculars and shouted, "We have to go help her!"

"We shouldn't be seen," warned Ceero. "We don't want criminal records. We've fought too long to regain our livelihoods just to spend them in prison."

Elto sighed. "Why is he attacking us?!"

"Cause he thinks we're with Oya trying to kill him," said Ceero, frustrated. "We should have considered how he'd react."

"Well I don't think any of us knew he had powers besides foresight," replied Elto. "But listen Ceero, I've got a plan. Let's send another blast in remotely. We'll direct it to explode from the center of the exhibit forcing everything outside."

"Why didn't we just do that in the first place?" griped Ceero,

"Because we didn't want to maim the little woodchuck," shrugged Elto. "But now he's not so much on my good side."

Elto aimed the hammer for the center of the exhibit and fired. The blast launched the toys, dirt, and tubing from the interior of the terrarium onto the exterior of the library. Thrud landed with her wings spread out on the cement. She seemed unconsciousness at first, but slowly caught her breath and made her way up onto her feet. She looked to her right and saw that Phil was convulsing on the ground beside her. The blast was too much excitement for the little rodent and sent him into a state of heart attack.

Thrud thought quickly and carefully lifted the creature off of the ground. She flew his trembling body over to the car where the boys could deliver CPR.

"God, I wish Thunderbird was still here," cried Ceero. Last time someone went into myocardial infarction they had thunderbird's voltage to reset the beating.

Elto tried to remember the CPR training he received from a paramedic while fighting hurricanes in Florida. He saved three children from drowning back in Tampa, but surprisingly the training hadn't stuck. And to make matters worse, the steps were surely different for a groundhog's much smaller circulatory system. He tried his best to compensate and speed up the chest pumps and lessen the pressure applied.

After four rotations, Phil suddenly shot up out of his fugue state and gave the boys a terrifying scare. He hissed long and hard at their faces and raised his fingers back up to the sides of his skull. But the boys begged him to stop and reminded him they'd saved his life.

Phil couldn't deny it was strange Oya would want him alive. He gave the boys a chance to explain.

"We came to get you to safety," explained Elto. "Oya's going to send a snow storm to freeze you to death. We've got to get you somewhere warm."

"If you're a psychic, couldn't you see us coming?" questioned Ceero.

"Are you a body of clouds coordinated by atmospheric changes in temperature and pressure?"

Ceero shook his head.

"Then you're out of my line of sight," shrugged Phil. "Because I'm sub-human, my psychic powers are each oddly limited in some unique way. My foresight, for example, can only show me the future of weather and that which is directly affected by it."

"So you can see Oya, though?" asked Ceero.

Phil nodded. "I saw her next move. Freeze to me death along with the rest of Western Pennsylvania. I feared there was nothing I could do to escape my zoo. After all, my captors would think I were crazy if I told them I were psychic. And then they'd think *they* were crazy for hearing a talking woodchuck."

"Why are you guys just staring longingly into its eyes?" asked Thrud, now back in human form. She'd be watching them from the back seat for a while now. Ever since the groundhog had recovered from its heart attack, it just stared strangely at the boys. And the boys stared strangely back, making silent facial expressions as though they were all speaking to each other.

"She can't hear me. We've been communicating telepathically this whole time," explained Phil. "But my telepathy only works with men, and I can't talk normally cause I don't have human vocal chords. But please, tell her to keep her talons away from me..."

Elto turned to Thrud and relayed the information. "He's not that good a psychic so he can only talk to boy brains. And he wants us to tell you thanks for saving him."

"Your welcome!" exclaimed Thrud from the backseat so Phil could hear.

Ceero took Phil in his lap and begged him to tell him his fortune. "Zeus wanted me to ask you something," he said. "How do I ultimately defeat Oya?"

"Let's see for ourselves," Phil took a deep breath to clear his mind, then grabbed the boy's hands. "I see... I see..." muttered the squirrel. "I see a horrible drought that decimates an entire country. It soaks up the rivers and the lakes. People go crazy trying to drink salt water and sewage. And only then, Oya dies in your arms, child, she's choking on her own vomit."

Ceero cringed at the thought of such an apocalypse. His ultimate triumph over Oya was nowhere near as glorious as he'd imagined. Killing Oya might come at the cost of an entire nation.

"Is my future the same?" asked Elto pulling Phil back over to his lap. He allowed the woodchuck to hold his hands and peer into his fate.

"I see..." hummed the groundhog. "There is a different storm in your future." explained Phil. "She's a sixteen-year-old single goddess."

"Wait what?" called out Thor from the confines of his hammer. As a male, he could hear all their conversations in his brain.

Phil smiled. "First you get with Thrud and then you have three kids that go on their own adventures."

"Noooo!" shouted Thor from his hammer, his howl made the whole car shake till the front windows cracked.

~

You set down your book and look at your phone. It's been buzzing annoyingly, cutting off your concentration. You flip it over and see you've missed two calls and a message from your best friend. They want you to go out with them. You feel kind of tired now that your caffeine's worn off, but you think it might be good to talk with someone about how your date went.

You've been gradually losing interest in the novel anyways and feel it might be dragging a bit to add filler. You wonder if perhaps you could just read the summary on Wikipedia and if it sounds interesting enough maybe you'll read the rest later. You don't mind having the plot spoiled after all; it didn't stop you from enjoying Se7en even though you already knew what would be in the box.

You open up a browser on your phone and bring up the wiki page for the At Most Fear series. You learn that the author, Q. Marlie, had first released a critically lauded essay collection from their time overseas in the military. These memoirs never met mainstream appeal, however. Marlie only got his big break once he switched publishers and tried something more commercial in the form of YA fiction.

You click to a linked page that lists all the books in the series along with their release dates. Another new one is due out next August just in time for kids to pick up for school reading. It's still untitled.

Beneath each release date is a one-page summary of the book's events. You briefly look over the synopses of Books 1 and 2 to see if there was anything important you didn't pick up on. You see that Book 1: No Sun in Seattle explained the origins of the Stratus family curse. It stemmed from the misdeed of their grandfather Bo Stratus who meddled with weather modification in the 1950's. He worked with William Reich to build a weather machine for the US government. It pissed off all the weather gods, but none more than Oya, who vowed to bury the invention, the inventors, and every last link of their bloodlines to make sure the idea never saw the light of day.

You then read through the summary of Book 2: Hurricane Oya where you see said goddess starting her mission to absorb other weather elementals to gain more power. They rescue Thor from his hiding place in a toolbox in the back of a Miami chop shop. Then they meet Zeus whose disguised himself as a card shark on a riverboat casino in nearby New Orleans. He bonds with the boys and Nim and performs a bunch of cool magical card tricks along the way, but is ultimately captured when Oya sinks the riverboat with a rabid squall.

You finally reach the synopsis for Book 3 just as you reach the bottom of your third frappuccino. You best not forget to brush your teeth before hitting the town tonight or your breath will taste like sour beans. You skip to the end of the description and see that you've read through most of the good parts already. After the heist there doesn't seem to be much action. It's just a bunch of warm, fuzzy dialogue as the team comes together to enjoy their first cheesesteaks in Philadelphia. Following that, the team decides their next stop should be Japan for whatever reason. And then, cliffhanger, Ceero commits suicide.

Wait. What? Ceero dies!? It's described in a single sentence at the end of the synopsis. "The morning after planning their voyage, Elto walks into their bathroom to find that Ceero has used the hammer to blow his own head off. You can't help but find this twist a bit jarring. From what you've read, the series has a whimsical tone fit for a middle schooler. But that ending is just plain dark. You wonder if perhaps it's been foreshadowed in the other books and only real fans would have seen it coming.

You try to clear it from your head and leave the bookstore. You get in your car and drive directly to your friend's place. It's getting late but you can stay the night. You really want to talk about Ceero's death with your friend, but you already know this friend hasn't read a book in their life. Whenever it came to school assignments, they've only ever read the SparkNotes.

When you first enter their apartment, they fix you a drink and beg for you to dish them all the details of your Tinder date. You're happy to oblige. You describe the parts that, in your opinion, went very well. You both played the same board games and studied the same major in college, but it seemed you both differed over matters of social reform. You being a stubborn egalitarian and them citing the Riot grrrl movement of the 1990's.

Your friend shrugs and asks if you liked her. You hesitate, but ultimately you say you do. You want to like her. It's just hard sometimes, because admitting it means that you can get let down if she doesn't want to see you again.

Your friend encourages you to reach out and text her first. It may seem early, but you should ask for a second date. Your friend grabs your phone from you so they can write it for you. They promise they won't hit send unless you approve.

Your friend unlocks your phone and smiles. "At Most Fear?" they chuckle. "They're gonna' make that into a Netflix series, I hear. The trailer looked good and it's made by the guy who made that movie Nightro I made you watch."

You remember Nightro. It was visually stunning, and the stunts were all done with practical effects. But god did that plot suck. Being chased by ghost vehicles just isn't that scary a concept. Even when they're exotic sports cars driven by undead supermodels.

"Are you thinking of reading them?" asks your friend.

You tell him you already have. You started reading them today and got really into it.

"Are you... okay?" he asks with genuine concern.

Your feeling tipsy at this point, but otherwise you're fine. You assure your friend you could handle more wine.

"That's not what I meant," explains your friend. "It's just seems like maybe you're using this book series as a bit of a distraction."

"I'm not distracting you from anything," you reply back with a little snark.

Your friend lets out a short laugh. "Whenever I'm stressed out about something, I'll often find myself using micro-obsessions to distract myself from what's bothering me. Sometimes I read guidebooks for games I've never played. Other times I'll listen to reviews for movies I haven't actually seen. Sometimes you just want to get lost in a phenomenon without fully participating in it."

"Micro-obsessions," you repeat it to yourself. You wonder what work or social obligation you could be running from. Your friend asks you the same question. Using the haze of the wine, you manage to draw out an insecurity buried deep in your subconscious. You take a deep breath and let it all out.

You tell him you're afraid you'll never find somebody who wants a second date. You're afraid that while your occupation and your friendships seem strong, your weaknesses may all lie within your ability to find love. It's a skill that needs improving and you're afraid to give it the attention it needs.

"Did your date really go as well as you described?" asks your friend. His tone is concerned, not accusatory. You assure him, the date went just fine in your eyes. But that's just it. You're so weak at the dating game you're not sure what keeps going wrong. But your last couple dates before this didn't go so well.

Your friend points out that you haven't had an awful lot of experience in relationships yet. "You're the one that wanted to stay single till you finished college," they remind you. "So you're just a little behind the rest of us. I've already had three year-long relationships in my life and I still fuck up from time to time. It'll go so much easier though once you take some L's and learn what works for you."

You take your friend's advice and decide to send a message to today's date. You ask for your phone back so you can type it out yourself. You decide on something short and to the point. "Lunch tomorrow?" It gets your friend's approval and you send it. Your friend then distracts you from the waiting game by playing a series of games with you involving shots of rum. When the time has come for the two of you to leave, you've completely forgotten about sending the message.

While in the back of the Uber, you realize that your phone's screen is lit up through the fabric of your pocket. You whip it out and see with your hazy vision that your date from earlier had texted you back. But the length of the text was immediately disheartening. You didn't even bother looking at it. You set the message to "read" so it wouldn't appear on your lock screen any longer. You then slide the phone back in your pocket and lean over towards your friend's ear. You give him a brief synopsis of what she replied, "It's a no."

Your friend pushes you to drink heavier than you normally would in order to help you bypass any hurt feelings that could get in the way of the night's plans. You accept his free libations but can't guarantee him you won't breakdown if your thoughts catch up with you. Determined not to let that happen, your friend grabs the bottom of your barstool and begins rotating. Slowly your perspective is turned clockwise. Your spun away from your friend and redirected to your other side. Here, you become face to face with a well-dressed young person. They turn to face you and smile. They seem interested enough and you decide to spark a conversation.

You zone in and out as your discussion advances rather rapidly. It seems, despite your impairment, you two are hitting it off. You fear however that they are falling in love with someone who isn't really you. This is just a drunk version of you spitting non-sense and half-truths at a beautiful face. For example, when they asked what hobbies you had. You said reading just cause its fresh on your mind from today's events. You proceed to ramble on and on about At Most Fear and exaggerate, saying you read all three books cover to cover today. You leave out the part where you were waiting for a date to arrive.

"Would you recommend those books?" asks the beautiful face.

You don't. You're actually quite bitter about them. They killed off the one good character and you're not afraid to shout angrily about it.

"Authors always do that. I used to write a little actually," explains the beautiful face. "People's attention spans crave a very specific degree of new. They want to try a new food but only at a restaurant they can trust. Or in other words, they want new stories, but they only trust the same franchises. In theory, when they want new characters and new settings they could pick up a new series. But instead, they stick with the series they know and love, and demand that the author introduces a bunch of new characters at the expense of the old ones. Every YA series is guilty of it to some degree. I'd say every major YA series is actually four or five separate premises tacked together under the same title."

"These is is paradox," you reply, drunkenly.

"Which paradox?" asks the beautiful face.

"Theese's... thieces..." you repeat, no clearer than the last time.

"Reese's... pieces?" she guesses.

You take a deep breath and try to control your tongue movements diligently. "The. See. Us. Is. Theseus's Paradox."

"Oh yes!" she laughs. "Yes, yes. Good point. The stories replace so many of their elements one has to ask at what point they are no longer the same series."

You nod. Your ecstatic they were able to articulate your drunken ideas so well. You just realize that something you'd really appreciate in a partner. More than just a shared interest in Gloomhaven.

"I guess new titles are too much of a risk when you can make spin-offs and sequels," continues the beautiful face. You listen to her theories till your mind has become undeniably overfilled. Majority of its volume has been displaced by liquor. Luckily, you *wouldn't have to memorize a phone number, thanks to the wonders of technology.*

The beautiful face says they like you and they're happy that you got to meet. After exchanging numbers, you promise them you'll message them in the morning, but you're far too intoxicated to attempt physical arts. The beautiful stranger tells you it's quite alright and bids you a goodnight with a kiss on the lips.

You're glad it worked out alright. You've been unsuccessfully trying to avoid mere hookups in order to put focus on sustaining a longer lasting relationship. You've learned over time that, although you like liberally minded partners, sleeping on the first night has failed to create anything consistent. You're happy you've managed to take it slow this time.

Satisfied enough with your night, you decide that it's time to call it quits. You find your friend at the bar and explain that you're headed home and that you'll pick up your car from their house in the morning. They understand; you're looking pretty wasted.

You Uber to your home and immediately dash upstairs to your bedroom. You pull your computer up off the floor and onto your lap. You partake in the enjoyment of pornography.

When finished, you check your social media accounts and see you've gotten a new friend request. It's from the beautiful face at the bar. You're ecstatic that she's found you, but don't accept it just yet. It's really late at night and you don't want them to think you think about them as you go to sleep. That would be weird. Especially if they knew you just masturbated.

Seeing the beautiful face reminds you of your long-winded discussion of Theseus's Ship and At Most Fear. You realize finishing Book 3 might not be a bad idea for the moment. After all, you're too dizzy to doze off. If you lie down and shut your eyes, you'll surely vomit all over your sheets.

You Google "AtMost Frar Book 3 free pdf". It's heavily typoed but Google knows what you mean. It immediately finds you a free copy of the story on FreeLib.lib. You wait for it to load then skip to the final chapter. You read it slowly through the blur of your alcoholic impairment, eager to understand Ceero's unjust ending.

~

"Hey so, your brother is really suicidal," explained Phil. "I hear his thoughts screaming in my head in the middle of the night."

"What's he so caught up on?" asked Elto with a look of confusion.

"Well mainly your dad and Thunderbird."

"But who needs them when we've got you and Thrud!" exclaimed Elto.

"Well that's just it, I think your brother is afraid the introduction of another new character will, next, mean the end of him."

"Well... why him and not me?"

"Remember when Ceero used to be afraid of thunderstorms but now he willfully goes storm chasing?"

Elto nodded.

"Well, that's him. That's his arc. He's fleshed all out. He's done," shrugged Phil. "You though, you just got a love interest. You and Thrud are set to reproduce and make a bunch of new adventurers for our time jump in Book 7. You're basically a guaranteed immortal."

"That's just awful," sighed Elto. "My feelings for her a still very much unclear."

Phil rolled his eyes. "Yeah well you're a sixteen-year-old boy. Trust me, one chapter on Sunayama beach leads to a page long description of her bathing suit, and it all becomes very clear."

"Oh," grimaced Elto. "Sunayama beach?"

"Oh yeah didn't I tell you?" said Phil excitedly. "We're going... to Japan!"

"Why Japan?"

"Zeus survived. Oya's given up on absorbing him and Thor. There's a new powerful entity she now seeks. Raijin, demon of storms. I fear this monster getting involved could be the first step towards the apocalypse I saw in my vision. Oya doesn't realize the pure chaos he'll instill her with. She'll be seeking more than just vengeance if they combine."

"But we don't have any money," griped Elto. "How on earth are we going to afford the plane tickets?"

"We're not traveling by plane, silly!" said Phil, gleefully. His exclamation was followed by a knock on their hotel door. "Oh, I think that's the captain. He's here early."

"Wait who is it now?" called out Elto as Phil jumped off his lap and ran over to the door.

"He'll be driving us to Japan via his personal watercraft. I predicted a hail storm that saved his life and his vessel. He owes me one," Phil reached up high and grabbed the door knob with his paws. "Presenting First Admiral Monsoon."

"No stop!" shouts Elto. "Please... don't let him in."

"Why not?" questioned Phil.

"Well I... I don't know," stuttered Elto. He stood up off the couch and ran to Phil's side. "Admiral Monsoon is quite the name, don't you think?"

Phil nodded. "Well he's a grizzled veteran who exclusively sails during the Eastern monsoon season. Hence the name." Phil adjusted his paws and turned the door knob. He pulled back on the door, but Elto quickly shoved it back closed. "Hey! What gives?" sneered Phil. "You almost crushed my little fingers!"

"Phil... what if this character is so cool and interesting that it becomes a more intriguing partner to me than my own brother."

"I don't know," said Phil, sounding frustrated. "I mean to me he's just a boring, old sailor. He only sails during monsoon season to assert his dominance over the harsh waves that took his son away long ago."

Another knock came at the door. "He's growing impatient!" shouted Phil. "He needs his introduction or we'll lose our chance to go to Japan!"

"Then let's just not go!" suggested Elto. "I certainly would rather keep my brother alive and happy then go to Japan to fall in love with the world's most dull demigod. For a shapeshifter, it's shocking she can only seem to muster one-dimension."

Elto turned his head over his shoulder towards the bedrooms. All the doors were closed shut. "She can't hear me thinking trash about her, right?"

Phil nodded. "Don't worry. My telepathy is still an exclusive men's club."

"Listen," suggested Elto. "How about you take Thrud with you and have the Admiral take you two for a spin-off in Japan. Me and Ceero can stay here and continue the main adventure on our own!"

"You've done enough in the States. It's time to go international or you'll lose intrigue." Phil fought hard against Elto's weight and tried to open the door for the Admiral. But his woodchuck strength could not compare to a human's. "Would you please let go?!" snarled Phil getting angry.

Elto still refused, so Phil let go of the door. He stuck his fingers to the sides of his head. Elto thought he was going to use his telekinesis to try and rip the door off, but instead a noise went off down the bedroom hallway beside them. It was a banging noise knocking on the door of Ceero's bedroom from the inside. With every bang, Elto heard Ceero let out a small oomph on the other side of the door.

"Open the fucking door in front you!" shouted Phil down the hall.

"...why can't you?" came Ceero's voice, muffled behind the door.

"I can only move living matter!" shrieked Phil. "It's another stupid limit on my powers."

Ceero opened his door reluctantly so Phil would stop smacking him against it. Phil was now free to levitate Ceero through the doorway into the bedroom hallway. Phil floated the child up to he and Elto.

"If you don't let things progress as they should," threatened Phil, "I'll snap the boy's neck just to speed up this whole process."

"You wouldn't..." pleaded Elto.

"There's no reason not to. It's only going to help you. I'm going to cut the only tether you have left to the past, Elto. And with that you'll join the rest of us in the future of this series!" shouted Phil. He began to spin poor Ceero around in the air like a gyroscope. Slowly rotating him around on his axes.

"My brother is a ten-year-old. How dare you assume he's got no development left for his character. It's not like he'll live happily ever after because he conquered a fear of thunderstorms. He's already showing signs of adolescent depression, that's something I would like to see him persevere!"

"It's a YA novel!" sneered Phil. "Suicidal types need to go through with it! Suicides are instant drama. Instant motivation. Keeping them alive is boring!"

Elto pulled out Thor's hammer from his back pocket. He pointed it at Phil and threatened to fire. "It's not boring, Phil! It's just mature. Its long, and its drawn out, and its meditative. Something this YA genre can't seem to understand." Waves of thunder crackled at the tip of the hammer, causing all the metal surfaces in the room to hum softly. "I think it's time to appeal to an older audience."

Phil let go of Ceero, dropping him to the floor. He then went right into trying to get a hold of Elto. Phil used his powers to bend Elto's arm toward the ceiling, directing the hammer upwards. Elto pushed through the telekinetic vice and fired twice, knocking down sheets of cement onto their heads. They all fell to the floor with heavy chunks of the ceiling weighing on their backs. Elto managed to wriggle out of the rubble, but Phil was not as lucky.

Phil couldn't move. He wasn't anatomically paralyzed, but he was stuck beneath a stone panel and his groundhog arms didn't have enough strength to lift it. With his telekinesis limited to only living tissue, he was stuck.

Elto picked back up the hammer and trudged over to Phil. Thrud, hearing the destruction, ran out of her bedroom to see what was happening.

"Oh my god is Elto safe?!" shouted Thrud as she ran towards the destruction.

Elto sighed aggravatingly and fired a sound wave down the hall right at Thrud's head. The blast bent her neck unnaturally far till the top of her head curled all the way back and touched the top of her spine.

"Nooo!" roared Thor from within the confines of his hammer. He wanted to burst out and kick Elto's ass, but the spell concealing him was too great for even him to unlock. He wept deeply, begging Elto to do no more harm to their friends.

"He won't," snarled Phil from under the stone panel. He managed to press his fingers to his head and activate his powers. "Not as long as I still have his brother." Phil tried to lift Ceero up off the floor, but the boy's body would not raise. "Come on! Come on!" shrieked Phil through his telepathy. "Why won't you budge, boy?"

Elto ran over to his brother's fallen form. He slid his arms under Ceero and lifted him from the hotel carpet. His body was limp and lifeless. Blood dribbled onto the hand Elto had supporting the boy's head. It was soft and wet. A piece of debris had smashed the back of Ceero's skull.

Elto wanted to cry out. He wanted to scream *Nooooo* or something else where the last vowel was really drawn out. But he really didn't want to come across as cliché. Thor sounded like a goddamn cartoon character when he did it. So instead, Elto said nothing and came across as cold. He slowly let down his brother's body and raised the hammer. It sobbed uncontrollably as thunder rumbled over its length. The thunder launched out like a missile and blew Phil's head into pink chewing gum.

Elto then walked over to the hotel door and opened it wide. First Admiral Monsoon was still waiting outside. His scarred, unshaven face was reduced to a trembling look of terror, "Are we..." stuttered the Admiral with a low, droll British accent. "Are we... still on for Japan?"

Elto raised his hammer and blew the Admiral to smithereens.

~

You suddenly wake up from your drunken slumber. There's a trail of slime on the side of your face. Drool that gradually slid from the corner of your mouth over the course of the night. You wipe it off and check your reflection on the blacked-out computer screen sitting in front you. You'd passed out last night with your laptop on top of you. You're glad it didn't fall in your sleep. You must have slept like a rock.

You click a few buttons on the keyboard but nothing lights up. The computer was left on all night, you should have figured it'd be dead. You close it up and slide it under your bed.

You peel the sheets and covers off of you. You go to the bathroom and fill a Dixie cup with water over and over till your throat doesn't feel so dry. You climb back into bed and try to go back to sleep, but your head hurts too much to get anymore rest.

Lying in your bed with nothing to distract you, you begin to recall some of your more painful memories. They've been coming up more often than usual. You've been drinking a lot more since it's the summer and that's surely been depressing you.

Your mind brings up memories from your longest relationship. It was all the way back in high school and it had only lasted a month. It ended when you started to bore them. They made that explicitly clear. They liked that you at first cause you used to apologize too much and get easily distracted during long conversations. But in that same month you dated, you began talk therapy and started new meds. It helped iron out those finicky flaws, but it also cost you a certain degree of quirkiness.

To stop your mind from spinning out of control, you message your friend from last night. You apologize for leaving so early on in the night. They text you back immediately asking you not to apologize for such trivial things. "You were drunk. You needed to go home." "You sound really sad. What's really bothering you?" You relay the thoughts on your first love and the damage they did to you. It was like they stopped loving you when your arc was finished. That's when you got stale. People used to say, "it's not just about the destination, it's about the journey." But nowadays it feels like it's just all journey with people. The destination is just as much fun as sex after the orgasm.

Your friend texts you back. "People do love an endless cycle of change," they admit. "But you're forgetting that humans quite naturally meet this demand. We never actually stop changing. We get better in one aspect while shirking on another. There's always room for growth and some new flaw that needs to be conquered. We're never perfect. Even the state of perfect needs further perfection; after all, now you have to struggle with no one seeing you as humble."

As you stare at the messages on your phone, you're stomach begins to upset you. When you're hungover, bright screens give you nausea. The only way to combat the queasy feeling is by filling yourself with coffee and dry food. You snack on cereal in the kitchen and keep your phone on silent flipped over on the desk in your bedroom.

You desperately want a distraction from your inner dialogue, but you need something that doesn't require a television or a computer monitor. You see the 3D puzzle you keep on your microwave as a form of messy millennial decor. You pick it up and spend a good two-hours pulling at its rings and strings. You finish off a whole carafe of sticky, black Folger's in the process.

You manage to free one the components from the rest of the puzzle. You get too excited start to get a little obsessive again. You begin to wonder how much these little puzzles cost individually. Certainly people sell them online after they've finished them. You could save a lot buying them used. Maybe you could even save money buying a whole set of little ones.

You run to your bedroom and grab your phone. You open Amazon and begin peaking at all the puzzles on sale. There's so many different types. Puzzle boxes where you can lock up your stuff in a clever maze.

In the corner of your screen you see an advertisement targeted at you based on your recent interests in At Most Fear. Book 4: Tickets to Typhoon is officially available for pre-order due out next August. You stare at the ad for a couple seconds as your dream from last night slowly plays out in your head. Then, a stinging feeling grows at the bottom of your throat. The glow of your phone makes you feel dizzy. You drop your phone on the kitchen table and run to the bathroom.

You vomit on the toilet's lid and collapse to your knees on the floor.

Pizza Crow V

I continued to run experiments until every metric of pizza was attached to a story element. I summarized my conclusions as follows: the crust controls the point of view, the toppings control the theme, the sauce controls the tone, and the cheese controls the probability of passing the Bechdel test.

All the necessary experimentation has had an unforeseen consequence so I had to put any further testing on hold. The bird is getting fat. I put the trials on hold for three months to put the bird back on a healthy diet of mainly corn and mealworms.

I spent those free months really thinking over the work I'd done so far. I tried to see if my notes up till then could find traditional publishing in reputable scientific journals. I ended up severely disappointed, so my original instinct to make money off this bird returned. Only this time, it was different. I was done testing different foods. I was sticking with pizza. I realized that with that alone, I had my very own publishing company. And a writer that will never run out of creative juices. As long as I had pizza, I had a writing machine.

Fantasy is hot right now, so I tried my best to create a combo that would capture that genre. It's really tough though to tune this thing to exactly what you want but I got close enough with a combination of thick crust, bacon topping, sweet sauce, and mozzarella.

F1

Pow! A cloud of smoke jumped from the tip of the farmer's weapon, sending a fat, copper slug up towards the stars. The blast laid the first layer of soot over the length of untouched rifling. This was a newly purchased .410-gauge shotgun; the first and only firearm of one Diego Garcia, carrot farmer.

Diego had not purchased this shotgun as a means of killing any human beings. So after hearing someone ransacking his stable in the dead of night, he decided to run outside and fire a warning shot just to scare the hoodlums away.

The blast was deafening. Diego hadn't realized just how dangerous it was to fire a gun so close beside his head without proper ear protection. He took a moment to fiddle with his ringing cochlea before continuing forward out to the tiny stable in his backyard. This building had two stalls, only one of which was occupied. Approaching the stable from the front, Diego saw that the padlock on the front door had been picked and now swung open freely.

Diego charged inside with his weapon extended, bluffing with the promise of a second blast, but there was no reason to pull the trigger, all the intruders had scurried away. The only soul left in the stable was its usual occupant and the property seemed to have been left unharmed. In the stall to the left, standing calmly and facing out the window, was Diego's one and only horse, an Appaloosa by the name of Barfly. Despite this magnificent breed, and her magnificent parents, Barfly was a piece of shit.

"They're trying to stop me from taking her head off!" griped Diego, or as Officer Paterson called him, Di.

"Di you don't exactly live close to town. Why would Dr. Greene travel forty-five miles to steal a blind, deaf nag?"

"First of all, she's not a doctor, she's a vet. A doctor would have some sense of mercy. Greene's got her own fucking agenda and when I asked her to come by with some needles to put down my horse, she refused," huffed Di. "She said my horse is too old. I raised it this long with its condition, I should keep it happy till it passes naturally. What the fuck is that?! That's not her choice to make. She has a responsibility to stop it's painful existence."

"And how exactly did you respond to her refusal?"

"I asked her directions to the nearest gun store." As sassy as that may sound, it was honestly Diego's only other option for euthanasia. Being on the edge of the Alaskan wilderness, Peter Post was the only town within driving distance. Just over two hours away. Diego was too far out for a house call from any other vet. So he had to take things into his own hands.

"So, you think she's trying to free Barfly?"

Diego nodded.

"Do you think she'll try twice?"

Diego shook his head. "Without too much detail, I scared her off... I don't need an arrest, but I want her to pay for the damages she caused. She chipped the paint off the front of my stable. Completely gutted my padlock. And broke the gate to Barfly's stall clean off the hinges."

Officer Patterson took down his notes; listing the many grievances along with some cost estimates he'd strummed up from his own time managing his family's farm in his youth. He promised Diego he'd be back with a check and a written apology and walked off to his police car. Patterson turned on his high beams and drove off down the long dark road. It was that time of year again in Alaska, midnight sun, where the sun never ascends over the horizon for a good two months. Instead, the sky stuck in a perpetual state of dawn. This was a contributing factor to Diego's penny-pinching.

When the sun was up for ninety days in a row, this everlasting sunlight would create large volumes of oversized crops. Nice, thick, juicy carrots. Plentiful enough to keep him economically sound. He uses savings from this period to survive the worst time for his business, when there's no light at all. Part of surviving this brutal bi-month was strict budgeting. One stipulation of such was no renovations, which now were required due to Greene's break-in. Diego required reimbursement, or the repairs would have to come out of his food money.

Diego's choice to put down Barfly was for related reasons. With one less mouth to feed, Diego could focus his funds on keeping himself healthy and happy in his sunset years. Diego was turning seventy next month. Diego had kept Barfly around as odd company on an otherwise lonely ranch, but she really never was the purchase Diego had expected. When he bought her as a young filly fresh out the womb, Barfly was predicted to be a champion. Her mother rose walls in barn construction and her father was a winning race horse. But somehow, all their best attributes filtered out when breeding Barfly, leaving latent mutations to blossom into malformations in Barfly's head and face. She grew to be fast and strong, but too hard to train by a novice rancher, as Barfly developed to be blind in one eye and deaf in the opposite ear. Without the money or the energy to sustain her, Diego honestly believed it was best to let her go humanely first thing this Summer season when the darkness comes.

With the officer on his way to Greene, Diego decided it was time to stop hesitating before anymore interference appeared. He slid a new slug down the barrel of his gun and walked out to his destroyed stable. Barfly had been tied down to the fencing inside to prevent her escape through the open wreckage.

Diego pointed the barrel forward as he crept silently into the stable. He approached Barfly from her blind side where she shouldn't have been able to see him coming, but as soon as he stepped through the front doors, she reacted. She yanked and tore at the vice around her neck as though she saw the barrel pointed directly at the side of her head. Diego lowered his weapon and ran over Barfly's anatomy in his head. Double-checking that he was approaching from the correct side. But it all added up as it should. He wondered if he was somehow caught in a reflection on her good side, but he couldn't make out any metal, water, glass, or otherwise reflective surface.

Diego marched up to his horse and pulled his cell phone from his pocket. He started the flashlight app and directed the beam into Barfly's bad eye. Diego was shocked to see it react so plainly, the large pupil quickly shrank towards the center.

"No way!" shouted Diego. The scream startled his horse further, sending her scurrying as far she could to the side of her stall. Diego tested his shout on her other ear and in return received a similar response.

In the remaining time before Officer Patterson's return, Diego tested Barfly's senses over and over, assuring himself he wasn't crazy. By the time Officer Patterson had returned, Diego had mounted Barfly and rode her out confidently to where the officer parked on the property.

Diego snickered as he galloped towards Patterson. "You know if I'd known Greene could have just fixed Barfly's issues right off the bat, she wouldn't have had to break in. I would have just let her have at it."

Patterson approached Diego with a look of confusion. "What are you talking about, Di?"

"She fucking fixed her up last night! Performed surgery in the dead of night. Restored her eyes and even her ears!" shouted

Diego with glee. "Why don't you go bring that check back to Greene and tell her, if anything, I owe her."

"There is no check," griped Patterson. "She's pleading innocent."

"Now what are *you* talking about?"

"Greene's got a solid alibi and we got no evidence it was her," explained the officer.

"...really?" said Di with surprise. "How solid an alibi?"

"Air tight, amigo."

"Really? Well then can you tell me what this means, then?" Diego led Barfly through a series of simple tests to demonstrate to the officer her miraculous recovery. Barfly followed commands whispered in her "bad" ear. And winced in panic when Di swung over her "bad" eye.

Before he was police, Officer Patterson was a farmer all throughout his childhood up until the age of twenty-two. His parents had owned a cabbage patch right next door to where Diego's family grew their carrots. It's how the two became such old friends. In all his years handling livestock, Patterson had never seen a lame animal suddenly spring back to its full potential. But that's not to say he'd never seen anything miraculous. His mother's shocking recovery from a year-long coma. His brother's safe return home after falling through the ice. And the sudden deaths of those ransackers just before they broke down the door. These events were always attributed to the Patterson family guardian angel. Officer Patterson wondered if such a force had now found Diego.

Officer Patterson put his hand in front of Barfly's eyes and tested her vision himself, watching her shutters carefully as his palm passed over her sight. She really did seem to be reacting accordingly, but Patterson did notice something else strange.

When Barfly reacted, she shook her neck, head, and tail, but kept her abdomen perfectly still. It reminded him of an old wives tale and sent him ducking down on one knee. Patterson observed the bottom side of Barfly and noticed that her udders were clearly dipping.

"You know, Di. It might just be my imagination, and it's been awhile since I've handled any horses but... I think Barfly could be pregnant."

"Well of course she's not, she's..." Diego leaned back in his saddle and gazed beneath Barfly's midsection. "Eh... no... that's not possible." Di was having a hard time believing it at first, so Officer Patterson volunteered to go fetch Dr. Greene after all. She reluctantly accepted the house call, despite having been accused by Diego of breaking and entering one day earlier.

Once they returned to Diego's ranch, Dr. Greene brought out a portable ultrasound and applied some jelly to Barfly's stomach while Diego kept her calm with some snacks. Dr. Greene showed on her monitor a big black and white mass growing in Barfly's uterus. She was, in fact, carrying a foal.

"You sure you didn't have a hand in this?" accused Diego. "I know you got a whole freezer full of animal cum."

Dr. Greene sneered in disgust, "That's for fertility testing and none of it is equestrian, Mr. Garcia." She began wiping the gel off of Barfly with a nearby rag. She then shut the monitor of the ultrasound and wrapped up the cables. "Officer can I please go home, now?

"Hold on a minute," replied Patterson. "Now, we still have a lot to figure out. Could a pregnancy alone have restored this horse's eyes and ears?"

"Of course not!" snarled Greene. "That makes no sense. Nothing could have brought back her senses short of ten-million dollars and cutting-edge animal prosthetics."

"Then explain this fucking miracle!" shouted Di, snapping his fingers in her once-deaf ears. It signaled the horse to rear.

"My professional opinion: She never was deaf. Or blind," grimaced Greene. "She just ignored this ignoramus till he pointed a gun at her face..."

"You bitch!" snarled Di. "Get the fuck off my property."

"Look I don't need a thank you, but not I'm leaving till I get paid," snarked Greene. "My time out of office is not cheap."

"I'll be taking care of that!" interjected the officer, attempting to cool the situation. "I'll write you a check when we're back in town. For now, let's just get you home." Dr. Greene nodded to the officer and hurried away to the back of his car. Before following after her, Officer Patterson turned to Diego.

"Stay off her back till she delivers," instructed the officer. "She's gonna' need plenty to eat the whole time so please call me if you don't have enough. Don't be stingy with her, I can cover anything extra you need."

Diego nodded, "I'll keep her safe."

A horse's gestation is normally about eleven and a half months. That's about a full rotation around the sun. Meaning a whole year's worth of resources normally go into a pregnant horse, but Diego lucked out. She only required a month's worth of attention before the baby had grown to full-size. Diego called up Officer Patterson as soon as the signs of labor were apparent.

"This is a miscarriage," shouted Patterson over the phone. "I've got to bring along Dr. Greene or you're gonna' lose the baby *and* Barfly."

"I don't want to see her, anymore," growled Diego. "Please. Just you."

Although Officer Patterson had delivered quite a few foals in his youth, he had no experiences with miscarriages. These can be messy, deadly, and might even require surgery; but Diego was clear that Dr. Greene was no longer welcome on his property. Patterson had no choice but to try his best to, at the least, keep Barfly from going under.

"Do you have anything roomier than this little stall?" asked Patterson as he raced out of his police car onto the property. "Can we put her in the fields?"

Diego complied. The carrots weren't growing this time of year anyways. He led the whimpering Barfly slowly and softly by her reigns. He comforted her in the center of the field while Officer Patterson tore into some hay bales and laid out a nice soft bedding for her to lay on.

Staring at the now comfortable mother-to-be, Officer Patterson found it strange how mundane the whole thing looked. Her stomach was the right size for a healthy baby to emerge, but it was so far ahead of schedule it seemed impossible. Patterson was picking up on a pattern of strange and unlikely events.

"Go get some soap and water, if this thing comes out okay, we're gonna' need her udders cleaned," called out Patterson as he eyed the horse's cervix from behind. "And get me something to tie her tail!"

As the two worked tirelessly to prepare for the foal, Barfly began to crown. A healthy-looking water bag broke as it emerged. The baby would be next. "Here's the head!" called out Patterson.

Through the transparent sheath around the foal, Patterson could make out a bright white coat on the coming baby. His forelegs came out next just as they should, prompting Patterson to breathe a sigh of relief. It was all downhill from here.

When he was fully emerged, Patterson tickled the nose of the foal to get it to sneeze. This assured it would start its breathing. He then cut the umbilicus and disinfected the cross section. To give mother and son some alone time, he and Diego then went to wash up and rest inside Diego's house.

The two sat down in Diego's living room. A dingy little corner with a cheap television connected to Diego's laptop computer. The two devices screenshared through a thick black cable. Diego put on YouTube and started a playlist of Looney Toons clips. He then got them both a mug full of green tea. After an excruciating spin class on the cycle of life, the two of them took a moment to relax and collect themselves.

"The thick feet, the broad chest, the massive mane," sighed Diego. "It's daddy was a mustang. Must have broke into the stable and mated with my poor Barfly in the night."

Officer Patterson shook his head. "There ain't no wild horses nearby. Our families both been in this neck of the woods for years. If there were wild horses, my daddy would have sent me out to break 'em and sell 'em."

"We're old men, now" chuckled Diego. "Fifty years is more than enough time for a band to migrate into the area. There's plenty of space."

"Old men, huh?" huffed Patterson. "Tell me Di, did you happen to catch sight of that big bump in its forehead?"

Diego nodded. "It's pretty gross. Felt hard when I touched it. Probably just a mutation from mommy's fucked genetics. Thank god it seems to have mainly taken after it's father," Diego shrugged while turning his attention back to the cartoons. "A bone spur ain't nothing to worry about. He'll just be a bit ugly," laughed Diego.

Patterson noticed a splintery box next to his recliner. The circular watermarks on top had him assume it was to be used as an end table. He rested his mug on top of one of the pre-existing marks. "I got a question for you, Di... was Barfly a virgin?"

The odd question prompted Diego to pause the running Pepe short. "Of course," he replied, turning back to his friend. "I mean, who would want to breed with her? You saw what it did to the kid. That's nothing any breeder wants in their product."

"Well then... I hope this doesn't come as a shock to you, but I don't think that foal's a purebred horse," warned Patterson.

"Think he's a mule?"

Patterson nodded. "It's called an Aelian mule."

"Alien? Oh no. But that makes sense!" said Diego, excitedly. "Good god those fuckers abducted my livestock!"

"a-*E*-l-i-a-n. *Aelian*," corrected the officer. "Aelian mules are half horse and half unicorn."

"Unicorn?" said Diego with a look of disappointment. "That's not real is it."

Patterson nodded. "I can attest to its existence better than any little green men."

"You mean you seen one before? Near our fields?"

Patterson explained his family's heritage. They were Gaelic, meaning they hailed from Scotland. His ancestor migrated over from the Shetland Islands. A benevolent spirit followed them over. A protector of sorts.

"A unicorn wanted my mangey mare?"

"They love virgins. And yours was probably the closest one for hundreds of miles," explained Patterson. He urged Diego to drop his drink and follow him back out. Patterson led them across the road to the patch of land that the Patterson's used to cultivate. Though they'd lost it to the state decades ago, their old home was never demolished. Being in the remote wilderness of Alaska, clearing the land was a low priority.

Patterson laughed as his old key still worked on the front door. He'd had the same key chain since he was a boy and he'd never thrown that house key away, holding onto it for sentimental reasons. As the two stepped inside, a cloud of silverfish quickly dissipated from the floorboards of the mud room. Patterson led Diego upstairs into his parent's old bedroom; here there were still many unclaimed items and heirlooms left behind. Patterson pried open the drawer beside the bed and pulled out the picture he was looking for. Considering his parents passed away long ago, Patterson decided to keep this photo to replace the copy he'd misplaced long ago.

"It's protected my family for generations," explained Patterson handing the old photograph to Diego. "Its acts are mainly unseen, but I saw it in the flesh twice before. The first time, at my elder sister's wedding."

"I don't..." Diego couldn't see a unicorn in the photo handed to him. Just the bride and groom surrounded by a mix of their respective families. Diego did however see a strange smudge at the bottom of the photo. As if something laying down in front of the bride and groom's feet was blurred out intentionally.

"It's an advanced defense against trappers," said Patterson. "Its will is incredibly strong. It refuses to appear on camera."

"It just... refuses?" asked Diego, touching the blur on the image. The spot felt warm, as though the film had been laying in the sun.

Patterson nodded. "They're powers revolve around the concept of absolute freedom. Scotland adopted them as a symbol of our fight for sovereignty in the face of England. We, like the beast, would rather fight to the death than lose our independence."

Diego handed the photograph back to Patterson. "I hope this isn't a problem for the little half-breed. Hopefully he didn't inherit all his father's powers."

"He may have..." said Patterson with a look of confusion. "What does it matter?"

"Advertising. Billboards and brochures aren't gonna' help if the star of the show is missing," griped Diego. "They'll think I'm a hoax."

"This isn't some sideshow... it's a holy animal," sneered Patterson.

"It's a tenant and it needs to pay rent," shrugged Diego. "It's not a big deal, Glenn. Every church has its collection box. All donations will be strictly voluntary and will simply go to keeping him fed and housed, happy and healthy."

At first, Patterson felt inclined to trust his old friend. But a week later, a request came through Facebook that cast doubt on Diego's integrity.

Patterson, of an older generation, was hesitant to create his online account, but he liked to use it to keep up with his nephews and nieces. He never had any kids himself. He didn't want the responsibility. Having grown up doing most of the farm work and parenting for his decrepit parents, he felt he already wasted enough of his life raising a family. His brothers and sisters, and now all their kids, are eternally grateful for his work.

They don't blame him for letting the farm go when he had the chance.

Outside of the family members, the only other people Patterson was friends with online were Diego and the sweet young lady who packed bags at the grocery store downtown. When Patterson saw the coupons suddenly appearing on his feed, he at first assumed it was from this store clerk, but upon closer inspection these were in fact invitations from Diego. $5 off your first tour and live feeding of Pinhead, the Amazing Half-Unicorn. The unicorn image on the coupon was most certainly not the real "Pinhead". It was grainy and its edges poorly cropped, clearly lifted off the front cover of a fantasy novel Diego found online. "Pinhead" must have inherited its father's camouflage after all.

Patterson arrived at Diego's farm just to see if this poor advertising was actually drawing anybody in. Despite its crude patchwork, a fair amount of people had shown. People get bored rather fast in rural Alaska and even a mundane hoax can be a rather entertaining show when compared to staring at piles of dirt and snow.

Many had come ironically, hoping to a get a chuckle out of the poorly plastered horn glued to the front of a white foal. But gazing at what was clearly a real specimen, these same folks now stared in awe. While many took turns staring through the window of the stable from the outside, Patterson could see a crowd of people being led inside by Diego for a private tour.

Patterson followed them in.

"Woah there! Excuse me sir, you in the back, I saw you! Pay up or head outside with the rest of the freebies."

Patterson glared at his friend angrily and squeezed through the crowd up to the front.

"Oh, Glenn," chuckled Diego. "Sorry I couldn't tell that was..."

"What the fuck is this?" griped Patterson holding the printed-out coupon up to Diego's face.

Diego panicked and asked the crowd to entertain themselves while he handled some business.

"Private tours?! Pinhead?!" shouted Patterson. "I thought you weren't gonna' turn that sacred foal into a fucking business!"

"You can look for free through the window. You only have to pay if you want to enter the stable."

Patterson rubbed at his face in frustration. "That's not donations, that's a business model!"

"I had to adjust things. Pinny's rent went up... he needs to pay for repairs."

Patterson turned his attention to the crowd. They'd begun swooning at the foal. Patterson walked up beside the stall and observed what was so cute for himself.

Pinhead kept trying to get to the stall door but was constantly blocked off by his mother. Every time he began walking toward the exit, his mother would nudge him with her head, instructing him to lay beside her and rest. Frustrated by Barfly's insistence, Pinhead would soothe his vigor by bashing his developing horn into the back wall of the stall. This wall was beginning to look like honeycomb with the number of holes bored into it.

"I think he's teething," said Diego coming up beside Patterson. Patterson could see that with each stab at the wall, the tiny stub of a horn lost some of the loose flakey skin around its base.

"Diego, don't you think this is a sign that maybe Pinhead's ultimately going to cost you more than he's worth?"

"Well... what do you expect me to do?" shrugged Diego. "He'll stop when the horns done growing."

"Maybe it's about time you let him go," suggested Patterson.

Diego shook his head. "I won't be able to find a buyer for a couple of months. I'll need real numbers first showing how much income this guy can bring in. I don't think there's a lot of traveling circuses still in business anymore. But maybe Cirque du Soleil? If I can get him to dance..."

"Fucking no, Di. Let him go as in just let him go. Into the wild. His pa's out there waiting for him."

"Without a paycheck?"

Patterson nodded.

"Glenn that's not fair. You said these beasts were protectors."

"What's your point?"

"So... it's protecting me. It gave me its young so I could save my farm from bankruptcy!" theorized Diego.

"Or... it was just acting like any other animal and participated in the mating season with the only suitable host!"

Diego begged Patterson to keep an open mind. "It's protects your family," said Diego, putting a hand on his friend's shoulder. "We've known each other for so long... aren't we like family?"

Patterson would nod after being put in such an awkward situation, but deep down that was not the case. Patterson raised his younger sister and three younger brothers practically by himself. He got frost bite and lost three of his toe nails while trying to milk their family farm for all it was worth. He only let the property go when he was sure the last of his siblings could start supporting themselves. That's a unique bond, somewhere between parenthood and brotherhood. It was not like the closeness he shared with Diego. Diego was not a kid that needed support, he was an old man that should be capable of survival without such silly tactics as exploiting a baby unicorn.

Despite Patterson's apprehension, he had enough responsibilities as an officer of the law. Too many responsibilities to be worrying about Diego's business integrity, even though it was most likely breaking a few laws.

Patterson would only return to Diego's cabinet of curiosities upon receiving another invitation online. This time it was not a coupon on his feed, but a private chat window. Diego had sent him a message begging him to come back. He needed advice on how to properly dispose of a body.

Patterson was terrified and hurried over as soon as his shift ended. "God dammit, Di!" he shouted in his car. "You really fucked up now!" Patterson pounded on his steering wheel. He was positive the damn foal must have gored one of the tour members. He might have to arrest his oldest friend for negligence.

Patterson stormed out of his vehicle and skipped the part where he knocks on Diego's front door. He knew where'd he be. Out in the backyard, in the stable. Patterson bursted through the stable doors with ease. They were never fixed from the unicorn's original breaking and entering. Patterson was shocked to see instead of a human lying in a puddle of blood and hay, it was instead poor Barfly that was slowly bleeding out onto the ground.

"No! Oh my god," whimpered Patterson.

"Yeah," said Diego, quietly. "I think we're gonna' lose her."

"What in the fuck happened!" shouted Patterson kneeling down beside Barfly's chest. There were a hundred tiny perforations all over her left side and underbelly. Tiny little stab wounds that clearly came from a tiny little horn. "Where the fuck is Pinhead?!" shouted Patterson.

"Little shit shanked his momma and escaped from his pen. Luckily, I caught him in the act and got him," nodded Di.

"You... got him?" questioned Patterson. "What does that mean?"

"Well I... you know," Di made a gesture with his pointer finger. "...I shot him."

"You shot a half-unicorn!" shouted Patterson. "One of the rarest species on this Earth?"

"He's a damn murderer, Glenn. He's lucky I only grazed his foot. He's just fine. He's healing up on a pile of towels in my living room."

"Ah god!" exclaimed Patterson. "You couldn't just lasso him?"

"I never learned how to do that," shrugged Diego. "My parents never taught me shit on how to run a ranch. Thank god picking out carrots is pretty self-explanatory."

"Okay, buddy. We need to have a serious conversation," scolded Patterson. "As soon as that boy's foot is healed, and I mean immediately afterward, you're letting him go!"

"But now that his mom's put down, he just cut costs in half. I can make more money than ever!"

"Di, he murdered his mom cause she wouldn't let him escape... if you do the same, he'll kill you too!" warned Patterson. "It's for your own safety; let him go!"

"You bring up a really good point," said Diego with a slow nod. "I got to protect myself. And the customers too, of course." Diego stood up from Barfly's side and held out his shotgun to Patterson. "I won't be needing this anymore. Do you think your department could trade with me? You guys get the shotgun, and y'all lend me some shackles?"

Patterson stomped his foot on the soft floor of the stables, but before he could yell his grievances, he was interrupted by a loud call coming from Diego's living room. It was a complex noise, beginning as a horse's whinny then ending as a metallic tinkle. Like someone strumming a tiny windchime.

"It's just the little one. He's been making that noise since he got hit."

"Oh my god. That's a cry for help," exclaimed Patterson.

"Then I should go check on him. After all, his mother's nearly dead. I'm all he's got left."

Patterson shook his head. "Not necessarily." Patterson ran out of the barn and got to his car as fast as possible. This time he'd brought his civilian vehicle, an old red sedan, that way he could carry a weapon in the trunk that wasn't authorized by his department. "I brought this along, in case you were in danger... it was my father's. When he died, it was left to me."

Patterson pulled out a sheathed weapon in his one hand. He pulled off the cover to reveal the shimmering blade, a steel dirk, a dagger about the length of a forearm.

"A unicorn can only be killed by the first swing of a steel blade," explained Patterson. "It seems these conditions weren't passed on to the half-breed. But don't go trying to use that gun of yours on the daddy, it'll just pass through him."

"You think Pinhead's calling his dad?"

Patterson nodded. "It seeks freedom at any cost. Its father will see to it that his son is untethered. That includes killing it's captor." Patterson began to jog towards Diego's front door. "The only way he may forgive you, is if you let his son go now. His father will probably be able to heal his injuries better than we can, anyways."

Under the deafening cries of the Aelian mule, a different kind of metallic glint caught Patterson's ear. This was not part of the hybrid call, but the cocking off a shotgun. Patterson turned around to face Diego, who had the barrel directed right at him. "No trespassing."

"Hey... now," said Patterson turning away from Diego's house with his hands raised. "We're... family, right? Family doesn't normally shoot each other."

"They also don't bankrupt each other," sighed Diego, putting his eye against the sight atop the gun. "Keep right where you are, facing away from the house."

Patterson did as he was instructed, while Diego walked around him to his front door. "I've got this gun pointed at the back of your head," explained Diego. "At some point, I'm going to creep inside and do what I need to do, but it's gonna' be quiet. So you're not gonna' know I've left. If you so much as turn your head to see if I'm still there, I'll blast you wide open. So stay still."

Patterson followed directions, giving Diego an opportunity to head inside and fetch the injured foal. Pinhead was growing fast, but he was still small enough for Diego to hold in his arms. He brought the crying foal outside and dropped him in front of Patterson.

Diego kept his gun pointed at Patterson's face. He reached down to the dirk Patterson had dropped when he raised his hands. While holding his gun in one hand, he examined the sword with the other. "Why did your parents have this if the unicorn was your 'protector'?"

"When mom and dad got sick, they knew they were officially a burden on the family. Extra mouths to feed with no added workhands. My parents feared our protector would protect the children before all else and get rid of the dead weight," explained Patterson as he stared into the white snow reflected off the face of the blade.

Diego bent down over the foal and held the dirk to its throat. "Daddy doesn't know what attributes you inherited. He'll think a tiny nick with this will put you down permanently."

"A hostage?" sneered Patterson.

"Yes. It's time for daddy to realize that his son's been properly adopted. He'll realize that if I ever see him on my property again, I won't hesitate to kill his son. Then he'll never get his freedom."

"That's not how it works," interjected Patterson. "It's freedom or death. It would rather die and have its son die then let either of them be slaves!"

"Be quiet. I hear something new," hushed Diego.

Patterson heard it too. It was the first time he'd heard it in forty years. The gallop of a unicorn always sounds like hooves on crisp cobblestone, even when its treading on soft snow and dirt. Each clop was a perfect pop as the unicorn drew closer and closer, appearing from behind Patterson's old house. It galloped so smoothly as if gliding on air.

When it got close enough it let out its own cry in response to its son. This cry was purely unicorn with no whinny at the front. It sounded like a forest of dream catchers with bells and emblems hanging from their bottoms, clanking and glinting as they lightly tapped one another in the breeze.

Upon seeing the blade held to its child's throat, a look of rage immediately glistened in its eyes. It lowered its head down to direct its fully-grown horn at Diego. The horn was bright yellow cartilage and it extended in a spiral pattern. Its point was well sharpened and extruded three full feet, a whole yard from the forehead. The unicorn began to charge.

"Shit!" shouted Patterson. "Stop being an idiot and run!"

Diego didn't budge, he held his ground and waited for the charge to get closer. He then raised the blade from the foal's neck and directed at the father. At the last moment, the father changed direction slightly and dodged Diego's swing. The first and only swing the dagger had ever had. The only swing that could kill a unicorn. "Drat!" shouted Diego. "Do you have another one of these?" he asked Patterson.

"Go fuck yourself!" replied the officer.

Diego raised his gun to Patterson and pulled back the hammer. "Then you've really run out of use." Diego fired a slug right into Patterson chest, shooting right through him and sending him onto his back.

Distracted by Patterson, Diego didn't notice that the unicorn's charge towards him wasn't as fruitless as it seemed. It wasn't an assault at all. It just needed to be in range to cast a healing spell on his offspring

Pinhead, its wounds vanished, jumped up from its slump and slammed its little horn into the back of Diego's leg again and again, shredding his calf and the tendons inside. Diego dropped down to his knee and shrieked in pain.

The father unicorn quickly made his return and bowed his head yet again. He charged at the fallen Diego and this time did not miss. The horn pierced right through Diego's esophagus.

Patterson was bleeding out on the snow from the shot to his chest. He was losing consciousness as he stared up at the tangerine sky. He did not see Diego's demise, but he heard the gory shank and the wet splash of blood that fell from the mortal wound.

Patterson waited patiently for the father unicorn to finish him off next. He knew it was coming. He was just happy this beautiful sky would be the last thing he'd ever see.

Instead of the father, Patterson felt a smaller horn stab at his heel. It was an attack by the mule. He felt the little horn puncturing through the soles of his feet. It seemed he'd suffer a slower, more painful death than he'd assumed. But after the sixth or seventh stab, the assault abruptly ended.

Unseen by Patterson, the father unicorn had persuaded Pinhead to stop and directed him to run off into the forest. Patterson could hear the cobblestone clacks as Pinhead ran off. They were slightly more spaced out than his father's, as only his front hooves produced the noise while his back feet simply crunched in the snow like his mother's would.

Before following after, the father unicorn knelt down beside Patterson and touched him softly with its horn. Like a magic wand, it filled Patterson's vision with a bright light. It lasted for a minute while his body was filled with a warm, intoxicating sensation. Patterson knew he had been magically displaced from Diego's yard and was now lying uninjured in his childhood home across the way.

He was laid down on the floor where his old bed used to be. But his bedroom had been emptied, the furniture sold off for a little profit long ago. Diego sat up and ran outside to catch the last sight he'll ever see of the unicorn or its son ever again.

Patterson limped after them. He saw the two of them galloping quickly into the distance while a faint resemblance to the

Northern Lights suddenly appeared over their heads. It twisted downwards like a winding rainbow and curled under the feet of the father and son, lifting them off of the ground onto a luminescent pathway leading high up into the stars.

"Woah," huffed Patterson as he recalled an old Lisa Frank notebook his sister had in her childhood. As the animals disappeared from sight, Officer Patterson wondered if Lisa Frank would have stuck with her original designs if she knew what a fucking mess these beasts really were.

Pizza Crow VI

My business model clearly needs work. "F1" didn't sell like I thought it would. I'm guessing it's because, while it shares some elements of fantasy, it stays mainly in the realm of surrealism. In fact, all the stories I've gotten so far reek of surrealism. I can't seem to shake it. The problem is I already mapped out all the parts of the pizza to the parts of the story. There's nothing left that could be tied to the degree of avant-garde. At least, nothing on the fundamental level.

I considered the parts of a pizza that aren't exactly tangible. What else goes into a pie besides the ingredients? That's when I thought about the heat. The amount of warmth inside a slice. I decided it might be worth experimenting with the temperature at which I serve my crow his meal. So I picked up a frozen pizza at the store and gave him a piece before it could thaw. I then cooked up the rest and gave him a hot piece of the same pizza the next day.

The stories I received in either condition were certainly different, but the temperature did nothing to adjust the strangeness. As you will see, both just keep getting weirder.

Nine-Tenths an Ape

Oliver Quitt is by far the most eccentric man I will ever meet. It's always such a shame that eccentricity is often the silver lining to mental illness and Oliver died just under a month ago. As I sat through his funeral, I reflected on his most respectable qualities. He was a shy genius, a Doctor of Anthropology who was a wonderful mentor to myself and the rest of our lab at University of Georgia. But it's tough to talk about him as a teacher, considering he was an even better friend.

During my time studying primatology as his graduate student, I learned Oliver had mastered a dark sense of humor, usually directed toward his own shortcomings. Oliver used to joke it was "an act of charity" whenever a woman would sleep with him, which might I add, happened remarkably often. He was an uncanny ladies' man, born with a physical deformity where his nose bent up towards the ceiling, exposing his nostrils entirely outward. But despite this disfigured face, women seemed to have an instant attraction to him. I wouldn't say it was charity; I'd say his personality just has this wonderful magnetic pull.

The funeral was a small affair, it was just myself, his immediate family, and another graduate student, Luie, who admired his work. After the ceremony, we were all ushered into a back room where a last will and testimony would surely bring-out Oliver's niche humor one last time.

To his mother, Oliver left his hunting rifle and an address he swore contained the residence of his deadbeat father. The acting attorney did not like this joke. And to his little brother, Oliver left a post-it note with a woman's phone number and the message "paid-in-advanced" beneath it. Once again, the attorney did not like this joke. To his older sister went his savings, an unexpectedly tender gesture meant to bandage some unknown feud between the two. And to Luie went an ensemble hat, shirt, pants, and boots, identical to the gear Oliver would wear on his research expeditions. The only difference is that the outfit was sized to fit Luie's far smaller proportions.

"Why did I get these?" she asked the attorney.

The attorney shrugged and gave her a look. "I think we can safely assume it's for something illegal."

That was not the case, but to explain the joke to Luie would take away any chance she actually wears the outfit, which I've got to see. It's how Oliver would have wanted it. Oliver realized Luie was both a good person and an excellent student. But he also recognized the difference between a fan and a friend. And Luie idolized Oliver like a boy-band. Not in the way that women seemed to flock to him, but in the way that Luie wanted to be Oliver. She joined his lab in hopes of one day emulating all his best accomplishments in anthropology.

And so, the suit he rewarded her was his way of letting her fulfill her fantasy. To become Oliver. I wondered if Oliver had an equally snide gift for myself.

With no one else left in the room, I eagerly awaited the attorney to fetch my own prize. Whatever it was, it was certainly larger than a survival jacket. It required the attorney wheel it in from another room. When he finally got it in front of us, myself and all the guests stared in bewilderment. Especially Oliver's family, who'd never seen the item before. Although myself and Luie were well aware of what it was, neither of us were expecting to see it pawned off into my possession.

"To Mr. Jonathan Vonmar" [that's me] "I leave my most renowned discovery for your own personal use... please provide him with Lefty."

Lefty is the basis for which all other evidence of Oliver's strange genius is founded. Oliver had discovered Lefty via his research in

Tanzania, documenting a particular troupe of chimpanzees for the last two decades. The troupe kept settled within the limits of a valley that offered them a never-ending supply of fig fruit. However, after a tropical storm had left the area flooded and uninhabitable, the apes suddenly uprooted from their familiar territory. Oliver tracked his apes twenty miles south to their new home, a rocky quarry with an oddly lush environment in its pit. It held an unusually diverse population of vegetation. Much more than the apes were used to. There were bananas, oranges, mangoes, and even melons vining out from the forest floor. If it could grow in the jungle, it was there. Ironically, the only fruit that seemed to be missing were the figs the apes had relied on for generations. The apes had to adapt to a new diet of, well, everything else.

In the center of this pit is where Oliver first saw Lefty. At first glance, Oliver wasn't sure what he was looking at. By the way the other apes left fruit at its feet, it seemed to be a newly established dominant male. But it appeared to be sick, skinny and starving, with large patches missing from its fur. Its face was grey and expressionless and its left arm was frozen in place over its head. The creature almost seemed to be stuck waving to some acquaintance in the distance.

Upon further inspection, this "leader" was long deceased. It's cause of death was unclear, but it may have been whatever people were responsible for its subsequent mummification. The creature had been dried and preserved in a method that set it in a cross-legged sit, with its left-hand waving, and its right arm laying in its lap. Strangely, this right arm was missing its hand.

Considering its apparent worship, Oliver was hesitant to steal away his troupe's idol, but returning the artifact to his lab was so tempting. Lefty was a mystery with value in every facet of anthropology. What culture made him, what for, and how so? Why were the apes so enticed by the idea of this figurine and why did they give it special treatment? Only Oliver's lab could help answer these questions, so while his troupe was distracted defending themselves from an intruding jaguar, Oliver made off with Lefty into the jungle.

"Oh, please don't tell me this is some sick joke?" barked Luie with a look of disgust. Knowing Oliver, it very well could have been. But this wasn't the first question to come to my mind.

"I'm sorry, but is this really Oliver's to give? I thought this belonged to our university?" I asked staring at Lefty's glossy black eyes, beautiful stones replacing the original organs.

The attorney shook his head. "It was rightfully his. And now, it's rightfully yours. The agreement between he and the university was that they were renting it for display in their museum. It was agreed that the lease would terminate immediately upon Oliver's death."

I glared at the ape in disbelief. The only thing that kept his ape from looking ghastly was his peaceful expression. The way he was positioned in front of me, it was as though he were happily waving hello.

Amusing only myself, I waved back.

Luie glared at me in offense, as though I were mocking some dead relative.

"Let me have fun, now," I warned her. "Or I'll dress it up in a suit and tie, and then you'll really be annoyed."

Luie rolled her eyes. "Can you please just donate it to the university, where it belongs?"

I shook my head. "Oliver was close to me and this is what I have to commemorate him. I'll let it go when I'm comfortable with the idea... but as for now, he wouldn't lend me this without reason. I've got to find out what this might be."

While Lefty is by far Oliver's most lucrative work, it was not a topic of conversation he'd entertain past his first meeting with you. It's a piece of pop-science that no longer interests him; Oliver's research on the subject concluded quite satisfactory leaving very little to entice speculation.

Lefty went through a process of preservation called saulmoning where the body is brined at the bottom of a salt-bog then wrapped in the leaves of a turnip-like plant called bibesh. The brining process dries the specimen while the wrap does an excellent job minimizing any warping of the animal's features.

The chimpanzee had cultural significance as a good-luck totem to several tribes with territories near Lefty's quarry. Oliver is quite certain it was the Almaj due to the stones used in Lefty's eyes. They're the same kind used in Almaj jewelry and decoration. The Almaj have long disappeared from Africa and integrated into the larger nations that now dominate the area. Estimating his creation sometime right before this assimilation, Lefty is at least two-hundred years old.

For Oliver, there was only one great mystery truly left unsolved, but it never seemed to interest him. Lefty's missing hand. Stitches on the animal's right wrist showed no signs of being brined with the rest of the body, suggesting the hand was removed only after the animal was preserved.

"He'd never talk about it," I said to Luie, pointing to Lefty's empty wrist. "Maybe he's it left for me to solve?"

Luie helped me move Lefty into our lab space, a bench outside of the "clean area" where casual experimentation could be performed.

"It is strange he's never pursued a clear answer. Maybe it stumped him to the point where it became an insecurity," said Luie. "Maybe it drove him to kill himself."

I shook my head. "No. He'd talk very clearly about the things that made him want to kill himself... the things he'd keep quiet about were the things that bored him. Maybe he's known the answer all along?"

Luie grimaced. "I would know if he did."

"*Cause you've read every last page of his every last paper?*" I sneered, rolling my eyes.

"But I have!"

"Then maybe it's not published work..."

Luie thought about that for a second, then motioned for me to follow her. She took me into Oliver's old office using a key we'd been given at the funeral. With Oliver's death, he'd left his records open-access to his surviving lab so that they may continue their work unhindered by his passing.

Luie took the keys to his office and his drawers. I kept the passwords to his computer and his email.

It was an arduous effort sifting through all his personal material. Not only was the volume immense, but the notes themselves were not filtered for professionalism, often transitioning into long accounts of personal trauma. A literature review of Eastern medicine was slowly replaced by Oliver's own anxieties on his declining health. A sketch of a ritual dagger they'd planned to carbon date was drawn peeling off the warped nose on Oliver's caricature. And a hypothesis on aboriginal grave decoration surprisingly shifted into a rough draft of the will and testimony we'd heard just yesterday.

"He mentions Lefty, right here," I said, proceeding to say the notes aloud, "*I feel it's powers have been squandered on me because of an egotistical request. But in the hands of someone*

*less morose, and more benevolent, it may prove valuable. I
believe Jon would be the proper choice."*

I stopped my reading and flipped the page. There was nothing
written on the back. I turned my head upwards to see Luie,
staring intensely at the page of a library book she'd found in
Oliver's belongings.

"He said it has... powers?" I said getting Luie's attention.

She nodded slowly, giving a cue to come over to her desk. She
directed my vision to the book she'd been examining. It was a
collection of short stories that looked to be perfectly intact albeit
a chunk taken out of one of the corners on a single page.

"It's a marker," she said, "for the Monkey's Paw..."

When I first heard the story of the Monkey's Paw, I was just a
child and so the unintended consequences of the wishes were
completely lost on me. All I really gathered was ancient items
didn't have to be magic lamps in order for them to grant you
wishes. This made shopping for antiques notably more enjoyable
when there was a possibility our purchase may hold the secret to
bending reality to my will. Life was more exciting after The
Monkey's Paw. Old objects, even people, suddenly became
conduits for magic. It's no wonder how I got into anthropology.

Of course, as I got older and gained access to real legendary
artifacts, used in real rituals, by real witch doctors... even those
turned out powerless. I had to accept the concept that
everything would one day grow old, and the chance of all that
everything becoming magic was extremely slim.

I was, therefore, utterly pessimistic. "So... he thinks the monkey's
paw came from Lefty?"

Luie never struck me as the superstitious type, but for some
reason, she seemed completely convinced. "If Oliver says it's true,

then it's true," she explained, comparing the sketching of the monkey's paw with the space on Lefty's wrist. "He's never been held back by the curses on all the tombs we've ever entered... he's very skeptical. He wouldn't believe it without evidence."

"It could just be a joke."

"But what's funny about it?"

"Maybe it's gone over our heads?"

"Nothing goes over my head."

"Well then why don't you go put on that suit Oliver gave you?" I suggested. "Maybe there's a clue inside it!"

"We don't need any more clues," said Luie stomping out of Oliver's office. She hurried over to the desk where Lefty had been waiting patiently for our return. "Look, Jon, we're like everyone else in this world. We're going to use the magic thing we've come across by fate. It's what humans do. Experimentation. It's just a matter of in what order..."

"Well, considering your excitement, you can be the first..."

"But it's *your* monkey!" said Luie. "Besides I'm apprehensive given the source material... I first want to see what level of ironic twist these wishes cost."

"Oliver seems to have suggested that a benevolent wish should have unforeseen consequences... so I guess I've got one."

I leaned in closer to Lefty.

"What are you doing?" griped Luie.

"I've got to touch it I think. That's probably why Oliver was fine with Lefty being displayed behind glass." I reached for Lefty's raised hand and wrapped my fingers between his. "That should do it."

I took a deep breath and made sure to word my wish properly. "I wish Dr. Oliver Quitt was back from the dead!"

"Wait no!" shouted Luie, but it was too late.

The lights went out. The sky outside darkened. Lefty's jaw dropped and a pillar of bright red light emitted from his throat. It glowed brightly on the neighboring wall where it cast a spinning triangle. A noise with no origin point enveloped the room and filled our ears with trees cracking and falling to the earth. It sounded like a giant trampling through a rainforest.

Immediately after making my wish, there was a strong pull keeping my hand touched to Lefty's. It lasted a minute before I could pull my arm back. Along with it, the light returned, Lefty's mouth had closed, and the noises had all vanished.

"Did you not read the fucking story?" shouted Luie in a rage. "It's about how you're not supposed to wish people back from the dead!"

"Of course, I remember!" I actually had not. I said it before, I was really young when I'd heard the tale and thought it was lot more like Aladdin. "But I don't see how anything could be more selfless than bringing back Oliver?"

"But have you read Pet Sematary?" asked Luie.

I nodded, lying to her once again. I'm really not well-read.

"He could come back like they always come back and be a vicious, mindless zombie."

Right on cue, a constant knocking began to rap on the lab's main entrance, a metal door that can only be unlocked with a keycard.

"Don't open that..." warned Luie. "He'll kill us both."

"Luie, grand scheme of things, we need to make sure any of our wishes go unnoticed."

"I don't follow?"

"If there really is magic in this thing, we should really keep that to ourselves, just like Oliver did. As anthropologists, we have a profound understanding of folklore and how when any human character gets their hands on a tool of great power there are world-changing consequences. So, unless you trust a university filled with egotistical mad-scientist types and the amoral businessmen running the school to not open Pandora's Box, we should really try to contain the consequences of our wishes..."

"So... you want to let the zombie in?" asked Luie.

I nodded.

"Then I'm gonna' go lock myself in Oliver's office," said Luie holding up Oliver's keys. "Try not to get eaten."

I nodded.

Walking up carefully to the lab's entrance, I noticed that the knocking didn't seem awfully nefarious. It wasn't loud or erratic. It was soft and timid, as though a shy undergrad was embarrassed that he'd lost his keycard bumping lines at a frat house last night.

I took my chance and pulled down on the lever on the right side of the door. The door creaked open, allowing the knocker to shove their foot through the crack I made. I quickly jolted backwards just in case and prepared a fist. If it were an undead Oliver, I'd bop him in his weirdy nose. That should incapacitate him. Like a shark.

"Oh no!" shouted the first person to enter. It was a plump man with a bushy white beard. "He's a hyper-evolved hostile. He sees us as primitive models that must be destroyed."

"uh... no", I said, lowering my arm. "I was just worried you all might be zombies."

"Is this a common pest in the future?" asked the plump man.

Two women shoved the plump man along into the main hallway of our lab. The first of the ladies to burst through was a black woman with a tilted hat.

"He's referring to the means in which he resurrected us," said this woman. "He's wondering why our souls did not return in our original vessels. Rotting corpses in the ground with deteriorated brains that would cause us to lash out like animals... the answer is magic, dear. It seems to have built us new bodies... or repaired what we had... hard to say unless you want to go dig us up. Either way, it seems magic didn't plan on eating you today. It must have something worst planned."

"Oh, that's disappointing," said the last lady to file in; she looked older and frailer than the last. With short white hair and plain white clothes. "I thought, with enough time, men would get a lot prettier. Seems you developed very little since our last encounter."

"Okay then," I replied, bitter. I personally think I'm very handsome, but uh, apparently, I'm alone in that notion.

Apart, these three seemed at first to be a group of casually-awkward traveling professors but seeing these three altogether in front of me brought back images of the front cover of a rudimentary textbook. "Oh my god. You're Franz Boas!" I shouted pointing at the plump man. "And you're Zora Neale Hurston!" I said pointing at the woman with the tilted hat. "And you're... I'm sorry I don't recognize you?"

"I'm fucking Ruth Benedict!" she hollered. "I'm solely responsible for bringing the idea of cultural relativism to a wide audience!"

"I'm just kidding," I laughed. "Sorry Dr. Benedict... but you called me ugly."

Ruth stopped her ranting and took a moment to calm herself. "I didn't mean for you to take offense, but... it's just sad to see some personal hypotheses about the progression of the sexes didn't pan out. I predicted an almost elven-like beauty amongst men and women as more aggressive traits phase out..." Suddenly, Ruth trailed off as the sight of Luie emerging from Oliver's office caught her eyes.

Luie, having not heard screams of horror, thought it might be safe to emerge. Seeing me huddled amongst a group of historical figures, Luie was relieved she would not be eaten by a zombie. Unless you count Ruth.

Ruth gave Luie a little wink. "A woman of science?"

Luie nodded.

Ruth looked towards me. "I see there's been *some* progress."

"The brightest minds in modern anthropology," smiled Luie. "Right at my fingertips."

"Stop!" snickered Ruth. "You're giving me ideas..."

"But why are they here?" I asked Luie. "That's not what I wished for."

Luie turned to face the resurrected anthropologists. "Would any of you have an idea?"

Franz Boas shook his head. "I certainly don't recall any sort of explanation. I was up in the clouds in the middle of dinner with

Frederic Putnam. Next thing I know, I'm sucked out of Heaven and shoved back on Earth with you people."

Zora stepped forward and lifted the brim of her hat so that we may look eye to eye. "I believe I may be able to assist you." Along with being an amazing civil rights activist, Zora is inseparable from her work documenting the Voodoo faith that originated in Africa. Her understanding of the paranormal trumped the rest of us. "When I collected ritual items from Port-au-Prince I had to create a method to determine their function. You'll want to make another wish, first. That way you have two inputs and their corresponding two outputs. From there you can observe a pattern and form a hypothesis."

"But what should I wish for this time?" I stared over at Luie. "My last wish almost gave you a heart attack."

"Something simple this time, please," begged Luie. "Something that you *could* easily gather even without magic."

I curled my hand back around the ape's fingers. "Alright then... I wish for a dog!"

Another squall suddenly appeared overtop our building. It's thundering lasted only a moment and was quickly replaced by the sound of a soft buzzing. It was the cell phone ringing in my pocket. I answered it and was surprised to hear another attorney calling me about another will.

I pulled the phone down off my face and looked over at Luie. "You're not going to believe this, but I think I just inherited a zoo."

"What, wait, which zoo?" exclaimed Luie.

"Kritter Bay. The one just down the street."

"Your family owns that zoo?"

I shook my head. "No, no. They said I was chosen at random. The former owner didn't have any family of his own, but more likely, and I think we can all agree," I pointed at Lefty and smiled, "I think he's selected me quite deliberately."

"Well then ask if there's any dogs," suggested Luie.

The attorney checked the list of animals I would receive ownership to and saw various canines including wolves, foxes, coyotes, and tanukis, but nothing like a domestic animal.

I hung up the phone and relayed this answer to the others. "He says if people want dogs they don't go to a zoo, they go to the park."

"So, you wish for a dog," said Luie. "And you get every animal *but* a dog."

"And when I wish for Oliver back," I said. "I resurrect every major anthropologist *but* Oliver."

"It seems that, if the monkey's paw gives you what you want," continued Luie, "the rest of the body gives you... everything else."

"That makes sense," I replied. "Oliver must have wished he could find his nose more bearable... Lefty made sure everyone else found it attractive, *except* for him."

"That's just terrible," frowned Luie. "That sort of cognitive dissonance between what you and everyone else sees... that would be maddening."

"Now *that* could have driven him to suicide," I sighed. "If it all causes is more suffering, this stupid ape is no better than its paw then?" I gave Lefty a pissy little shove. It knocked the animal onto its back.

"Well that's just how all magic is," said Zora stepping forward. "That's its modem operandi. Magic is a purely sociopathic energy. It only gives you a gift, if it's planning on killing you."

"So, it gave Oliver ladies... cause it knew it would drive him to suicide?"

Zora nodded. "I've studied some of the most benevolent healers and some of the most terrifying witches. No matter how the magic was used it always sent the user to Hell. Even one-time users are destined for eternal damnation. Myself included."

"Zora... we rescued you from Hell?" I asked.

Zora nodded with a grim expression. "Any intimate contact drags you down I'm afraid. And I wanted to experiment with some voodoo doll. Just like we are now with Lefty."

"So, I'm bound too, now?" I asked, sullenly.

Zora affirmed it. "As soon as you summoned us, there was no going back."

"So then is Oliver *down there* too?" asked Luie.

"Unlike my colleague here," Zora pointed to Franz, "I don't get to have heavenly dinners with my fellow dead. But in Hell, I've shared plenty of torture devices with some notable academics. Me and your Oliver shared a fine conversation on the development of basic human rights while we were both flogged on neighboring racks."

Luie shook her head. "That isn't fair."

Zora agreed. "If you want a just energy, you'll have to go with karma. And if you want something purely benevolent, go with luck. Cause when it comes to magic, magic is intentionally unfair. It wants to be. It was *born* to be."

"So then, what if I use it to contradict itself." I wrapped my hand back around the palm of Lefty. I hoisted him back up right.

"Easy now!" cautioned Zora. "You may already be hell-bound, but a half-baked wish could have dire consequences for everyone else as well."

"I want to use it to turn everything around," I suggested, "We have a rare opportunity here, Zora. Most people don't know what magic does to them, but I've got you here to spill the beans. We can use Lefty to avoid the fate of all magic users... I just have to word it right."

I held on tight to Lefty's hand and smiled at Zora. I was going to set her free, with the appropriate contrary demand. "I wish you were in Hell!"

I swear my intentions were good. I fully intended for her to go to the opposite of Hell. One would assume Heaven. But I was only half-right.

Lefty's mouth opened again and released his symbol into the encompassing dark. As the thunder of lumber echoed in our ears Luie and myself turned our attention to Zora's transformation. Slowly, a single wing began to climb out from behind the left-side of her back.

"Wow," said Zora with a warm smile. "It's... incredible." She eyed the beautiful angel wing as it fully expanded. Its feathers began to glow bright white. A thin string of tears rolled down Zora's left cheek. "Is it really that simple? Am I free just like that?"

Zora then looked to her other shoulder and waited patiently for her second wing to arrive. But as Lefty closed his mouth and finished the spell, another wing never came. Zora's face dropped from ecstasy to utter confusion. "Well what happens n-"

Suddenly, the left side of Zora's body vanished, wing and all. This disappearance vivisected her down the middle and left her lifeless right half standing bewildered in the middle of our lab. Blood slowly began to ooze from her opening. Her body gave way and collapsed to the floor, spilling out the right half of her brain. It rolled over to our feet.

"Jon..." whimpered Luie. "What did you say?!"

"God dammit!" shouted Franz. "Did you forget everything else besides Hell... *includes Earth*?"

Heaven *and* Earth. Lefty had spread her out evenly across the two. Right down the middle.

Ruth stepped forward and tapped the remains of the body with the tip of her shoe. "Way to go kid, you cut a civil rights hero in two... you couldn't have tried that little trick on yourself first?"

"I thought... I thought maybe..." I kept stuttering. I had thought it would look sweet if I helped her out first, her being a wise grandma type and all. But the plan had backfired horribly. I had no excuses for my mistake. I hadn't thought it through and I messed up bad. "If that didn't work, I'm not sure what wish will."

"Well don't you go trying that shit on either of us," sneered Ruth.

"He might have to though," sighed Franz. "I just realized, our spots in Heaven may not be guaranteed upon our return to the dead..."

"Wait. Why wouldn't they be? Margaret Meade's waiting for my return with a glass of Dubonnet and all six gold medalists from the Olympics of Grace," said Ruth, practically drooling at the thought. "I can't miss that!"

"Well poor Zora made it clear that just a little bit of meddling with the unknown can damn us. And if we were summoned back to Earth by that thing..." Franz pointed to the ape. "I'd call that intimate contact."

"You're saying that by bringing us back... these two damned us?" snarled Ruth. She turned to me. "Move out of the way..." Ruth shoved me to the side and wrapped her hand around Lefty's neck. "If you can't fix this then I will."

"Wait," I begged her. "I know you're scared but-"

"Relax..." called out Ruth tightening her grip. "This wish will help you too. None of us have to burn." Ruth shut her eyes and concentrated on the wording. "I wish Hell was for magic-users!"

Lefty ran through his routine once again. His jaw gaped, his light shined, the storm appeared, and the sounds roared. When it was all over, there was no visible difference to reality. But judging by the look on Luie's face, I knew something had gone wrong.

By contrast, Ruth's face looked quite satisfied with herself. She let go of Lefty's neck and smiled. "We should be safe now."

"Ruth... what have you done?" huffed Luie.

Ruth shrugged. "What's wrong? I just made Hell no longer for magic-users..."

"But now it's for everyone else!" shrieked Luie. "You just damned something like ninety-nine percent of the total population."

"You know that doesn't have to include you, love," suggested Ruth, pointing towards Lefty. "If you make a wish, you can come join me in Heaven too... I'll make it worth it."

"Really?" snickered Luie, bashfully. "Well you know, maybe it wouldn't be too bad..."

"Don't give it to her!" shouted Franz. "It's just a trick." He quickly ran up behind Lefty and shoved his hands under its arms. He lifted Lefty off its counter and backed away with it into the corner of the room. "Ruth, you fucking horndog, she'll just undo *your* wish with *her* wish. She's a goodie two-shoes, we can't let her touch the ape."

Luie took a chance and dove into a sprint towards Lefty, but before she got too far Ruth reached out and snatched Luie's wrist. She pulled Luie backwards and stuck her in a firm vice. "She's clearly not thinking it through," growled Ruth, holding tight onto the wriggling Luie. "If she makes a wish she's a magic-user, and if she wishes all magic-users back to Hell that will include her."

"That's literally the right thing to do!" shouted Luie. "I don't think that highly of myself to damn a whole world over me."

Ruth looked confused. "You are in academia, aren't you?"

"Luie... you don't have to sacrifice yourself," I sighed. "I'm already hell-bound as it is... let *me* make the wish."

"Don't fucking do it..." sneered Ruth. "Come on, boy! Think about yourself for once. What's this girl done for you that you need to save her ass?"

I shook my head. "Look, it's not for me, but it's also not for her. It's the only thing I can do to make Oliver's afterlife a little more bearable."

"Wait. What's that mean...?" questioned Luie.

"Well... no offense Luie, but I honestly believe Oliver would enjoy any afterlife far away from you..." I explained carefully. "It's not that he hated you, but he wasn't a big fan of... well... his fans. And he considered you the queen of said fans."

Luie's face looked to be in disbelief. "So, you're going to keep me from Hell in order to block me from ever seeing Oliver again?"

I nodded. "I mean, you also get to go to Heaven so... everybody wins!"

Luie looked defeated. She went limp in Ruth's grasp. Ruth got agitated holding all of Luie's weight and shook her around till she bucked up out of her catatonic state. Ruth then looked over at Franz. "You've got to kill him, Franz!" she shouted. "Use the ape."

"Uh... what? No!" stuttered Franz, with a look of offense. "I'm no murderer!"

Ruth rolled her eyes. "You buffoon. We've already done a lot of worse things today than kill people!" shouted Ruth.

"No way am I doing that..." frowned Franz. "It's a morality thing. I can reprogram the afterlife, but I can't just take lives."

"God dammit," Ruth looked frustrated. She pointed at Lefty. "Fine then, just wish for something so he at least can't wish for anything!"

Franz nodded. He could do that much. He ran his fingers over his mustache and began thinking of the correctly worded wish.

I wouldn't give him the chance to muster an answer. I stepped forward and began to charge at him. I was going to knock Lefty from his hands.

Frightened, Franz hurried his thoughts. He couldn't think of anything he'd consider perfect, so he made a desperate attempt. "I wish..." I tackled him and Lefty against my chest. Franz screamed out as I toppled him to the floor. He wheezed out the remaining words under the crushing force of my and Lefty's combined weight. "I wish the Jon in this room had a mouth!"

I felt a sudden pressure build against the walls of my cheeks from the inside of my head. All of my oxygen exchange was quickly redirected in and out of my nose. I tried to scream in discomfort and disgust, but my lips weren't just sealed, they were completely replaced with soft pale flesh. It was like I'd never had a mouth to begin with.

In my panic, I loosened my grip on Franz just enough for him to regain control and shove me off of him. He began to laugh, "H-heh... *it worked*... it worked!"

Ruth began to laugh as well. "Excellent, Franz! I knew you had it in you. Now help me neutralize this one too." Ruth pointed to Luie, still trapped in her vice.

Franz picked up Lefty off the floor and stood him up straight. He placed his palm against Lefty's hand and shut his eyes.

But before Franz could utter another word, a long red tentacle wrapped around his face and shut his lips tightly. It coiled around his head and tied his jaw shut as he attempted to shriek in pain. Slowly, Franz was being lifted into the air by some vile chimera that had grown from my body.

When Franz had wished I had a mouth, it took it away, then gave me *everything else*. That included every appendage nature could develop. I had tendrils to toss Franz around in the air and claws to shred at his arms till he dropped Lefty to the ground.

"No!" screeched Ruth. She threw Luie to the side and leapt for Lefty. I quickly stopped her by lassoing her midair with one of the many tails now growing out of my back. I coiled her inwards towards my body and stuck her a few times with a scorpion's stinger to keep her paralyzed while me and Luie tried to fix things.

"Holy smokes, you're ugly," snarled Luie. I could sense she was still mad about the whole 'keep you as far away from Oliver as possible' thing. "You know I don't have a lot of motivation for changing you back."

Having no mouth, I couldn't really argue with her, so I decided to verbalize my disapproval by rattling a snake tail.

"Don't threaten me!"

I really wasn't trying to. I was being misread. I should have chosen a less threatening appendage. I tried to show her I meant no harm by switching over to a small dog tail. I gave it a little wiggle.

"Wait. Are you trying to apologize?"

I wiggled even harder.

"It's not that simple," sighed Luie. "I can't help but appreciate you trying to keep me out of Hell, but your reasoning sucked, dude. I always wondered why you and Oliver were always trying to ostracize me and this finally confirmed all my phobias. Why is it so wrong to geek out about my professor?"

I had an answer, but unfortunately, I didn't have an appendage that could symbolize such a deep, complicated response. I just kept wagging.

"Dammit, I need a real answer out of you!" shouted Luie. She ran over to the ape and held onto to it tightly. "How about... ugh. It's like being on Jeopardy! I know what I want but it's all about how I say it. Maybe- maybe this will do it... I wish the Jon in this room spoke Japanese!"

With each bolt of lightning that flashed thereafter, another mouth would fill in the gaps between my countless arms and legs. When the storm had fully passed, I could feel a thousand or so new orifices opened up across my skin. They were rambling madly, translating my thoughts into a thousand different languages.

"One at a time!" shouted Luie.

I struggled to get my mouths under control and when I did it was just as difficult finding the one that could speak English.

"Ti les gia aftó?" I spoke out of a hairy lip tucked between two crustaceous claws.

"Ose ndoshta është kjo?" came a thin mouth perched over a dove tail.

"Well how about this?" It wasn't my usual voice, but this mouth could speak English and that's all that mattered. With my speaking abilities returned, I could finally give Luie a proper apology. "Luie, it's not fair for us to act cold towards you and for that I'm sorry. I know I say you were a fan, but what that really means is... you didn't mesh well with our misery."

"You're... miserable?" asked Luie.

"Si!" "Jes!" "Hoàn toàn!" My mouths all answered at once, venting my frustrations with myself and the world. I shut them all up and tried to continue. "It's even more frustrating knowing that the one person I could relate to the most had to go and be a selfish prick. He left me to suffer all on my own."

Luie sighed. "So, you two have a grudge against me for... having hope? Smiling too much? Not being a mopey bitch?"

"Sort of. I mean neither me nor Oliver could really 'geek out' about anything the way you could. It kind of made you the black sheep."

Luie shook her head then turned away from me. She walked up to Franz Boa, still bleeding out where I'd tossed him. He'd broken too many bones in the fall to stand back up. "I'll admit. Maybe I do idolize too much. I realize that especially now with two of the greatest anthropologists of all time bleeding at my feet for being completely heartless assholes."

"Zora was pretty cool though..."

"Agreed," nodded Luie. "But we got to do something about these two."

"And if you could also change me back to normal in the process... I yearn for my days as a simpler organism."

Luie nodded and grabbed hold of Lefty yet again. "If only there was a way I could make it that Lefty's wishes never worked. That could rescue all of us from Hell... and maybe even keep Oliver from suicide."

"Perhaps you could use something else to wish on!" I suggested. I quickly slithered a free tentacle over to Lefty and made a new wish. "I wish for Lefty!"

"For Lefty?" questioned Luie. At first it didn't make any sense, but when the storm settled, and my *real* wish came true. Luie nodded while staring with apprehension at one last appendage added to my form. "The real monkey's paw..." she said softly. By wishing for Lefty, I could only get the one piece not included. "You really think this will be any better?"

"They're both evil, don't get me wrong, but Lefty is just too tricky to work with. You have to do too much thinking in reverse and loose logic. The monkey's paw is a total bitch, but... it should be more straightforward. The key will be being as specific as humanly possible."

Luie reached out and grabbed the monkey's paw from my tentacle's grasp. She shut her eyes and took my advice, making sure to be extremely detailed. "I wish the Jon in this room was the exact same person he was at the start of today, but with his current memories intact!"

Instead of a storm, the monkey's paw caused the ground itself to roar. The tremor lasted only seconds, before blue light beams shot out from the paw's finger tips. Once they faded, I felt a sharp pinch in my side. Suddenly, my height and weight began collapsing inwards. I could feel my body shrinking rapidly. The mouths along my skin sealed up and disappeared. The limbs along my sides fell off and smoothed over. I was soon back to completely normal again. I felt around my body and, despite all I'd lost, everything I wanted to have seemed to still be in place.

"Fantastic!" I exclaimed. "I mean... thank you, Luie. I really mean it. Life may be miserable sometimes, but it would have to be a lot worse stuck as a giant everything-beast for the rest of my life."

"Yeah well, now that that's through, how about you help me correct the rest of this awful day."

I agreed and took the paw out of Luie's hands. "I wish the bodies of Franz Boas and Ruth Benedict were out of this lab and back in their graves!"

The two were gone as soon as the floor stopped its rumble.

"Wait, Jon, you left that wish completely open to an evil interpretation. They both were totally just buried alive!"

"Oh... yeah, I know," I shrugged. "They kind of deserved it."

Luie's look of shock waned. She agreed. "Well at least make sure when they suffocate, they don't go to Hell..."

I wished for famous anthropologists Franz Boas and Ruth Benedict to go to Heaven when they died.

"And add Oliver Quitt to that list of course!"

I wished for famous anthropologist Oliver Quitt to go to Heaven from his current residence in Hell.

"Oh, and don't forget us," suggested Luie.

I did the deed.

"And, while you're at it, how about all magic users from now on..."

I rolled my eyes. "I think I draw the line there... it may not be a perfect system, but I'm sure that rule does catch a lot of child-eating warlocks."

"*Fine*..." groaned Luie. "Well then just top it off with a lab cleanup. They left blood and you left scales and feathers all over the place."

I wished the lab was spotless... except for the chairs, machines, and chemicals we used for experimentation. Fucking paw would have probably stolen all our shit if I didn't specify that.

"That's all I can think of," sighed Luie, wiping the sweat from her brow. "You got any other ideas?"

I looked down at the paw and cringed. "We definitely shouldn't use this thing too liberally. Every wish we make is a roll of the dice. It's like Zora said, it's only giving us these gifts cause it intends on killing us somehow."

"Hmm..." huffed Luie. "You don't think it's already set something up, do you? Like with all we've already given it?"

I shook my head, although to be perfectly honest, I wasn't entirely sure.

For a long period of my life thereafter, I would believe we'd actually fooled the system and gotten our names off of Hell's records. But as I grew older and neared death, I realized something was still not quite right.

I don't know if it was just the anxiety of old age, but I suddenly became paranoid. I began to reconsider those last four wishes I'd made on the monkey's paw. I began to run them over in my head again and again up until the very last minute of my life. By then, I was completely captured in my fear, unsure of what fate awaited me on the other side.

When death came for me it wasn't painful. My chest felt cold, then moments later the world around me was going dark.

When the light returned my soul was hovering amongst the shiny blue ghosts of familiar faces. I saw Franz Boas and Ruth Benedict. And Oliver and Luie. They were all smiling in their incorporeal forms and were surrounded by a beautiful green landscape with deep blue mountains on the horizon.

"So, we made it to Heaven after all?" I asked, followed by a sigh of relief.

Luie came to my side and patted me on the back. "I mean... close enough." She pointed to a nearby road sign: *Swede Heaven, Washington*.

I shrugged. "Well... it certainly beats Hell."

Lethe

The folks in Hul's Square often get asked why they haven't ventured too far away from their roots. We've got cars and trucks, we've got money to spare and good health to travel, but we all stay put.

"Why would they leave?" say the tourists. "They've got it all right there." They're referring to our jobs. Our families own the heart of agriculture in the state. We have a fair amount of wealth but that's not why we stay. We stick around for the warmth. It's sunny two-hundred-and-fifty days a year in Hul's Square. It's something to do with our distance from the mountains. Every day feels like the last week of Autumn, breezy and warm. This all leads to happy crops, happy livestock, and most importantly, happy citizens.

Hul's Square is a tight community; a perfect place for kids to feel safe. I know everyone here by name and they all know mine. There's a level of trust here you can't find anywhere else. One man's business is everyone's business.

We kids take advantage of such a cozy environment. We're always outside whenever we can be. We're off playing some game or exploring some new neck of the woods. And we're completely self-supervised.

It's no surprise then that my earliest childhood memory would be playing outdoors. I remember a remarkable full moon overhead. There were no curfews in Hul's Square, so playing after dark wasn't uncommon. In fact, nothing about the memory is all that unique. It was just midnight tag. I've done it a million times before. I only know it's the furthest back I can remember because of the faces.

The memory starts with Theodore tagging me in the back. He's how I can place the chronology. It was one of the last times we'd play together. He'd move away a month later. I was ten years old at the time.

Theodore found me hiding between the barbershop and the pizzeria. He snuck up behind me and tagged me so hard it sent me to the ground. It wasn't his fault, Theodore had matured earlier than the rest. He was twice my size and didn't know his own strength. "I'm sorry," he said, before running off. I didn't bother trying to chase after him. There were no tag backs.

Instead, I went directly to the tobacco shop. I knew Maggie would be hiding inside. I shared my secret entrance with her earlier that night. I had a bit of a crush on her and wanted to help her hide. In hindsight, betraying her seemed like an awful way to share my affection, but I wasn't very fast. I needed an easy target or I'd be stuck being *it* all night.

I found the open window in the back of the shop and crawled through. I found Maggie ducked under a display table of cigars. When she saw me, she smiled. It quickly faded as I leapt forward and planted my hand on her face.

My memory ends there. I'm not really sure why it's stuck with me. I wasn't particularly proud of myself for betraying Maggie. But I wasn't devastated by the guilt either. We were just stupid kids and it was just a stupid game. The memory only stands out because everything before it is blank.

On average, childhood amnesia ends sometime around the age of six. Having my earliest memory placed four years after that never struck as me strange. But once I leaked the truth, people around me started treating me different.

I remember sitting around the dining table with my family: my father, my mother, and my two older sisters. I'm the youngest sibling.

The family was excited about the upcoming trip to Trollemon's, an old-fashioned amusement park an hour away from the farm. It's built into the center of the Ghenny Forest, meshing in nicely with the rest of nature. If you hold out your hands on the tall rides, you can touch the branches of the neighboring trees.

I couldn't wait to ride Odin's Ravens. It consists of two dueling roller coasters running side by side. I told my younger sister, Marceen, that we should race. We'd each sit in the front of one of the coasters and pretend we're driving head to head.

"You won last time," she smiled, "but that's cause my cart got weighed down by Dad. He can sit behind you this time."

I nodded with a look of confusion. I had no clue what 'last time' she was referring to. I thought this would be my first time on a dueling coaster.

"Oh, I'm not sitting with Jerrit!" laughed my father. "He got sick and sprayed all over the poor little girl behind him."

My father began laughing uncontrollably. The rest of my family started to join in. I, however, had no memory of getting sick at Trolleman's. Or having ever visited there before.

My mother scolded my father. "Ah, he looks upset. Stop embarrassing him," she asked. "He was so young, he didn't know his limits!"

"Oh..." I stuttered. "Did we go to Trollemon's before? When I was little?"

"Uh... *little*?" exclaimed Joyce, the older sister. "You were nine I think."

"That's little!" I laughed. "Did I enjoy myself at least?"

My dad suddenly looked as though he were insulted, "*Did you have fun?* Of course you had fun! You're the reason we keep wanting to go back."

My mother turned to me with a concerned look on her face. "We'd never seen you in tears before. You rarely cried when you were sad. But that night, you were welling up the whole ride home. You couldn't stop giggling. It was your fondest moment..."

"How can't you remember?" They kept asking me it all night. All I could do was shrug. I wasn't sure how the mind worked, but mine clearly matured a bit differently. It couldn't recall anything until I was ten. It didn't strike me as a reason for concern, but everyone around me seemed so worried. I didn't become worried myself until I noticed my father started ignoring me.

He wouldn't speak to me again until the day we went to Trolleman's. At this point he couldn't keep up with his estranged behavior or he might ruin the trip for everyone else.

As we waited in a line of cars for entry into the parking lot, my father asked my mother, "What ride do you want to do first?"

"I'm going straight for the K'Thume!" she replied. "You're welcome to join me."

"I don't wanna' get wet," he laughed. "What about you Joyce?"

"I'm melting back here," she replied. "I think I'll join Mom on the K'Thume, then I'll start my tour of the carnival games."

My father nodded. "How about... Marceen?"

She thought hard about her answer. "I think..." She paused. "...maybe, the bumper carts."

I was disappointed to hear her say that. It sounded like she remembered our plans to ride Odin's Ravens, but changed her mind at the last second. I don't think she even liked bumper cars. The line's always too long for such a short ride.

"Go extra rough on 'em!" exclaimed my father. "These tourists think we Hullers are a hokey bunch of pacifists."

There was a noticeable silence before my father finally brought his line of questioning onto the only remaining passenger. I wondered if he'd even ask me or just continue with his silent treatment.

"Jerrit?" he said, softly. A thick silence filled the car. All he had said was my name. Was I supposed to assume the rest? I guess he'd already asked it to everyone else, so I just took the lead.

I saw my sisters out the corner of my eye. They were both glaring at me. I stuttered, "I'll, uhm... I'll probably get in line for Odin's Ravens."

"*Odin's Ravens*?" exclaimed my dad with a look of surprise. A warm smile came across his face. "You're gonna' get sick again!"

My father started cracking up. We made eye contact in the rearview mirror. He was acting like there was never any tension between us. I was lost for words. I just decided to go along with it. I, too, didn't want to ruin the trip for anyone else.

"I'm trying to get it all out early on!" I replied. I put on a smile and laughed along with the rest of the family.

"Great," grinned my father. "Then I'll go with you."

The car was oddly quiet after that. There was silence till we found our parking space and bought our tickets. That's when my father's arm went around my shoulder and led me off from the rest of our family. I was being led to the longest line in the park. It was a thirty-minute wait before we could ride the Ravens.

It all seemed very normal at first. My father smiled and hummed as we inched closer and closer to the end of the line. Every now and then he'd sigh and take the weight off his feet by sitting on top of the metal barricades. I'd join in and find a comfortable seat.

I can't be sure of it. But I think my father was waiting for a line to build up behind us. That would make it harder for me to slip away.

After waiting for about fifteen minutes, my father turned to me. "You know what's in your room, right?"

It was a strange question, but I nodded. "More or less. Why?"

"Can you start naming some of the things inside it?"

I had an uneasy feeling about all these questions. It felt a lot like the dinner table a few weeks back. I decided to just comply. I started spouting off everything I could remember. "Violet wallpaper. Baby blue sheets. A knit blanket."

"And what's on the shelves?" he asked.

"Lots of stuffed animals. They're all at the bottom. Then there's books above that. And some memorabilia at the very top. It's from shows I like."

My dad started nodding. He seemed satisfied enough.

"Is this a game?" I asked him.

His eyes squinted. He glared down at me. I never realized how much taller he was than me. I'd gotten my mom's proportions. Short and skinny.

"It really isn't a game," he said softly. I could barely hear him over the roar of the crowd and sounds of the rides. He didn't want anyone to hear him but me.

My father continued his questions. "Andy Malt. Why's he on your shelf?"

"What?"

"Andy Malt. He's the puppet on your top shelf. He's got a straw hat."

"Oh!" I exclaimed. "He's from that old cartoon. You showed it to me. We watched all six seasons in two weeks. I really liked him."

"But where'd you get it?" he prodded.

"I don't... I mean... didn't you get me it?"

"Good. Very good," affirmed my father. "I got it for you when you turned twelve. Now, how about Garnzo?"

I tried to picture him. He was a stuffed rabbit. Designed to look kind of secondhand and ragged. He was made from blue crochet. He looked just like the character on an old book I used to have.

"Garnzo at the Carrot Faire!" I remembered.

"*What?*" huffed my dad.

"Garnzo at the Carrot Faire... it's a book. You read it to me. I became obsessed with him."

"No," grumbled dad. "Your mother read it to you. She bought you the bunny *alongside* the book. You had no obsession with it."

"Well I mean... I guess I was too young to remember that."

"No, you weren't!" griped my father. He looked frustrated. "I told your mother not to get it for you. You were too old. You were nine. You liked trucks and superheroes. That's why it's gathering dust on your shelf."

"Oh... "

"Chewball!" My father raised his voice. The crowd could hear him now. Some of them began to snicker. "What can you recall about Chewball?"

"I uh... who?"

"Chewball!" my father repeated again. The tourist behind us pulled out their phone. They thought we were amusing. Hullers losing their temper. What a novelty.

I explained to my father that I had no memory of Chewball.

"He's the town mascot. For the baseball team. It changed to a fox when you were eight and you were devastated. You made me wait till the end of his last game to get his autograph. It's on that doll!"

I kept trying to remember. All I could put together was that Chewball must be the big baseball-headed creature on my top shelf. I stuffed it near the back forever ago. It's big eyes and rosy cheeks started to creep me out.

"Start listing Halloween costumes," demanded dad.

"Starting with?"

"Last year!"

"I painted a bunch of boxes silver. I went as Robo-Jerrit."

"When you were 13?"

"I was a boy version of Chun Li."

"12?"

"A unicorn-wizard."

"11?"

"A preacher. Who hunted demons."

"10?"

"A ninja."

"9?"

...

"9?!"

...I had nothing. It was a total blank.

"Just say any other costume," demanded my father. "Anything before nine."

"I was... a hippie?"

"Your sister was a hippie. Two years ago."

"Wasn't I a superhero?"

"No..." His voice fell flat. "No one was ever a superhero." He looked up towards the front of the line. "Well look at that. We burned a half-hour."

His voice suddenly returned to normal "Come on son. Let's race." He patted me on the back. I took the front seat of the coaster on the left. My father took the front seat of the coaster on the right. Before take-off, he turned his head to me. "If you finish first, I'm urging you, don't run away." His face turned deadly serious. "If you do, there's no more interrogation needed."

The rest of the trip my father breathed down my neck. He encouraged me to try and enjoy the rest of the day because, when we got home, he and I were headed straight to church.

As we left, I couldn't help but pay attention to all the gawkers. They were unusually present at the park. I overheard one of the tourists speaking with their friend. "Well yeah, they're sweet," said the tourist. "But no, I'd never live there." But that's only because they can't.

It's an honor to work for our farms and ranches and so all our openings are offered only to family. And that family always accepts.

The shops and services downtown are run mostly by old folks who've become too achy to continue working in the fields. No one likes to retire around here. So when your legs get too weak to push a wheelbarrow, you get a job sitting-down as a cashier. There's always something somebody can be doing.

Lauren Kost became our preacher when her hearing went bad. Deaf employees take a toll on our labor. They can't hear calls from their fellow workers. The can't hear when a machine needs oil or repair. And they miss dire calls from livestock in danger.

Lauren certainly didn't need perfect hearing to preach. She could read just fine and speak just fine and that's a fair amount of all preachers do.

Lauren watched me closely as I took a seat in her study. I sat at an oak table with a thick, red tapestry draped across it. The walls around us were covered in old sacred texts. Their authenticity didn't match with the plastic candles on the window sills. Each candle was topped with a flickering light-bulb encompassed in a translucent orange shell made to look like a flame.

Lauren asked my father to leave the room. She gave him a list of my friends and asked him to go fetch them and wait outside the door. In the meantime, me and Lauren would be having a private conversation to discuss my ailment.

"Memory issues," said Lauren taking a seat in front of me. "You're suffering from memory issues that could arise from a handful of illnesses. Some physical. Some mental. The cause for alarm is that there's also a chance for spiritual infection."

"I'm not light on myself," I tried to explain. "I make mistakes and I ask for forgiveness. I haven't felt especially enlightened lately, but I don't feel *possessed* if that's what you're suggesting."

"Your father's suggesting that Jerrit's memories end where yours begin," explained Lauren. "At the age of ten you, whatever you may be, entered his body."

"So, he thinks I'm just a ghost speaking through his kid?" I snarked.

"It's happened before," shrugged Lauren. "I've heard your earliest memory from your father... so then you must remember Theodore, correct?"

"Of course," I said with surprise. "He moved away..."

"He was forced away," she corrected, "and it's worrisome seeing his name associated with the matter at hand."

Lauren dropped a clasp envelope onto the table. It had the name Theodore Teufel written in pen along the flap and a red five in the bottom corner.

"I wanted to review his old file with you."

Lauren undid the seal and pulled out a series of drawings. She fanned them out along the table.

"These are from fifth grade," explained Lauren. "We keep samples of all your work for psychological evaluation. We first noticed peculiar behavior in Theodore through the pages I have here in front of you."

"*That's* why you had us draw?"

"Everything we have you do as kids is deliberate," answered Lauren. "Athletics predict your future job performance. Show and tell predicts social behavior."

With a skillful swipe, all of the drawings were flipped over onto their backside. I could see notes written in blue pen. There were ten stages of an evaluation. I've summarized them below.

* Color Count- One, Many, Null

* Color Majority- Hots, Colds, Natures, Fleshes, Shimmers, Primaries, Null

* Tool of Choice- Pencil, Pen, Crayon, Marker, Paint, Other

* Where Am I?- Behind the camera, In the photo, Nowhere

* Who is that?- Circle all that apply: Family, Students, Teachers, Animals, Gods, Celebrities, Uh-ohs, Others

* Holiday- Yes (_____), No, Unknown Ritual

* Shapes- Abstract, Structured

* Skill- Match, Too Mature, Too Immature

* Humor- Funny to them (y/n), Funny to other kids (y/n), Funny to me/adults (y/n)

"In Theo's, there's not an obvious red flag. There's no coloring-in with thick lead pencil. There's no overuse of red. Every character used is accounted for and currently living. The only consistently odd detail is an unusual amount of drawings related to Christ's Reunion."

Christ's Reunion came right after our big corn harvest. It aligns fairly well with the other winter holidays and practices similar customs to Christmas. Every year, it's tradition that our fathers hang up decorations on their roofs.

"Theo's obsession seems normal enough," I replied. "His dad was just as nuts about it. He had the best display in town. With a big, light-up Jesus three times my size. They had it blink to the tune of Cerulean Night."

"But it went on and on! He was drawing these well into the summer. And just look at 'em..." Lauren directed my attention to a string of crosses and candle-lightings dispersed throughout the pictures. "These aren't the aspects kids obsess over. It's not toys or trees. It's detailed religious ceremony. And drawings of baby Jesus. It's trying a little too hard, don't you think?"

"It's just... childhood fantasy. Christ's Reunion every day."

"It's overkill, Jerrit. He wanted to look devout, too devout for a bad spirit." Lauren restacked the drawings and slid them back in their envelope.

"You banished a nine-year-old for loving Jesus?"

"Of course, not. The pictures just brought him to our attention. Much like your memory loss. Our suspicions weren't confirmed until Theo's sudden growth spurt. It didn't align with his family's traits. His mother wouldn't admit to an affair, so the only remaining explanation was possession. Demons are an uncanny source of nutrients, they're made of special elements that can overwrite deformities. The girls get more beautiful than their mothers and the boys get more fit than their fathers. Demons like a perfect specimen and can mold their habitat to their will."

"Well... I suppose I *am* better than my father at hoop, but that's only cause he hurt his foot when he was a teenager. If he hadn't, I'm sure he'd win."

"Oh don't worry, Jerrit," smiled Lauren. "*Your* stature is nothing alarming."

"Oof."

"Oh, don't take it offensively. It's a good thing. Your height and weight are your best defense at this point," explained Lauren.

A knock came at the door.

"The clincher will be your friends' testimony." Lauren invited them inside. "You've known these three your entire life. They'll be able to remember a notable change in your personality."

I wasn't surprised by the first two friends they'd selected. It was Maggie, my current girlfriend, and George, my current best friend. Together we were a good trio. We had a good balance of attributes. My part being the timid brain.

The third selection however was a bit unfamiliar. We've shared the same group for a couple school projects, but we've never hung out after school. He was definitely the odd choice of the bunch. I believed his name was Grayson.

The three filed into the room and stood uncomfortably still beside our table. They all looked nervous. George kept his eyes focused on me and gave me a confident smile. Maggie, on the other hand, looked down at her feet, as did Grayson.

"So," said Maggie, rubbing at her arm. "How do we, *prove* things? Like did we need to bring evidence with us?"

Lauren shook her head. "Your word is enough for me. I mean why would any of you lie, we're just trying to help our friend

Jerrit, here," explained Lauren. "After all, the real Jerrit *could* be trapped in his own body."

"I don't think that's the case," chuckled George, shaking his head. "I've known this guy since preschool, Jerrit's always been an outspoken kid with good grades. He's a pretty simple concept. If he would have changed at any point, I'd still be in elementary school. I needed my smart guy for help."

"What do you mean by *help*?" asked Lauren.

"Well when we were younger I'd just cheat off him, but as we got older he noticed I was struggling and he volunteered to be my tutor."

"That's really sweet," said Maggie. "I never knew that."

"Just when exactly did this change occur?" demanded Lauren.

"I'd guess around ten."

"Well look at that," exclaimed Lauren. "That aligns perfectly well with when we figure the demon took over."

"I'm sure that's just a coincidence," countered George.

"He's just matured!" affirmed Maggie. "And it wasn't just at ten. He's made a huge change just over the last year. It's why I started dating him. He started taking better care of his hygiene and he got way less shy. Are you telling me every adult skill he learns is just another demon moving in?"

"That's a fair point," admitted Lauren. "I won't disregard the effects of puberty. But *one* of the three of you saw some changes in our friend Jerrit that I don't think any of us would call *mature*." Lauren pointed to Grayson. He stepped forward.

"Wait, I'm confused," said George. "What's your son doing, here? He's not in our friend group."

Grayson looked up at me and stared at me through these big sad eyes. I felt guilty, but I didn't know why. It really looked like I hurt him, but I swear we've never spoken before.

"We, uhm... I, uh..." Grayson was as soft-spoken as he appeared. "I might have been in your friend group if Jerrit didn't just cut off our friendship out of nowhere."

"Tell em' exactly when it happened," encouraged Lauren.

"When we were nine, we used to hang out every weekend. But then sometime after ten, you just lost interest. I called you for a sleepover and you never called me back. Or visited me. Or talked to me in school. It felt like you were ignoring me..."

I was amazed at how legitimate Grayson's sorrow looked. It felt like he was telling the truth, but I couldn't recall any of it. He was a stranger to me.

"It hurts a lot less knowing now you just forgot me," explained Grayson. "At least now I know I didn't do anything wrong."

Lauren hummed. "To me, it seems like the demon kept most of Jerrit's friends. But, for obvious reasons, dropped the one with a priest for a mother."

"That's ridiculous!" I shouted. "There's a much easier explanation! I probably dumped your drab kid and just gravitated more towards George. I mean George is George! His confidence is hypnotic."

"Hey maybe I'm the demon!" jested George. "No really I'm not good with pressure. Don't do this shit to me too."

"Don't say *shit* in front your priest, George," scolded Lauren.

"So then, what *is* the furthest back you can remember, Jerrit?" asked Grayson. "What really took precedence over our entire friendship?"

I shook my head. "I won't lie to you, it's so... uninteresting." I went over all the details, explaining the scene as well as I could. We were in the fourth grade. It was midnight tag. Theodore found me in an alley. He got me good. I found Maggie waiting in the tobacco shop. And tag. She's it.

"Wait a minute... ah no," grumbled George, softly. "Excuse the language, Lauren, but there's something really fucking with me." George thought about it carefully. "Maggie... was that really the same night?"

Maggie nodded. "I thought it sounded familiar too. But what does *that* mean?"

Maggie and George looked too terrified to admit something. But they'd already hinted at it, they had no choice but to explain.

Maggie sighed, sullenly. "George and I remember that evening too. It's how we became friends."

"We had a *huge* fight!" exclaimed George. "She drew blood..."

"We were mad cause the game ended and me and George were both somehow *it*," explained Maggie. "I called him the loser. He called me the loser."

"We tried to trace *it* back to the error but too many kids went home," replied George.

Maggie frowned. "I think I might know where the second *it* came from now...."

"What's that mean?" I asked, hesitantly. "What are you two getting at?"

"I'm so sorry Jerrit," said Maggie, tears filling up. "I don't think Theo was ever *it* when he tagged you."

"Maybe..." George shut his eyes. It was hard for him to admit it. "Maybe that's actually when he got you, man."

Lauren started waving her hand towards the door, beckoning for my friends to flee the room.

"You're all dismissed," said Lauren. "Spare yourselves. Keep far away from the doppelganger."

Maggie finally looked up at me. "I don't want to believe it. Is it wrong if I find it so convincing?" She turned to Lauren. "Does this mean I'll always fall for imposters? Can I not sense the good in people?"

"I won't lie to you," sighed Lauren. "It may be hard for anyone of you to trust your friends again after this ordeal. It's not your fault, he's ruined you. We'll have to work on the damage it's caused," Maggie motioned again for them to leave the room, "but at another time."

Grayson followed his mother's orders immediately. Maggie couldn't suppress her weeping any longer, so she left to bawl in privacy. All that was left was George. "What's gonna' happen to him?" he asked Lauren.

"Well, we normally leave that up to the child's mother," explained Lauren. "Theodore's mother decided to move them all away... and we never bothered them again."

My mother is *not* a superstitious woman. But her decision wouldn't be based solely on her belief in demons. It would be based on her belief in the outside world. If she chose to leave, our whole family would have to assimilate with the rest of America. Which, in the past, has tempted each and every one of us. But as times gone on, we've felt a rise in the adversity.

It became particularly discouraging during the last dinner we hosted for the outsiders. They visit our farms in the summer for personalized tours of our facilities usually followed by a traditional home-cooked meal. My family stopped volunteering to host after Mom caught our last guests discussing some offensive postulations about Hul's Square.

A couple kids from the local college were watching me milk the cows. Assuming I was far younger than I really was, they were speaking quite freely around me. My mother walked into the barn to inform us the meat was done broiling, just in time to catch their gossip.

"It's just a different lifestyle," said one of the tourists. "Sure it's conservative, but so are *my* parents."

"What's really the difference though," asks their friend, "between this and a cult?"

I waited in Lauren's office for just an hour before my mother had decided. Despairingly, we would not be leaving town. Instead, we needed to stay for an exorcism.

I wondered how much of my mother's decision was her own. She had two other children to think about and taking them away from here would obstruct all their plans. Marceen had accepted a promotion to breeder and Joyce had a marriage coming up next autumn.

My father certainly had some unofficial say in the matter as well. He probably threatened to stay behind if my mother were to leave. My mother was incomplete without my dad by her side. His absence alone would persuade her to stay.

When Lauren returned with my mother's decision, she gave me an opportunity to cooperate. As long as I willfully followed her directions there would be no need to bind or imprison me while the exorcism was prepared.

In the meantime, I would live in the mess hall in the basement of our church. They supplied me with a sleeping bag and bathroom supplies. I was to take sink baths in the attached lavatory. All my meals would be microwaved and for entertainment I was allowed to watch the VHS tapes in the storage closet.

"Licht 2:16 asks us to forgive our family *before* we ask them to change," said the opossum to his nocturnal friends. "When your brother knows you don't hate him for it, it'll be easier for him to stop stealing your toys."

Stouffer's pasta dripped down my chin as I watched a full season of Creed Critters on the VCR. I was trying to keep distracted by revisiting some old cartoons, but they quoted so much scripture that I couldn't help but feel like they were administering my last rites.

I wasn't necessarily going to die, but exorcisms were precarious by design. I'd heard the process from an older boy at a bonfire. He told me about the idea of a sinking ship and a loyal captain. When things look bleak for a body, a human soul goes down with the ship, but a demon can betray its vessel and escape.

A date and time would be set, and news would spread by word of mouth. Everyone would gather at a ceremonial ground and watch as I'm placed into a perilous scenario. It's different every time, but the concept remains the same. There's a chance I'll survive, but the odds are so low the demon won't take the risk.

I spent two nights under the church emptying the freezer and watching small mammals discuss scripture. Most of the time I was too preoccupied with my dread to concentrate on the programming in front of me, but one episode in particularly kept my attention.

Two voles wanted to stay friends, but one isn't a Huller. Our church does not forbid outside relationships, but stresses how hard they are to keep. Our traditions don't align with Western standards. And sometimes they think we go too far. I wondered if I were born somewhere else if my amnesia would be less extraordinary.

When the town came to collect me, they sent a pair of strong hands to make sure I'd come peacefully. I recognized one as my old gym teacher. As we drove to our destination, I asked him if there were any signs I'd end up like this. He turned around and looked over his headrest. He shook his head. "Your time in my class suggested you'd live to be a hundred."

I was dropped off at Bunny Lake where the whole town was waiting in the shallow end. Bunny Lake isn't all that large, but there weren't that many Hullers to fit. I was led to a cliff overlooking the water. The deep end was thirty feet below me.

I looked across the crowd trying to spot any of my family. I wondered if they'd all be watching or if some couldn't bear to look. From a distance, it was hard to tell any of the crowd apart. The men all wore the same pair of shorts and the women all wore the same russet one-piece. These were the bathing suits provided by our church in the summer. They'd handed them out early this year just for the occasion.

There was usually rope hanging from the tree to my right, people would use it to swing closer to the surface before letting go. The rope had been removed, however, and was now being used to tie my wrists and ankles. I stood up tall, hogtied at the edge of the cliff. An anonymous executioner rested their foot on the small of my back.

"This body will be submerged for five minutes before we fish it out," explained the executioner. I tried to match the voice to a neighbor, but their whispering kept it masked. "I'll drop you in when the speech is over."

Down below, I saw a pickup truck pull up to the side of the lake and deliver a pair of speakers and a microphone to the front of the crowd. One of the swimmers got out of the water and dried herself off. She grabbed the mic and called out to the crowd. "I want my brother back." It was my sister's voice, Marceen.

The audience responded with an uproar. Some screamed for my return. Others begged for the demon's death. "My family loves him, but the size of our family is not limited to sisters and brothers, it is said in the book of Hoffen that our family includes our teachers and our doctors, our leaders and our laborers, our preachers and our strangers." The audience cheered louder than before. "When young Wilheim got lost in the woods, he couldn't hear his mother's calls, but when the whole town joined in, together, they led him home."

I heard my name being shouted softly. Then it grew to cover the whole crowd. They were rooting for me. My sister joined in over the sound system. Encouraging them to grow louder. At this point, it was tough to hear what the executioner was saying. They had to bring their lips right up to my ear. "It's time," they shouted, right before digging their heel into my spine and sending me over the edge.

The fall came so suddenly, I barely had time to react appropriately. By the time I had to seal my lips, I'd only filled my lungs partway. This left me with very little air to spare. I wasn't going to last the five minutes. I'd doubt I'd make it past sixty seconds.

The only way I'd survive is if I escaped my bondage. I decided to take the risk and use all my strength to wrestle against the ties. But even with my best effort, I just wasn't strong enough.

I got so tired I couldn't fight the instinct to catch my breath. I opened my mouth and the water flooded in. I felt it enter my lungs and force me to gag. My chest started to tighten up and I felt a sharp pinch in my abdominals. My core was burning and there was nothing I could do to stop the pain. I had to wait for the lack of air to finally kill off my brain cells. That's when the numbness finally kicked in.

At this point the mysterious effects of death on the human conscious began to unfold before me. They say you'll experience your life flashing before your eyes. But I saw many.

First, I saw Jerrit's. I saw his first kiss with Maggie in the back of the ice cream shop. I saw Marceen teaching him to play chess. I saw his father patching him up after a fight with George. It was the only time he refused to give him his homework.

Then I saw Theodore's. I saw the nights he'd spend with his friends. His hiding spots in the park. His hiding spots at home. I saw his wins on the football field and all the injuries he's caused. I saw his father eyeing him suspiciously. And his mother singing him off to sleep.

Then I saw Maria's. She's far younger than the first two, just a toddler carried around on her parent's backs. They took her across the world just to see Hul's Square. Her father wanted a photo in one of their straw hats.

Then I saw Philippe. Then Daniella, then Reni. Then I saw a boy on a large ship from a long time ago. Then I saw a girl being lowered into a pit of servals. Then I saw a newborn crawling across the sea.

Then I saw a pit of fire that took up everything in my sight. Maybe it was just the chemicals thrown in the lake burning away at my bulging eyes. I can't shut them, I'm panicking. Or maybe it's the lack of oxygen flowing to my head, I'm "seeing stars" as they say. But these stars look more like burning pillars. Colorful blues and ambers swirling upwards. I swear I can see people behind the flames. Black shadows with too many arms and pedestals for legs.

Suddenly, I feel like the world's gotten larger. I'm trapped inside of a pant leg and manage to escape through a hole in the knee. I'm swimming away from what I recognize as my old body. But it's already growing harder to remember it's past. I see a whole new chapter before me. I'm racing towards the shallow end of the lake towards a hundred new possibilities. I need to touch their leg before they make it out of the water

Pizza Crow VII

The temperature did something, but I'm not sure what. I don't have the time to think on it.

I was becoming desperate. I'd sunk a lot of time and money into trying to start this publishing company. But I couldn't get a story to fit the times. People didn't want surrealism. They wanted magical realism. And non-fiction. And true crime. Down-to-earth shit.

I tried to fiddle with the shape of the pizza. I tried changing the triangular slices into squares. But nothing changed. I went to the extreme and flipped the whole thing inside out, turning it into a calzone. But still it had no effect.

I began to wonder if the bird knew he was ruining my life, or if perhaps he had control over what came the whole time. It just seemed like every time I came close to cracking the code, to getting something normal, the next work would come out stranger than the last. I couldn't find the pattern.

My financial situation is really starting to sour. Running out of money for groceries, I've had no choice but to eat half of every slice I give to the bird.

I've nothing to entertain me except the hundreds of stories that failed to publish. I've mostly just skimmed them, so I've decided to use my time reading them thoroughly instead of being bored. I've found a few I genuinely enjoy. They keep me my mind off the bitter failure.

This next one's my favorite.

The Bright Idea Room

It's not a psychopath or a monster that kills an innocent victim; it's the environment that surrounds them.

It needs to be in close-quarters. In an open field, a lumbering zombie is quickly outrun by the superior speed of the uninfected. Same goes for a psychopath. Weighed down by steel weapons and the occasional bulky costume, he'd never catch his victims out in the open. These enemies require the element of surprise provided by a haunted house. They need something like the dead ends of a corn maze to keep their victims in place for dismemberment.

The environment also needs to be relatively "middle-of-nowhere". If a werewolf were to change on a street in Manhattan, the cops would mow him down before his first howl. The key is to be in an area of lawless isolation like a dark, forgotten forest or a non-profit bookstore.

If the environment doesn't first fulfill these requirements, villains can be otherwise shrugged off. After all, what was the minotaur without his labyrinth? Half a farm animal, and not even the fast parts. And what are snakes without their plane? Scaly worms who would much rather be chasing field mice than airsick commuters.

In other words, don't be afraid of killers. And don't be afraid of monsters. Be afraid of tight spaces. Claustrophobia is really the only phobia with any sense. After all, there's no need to fear a four-inch knife, unless it's five inches away.

Now, there were no knives amongst the four professors that suddenly found themselves trapped in the Bright Idea Room. Of the four, three were practicing pacifists. Of the remaining, only two owned knives, and of those two... only one carried it in his pocket. He'd carry it every day and everywhere. Even to the classes he'd teach. His name was Dr. Stanley Heit and he studied American Espionage.

Stanley's knife was named Company. It was a smatchet, a blade commonly used by the CIA-precursor, the OSS. Stanley panicked when he felt around his cargo shorts and realized Company had vanished. He realized he had no recollection of passing out. He was positive he'd been knocked out by a thief who'd made off with his priceless artifact.

Stanley quickly flung himself off of the floor. He was surprised to see he was surrounded by pitch black. The last thing he remembered was being under the luminescent lights of the largest lecture hall in Temple University. In the dark, it was difficult to see where he'd been carried.

Stanley felt around the area. The floor felt like cold linoleum. Reaching behind him, he found a nearby wall, smooth and dusty. He pressed his hands firm against the wall and hoisted himself up to his feet.

He began to follow along the wall, slowly strafing with his arms spread out. He'd taken only six steps sideways when he came across a cold metal bar. He gripped on tight and followed the bar to its top. There he felt a silk shade encasing a glass bulb.

Stanley had found a lamp. He twisted the tiny metal knob beneath the neck of the light bulb.

Clink. The lamp shot to life. It stood at the same height as Stanley. It's base and body were crimson steel and its shade was a matching, brick red. The bulb inside emanated a clean white glow. It lit precisely ten feet from its base.

Stanley could see that the lamp was placed in the corner of the room. The corner was otherwise empty, except for a wire that led from the foot of the lamp off into the dark.

Stanley considered following the wire, but he was stopped by a sudden noise.

"Oh!" cooed an eloquent voice from the shadows. "Have I begun to dream?"

Stanley heard footsteps slowly approaching from out of the dark. A body began to take shape as it stepped into the light of the lamp.

"Are you my captor?" asked Stanley to the well-dressed man standing in front of him. "Or are you a prisoner too?"

The well-dressed man wore a casual grey sport coat over a baby blue button down. His face was thin and hairless. He was a young man of his mid-thirties.

"I surely didn't capture anyone," replied the young man. "But I don't recall being held prisoner either. I'd assumed for the last hour I was experiencing the effects of a mescaline trip, hence the memory loss and surreal darkness. But then I heard some shuffling and you've now appeared out of nowhere. Are you a hallucination?"

"I can assure you I'm real," replied Stanley. "And I guess I might be jumping the gun calling us prisoners. There could be a door. I just can't see much in here."

The young man nodded his head, then stared curiously at Stanley and the lamp. He then approached the wall beside them and ran his fingers down the colorless surface. He began to snicker.

"Wait. Have I wandered into a deco while high again?" chuckled the young man. "Is this a performance piece... you're an exhibit?"

Stanley looked confused. That's when he realized that the white walls around them did in fact look like the plain backdrop one finds in an art museum.

"An old man with a red lamp..." pondered the young man. "This is a blunt metaphor for a conservative."

"Uh..." droned Stanley, thinking back to his twenties abroad in the UK. Memories of Enoch Powell and lighter fluid flashed before his mind. "...that's not accurate-- in more ways than one."

"*Am I the captor or the prisoner?*" said the young man, paraphrasing Stanley. "I sense some subtext about veterans, but I can't put my finger on it."

"Listen son," groaned Stanley distancing away from the red lamp beside him. "I know you're confused, but I am *not* a piece of art."

The young man stroked his chin, "Are you not a piece of art? Or are you just a piece of art that says it's not?"

Stanley sighed in frustration, "Look, just name one thing a performance piece can't do."

The young man shrugged, "Well... without a waiver, you can't hit m-"

Smack! Stanley slapped his palm hard into the young man's pale cheek. The young man's eyes went wide. He began glaring around the room with his jaw half-open.

"It seems my pain receptors are fully functioning," said the young man beneath his breath. "...I am truly sober." His eyes locked on Stanley. His face became deadly serious. "Forgive me, sir. It's logical to process the surreal as, well, surreal. I've mistaken fiction for reality before and that embarrassment has made me cautious not to do it again."

247

Stanley motioned to their unusual surroundings, "I can't blame you for finding this place... unreal. I'm trying to get a better feel for exactly what it is. I'm most afraid it's some modernized cell. Perhaps a Swedish prison. But I've got no memory of being detained."

"Nor do I," said the young man. "The last thing I remember is attending a lecture on web design."

"Do you study computers?"

"Oh no. I'm a Doctor of Contemporary Art. The debate was on whether web design qualifies as modern architecture. I couldn't follow a lick of the technical jargon."

The young man reached into the front pocket of his sport coat. But he looked surprised to find nothing inside.

"I usually have cards," said the young man peering into his pocket from above, "but it seems my jacket has been emptied... well anyways, I'm employed by U Penn. My name is Ethan Wyth."

"Well I'm Stanley," replied Stanley. "I'm not far from U Penn, myself. I work at Temple's history department."

"You're a rabbi, then?"

"Uh... that's the... that's not the right Temple."

"Tell me Stanley," interjected Ethan. "How much of this place have you explored?"

"I've only taken a few steps really. I wound up in this corner." Stanley motioned to everything the lamp's light encompassed. "Perhaps we should continue exploring. We should split up and each take a wall."

Ethan nodded. Ethan shimmied into the darkness, exploring the wall to the left of the lamp. Stanley did the same, taking the wall that led back to where he'd first awakened.

For the next five minutes the two searched in silence. At the sixth minute, Ethan cursed out in pain.

"Sorry!" shouted Ethan "I just stubbed my toe on some big fucking obstacle." Ethan knelt down and felt around whatever his toe had just failed to penetrate. "I think it's just a giant box jutting out of the wall."

"Really?" replied Stanley, shouting back through the dark. "And just how big is it?"

"Tall as a desk. Wide as one too. I can't feel a crack beneath it or behind it. I think it connects with the wall and the floor. It's made of the same material."

Stanley heard a series of soft thunks in the dark.

"I think it's hollow too," said Ethan wailing on the top of the block. "Wait, now. I think... I think I've brushed something. Now what in the hell is this?"

Stanley could hear Ethan fiddling with the object in the dark. He could hear his palms sliding around the structure, learning its shape. He heard a couple light pats, some faint creaking, then finally, a crisp snap.

Suddenly, the image of Ethan and the cube popped out from the dark. They were both caught in the white glow of a second lamp. This one was smaller than the last. It was one of those gooseneck desk lamps. Like the little Pixar mascot. Every piece of it was the same shade of forest green, the cone around the bulb, the plate around its foot, and each segment of its bendable neck. Its palette was vibrant against the white block it sat atop and the white wall behind it.

Though smaller in size, this lamp lit about the same distance as the red lamp from before it. It was able to illuminate the entire block beneath it and then some.

Ethan had his hand on the base of the lamp. His finger sat atop a rectangular rocker switch. He clicked the switch back and forth a few times, strobing the desk lamp.

"Having fun over there?" jested Stanley from the dark.

"I'm sorry," replied Ethan, "it's just got this nice tactile fee-"

Smack! For the second time since meeting Stanley, Ethan's face had been assaulted. An unknown assailant had rushed out from the dark and landed a fist into Ethan's jaw. Ethan and this attacker both fell to the floor.

Rolling around, Ethan wrestled with a man half his size. Ethan was pinned. The assailant held Ethan's pencil-thin neck between his little hands. He was choking the life from him.

Ethan had never been in a fight before so his first response was to try and take in all the nuances of the new experience. He enjoyed the surprise of the attack. That was a fun, little rush. And the lightheadedness he felt was nearly identical to the first six minutes of a salvia trip. How nostalgic. Ethan didn't like the pressure around his neck, though. It brought back a bad memory from Catholic School, when the head nun thought his scarf was sacrilege. It had a picture of Bugs Bunny in robes and a crown of thorns. Ethan came home with a ring of bruises over his throat. He lied to his mom and said they were hickies.

Stanley really thought, at first, Ethan would be able to easily fight back against the small man slowly killing him. He sat back in the dark waiting for Ethan to strike back at the attacker. But the young professor just kept still on the floor. Ethan was too busy in his thoughts to retaliate. Internally, Ethan had begun comparing the attacker's breath to that of his neighbor's Chow Chow.

Stanley sighed. He would have to help. He quickly rushed over to the white block and grabbed the green desk lamp. He raised the head of the lamp above the attacker's twisted grey locks, then slammed downwards. The spherical cone of the lamp wedged atop the attacker's head like a yarmulke. The force of the blow shattered the lightbulb inside the cone against the attacker's scalp.

The desk lamp had been broken. The whole scene around the three men had returned to black. But Stanley could no longer hear struggling in front of him. Instead, he heard Ethan wheezing in the dark, returning air to his alveoli.

Stanley tossed the shattered desk lamp to the floor and grabbed the attacker by his shirt. He picked the little man up off of Ethan and hauled him over into the light of the red lamp in the corner. He propped the man against the wall. Looking into his eyes, Stanley saw he hadn't passed out. In fact, the man barely looked dazed by the blow to his skull. His face was simply complacent.

"Ethan," shouted Stanley over his shoulder. "Have you finished recovering? Are you injured?"

"Honestly, I can't say I'll ever be the same," muttered Ethan to the ceiling. "I learned so much."

Stanley rolled his eyes. "Just get over here, right now! I'll need some help with this guy. We need to find out who he is."

"I can just... tell you..." muttered the short man softly. His eyes looked glassy, they stared arbitrarily into the darkness behind Stanley. They were shielded behind a pair of rectangular spectacles. "My name... is John... John Lang ... MD... PhD..."

"Oh lord, that combination always follows one career in particular," sighed Stanley. "You're damned Psychiatrist, aren't you?"

John nodded. "As a doctorate... I research neuropathy... and as a doctor... I treat it."

"Do you treat all your patients with chokeholds?"

John turned his eyes to meet Stanley's. "I'm sorry."

"You're sorry?" scoffed Stanley. "Apologies aren't capable of absolving a murder attempt."

"It's currently the only means I have of garnering forgiveness," droned John. "I'll find a more meaningful redemption if you give me some time."

"Well how about instead of an apology, you redeem yourself by explaining why you attacked in the first place?"

John's eyes turned towards the floor. He raised his shoulders. "I haven't the slightest idea."

Stanley's jaw dropped. "You won't tell us... should I assume it has something to do with why we're all trapped in here?"

"Are we trapped?" asked John peering out into the darkness. "I hadn't realized that much. I woke up to you two shouting at each other through the dark. That young man, I believe you've called him Ethan, he switched on a light and I was able to see his face. Something clicked. I went into a tizzy and I socked him to the floor."

John looked over Stanley's shoulder. He stared into Ethan's face. John shrugged.

"It's gone," sighed John.

"What's gone?" groaned Stanley.

"The urge. Whatever compelled me to attack him. It's just not there anymore. And I have no memory of what it was."

"I can't believe that," huffed Stanley.

"And why is that?" asked Ethan coming forward. "Both of us are having quite a bit of memory loss as well. Yet we're exonerated of having any part in us being here."

Stanley turned his attention to Ethan. "He tried to kill you, son. Don't you care? He left a massive welt on your face."

"Actually, that was from you," replied Ethan with a bashful smirk. "You both assaulted me. And you both have memory loss. Your differences are slowly diminishing, huh?"

Stanley shook his head in anger. "You're taking this too lightly, kid."

"You two are having memory loss as well?" questioned John, crawling up the wall behind him up to his feet. "How so?"

"We have no memory of why or how we've gotten, here," answered Ethan.

"Stop giving him our info!" scolded Stanley. "Anything you say he can use against us."

"I have no recollection of coming here either," explained John. "My most recent memory is grading papers in my office. I teach at Drexel University if you've heard of it."

John was about to assure him, they had. They were all teaching in the Philadelphia area. But John kept his mouth shut. He could feel Stanley's gaze aimed at the side of his face. He took Stanley's advice and kept their origins a secret for the time being.

"I can't recall what triggered my amnesia. In many cases where people are drugged they can remember the event of consumption, then the following memories are obscured. But if none of us can recall the events leading up to whatever has caused our memory loss then this may be related to head injury or even a shared disease. Have you checked each other for signs of head trauma? Bruising? Lumps? Perhaps stitches if treatment followed?"

Ethan ran his fingers through his soft blonde curls feeling for any swollen regions or painful spots. Stanley reluctantly did the same, checking the innards of his short silver crew cut. They both found nothing out of the ordinary.

"Exterior signs of head trauma aren't needed I suppose. Just a small, precise knock could have caused our amnesia. Or perhaps we've been out so long any outward signs of abuse have already healed," explained John. "A bump on the head wouldn't explain my sudden fit of rage though, I'll admit. Along with memory loss, dementia can cause some unexplainable mood swings and aggression."

"But we're not all taking sudden swings at each other... that's just you," replied Stanley.

John nodded. "I should only speak for myself, then. Although, it's worth noting I may just be experiencing more advanced symptoms than you two. Dementia can move at vastly different paces per patient"

Stanley turned to Ethan and motioned him to follow into the dark. He led them far enough from John that they may talk in private.

"I wanted your thoughts away from him," said Stanley. "Just tell me what you're thinking."

"I'm not really sure," sighed Ethan. "I wouldn't bother with my take on it though. I've never been good at spotting a liar. Art is all fiction. My mind's been trained to just take it in without hesitation. It helps me get lost in the piece."

"I don't care if it's the truth. I just want to hear your thoughts. They matter," assured Stanley. "Let your imagination run wild."

"Okay," nodded Ethan. "Stanley, I think we're in an asylum. I think we all have the same debilitating disease and it's all given us severe memory loss. I believe this room keeps us from hurting others on the outside. And I believe it was designed to keep us as calm as possible, hence the bright colors and extremely satisfying switches."

"Would a calming design allow me to beat a man with a desk lamp?" questioned Stanley.

"Fair point," nodded Ethan. "You see. My thoughts are worthless fantasies. I don't know why you'd want my theories."

"Well frankly, I don't," answered Stanley. "I mean if they were any good I'd consider them. But right now, I mainly wanted to see how John would react if we left him alone. We need to remain talking naturally to seem distracted."

Stanley peered over at the lit-up corner by the red lamp. John hadn't moved from his initial slump against the wall. His eyes were shut. He looked as though he were resting peacefully.

"John is free to move and he's only a few steps from perfect dark. If he wanted to lose us, he could," explained Stanley.

"I mean could he really?" asked Ethan. "We still don't have a clue how big this room is. Or if there's even an exit he could escape through. We should figure out the rest of the layout before we make any more assumptions."

Ethan awaited a response from Stanley.

"How's that for a good idea, huh?" continued Ethan. "I guess I have some quality thoughts, huh?"

Still no response.

"Uh... am I wrong? Am I still being stupid?" questioned Ethan. "Your silence is kind of hurting my feelings man. I'm really proud of myself right now. And I've really learned to respect your opinion of me over the last couple of..."

"Shut up," came a nasally voice from the dark. Though it came from right in front of Ethan, he recognized this did not belong to Stanley.

"What... who are you?" asked Ethan. In the pitch black, he could not make out who had taken Stanley's place before him.

"Shut. Up." demanded the voice. "You will shut up and follow my exact instructions. Or I will slit your friend's throat."

Ethan wasn't sure what was going on. He had no reason to believe the voice. But, as he stated before, he was prone to taking people's stories without question.

"Reach forward a few inches and you should feel the dull edge of something metal," droned the voice. "You'll see I'm not lying."

Ethan never thought the voice was lying. But he followed instructions as demanded and touched the knife.

"Good. Now, my other hand is over your friend's mouth," continued the voice. "He's already put it all together and stopped talking. From now on you'll do the same."

Ethan kept quiet.

"Good response," said the voice. "Now, I want you to follow this simple set of instructions. It's a series of tasks that upon completion will assure your safety and the safety of your friend."

Ethan continued to keep quiet.

"I need *you* to lead that man sitting in the corner, there. Have him follow you into the dark. You will bring him right to me."

Ethan said nothing.

"Tap my knife if you understand."

Ethan reached out and did as commanded.

"Excellent," said the voice. "It doesn't matter precisely where you lead him. Once he's in the dark, I'll catch him with my knife by surprise. I just need to remain unseen. You understand? After that, you, me, and your friend here can all have a chat about our current predicament."

...

"Tap my knife if that sounds okay."

Ethan did as he was instructed.

The Man in the Dark had determined Ethan as the less dominant of the two inhabitants he'd been observing from the shadows. Taking Stanley hostage was a power move in order to subdue the most likely interference with his plans. Ethan would, on the other hand, become a valuable pawn.

Ethan stood in the blackness mulling over how he should proceed. While protecting Stanley was the highest priority, Ethan didn't want John to get killed either. Even if there was some truth to John's malice, the Man in the Dark came across as desperate and unhinged. In the narrative world, Ethan recognized the Man in the Dark as a force of chaotic good. He was a loose cannon with good intentions but acting out of spite. Ethan would therefore have to act as the lawful good counterpart, but he was running out of time to devise a plan. As soon as he walked out of the dark, he was expected to follow his role as bait. He had only ten steps left in the shadows to devise an alternative course of action.

If Ethan wanted the ending he desired, he'd have to play off of what the Man in the Dark didn't know and use it to his advantage. What he *did* know was that John was in some way the bad guy. But he only assumed Ethan and Stanley were equally victims of John's malice. Ethan could very much be John's partner in crime, leaving the Man in the Dark with a knife to his only true ally's throat.

There. That was the story Ethan needed to sell.

All Ethan had to do was put on his best impression as the true "mastermind"; an impression that Ethan immediately began to second guess. Unfortunately, Ethan's experience in theatre was always as the fool. A type-cast that fit his real-life jolly and preferably intoxicated persona. To put on the mask of the villain, Ethan would have to tap into the closest role to an antagonist he'd ever performed: A Flying Monkey in his eighth grade Wizard of Oz.

Ethan internally recalled his stage directions. *Look imposing. Chest out. Chin up.* Ethan tried to elongate himself height-wise as much as humanly possible. *Approach Dorothy menacingly. Your face should look vicious.* Ethan marched out from the darkness slowly. His face twisted into something fearful. *Now, growl!* "I'm afraid the experiment has been compromised, Professor Lang," droned Ethan, slow and guttural. "Subject A has somehow obtained a weapon. It's being held to Subject B's throat."

John glared at him strangely. "Uhm... are you okay?" he questioned. "You keep peeling back your lips like an ape?"

Tone it down. Tone it down! Ethan returned his mouth to a normal state, but kept his eyes squinted and piercing. "An evacuation route should be opening for us now," said Ethan pointing into the dark. He quickly latched onto John's wrist. "We have to make moves before the subject becomes self-aware!"

"A way out!" shouted the Man in the Dark. "Help me stop them!" He shoved Stanley forward and directed the two of them toward Ethan and John's "escape route".

Hidden in the black, Ethan and John had simply crouched down in the corner of the room diagonal to the red lamp. While Ethan sat still listening carefully to the other inhabitants' movements, John explored the corner, pawing up and down at a strange structure to his back.

"bek..." Ethan heard what sounded like a duck's quack. "gyyet. off. ub. me!." hissed the Man in the Dark. His throat was being squeezed, disrupting his voice. A metallic sound bounced around in the blackness, emitting its clanging further away from the scuffle in the dark.

"Get the knife!" shouted Stanley "Find it. Quickly. While I still have him."

Ethan felt John squeeze his shoulder. "I think I've found something that should help." A beam of white light shot upwards from beneath John's chin. It was a Pepsi-blue flash light. The bulky type with a handle on its back. John turned the pillar of light onto another blocky extension of the room. This white cube held a homogeneously blue charging station where the flashlight could be lain. John illuminated the path along its chord where it ended at an orange outlet.

"Shine it over here," Ethan had moved across the room to wear the knife had banged on the floor. John shined the flashlight in the direction of Ethan's voice and found his head. He lowered the light down to the floor and swiveled it around until the blade of the knife reflected the light upwards at the ceiling. "Got it!" shouted Ethan grabbing the knife's handle.

"Company." cooed the disembodied voice of Stanley, still pinning down the Man in the Dark. Stanley's voice was soft and reminiscent; like they'd just uncovered his long-lost love. "Bring her back to me, please."

In the glowing beam of the flashlight, Stanley, John, and the Man in the Dark all watched Ethan like a performer trapped under a spotlight. Ethan's face suddenly changed before them; it looked like he'd caught stage fright. His eyes went wide and tears began to roll down his cheeks. He began to sob wildly.

"The boys gone mad!" shouted the Man in the Dark.

"What's upsetting you, boy?" called Stanley.

"You- you are," whimpered Ethan. "You fucking stabbed me..."

The other three men went silent, trying to understand what he meant.

"You're the one holding the knife, boy," called out Stanley.

"I don't think that's what he means," followed John.

"Dr. Heit... you murdered me in my office. I can remember, now. I think it's the knife. It's bringing back the memories..."

"I've never met you before this," assured Stanley. "And if you were murdered how are you right here in front us alive and well?"

"That's what I've been trying to figure," called out the Man in the Dark. "I too was murdered before this... by the fat man with the flashlight! The one you call John..."

"I've never met you just the same!" shouted John. He would have remembered such a distinct voice. But he pointed the flashlight at the Man in the Dark, just to be sure he'd never seen his face. It was certainly memorable. Pudgy and pink, with pockmarks digging into his cheekbones. The man had no hair atop his head and one large red eyebrow arching over a freckled nose. His voice seemed much more intimidating than his face now contradicted. "What is your name?" asked John.

"No name," grumbled the Man in the Dark. "Just call me Tim."

"Without your real name, I can't tell if I've even *heard* of you," replied John.

"You busted down my door and sicked a big black dog on me!" screamed Tim. "It tore my throat out!"

"Muggy?" laughed John. "I do, in fact, own a black dog. But she's not violent. And I've never trained her to attack even an intruder."

"Two murderers. Two victims," stuttered Ethan, still shaking with the knife in his hands. "My imagination is beginning to churn. These themes are familiar and they usually point to a secret setting in the afterlife. What if this is Hell?!"

"It can't be," sneered Tim. "Victims don't follow their perpetrators to Hell. We might be dead, but this is more likely a Purgatory stage before we're sorted by virtue."

"This does seem to be like a playroom," replied Ethan. "A purgatory is often like a game or a puzzle. Where a 'win' usually pushes you to your final resting place." Ethan stood up and examined his knife. "But then what is the winning condition."

"Well Ethan, allow me to include you in my current theory," began Tim. "I believe, upon our deaths, our souls have been waiting here in a state of unconsciousness until our murderers could join us in the afterlife. Now, in order to pass on, we must satiate our emotional baggage and enact sweet revenge on their souls with that knife."

"Now just hold on! *When* and *where* were you two murdered?" asked John. "If the timeline was clearer, me and Stanley might have perfectly reasonable alibis."

"You can't *prove* an alibi from in here," replied Tim. "Regardless, I don't know the *when*. But I know the where, my office in Chestnut Hill. That's just short drive away from Drexel, John."

"Stanley and Ethan both work in Philly-area too, so they too are within range of each other," grimaced John. "Can *you* supply us with a time of death, Ethan?"

Ethan shook his head. "I can't even see the time of day outside my window. Or the papers on my desk. I could have been preparing slides in the morning. Or grading papers after class. All the details are in the attack itself. I see Stanley's face. And Stanley's knife."

"Then this trial is looking pretty pointless," said Tim, confidently. "How about you lift yourself off of me Dr. Heit, before Ethan here guts you."

"No, no. You stay put Stanley," commanded Ethan. "Even if I was attacked, I'm not executing anyone until I know there's not a fair trial awaiting us outside these walls. We can't let our fantasies get the better of us, Tim. First things first, I need to see the full picture of this room. There's still a dark corner we've yet to uncover..." Ethan pointed his knife to the unexplored space. John moved the lens of his flashlight off of Ethan and lit the area.

In the flashlight's beam, appeared another white extension from the wall, but this one wasn't a simple block, it was shaped into a staircase. The steps led upwards close to the ceiling, and next to the highest step was a bright orange contraption hanging from the ceiling. A cylindrical stage light mounted in a harness with two degrees of freedom. Its coating was bright orange plastic all over. The warning color you'd find during deer hunting season.

"Turn it on," encouraged Ethan directing John to climb the stairs. Ethan wanted to fill the room with as much light as possible. He was sick of people hiding in and out of the shadows.

John climbed the staircase and found the control panel on the back of the light. There were two red dots, a switch, and a knob. He started with the obvious and flipped the switch to the 'on' position. Compared to the flashlight, the beam emitted was whiter, powered by an LED instead of an incandescent bulb. The beam was also brighter and more condensed, lighting only a small circle at the end of its path. John wondered if the extra knob allowed him to adjust the circle's radius.

The knob twisted with a sharp click. Suddenly, the stage light began flickering rapidly. John had turned the knob all the way up to its highest setting. It became apparent these were actually the controls for a strobing effect.

Stanley began to scream out in pain. Taking advantage of his captor's weakness, Tim shot his elbow backwards and knocked Stanley off of his back. He ran over to the tall red lamp and grabbed its metal bar in his hands. He ripped off its lampshade and lifted it off the floor "Keep your distance from now on!" shouted Tim, prodding the lamp forward like a spear. "Or I'll break this bulb off in your chest!"

As Tim overturned the light, he redirected its aura forward towards the center of the room. Stanley could be seen convulsing at the edge of its glow. He writhed around on the floor, his hands stuck to his head, pulling at his short grey hairs as he wailed in agony.

"Shut it off - shut off!" shouted Ethan. "He's having a fucking seizure."

John panicked and quickly flipped the switch on the back of the light; shutting it off entirely. "I'm so sorry. I'm so sorry," pleaded

John from his perch on the stairs. "You've got to believe me; it wasn't on purpose! I had no idea poor Stanley was epileptic."

"I'm not!" hollered Stanley, bringing his wriggling body to a rest. "It wasn't... like that. It felt like... I had an idea."

"What was the idea?" asked Ethan. He was tempted to run to his murderer's side. But the memory of his death made it too hard to trust poor Stanley at such close distance.

"It felt like a memory was being thrusted in and out of my head. It would be on the tip of my tongue, to the point where it would begin to unfold before my eyes. And then, poof, it would vanish. The image kept flashing in a rapid cycle. Never developing fully. The frustration snowballed into a headache, then dizziness. I was close to a blackout."

"Ethan, may I turn the light back on?" asked John from his perch atop the stairs.

"Are you trying to kill *me*, now?" shouted Stanley.

"I'll leave the strobe off this time," assured John. "But I want to test if the light still has power over you even with the strobe off."

"Sorry Stan," frowned Ethan. "But I'm curious too... give it shot, John."

John made sure the knob was all the way off to prevent any more blinking. He flicked on the switch. "Are you okay?" called John.

Stanley breathed a sigh of relief. But instantly, it changed to a look of surprise. Stanley turned to where Tim guarded himself in the corner. "It's certainly different this time," explained Stanley. "The memories coming in clear. Tim isn't a good Christian after all."

John quickly shut the light back off.

"dah." muttered Stanley. "...uhm... wait."

"What were you going to say?" asked John.

"Well now I can't remember," shrugged Stanley.

"Precisely," confirmed John. He switched back on the light. "Four lights. Four of us. Guys, I think these lights are tied to the memories of the murders. When they're on... we remember. When off, we can't recall."

"But that begs the question... are the memories real?" asked Ethan. "If they're tied to these devices, I'm willing to believe they're being transmitted into us. Or in other words, they're fake."

Tim began to growl. "Psalms 119:105 'Your word is a lamp to my feet. And a light to my path.' Truth and light are synonymous in the Bible. These lights around us are just another metaphor built into the larger message of purgatory. Discover the truth. Accept the truth. And move on."

Tim stepped forward into the center of the room, arching his back like a Roman soldier on the front lines. He turned his head to face Ethan. "You're more than happy to stick around, here. But the puzzle's been solved and nothing's changed. Which means you only get the good ending exactly how I first imagined it... first one to kill their killer, leaves."

"You're delusional!" shouted Ethan.

"There's no other way to be in this place!" screeched Tim. He rose the lamp over his head like a bo staff and looked prepared to charge his killer, but before he could race forward, the world around him turned to black, except for the stage light that shined a small oval right over top of his face. Everyone watched as his expression turn from fury to a baffled defeat. "no..." he whimpered.

"What's wrong," snickered Ethan. John shined his flashlight in Ethan's direction. Ethan was twirling a cherry red wire in circles. He'd unplugged Tim's memory. Ethan kept his knife extended in his other hand, warding off any advances by Tim to fix the dilemma.

Tim groaned in frustration and smacked his fleshy scalp over and over with the top of his palm. With the memory in his head shut off, he couldn't remember which of the men he had to kill.

"Still coming to get me?" laughed Ethan.

"I thought I was a goner for sure!" shouted John.

"Don't let me get away," joined in Stanley. They all broke out into a smile as Tim's aggravation grew into a fit of stomping and self-bruising.

"I might just have to kill all three of you, then!" snarled Tim, but before he could make another move a twinkle appeared beneath Tim's illuminated face. Ethan had curled Company beneath Tim's chin, prompting Tim to relax his weapon. He dropped the red lamp and chuckled nervously. "Easy there, friend. Remember *were* the victims, here. You and I."

Ethan shoved him forward. "I'm going to show you, your wrong," said Ethan. He kept pushing Tim along till the two of them reached the corner with the broken green desk lamp. He directed John to shine the stage light on the desk lamp's outlet where it was plugged. "I noticed earlier that the outlets in this room were the same four colors as the lights," explained Ethan. "But they don't match the light that's plugged into them." Ethan pointed at the outlet the green desk lamp was plugged into. It was blue, instead. Made from the same blue material eerily similar to the blue charger and blue flashlight in the other corner.

Ethan unplugged the green desk lamp and plugged in the red lamp in its place.

As the red lamp lit up again, Tim let out an airy gasp. "I can see it, again. *You* killed me, Ethan!"

Ethan shook his head. "Earlier you said it was clear as day... *John* had killed you. Don't you see? The outlet determines the murderer in the memory."

Tim struggled to believe. "I can only take your word as to what my memory was in the other outlet. I don't have any evidence this isn't a clever way to sway me from my mission."

"Fine then..." said Ethan with a devilish smile. "Then we'll see if you believe these memories are real, when you burst into your own office and become your own murderer!" Ethan unplugged the red lamp. He shoved Tim along till the two of them stood in front of the staircase on which John stood. Ethan unplugged the orange stage light from its red outlet and plugged in the wire to the red lamp. "Do you believe us now?"

"oh god..." whispered Tim. "no. I'm a fucking abomination."

"Relax. You're just panicking in a strange situation."

Tim flung his hands upwards onto the arm Ethan had raised. "*Lord forgive me*!" Tim shoved Ethan's hand inward, pressing the knife tightly to his flesh. Tim quickly jolted his body just slightly to the left, enough to slide his neck along the edge of the knife, slashing open the bottom his own throat.

"Oh my god!" screamed Ethan, dropping Tim's body in a panic. He watched as Tim fell to the floor and began to homogenize with the red lamp fallen beside him. His crimson flood flowed down his neck, soaking into his shirt before it could corrupt the otherwise immaculate floor.

John stared down at the two of them from the top of the staircase. In all his years of psychology he'd witnessed violent ends like this a total of twelve times. But it was rare he saw anything else but the results. Seeing the guilt in the man's eyes was consistent with what he'd always imagined his departed patients expressed in their final moments.

"What did that do?" whimpered Ethan. "What did /do?" Ethan dropped Company into the puddle of blood and backed away.

"It was a mistake," assured Stanley. "It's like me and the strobe light. You weren't trying to hurt him."

"I had a knife to his throat..."

"To protect me, remember?" called out John. "He wanted to kill us all and so you wanted to keep him contained. Don't blame yourself." John turned to face Tim's bleeding body. "Although, my academic mind does make me morbidly curious as to what that lamp ran through his head to cause such an outburst."

"We can find out," said Stanley. He walked over to pick his knife out of the blood. He wiped it off on his clean shirt and handed it up to John. "You keep this safe. Let's try a new experiment."

Stanley walked over to where Ethan was trying to keep himself together. Stanley hoped Ethan could accept being in his vicinity again. Stanley crouched down and patted Ethan on the back. "I want to figure out what went wrong," explained Stanley.

Ethan's eyes went wide. He shook his head. He wouldn't help cause another man's demise.

"Tim believed there would be a winning condition to get us out of here. He thought we solved the puzzle already, but I think there's still some secrets left to uncover. You agree?"

"I don't want the answers to cost you your life."

"Then, hold me down. John's got my knife for safe keeping. Once I'm plugged into my own outlet, I'll describe whatever crazy shit enters my mind."

It was difficult for Ethan to participate, but there was no way short, little John could keep Stanley down. And Stanley would definitely try it on his own, if no one would help him. Ethan minimized conflict and went along with the plan. Gripping Stanley's arm tightly behind his back. "Hold them exactly as I've instructed," commanded Stanley. He taught Ethan a valuable war tactic from Nazi Germany, on how to subdue an enemy without any rope on you. The position could be done with one arm free, so Ethan could be the one to plug the orange stage light into the orange plug.

Sparks flew from its prongs as Ethan shoved it inside the outlet. The stage light shot on and so did Stanley's memory. Ethan let go of the orange plug and returned it to the back of Stanley. He needed both hands to keep the man under control. Stanley was struggling way harder than either predicted. It was like Stanley had just been strapped into an electric chair. All his muscles were firing in a desperate attempt to end his life.

"Oh god..." wailed Stanley. "I hung myself... in the closet of my office... it seems so real!"

"But why do you want to repeat it!" called out John.

"It's trying to be so authentic that it gives you motives for doing it... really. good. motives."

"What's *your* reasoning?" asked John.

Stanley shook his head wildly. "If I could tell you, they wouldn't be that bad, would they?" shouted Stanley. "Let's just say when I was younger... I did something in poor taste out of desperation."

"Be a good shrink and get him to settle down!" shouted Ethan, struggling to keep Stanley's arm from flailing out of his control.

John had nothing he could say. It takes months of extensive trust building to get his patients to reveal those aspects of their lives that fuel self-harm. John instead hurried down the stairs with Company outstretched in his hand. Stanley roared in anger and jolted his head downward towards his lap, flipping Ethan over his arched back. His arms freed, he ran toward John and tried to impale himself on Company's point. John was able to dodge Stanley's attempt with a quick side step, but fell to the floor in the process. Stanley reached down and grabbed John's ankle. But before he could lift him into the air, John slid Company's edge along the stage light's orange cable. The light quickly fizzled out, as did Stanley's panic.

"Well I... uh..." Stanley held a hand to his face. He was embarrassed. "...let's help you two off the ground."

Stanley reached and lifted John up off the floor. He then walked over to Ethan and did the same. They all agreed they wouldn't perform any more tests like that again.

"I'm kind of disappointed," sighed Stanley, wiping sweat and tears from under his chin. "After facing all that, I'm still stuck in here." Stanley turned to Ethan. "Wouldn't that of made a great conclusion. The protagonist faces his demons and wakes up from the nightmare."

Ethan shook his head. "I'm not convinced there even exists a winning condition. I don't think anything is going to let us out. I think we have to escape." Ethan pointed to the lights around them, some destroyed, some still intact. "I think these lights are supposed to be the death of us. They're booby traps, obstacles to get in our way. And we got to stop playing with them. They will do us in before we can get away."

Stanley sighed. He took Company and tried to stab it into the ground. But floor was too solid and reflected the blow. He repeated his strike on the wall to his back, showing that that too could not be punctured. "This place is impenetrable. We've tried all the buttons on all the mechanics. I don't think there's a secret door that we're not seeing."

"But there might be a weak point," suggested Stanley pointing toward one of the outlets. "These outlet covers are screwed-in. Why don't we use the tip of the knife like a screwdriver? Maybe we take this place apart if we can get inside its circuit system."

Ethan nodded and handed Stanley his knife back. "It's your outlet. You should do it." Stanley nodded. He was happy to have Company back in his possession. He knelt down to reach the orange outlet and began to unscrew it. It took a bit of force, but Stanley actually managed to get it to budge. Turn by turn he unscrewed the top screw till it fell to the floor. Then, he undid the bottom one. Free from its constraints, the cover slid off.

The network of wires inside could have been mundane or completely alien, but it was impossible for any of them to tell the difference. Of all the experience shared between them, none of their professions required any sort of knowledge of circuit design.

"I was hoping for something dark or mystical," said Ethan with a look of disappointment. "A bottomless void or organic nerves meshed with the electronics. I can't make any sort of conjecture of something so... nonfiction."

"I'm no expert myself, but there *is* something worth noting, even to an amateur." Stanley pointed the tip of his knife to a little red wire. "These are English characters." XHHN. The code was typed in a faded white font that was almost invisible in the room's subpar illumination.

"English characters means no aliens," suggested Ethan. "Good to know this isn't some sick form of entertainment for some unknown species."

"Who's to say it isn't?" snickered John. "Not to be pessimistic, but this whole scenario screams human entertainment boiled down to its most basic elements."

"Mystery?" asked Ethan.

John shook his head. "Revenge. We're living in a revenge generator. A hurts B, so now B hurts A back."

"It's a classic," replied Ethan. "No matter how often it's repeated, it stays effective. It's a great way to show off your style without having to put too much energy into the plot structure. It's Sweeney Todd and it's Kill Bill. It's fucking Hamlet. It's the barebones approach to storytelling."

"So then... what'll happen if we don't comply?" asked Stanley. "By the way we're talking, it sounds like we're not going to be flicking on anymore lights... so then what?"

"Simple. We bore them!" exclaimed Ethan. "I mean whatever or whoever they are, we shouldn't give them what they want."

"Inaction?" repeated Stanley. He motioned to the darkness surrounding them. "There's no supplies here. No food or water. Inaction will still kill us, just slower. And with further pain and suffering. It's not smart to do nothing."

"But it's *our* revenge. Real revenge," suggested Ethan. "We can stick them with an anticlimax."

Stanley shook his head. "I'm not so sure I want to go out that way... before I got my life together I spent the first half of my twenties on the streets. I was always on the brink of starving. I have too much pride to let it get me now."

"Come on Stan," said Ethan with a smile, he tried to comfort his new friend. "This is the only possible ending where we die heroes."

"We avoid becoming victims, but we're not heroes," griped Stanley. He got back down on one knee and faced the wiring behind the outlet. "Hero should be saved for the ending where we escape."

Stanley held his knife back over his shoulder and swiped down with a confident thrust. The swing cut deep into the layers of wires. It dug in as far as it could and stuck when it reached the backside of the hollow. Sparks shot out in all directions as the wires completed their circuits using the metal in the invading blade.

Far outside the Bright Idea Room, a small Norwegian teenager playing on a swing set with his girlfriend has a premonition of Stanley stabbing him to death. He freezes in place at the horrible vision and forgets to catch his girlfriend in his hands as she swings backwards. She knocks him to the ground and knocks out his two front teeth.

The boy would wake up within five minutes with no recollection of what had caused his mind to error. In this same timeframe, Stanley had drawn backward in fear of the sparks flying towards his face. He removed his knife from the workings of the outlet and wouldn't consider doing it again. "Last thing I want to do is cause an electrical fire, there'd be nowhere to escape."

"Then will you please take a break and reconsider my idea?" asked Ethan, he put his hand on Stanley's shoulder. "Wait it out with us. The more you struggle the more you're just satisfying their interest."

Stanley shrugged off the boy's vice and stood up onto his feet. "I'll wait, but not till until I'm dead. I'll wait until I'm too hungry to stand, but then no longer. I'm just curious if 'boring them' will work out sort of like a strike. Perhaps if we ignore their plans long enough, they'll replace us with someone more capable of falling for these traps."

"Good enough for me," replied Ethan.

John agreed. He invited them all to join him in the corner under the orange spotlight. There, they could wait patiently, maybe share some stories to pass the time. They each got an opportunity to share how they got into their respective fields.

John was diagnosed with bipolar at a young age and took interest in the pill regimens he'd been prescribed to satiate his paranoia. He was happy to pursue the same field as his doctors and help others like they helped him.

Ethan on the other hand only got into art because of a disinterest in anything else. He hated math, science, business, and politics, but his parents insisted they pay for him to go to some college. All he could bare to attend was art school and he ended up loving it. It captured his imagination and got him to apply himself to the extent where it turned into a career.

Stanley had by far the most interesting origin story of the three. While homeless, he sought shelter in a history museum that agreed to let him stay the night in the winter as long as he didn't touch anything. While staying there, he perused the artifacts to pass the time and gained enough insight from the exhibits to form a legitimized opinion on the effectiveness of warcraft throughout the ages. He borrowed a computer from the local library and wrote an impressive paper that catapulted his opinions into publication. From there his struggles finally began to wane.

"As you can imagine, I'm willing to take great strides to escape a poor situation. And so, it pains me waiting around here doing nothing," Stanley cupped his hand under his shirt and felt his stomach rumbling. "It pains me in more ways than one. I'm afraid

I might start looking for more alternatives if things continue the way they are."

"You're not gonna' get anywhere sticking that knife in every outlet," sneered John. Being away from medication so long, combined with his growing hunger, had begun to make him irritable. "Can you just sit down and work with us, here? It's not like any of us feel any better than you do."

"Then what are we waiting around for?" sighed Stanley. "Time clearly isn't opening any doors for us, so let's consider route B... we kill ourselves."

"No, no, no!" scolded John. He rubbed his palm over the ridge of his nose, aggravatingly. "You're not bringing that up while my heads like this."

"Well that's the beauty of it, your head doesn't have to be like that," said Stanley slowly picking himself off the ground. "It can be... satisfied."

"What are you talking about?" questioned Ethan. He'd been passing in and out of consciousness for the last hour. He wasn't sure if he was slowly dying or perhaps he just needed sleep. It was impossible to tell the time of day, but it might just be approaching his bed time. Or perhaps bed time had long passed, and his body was simply breaking down.

Stanley walked over to the orange chord that went with the lights over their heads. He dragged it back over to the orange socket. "If I just pull these two together, I could make my final moments at least feel sort of *meaningful,* you know? I could trick myself until at least thinking death is what I really want. Which beats struggling against it... and inevitably losing a sad, sad, fight."

"You'd rather die the victor, huh?" said Ethan, pulling his face off the cold ground. He managed to sit up straight using the wall behind him for support. "It's not the worse idea actually."

"We had a plan," griped John, "to disappoint whatever voyeur is watching us suffer. You want to give in?"

"I guess for a little time I kind of thought like Stan did. Perhaps they'd just let us go if we refused to do anything fun, but now I've waited long enough to see otherwise. Whatever sealed us in here, human or not, has capabilities to seal men in sealed boxes and create machines that change your memories. It doesn't play by normal rules. It doesn't have to be entertained by such earthly delights such as vengeance. It could just want to test its powers on us in general. To trap and to torture. Stabbing or starving. Perhaps it loves to see us die all the same."

"Maslow's hierarchy of needs," suggested John, "You're just hungry Ethan and it's clouding the rest of your judgement. If I could just get you some sustenance, you wouldn't side with Stan's erraticism."

John peered out into the darkness where Tim's body was supposed to be rotting.

"You should at least allow me to exhaust every other possibility before committing suicide, because there's no more chances after that!" begged John. "We could buy a little more time if we considered eating the dead guy."

"The psychiatrist is the first to suggest cannibalism, how fitting," snickered Ethan.

"I was thinking just the same," said Stanley.

"It's not like he's still alive," argued John.

"But it seems counterintuitive," replied Ethan. "I mean you're trying not to cause a spectacle for our audience... but then you wanna' go eat a corpse?"

"Just take three bites and I beg you to reconsider whose side you're on," said John to Ethan. "You'll see just how pointless suicide is right after that first bite hits your stomach."

John crawled into the dark and began to feel around the floor for Tim's body, but he panicked when it proved more difficult than he imagined. "Whoever has the flashlight, please shine it over here. I can't find the damn guy!"

Stanley begrudgingly accepted the request and picked up the blue flash light from its place on the floor. He shot its glow in John's direction till it landed on what seemed like a body but was way too small to be Tim's.

"Oh my god," said John with shock and disgust, "It looks like it's fucking shrinking."

"Let me see!" shouted Stanley. He trudged through his stomach pains and plopped down beside John. He stared at the doll-sized body on the floor. It looked like equal parts had been stolen from every vital tissue, depleting the corpse without distorting its size ratios. "What does this mean?" asked Stanley.

None of the men were biologists but they understood that when matter disappeared it was likely being stored somewhere else.

"It's sapping him up like a prune," suggested Stanley. "Perhaps, this room is alive!"

"What?" called out Ethan from his sprawl along the floor. "You think it's eating him?"

John nodded. "The lamps and lights. They could be like teeth, crushing and killing the prey before the stomach absorbs the softened remains."

"But how does that help us?" questioned Ethan. "It's just as hopeless, John. So we're not stuck on a sadistic game show... now we're *just* stuck in the belly of a carnivorous pocket universe."

"But it *does* matter," said John, staring down at the little body on the floor. He picked it up and held it in his hands like a toy. He then pushed his head forward and bit a hefty portion off of the body's shoulder.

"Oh, nuh-uh!" hollered Stanley. He blocked out the grotesque sight by pressing his wrist to his eyes.

Ethan, on the other hand, couldn't look away. "...it's like Saturn Devouring his Son." John took in bite after bite, cringing through the disgusting flavor and accompanying fluids. The blood mixed with the bile and formed a tan mixture that dripped down his bottom lip.

The nightmarish feast only lasted five minutes. By then, the child-sized man had been entirely masticated and stored in John's chest. Stanley unveiled his eyes and saw a conflicted look upon John's face. The eyes looked sunken and guilty, while the lips licked and smacked with satisfaction.

John came out of his trance and twisted his head back and forth in a panic. He switched gaze between the two other men in the room. They both were glaring at him like they'd witnessed a murder.

John cleared his throat. "...I uhm, I assumed none of you wanted any of that."

Ethan nodded. "I think I'd rather starve."

"Well..." smiled John, "that won't be necessary now."

"What are you talking about?" questioned Ethan.

John wiped the brown mixture off of his chin and looked down at where the body once lied. "He's got to reset, now. I forced his hand."

"What makes you think that?" asked Stanley unsheathing his eyes.

"With the rest of Tim inside me, I've stolen the room's only meal," explained John, pointing to the blood stain where Tim's body used to lie. "As long as we all keep alive, we can starve the room before it starves us!"

"But why wouldn't it just keep us here?" asked Stanley, he stood up in excitement.

"It can't wait that long. It's big. It needs nutrients quite consistently to sustain all this mass. It'll reset its room and get new players to fill that need. And it won't want us around to spill the beans on the room's secrets."

"So then. what's it going to happen with us?"

John was prepared to explain, but Ethan answered for him. "...we'll be vomited."

"And what's that going to be like?"

"Oh who knows? None of us are physicists. Or, just as well, biologists," John shrugged. "I imagine it'll be like being squeezed out of an amoeba."

When the time came, none of the prey trapped inside the Bright Idea Room would have any recollection of their physical escape. Much like how they were captured, the memory of their return would go completely unremembered. Which is for the best, the process of rising from a subuniverse has been compared to having your entire body passed through the tip of a tube of toothpaste.

Without any recollection of their time spent in the Room, all the professors besides Tim would reappear exactly in the moment from where and when they were removed. Tim, on the other hand, would disappear in a sudden blip. Luckily, there was only one observer to witness such a surreal event and they were just as much a religious fanatic as Tim himself. The abrupt phasing from reality simply helped to bolster their faith in a higher power. Being the last one to see Tim alive, this same man would be tried for murder, a challenge that would further bolster that high, high faith.

As for the fate of the Room itself, its hunger still needed to be satisfied. It has a favoritism towards swallowing up professors due to the extra pinch of salt in their brains. They're richer supply of neurons comes with an equal increase in sodium ions to fire them off.

The Room would prey on a whole new bunch of educated elites. Another four. All doctorates but this time in STEM fields. The Room always picks on them when it's time to be desperate. For some reason, they're far easier to chew. Especially the Chemists. Their egos tend to get in the way of any of that pesky communication that makes it hard to swallow.

Pizza Crow VIII

I can no longer afford the pizzas, so I'm no longer using the bird for pages. I need him for food, now. I've resorted to feeding the bird inanimate objects. In exchange for pencil shavings, he gives me steak fries. In exchange for pocket change, he gives me half-eaten hamburgers. And if I really get lucky a loose bolt will fall off my bed frame, and for that he'll trade me a whole head of lettuce.

I'm surviving, but I'm afraid the pica is driving the little bird mad. His feathers are falling out and his beak's turned green. The food deliveries are becoming dramatically different. The color was missing from the french fries, the burger meat tasted like wood, and the lettuce was screaming uncontrollably.

Soon everything turned unpalatable. I tried to stop feeding the bird the inanimate objects. I went back to corn. But it was too late. The damage was irreversible.

The bird died. And it's my fault. Usually when I fed him corn, all I'd get in return is a drill bit. I have a lot of rusty, old drill bits. But that last day, when I fed him the corn, I got a flower. Now perhaps the illness had warped the reality around the drill bit so much that it's shape and size had turned into a flower. Or perhaps that bird thought of me as some sort of friend. Which maybe makes me even worse for killing it.

I would like to leave you with the last story the crow ever delivered. This was right before I ran out of food. Back then I was eating half of every slice, so it was my favorite pizza. Thin, crispy crust. Sausage on top. White sauce. Mozzarella. Served hot in big triangular slices.

Satan's Spies

It was my senior year and I was set to graduate with a Bachelor's in Biochemistry. While my graduating class all seemed to be set on pursuing PhDs, I was more eager to head right into industry. This came as a shock to both my friends and family who'd witnessed me sacrifice so many precious nights and weekends to work as an unpaid lab tech. Getting that much lab experience was a prerequisite for anyone wanting to be considered for graduate school. Why else would you miss out on all those parties and poker nights?

I guess the way I see it, whatever merits I have in academia mean twice the value in industry. I have my name on three Nature papers and recommendations from two of the top professors at Johns Hopkins. In academia, that comes across as impressive. But for any industry position, that's practically "congratulations, you're hired".

I've been trying to get a job secured *before* I graduate. My first round of resumes was, naturally, a wide success. I reeled in six phone interviews and three on-sites right out the gate. That had my confidence soaring.

My top three choices so far are Mintland Gum, Glexmann Super Glues, and Nimsler Frozen Foods. None may seem like a game-changing, cancer-curing tech-empire, but all of these small players have CEO positions within realistic reach. And once I reach the top, I can switch our R&D teams to any product I want. I'll make the next Nestlé. Selling Crunch Bars today. Simulating serotonin reuptake tomorrow.

Nimsler was the first of the three on-sites. They were interviewing me at their new headquarters in Doot-in-Root, Pennsylvania. It's a town smaller than a small town about four hours from Cincinnati. It's PA-rural which means cornfields and forests checkered side-by-side. Besides Nimsler, the other factories here are unoccupied and decaying. They're crumbling monuments to outdated industries waiting to be reclaimed by the growing cityscapes to the east and west.

Nimsler treated me like a rock star. They paid for my rental car and booked me a one-night stay at the Doot-in-Root Motel & Lodge. I reached the motel by 6PM on the night before my interview. The motel wasn't as dilapidated as the surrounding town, but that's not to say it was fancy. It was a single-story structure in the shape of a large L. No hallways, no commons; just two dozen rooms bordering a parking lot.

I checked in at the main office where the two arms of the L intersected. I told them my name and got the keys to my room, 12B. The manager pointed me to the row of rooms parallel to the highway. My room would be at the very end. I had to wheel my luggage past the front entrance to every other room between mine and the office. I examined the numerous occupants that stood outside their quarters. Most were outside to smoke and one was trying to get a better signal on her cell phone. None of them made any effort to move out of my way as I wheeled my suitcase around them. They each ignored me, tending to their own devices, keeping their eyes on the highway in front of us.

When I got to my room, I was surprised to see Nimsler had booked me two beds by mistake. I claimed one for myself and laid out my suit for tomorrow on top of the extra. At this point, I considered jumping under the sheets and heading to bed early. It was a long drive and I was feeling the come down from all the coffee I'd drank. But as I plopped down on the mattress, I opened my eyes a little and caught the time on the digital clock on the nightstand. It was only six-thirty, and with my interview at nine in the morning, over twelve hours of sleep seemed slightly excessive.

I wondered if there was anything amusing I could do to kill some time. I could have played on my computer and made use of the free Wi-Fi, but something inside of me kept trying to coax me outside. I'd been so stuffy in college, I'd barely been able to celebrate my right as a 21-year old to enjoy a night out drinking. Considering I'd done so well acquiring all these interviews, I finally felt like I deserved to let off some steam. Considering Nimsler would be paying for all my food and beverage, this seemed like the perfect opportunity to blow some money on binge drinking.

The more I thought about it, the prospect of getting hammered in a small town was oddly enticing. Especially for someone like me who'd never traveled too far from home. I felt like I was in a sandbox simulation where no one knew me and the rules were murky. I was getting excited. My first thought was to head to the nearest bar and pick up whatever MILF took a liking to me. But with the lack of these facilities at the motel, that would require travel to some shady dive on the edge of town. Being so young, and not so intimidating, going alone could open up the possibility of danger.

Certainly, I'm not the only one interviewing, I thought. *Perhaps if I found another candidate, he, or even she, may accompany me for some fun.*

I stepped outside my door and took a better look at some of the occupants I'd passed. Unfortunately, none of them looked like the type. They weren't groomed or shaved properly for an interview in the morning. Plus, most looked too old to be filling an entry-level position.

That's when I heard the music. The type that my generation tends to play obnoxiously loud. I looked across the parking lot at the row of rooms perpendicular to my own. Three rooms down from the main office, I could see several gentlemen in nice suits standing outside their open door. They were blasting 90's hip-hop hits from inside, while they pumped a keg on their front step.

Coming from a college campus full of overindulging aggressives, I wouldn't normally crash a party in fear of intruding over a primitive's territory. But these men weren't guarding an exclusive frat party with a strict gender ratio. They were a small gang of all men that could use a willing participant. Their festivities spilled out through their open door suggesting that the rest of the motel may join-in if they pleased.

I took their bait. I crossed through the parking lot and was immediately noticed by one of the gentlemen out front. He was unusually tall, six and a half feet, but his body bore little width in reciprocation. As he filled a plain white mug with beer from the keg, he stared at me through a pair of thick black sunglasses.

As I closed in, the man greeted me with a welcoming smile. "Hello stranger, how's it hangin'." Despite us being on the exterior, his voice had a strange reverberation surrounding it, as though his hand were cupped over his lips. "Would you care for a drink?" The tall man lifted his frail arm upwards and held the keg's spicket over my head. I was worried he was about to douse me. "Open wide."

I stepped back from under his aim. "I'll take a drink... but maybe with a cup?"

The man formed an open smile. His yellow teeth displayed a weakness in his hygiene. The lanky man pointed his long arm into the interior of their motel room. "Help yourself."

I walked inside to find two more gentleman conversing beside the sound system. They dressed in the same black suit as the man out front, but in appropriate sizes for their diverse body types. The shortest of the three was swaying drunkenly beside the speakers, while the other, the widest of the three, seemed to be selecting a song on the attached phone. I asked the short one where I may get a mug like theirs. His head turned upwards to face me, but I couldn't see his eyes. Looking down at him, his face was obscured by the brim of a black trilby tipped downward over his forehead.

"We took all the, the... all the mugs out of our cabinet," said the short man. This man's voice had the same strange echo as the tall man outside, but it was far more slurred. I could smell the alcohol rising out of his throat. "Do you have a rup... rup... room, here?"

I nodded.

"Then go get your own!" shouted the short man. As he waved his arm towards the door, he almost tipped over from the force of his own swing. The portly man beside him reached over and saved the short man from falling.

"You don't have to get your own," said the portly man, setting his friend back up straight. "There's some paper cups under our sink. Feel free to indulge."

"Thanks," I replied, trying not to stare at the portly man's strange hairstyle. Long black bangs hung all the way to the top of his nose, like a teenager's dark phase. "Are you guys just in town for the day?" I called out as I rummaged through the supplies hidden beneath their sink.

The portly man nodded. "We have a bunch of meetings all through the evening."

I grabbed a soft, plastic cup usually used for rinsing after brushing. I closed their sink's cabinet and stared at the portly man in confusion. "You're pregaming a business deal? Or is this some kind of conference?"

"We're here for The Cove!" shouted the short man, flailing his drink in the air. It spritzed onto the phone laying on the speakers. The portly man grabbed the device and dried it off with the wing of his blazer.

"The Cove? Are you talking about a tradeshow?" I asked. "Do you guys sell yachts or something?"

"Oh no, no," chuckled the portly man. "It's a strip club, my friend. You're more than welcome to join us."

"Really?" I exclaimed. That was quite the nice surprise. A strip club could be exactly what I was looking for. A little shady, a little gross, a lot of booze. I smiled and held out my hand. "The names Nathan. Nathan Lin. Yourself?"

"Oh! It's right here," the man pointed to a nametag on his jacket. I noticed the tag earlier, but I thought it was utter gibberish at first glance.

"How... how do you pronounce that?"

"Like Ste, then Ven. Ste-ven." He enunciated over the loud music blasting behind us.

"Just... Steven?" I repeated back to him. He nodded, but the nametag on his chest didn't seem to match. Several of the consonants had umlauts overtop of them and the e's looked more like 6's. "Is that Icelandic spelling?"

"No! No... it's just southern."

"Oh..." I shrugged. "So then, who are your friends?"

Steven pointed to the short one. His name was Boonie. And the tall one outside was Raphael. "There's also Mike but he went out to get some cigars. He's not much of a drinker, so he'll be our DD for the night..." Steven went suddenly quiet and asked me to do the same.

We could hear Raphael outside slurping loudly on the head of his beer. Footsteps were fast approaching him from the parking lot. They were men's slip-ons; their rubber heels were banging against the asphalt at a manic pace.

"what the fuck!" shouted someone from afar.

"Oh... speak of the devil," said Steven pointing towards the door to their room. Raphael was violently shoved inside, his arm grasped tightly by a fourth man in a suit. I stared at his nametag. It didn't look a thing like Mike, in fact it looked more like braille interspersed with mirrored wing-dings, but I could tell from the very sober, very agitated glance, this was the DD for a bunch of obnoxious drunks.

"God dammit, Steve," growled Mike. "If these two can't stand up straight they won't fucking let us in. I told you not to let them get too drunk!"

"Raphy?" called out Steven. "How much did you drink?"

Raphael's head drooped. "beer."

Steven frowned.

Mike threw Raphael hard into Boonie. They both collided with an *oomph* and fell into a pile on the carpet where they both began to moan in discomfort. With his hand free, Mike reached into his grocery bag and tossed a pouch of coffee grounds at Steven. "There's a coffee drip in the closet, go plug it in and get to work!" demanded Mike. Mike then turned his attention to me. His eyes had a strange sheen overtop of them, although they were made from plastic. And the frosty blue color of his retinas seemed unreal.

"Are those... colored contacts?" I asked.

"Who the fuck is this genius?" barked Mike, glaring at me with rage.

"Uh..." Steven stuttered. "He's just a... drinking buddy. He's staying the night here too, right?" Steven turned to me for confirmation.

I nodded. "Got an interview in the morning. Couldn't get to sleep."

"Well we're not sleeping, here," warned Mike. "We're going to be up all night working."

I frowned. "So then... no Cove?"

"Not till we're done at The Show," said Mike.

"What product are you showing?" I asked.

"It's another strip club!" shouted Steven, pulling the carafe from under the coffee maker. It was done brewing. He ran it over to his friends on the floor and helped them drink it straight from the pot. "We've got four clubs we've got to hit before morning. First The Show. Then The Cove. Then The Lounge. Then finally the big finish at Almighty Al's Sequin & Leather Cabaret."

"And there's no return till it's all finished," warned Mike. "So if you're not prepared for all four, you better be comfortable walking yourself home."

Four clubs did seem a bit excessive, but I was eager to try excess for once in my life. I really wanted this. As I'd reached my senior year, I began to regret some of the fun I'd turned down throughout college. I felt I'd passed on a lot of risk I might have enjoyed. I felt like, for all that output, I definitely earned more than just a nice job or an interview. I earned this night.

I helped Steven try to sober up Raphael and Boonie, while Mike huffed on one of his cigars outside trying to calm his nerves. After a substantial amount of caffeine worked into their heads,

Raphael and Boonie were able to lift themselves up without our help.

"Great," groaned Boonie. "I'm starting to feel sober again."

"There's still half a keg outside," grinned Raphael. "We can fix that."

"No. No. Wait till we're in the club," begged Steven. "Mike's concerned."

"For no reason," laughed Boonie. "This isn't the city. I doubt there'll even *be* a doorman."

"I know. I know," said Steven softly. "Just... humor the guy. You won't have to wait too long to drink again. The first club should be open in like fifteen minutes."

When Mike was done with his cigar, we followed him out to the car and piled into the back two rows of a Chrysler Pacifica. The drive to the first show was only ten minutes. We passed by a diner and a half-dead strip mall along the way. By the time we parked, The Show had just opened its doors and started letting people in. Being a relatively desolate area, there wasn't much of a line to get in. There was a doorman, though, despite Boonie's suggestion. But he only stopped to check me, being the only party member that looked to be under 35. By the time I passed inspection, the other guys had already found their seats. Steven, Raphael, and Boonie had all sat around the main stage, while Mike found a table near the bar. I walked to the floor seats and sat in the empty space beside Boonie.

"Do you need any ones?" asked Boonie, fanning out a dozen or so singles. His breath shot notes of ginseng and vodka into my nose. Looking down at his elbow rest, Boonie already had two empty cups in front of him. And his third drink was half empty.

"You drink fast," I said with surprise.

"It's just to break my twenty," he smiled. Boonie folded his ones back into a neat stack and split it in two, giving me half. "That should be *eck* enough... as long as you don't tip the ugly ones."

"Please. Tip. Everyone!" scolded Steven from the other side of Boonie. "If you sit up front, you tip. Them's the rules. And we can't risk getting thrown out."

"fine..." frowned Boonie. "I'll go split another twenty. That way you can at least tip the good ones two dollars. It still makes the statement clear... you want something while I'm up? SoBe & Vodkas are 1$ special right now."

I nodded. I'd ended up having five or six of these as the night progressed. Boonie wasn't kidding about the questionable quality of these strippers. But as the drinks flowed and my inhibitions narrowed, I found myself enjoying a one-eyed hooker's breasts in my face. I slipped the dollar under her eye patch. She winked at me with her good eye.

"Just wait," Boonie threw his arm around and held me in close. "At the end of the night is Al's. It's not too far from Harrisburg... the girls drive in from the city and they're *waaaay* hotter."

"Oh really," I said drunkenly.

"Al's is... it's just incredible. And if you don't like a girl... you can go to another. There're four stages! One for every fetish."

"There's only four fetishes?"

"Well yeah," assured Boonie. "Leather. Pregnant. Ethnic. And cowboys."

I nodded. That sounded right.

"Boys!" Mike suddenly appeared between our faces. He latched his hands tightly onto our shoulders. It startled me and sobered me up a bit. "Leaving in five minutes. Next stop is twenty minutes way. If you need to piss... Do it. Now." he said sternly. Mike then disappeared and repeated the message verbatim to Raphy and Steve. He then pulled out a cigar, popped back down at his table in the back of the club and puffed patiently. His face stared vacantly at the center stage.

"Why does he even go out with you guys if he just sits at the table the whole time? Is he just shy?"

Boonie shrugged. "None of us actually have to interact with the strippers. Our job is just to see them in action whether it's up close or from afar... but it's-*eh* fun, easy assignment! Not all of us get those. So, we have *smph*-fun with it, while we can. We could be transferred any *eck* day."

"Transferred to what?"

"Some other sin," shrugged Boonie. He then stood up from his seat and motioned for me to follow him. He led me through the club to the bathroom near the entrance. We stood side by side at the urinals and relieved ourselves. Boonie kept his head forward as he explained further, "Before this. I used to be in false idol worship. It was way more serious. And there was too much long-distance travel. It ruined travel for me! I used to love vacation, now I hate even the thought of planes."

"So wait, your job is... witnessing sins?"

Boonie nodded and buttoned up his fly. He waited for me to button mine before looking me in the eye again.

"How'd you get that job?" I laughed. "I want in."

Boonie shook his head. "Sorry, but you've got to be born into it." Boonie lifted the brim of his hat, removing the dark shadow that always obscured his eyes.

If I hadn't been under the influence, I would have started shaking. His eyes weren't human. Not even close. They were bright yellow, with several golden rings concentric with a tiny black pupil in the center. The eyes bulged out of their sockets and rotated wildly, scanning the room independent of one another, like a chameleon.

"You're all like this?" I asked.

Boonie nodded. "Listen, I hope this doesn't change our relationship... despite how it looks, we're completely harmless... unless you're a stripper of course."

The bathroom door slammed open and Mike rushed in to get us going. He caught Boonie in the act of showing me his reptilian peepers. "Exposing yourself in a strip club bathroom," grimaced Mike. "You disgust me, Boonie. Let's get the fuck going. Is the mortal still coming or did you break his little brain?"

I shook my head, "A few minutes ago, I just let a grandmother touch me intimately. I don't think a pair of googly eyes are going to ruin my night."

We left the bathroom and headed out to the car. On the way to The Cove, I shut my eyes and tried to process what exactly I'd just discovered. I ran it over in my mind again and again. I couldn't make heads or tails of whether this night was as liberating as I first thought. On one hand, I stumbled over something wholly rare. On the one night I let loose, I end up palling around with a band of fucking lizard people.

But on the other hand, this was now just another day at the office for these creeps. And I was practically an unpaid intern shadowing some old men on their daily grind. That's a sad way to see it, but it was true. Their drinking was just a distraction to make their routine a little more bearable. No different than the bosses who sip from a scotch stuffed under the desk.

By the time we reached The Cove, my enthusiasm had begun to take a bit of a downturn. I decided not to sit up front this time with the rest of the drinkers. Instead, I decided to sit with the shy kids and pulled up a seat across from Mike. He stared at me through his glossy lenses. "I'd rather you not sit there," he said blowing smoke in my face. "You might distract me from the girls."

"Mike, how do you keep so focused without having any fun?" I asked sincerely. Mike stared up at the stage and checked that there were no performers yet. He then looked back at me.

"It's like how you humans get a paycheck. We get paid with a continued existence. That alone keeps me going. It's like breathing. It's the things that keep you alive that become autonomic."

"Why's that not enough for them?" I said pointing at the drunken members of our party fetching their drinks before the show starts.

Mike lowered the cigar from his lips. "I guess they can enjoy it. So why not? But me... I don't really like girls that way."

"Oh." I sat up straight in my chair. "Does that mean you all switch roles when you get to a Chippendales?"

Mike shook his head. "Either way, I don't like strippers. They're sinners, and sinners need to pay." Mike's face broke out into a long creepy smile. "If you really want to know where I get my job satisfaction, it's knowing that, because of me, sinners don't get away with their crimes. That's what keeps me buzzed. And it always has, long before SCOUT."

"SCOUT?" I questioned.

Mike nodded while ashing his cigar. "It stands for Strip Club Observation UniT. There're units assigned to each of the numerous sins of mankind. Before SCOUT, I tracked rapists in ROUT. And before that, I tracked litterers. And before that, I tracked black metal."

"Wait. That last one is kind of cool," I smiled. "You got to go to rock concerts for a living?"

Mike hissed at me. "Don't call them *concerts*," he snarled piously. "It's unholy."

Mike glanced back at the stage and refused to give me anymore more attention. The show was starting and, therefore, Mike's shift. Mike kept his eyes frozen in place pointed towards the stage.

We only got through two of the dancers before the lights unexpectedly came on at 11. The DJ shut off the music abruptly and came in over the microphone to apologize. White Lettuce and Kisha Cold hadn't shown up for work, so Derrah Muffin and Vitamin Ultra would be filling the time slots. These two had gone on earlier and would simply be repeating their acts.

"There's no point in seeing it twice," said Steven.

"So then, we're done ahead of schedule!" exclaimed Raphy.

"Which means there's time to stop for food!" shouted Boonie.

The three dragged me from my seat over to Mike's table, where they begged him incessantly for fast food. He gave in just to stop the annoyance. I could tell the night was gradually wearing down Mike. He was putting up less of a fight, trying to conserve his energy.

"I'll take you, but we stop at the first thing that comes up," grumbled Mike. This turned out to be a Sheetz five minutes west of The Cove. Sheetz was a staple in Pennsylvania. It's a gas station with above average fast food and the best egg salad sandwiches on the East Coast.

I ordered their appetizer platter. That's twelve nuggets, six mozzarella sticks, four fried mac & cheese squares, and a small cup of curly fries. I then bought a red slushie to help wash it down.

After ordering, I took my receipt and waited for them to call my number. I saw the rest of my crew through the window, they were standing outside the restaurant discussing something in deep detail. But as I stormed out the door and approached the men, I noticed something looked off about them. At first, I thought I was just being drunk, but the longer I stared it became increasingly obvious. This wasn't SCOUT.

"More googly eyes?!" I exclaimed, embarrassingly. It seemed my drinking had left my lips permanently loose till I got some sleep.

"I'm sorry?" muttered one of the men in suits. "Did you just call us 'googly eyes'?" This particular man looked a lot like Raphael. He was hiding his strange peepers with a pair of dark black sunglasses. The only difference was in their hair style. While Raphael had a greasy rat tail, this man was entirely bald.

"Sorry," I said, covering my lips with my palm. "I'm here with another group of... observers. I've only just become aware of your existence. I'm shocked to see even more in the same night."

"That's understandable. We're always around you mortals. But until we're properly introduced, we just kind of blend into the background."

"It's the suits," laughed an observer with a casino visor perched over his forehead. "It's human camouflage." This observer came up to my side and pointed through the window of the Sheetz. "So, who's in there?" he asked me.

"SCOUT," I said, pointing at my crew. They were sitting at a table just behind the divider between the checkout line and the dining room.

"SKOUT... as in serial killers?" guessed the man in the visor.

I shook my head. "Strip clubs."

"Oh... with a C," said the visor man nodding slowly. He then spun around away from the window and pointed to his men. They were all wearing various sizes and shapes of suits. And they all had their eyes impaired by some mundane means. "I'm with SHOUT."

"My turn to guess," I jested. "You guys do... selling heroine?"

The men all shook their heads. Visor guy spoke up, "Something more dangerous."

"Self-harm?" I guessed.

"Pretty much the exact opposite," called out an observer in violet teashades.

I shrugged. "I'm out of guesses, guys."

The bald observer with sunglasses bent down to my ear so I could hear him say it softly. "*shootings.*"

"Guns?" I muttered. I looked over my shoulder through the wall of windows lining the Sheetz. "Guns."

Shots rang out at two different rhythms. They overlapped. One was an Uzi directed towards the kitchen staff in the back. The other was a semi-automatic pistol firing point blank into the two cashiers.

The shooter was a frail man in tattered jeans and no shirt. He looked like he was starving; I could see his heart beating through his rib cage. His motives were unclear from his loud ramblings. "Making money... making money!" he hollered. "Michigan Containment Device 1986. Your governor works for the project!"

The shooter spun around and pointed his gun at SCOUT. They looked completely helpless. Poor Boonie ducked under the table with Mike, while Steven struggled to squeeze his large body out of his seat. Raphael sat patiently awaiting death; either entirely at peace with his coming demise or so blackout drunk he couldn't react.

I shrieked. I balled up my fists and started pounding on the window. I needed to shout something that would get the shooter's attention. "Heeeey!" I screamed. His mission was an illogical mystery, so I wasn't sure what phrase would bother him. There's always some degree of homophobic insecurity marbled into these ideologies, so I went for the low hanging fruit. "Fuck you, faggot!" I flipped up my middle fingers and pressed them on the glass.

The shooter's head turned to see me cursing him. Roaring in anger, he fired a burst of three shots. It tore through the window just to the left of me taking down a SHOUT agent right beside me. I quickly leapt to the grass below the window out of the shooter's range. He kept firing. More bullets burst through the window. I kept my head covered so the falling glass wouldn't cut me. When the shattering stopped I could hear the gunman's weapon still clicking. He'd run out of ammo.

I heard him shout some incoherent speech about the Senator killing his daughter. Then I heard a car screeching away. I refused to stand back up till the sound of the engine was too far down the road to hear.

When I thought it was safe I got up off the sidewalk and looked through the window. One by one I watched the agents of SCOUT pick themselves up off the floor. I was happy to see they'd all been uninjured.

As Mike lifted himself up off the floor, he sneered, "What the fuck did you do!" Mike was furious. He charged at me, coming outside and lifting me off of my feet by the neck. "Look what you did!"

"I..." I could barely breathe through Mike's superlevel strength. "I - saved - you."

Mike tossed me down a few feet from the Sheetz's outer wall. I landed beside what seemed to be discarded clothes. It was a black and white suit, completely emptied and spread out like someone had suddenly disappeared from inside it. There was small lump beneath the back of the sports coat. Mike bent out and reached inside, pulling out the cause of the bump.

He pulled me up off the ground so fast I almost vomited. I held my head stationary and tried to focus my eyes on what Mike held in front of me. "It's a lizard," I said.

"It's SHOUT," growled Mike, "and they're fucking dead because of you." Mike held the chameleon by its uncurled tail and shoved it in my face. Its webby hands fell lifeless towards the ground.

I looked around me and realized that none of the members of SHOUT had survived the shooter's spray. Four emptied suits laid just outside the broken window. All of them containing an agent reduced to, what I assumed to be, their original form. I wanted to ask how exactly that worked (were they born as lizards, then later got employed?) but I figured this wasn't a good time for uncovering lore.

"Steve!" called Mike. "You make sure the mortal doesn't go anywhere." Mike began reaching into all the pockets of the discarded pants. As he pulled out wallets and keys he tossed them aside.

Steven came up beside me and grabbed lightly onto my arm. "You screwed up, kid. You screwed up bad."

"But you're alive because of me!" I griped.

Mike stood up from one of the suits with a cell phone in his hand. He nodded as he played with the buttons. The device was still functional. "One appointment left for the night. Two hours from now," Mike gripped the phone tightly till the veins on the back of his hand stood out. I thought he was going to snap it in two.

I begged for forgiveness. "I'm not sure what I did wrong, here."

"You killed the wrong people," said Steve sullenly.

"Because of you a murder is gonna' go unwitnessed in two hours. There's no way Satan can get a new crew out here that fast. Chameleons aren't a native species. It'll take too long to fly them in from Florida..."

"So what?" I hollered. "Who cares if Satan misses one murder? Can't he just watch something else for fun."

"Kid's a fucking moron," huffed Mike. "We don't watch this shit for entertainment..."

"If we don't see it," sighed Steve. "They don't go to Hell."

"Wait. You guys are sending strippers to Hell?" I whined. "I don't know if they deserve that..."

"Well what about a murderer?" snarled Boonie, he'd finished his cheese fries and came waddling outside. There was orange slime still stuck to the corners of his mouth. "I think all of us would have preferred a murderer get eternal hellfire over a couple working girls. But you knocked on that window, you fucked with fate."

"I didn't know he'd kill them," I pleaded.

"Well then, you're just going to have make up for your little mistake," said Mike. He reached into his pocket and tossed me the cell phone he'd excavated from the empty suits.

There was an event blinking of the main screen. 1:33AM. 42 Almond Road. Baker Township.

"I can't do this." I whimpered.

"Oh yes you can," said Mike with a tiny grin. "I didn't see you have a single drink at the last bar. You're in way better shape than *my* men. After all, you already dodged some bullets."

"You could come with me?" I begged Mike. "You haven't been drinking either!"

"Al's got four stages. We need all hands if we're gonna' witness all the girls."

I stared at the phone. Tears fell from my eyes onto the screen. "I'm scared." I turned to Steve. "Please don't let him do this."

Steven turned his head to the ground and walked back into the tattered Sheetz where Raphael was practically blacking out on the ground. Steven picked Raphy up and brushed straw paper and crumbs of his coat.

"We've got thirty minutes till our show," continued Mike checking the time on his Mont Blanc. He lowered his wrist and pointed towards the car. "Given it didn't get hit in the crossfire. I'll drop you off. Then we'll pick you up after Al's closes."

I cringed. "But... but I don't have the eyes. I thought I had to be born into the profession."

"Hey genius," Mike snapped his finger and pointed at the phone in my hand. "Record it. The boys and I will see it when you're done."

"And that counts?"

Mike smiled. "Yeah. It counts. We have some units that solely work from home, watching every porn that's ever touched the internet." Mike chuckled. "God, wouldn't that have been easy to replace. You really chose the worst unit to kill."

On the ride to Baker Township, I spent the whole trip looking down at my knees. They were covered in dirt from when I dropped below the shooter's aim. I'd barely dodged those bullets. The first couple shots had missed me by pure luck. And now, I'd have to do it all over again.

"Can I get more info on my mission?" I begged the guys. "Like the *who* part?"

"The phone gives you all the info you need upfront. If it's not listed, it's not necessary," explained Mike. "When I worked for ROUT, I'd never even get an address. I'd get the name of a park and a landmark near the scene of the crime. If I was lucky, I'd get the color of the rapist's mask."

"Who sends you all this intel?" I questioned.

Steve, squeezed into the center seat beside me, leaned into my ear. "*Angels,*" he whispered.

"Angels as in... Satan?" I wondered.

"*Yeah. They're like Satan,*" nodded Steven. "*They're all exiled and trapped beneath the Earth.*"

"I mean... so we think," spoke up Raphael. I'd barely heard from him most of the night, so it was surprising to hear his voice. His meal must have sobered him up enough to speak again. "We really only know as much about the afterlife as you mortals do. None of us have actually been to Hell. Or talked to Satan. We just follow what the cell phones tell us to do and that keeps us alive.

The *why* part has always been just been assumed amongst us. It's legend."

"It's only legend if you don't have faith," growled Mike, rubbing on the black layer of foam on his steering wheel. "*I know what's real.*" Mike slammed on the breaks, sending Steven flying up into the front seats. The middle seat didn't come with a seat belt.

"We're here," said Mike. He unlocked the car doors. "Get out!" he commanded. I did as I was instructed.

As I stepped out of the vehicle, I asked them all, "What if I just ran away right now and never saw you guys again?"

Mike coiled up his pointer finger and set his thumb over top of it. He touched his knuckle to the window beside the driver's seat. "We know where you're staying tonight and where you parked your car..." Mike flicked his window and shattered it into pieces. "Do as instructed or we'll fucking kill you in the night. Go to the cops and you'll find they won't believe you. Leave it all behind and you'll find creating a new identity is fairly difficult in 2019. Especially for a cushy little millennial like yourself. You'll lose your degree and die homeless on the streets. Your options are so very limited, so I suggest you follow our orders and get this night over with so you can move on with your life." Mike busted out a warm smile while shutting his eyes blissfully. He raised his cell phone up in the air. "I'll be keeping in touch."

Mike pressed down hard on the gas and sped the car away, making no effort to keep my arrival at the residence clandestine. I stood alone for a moment considering all that had just transpired. I held my breath and looked off in the distance. The residence I was to invade was a beautiful two-story country home in the middle of a vast field of alfalfa. Despite the late hours, the lights were all on. I decided to approach the residence from its side. There would be less windows facing my direction.

From the side of the house, I sidestepped along the wall and peered around the corner. The front porch was empty. I climbed over the railing as carefully as I could. I tried not to put too much pressure on the panels. I got beneath the nearest window and slowly rose my head till I could make out the homeowners on the other side.

There were two. An old man and his wife. Both carried firearms tucked into their belts. That made it hard to tell who the victim would be and who would be the shooter. I suppose it didn't matter as long as I got both on camera.

I pulled out the phone and activated the backlight. There was a new message on the screen. A text from an unknown number, 305-501-3251. It read: [Out the car. In the club.] It was Mike. I added his name into the contacts.

I messaged back: [sending perps]. I clicked "attach" and selected "new video". The camera on the back of the phone began to record. I raised it up until the wife appeared on the feed. She was sprawled out along the couch and footrest. I slowly panned left and got the husband into the shot. He was reclined peacefully in his leather chair.

I paused the shot and lowered the phone. The footage wasn't perfect. Without the flash on, it all looked murky. But their faces were sharp, and their guns could be seen resting in their holsters. I decided to send the message.

Thirty seconds later, I received two buzzes. [nice try] [need the moment the gun goes off].

Fuck. I didn't know it would have to be such a specific moment. That managed to make things even more nerve wracking. I checked the time. It was 12:50. I had a little over half an hour till the shooting. I was anxious and I didn't feel like waiting. I was also freezing. It was the middle of November and all I had on was a loose button down with no undershirt.

I tried to keep distracted by keeping my eyes on the couple inside. I paid attention to their every move. Gradually, they're behavior transitioned. They changed from relaxed television viewing to a heated argument. It seemed as though the setup to the kill was beginning to unfold.

"It's your responsibility," shouted the wife. I watched her hands to see if they reached for her gun. But they stayed put, holding onto a pile of snacks in her lap.

"That's just cold!" replied the husband. His hands kept grasped onto the arms of his chair.

"You're treating your family like dirt!" screamed the lady. My heart raced as her arm lifted up! But it just landed on the remote and shut off the tv.

"Don't guilt me dammit!" The husband reached his hands up towards his belt. Close, but no cigar. The husband found his pockets and buried his hands inside. Harmless defensive body language.

The wife got off her couch and flipped up onto her feet. She shook her head in disappointment, then hurried into the adjacent kitchen. She walked up to a door beside their fridge and opened it wide. That's when I saw her descend into a basement level.

The husband was all that was left in my line of sight. For a moment, he considered staying put, but in the end, he gave in and followed his wife. He leapt from his seat and walked into the kitchen. He stood at the doorway to the basement and stopped in his tracks. I watched as his hand raised and, finally, brushed against his holster. It was a subtle gesture, but it's meaning was clear. He was preparing to reach for it. The idea of murder was running through his head.

The husband disappeared down the steps, leaving me with no one left to witness. I checked the time. Fifteen minutes left till the murder would take place. I began to panic. I scaled down off the porch and rush around all four sides of the house looking for a cellar window. But there was nothing.

[they're out of sight. What do I do?] I delete the text before I bother sending it. There was no point. I could already guess the response I'd get. *Hurry up. Go inside.*

I cursed internally at the thought of breaking-in. The googly eyes may not have to worry about the law, but that's because most people don't know they exist. I, on the other and, am very real and very liable. But I had no choice.

I crawled up to the front door and tried to the turn the knob. No luck. It was locked. I walked back over to the window I'd been peering through. I grabbed its edges and gave it a little shake. The panel was loose. I pressed my hands on the glass and slid it upwards. I was relieved I'd found my entry, but the next part was going to suck. And there was no stopping it.

I stepped inside. Luckily, the floorboards were relatively silent to step on. I slowly walked over to the basement door. I peeped around the corner to make sure no one's standing at the bottom of the steps. The coast was clear.

I stood still for a moment at the top of the step. I examined the stairs closely. They were noisy; I could remember hearing every step the husband and wife had taken. I would have to be quieter, so I thought back to my childhood. I recalled my strategies for that game everyone played, 'red hot lava'. When descending a staircase, I would wedge myself between the walls to the left and right of the stairs and shimmy down without touching a single step.

I tried to repeat my strategy. I leaned my back against the wall on the left then placed my feet up on the strip of molding on the right. I shifted my weight around to test for any creaking., but my approach seemed solid. I began to descend, softly shimmying closer and closer to the basement floor.

At one point, the wall to the right of the stairs discontinued and a railing began. If I descended any further, I'd be exposed. I kept still and carefully took the phone back out of my pocket. I leaned a little to my left to position the camera right over top of the husband and wife. I was lucky; both their backs were turned away from me.

I turned on the camera app and started a new recording. I zoomed in on their waists; their holsters were empty and both their guns were drawn. But from their backs it was impossible to tell what they were aiming at. Surprisingly though, it wasn't each other.

They both began to fire over and over into their victim. They shot and they shot until their clips were emptied. I took advantage of the loud bangs and scurried up the stairs, ignoring any careful footing. I booked it over to the window I'd crawled through and leapt outside. Lying on my stomach, I tried to catch my breath with the painful Autumn air. When I could manage it, I sent the video over to Mike and rolled over onto my back. My head began to feel warm and I felt the veins beside my eyebrows quivering. Colors, ambers and purples, layered over the awning above me. I felt like I was going to pass out, but before I could lose consciousness, a loud bang to my right shook me out of my half-sleep and sent my arms folding over my face.

I whimpered; nothing in life prepared me for the anticipation of a bullet cutting through my face. Careful planning, meticulous study, and extremes in adolescent self-control were supposed to prevent any such experience from ever occurring. I had no context for which to react; the event had never played out in my head.

And yet, I felt no pain. Perhaps my nerves had been damaged with the wound. I kept reaching all around my body looking for a wet spot, but nothing came up. My head was one piece. My body was fully functioning. I could stand myself up off the ground. But I only got to my knees. Just enough height to peer into the window to my right. The husband had shut it tightly. His wife was nowhere to be seen, but he stood crying in the middle of their living room. He wiped the tears way with his hands and left the room. Shutting off the lights behind him.

He'd shut the window in such a humor; he hadn't seen me laying only inches below it.

Two buzzes in my pocket suddenly went off and shook me senseless. I had to get a grip. It was just the cellphone. I stuck my trembling hand into my pocket and reached for the phone. I had two new messages from Mike.

[victim]

[victim?]

I bit down hard on my thumb nail. The footage still wasn't a good enough. I needed the fucking victim too. The thought of going back in made me want to vomit.

I held my hands back up to the window and pressed my weight against it. I pushed upwards but it wouldn't budge this time. When the old man shut it, he locked it closed.

I checked the front door again. It was still locked. I shivered nervously. I needed *another* entryway. I had no experience in theft and couldn't think of anything obvious. I wondered where most people would forget to secure themselves. I had one idea, but it wouldn't be easy.

If they left one window unlocked, there'd probably be more. Especially those on the second floor where one wouldn't normally be so careful.

I leapt onto the railing bordering the front porch. I was lucky to be lightweight or the bars would have cracked as I lunged upwards onto the awning. Using a source of adrenaline I'd rarely tapped into it, I was scaling the couple's house like a professional heist. From the awning I was able to hoist up onto the first slope of their roof, then quietly slide over to a window to my left. Reaching out to the window, a light touch sent the glass panels folding inwards on a hinge. I peered in. It was too dark to make out most of the decor, but there didn't seem to be anybody inside.

I toppled through the window and landed on something hard inside. It knocked the wind out of me. Feeling around its sides, it seemed to be a big plastic crate. I slid off of its roof and tumbled onto the floor. I landed on a pile of wet rubbery items laid out on a tiny rug. My impact condensed one of the objects and as I stood up it reinflated, letting out a long, loud squeak.

That small noise was enough to call for the attention of the couple. I heard someone dashing down the hallway from their bedroom. I quickly threw myself inside a nearby closet for cover. As the old man came charging down the hallway. He paused before entering. I heard him let out a long, anguished sigh before stepping inside.

As the lights came on, I could see through the grates of the closet door. It seemed I'd entered into a guest bedroom converted to house a family pet. I could see that the box I'd landed on was actually a large kennel. And that the plastic object that had sounded was a squeaky toy.

The wife suddenly rushed in behind her husband. She scolded him. "You're just hearing things!" she snarled. "It's just your head processing it all. Please. Come back to bed."

"I think... I'm hearing ghosts," said the old man sullenly. He sighed again, then followed his wife out of the room. That was my cue to step outside the closet. I waited until I heard them shut their bedroom door, then carefully slipped into the upstairs. I tiptoed over the staircase and laid out flat. I slid down the steps like a slide, allowing my body weight to be spread evenly along several stairs at a time. This prevented any creaking as I quickly descended to the first floor. When I reached the bottom, a noise called my attention back to the top of the stairs. I quickly shot up onto my feet and felt around at my pockets. *Fuck.* My phone was gone.

Bzzzz. Bzzzz. Bzzzz. The cell phone's buzzing was echoing all throughout the house. It must have slipped out when I'd fallen onto that kennel. It was vibrating against something metal nearby, amplifying the noise for the whole house to hear.

"Now you hear *that* don't you?!" shouted the old man from his bedroom. I heard the springs of his bed, then the slam of his door. I quickly ran away towards the basement. I was running out of time. It was a race against his realizations.

I scurried through their kitchen using their shouting upstairs to mask my moves. I opened their door to the basement and slid down on my back. I then spun around towards where the shooting took place and sprinted forward into the darkness of the cellar. I began to feel around with my hands and knees on the floor. I was looking for a cold body or a wet patch of blood. Eventually, I found both. Although, the body wasn't as clammy as I'd imagined. It was more fuzzy. I squeezed the parameters of the victim from top to bottom till I realized what I was dealing with.

They'd killed a dog. *Their* dog, I presume. I could feel the bullet wounds running along its skin. It had been shot a dozen or so times. Without my phone, there was only one way left to show the body to the observers. I'd have to carry it to them. Thankfully it wasn't a full grown human or I'd never be able to carry it.

I slid my arms under the dead animal. My sleeves immediately absorbed a fair amount of cold blood into their fabric. It made me shiver in disgust. I lifted with my legs and hoisted the dog all the way up and over my shoulder. As its head hung down over my back, I felt a trail of fluid begin to leak out of its mouth and down my spine. I fought the urge to vomit and began my final charge out of the house. But as I reached the top of the stairs, I noticed that the kitchen lights had been turned on and the couple was standing with their guns drawn.

Click-click-click. Click. Click. ...Click. The wife and husband pulled their triggers, but they'd forgotten to reload after pumping their pet full of lead. The front door to their house was behind me; all I'd have to do was outrun them through their living room. But for some reason, I began to consider their back door instead. It was right at the couple's back.

At this time, my trust in my risk analysis was definitely broken. I measured the risk-reward ratio of tonight's debauchery all wrong, but there's some evidence that it may not be all my fault. After all, before tonight, reality was a constant and now it's suddenly become a variable where humans are only sometimes human and damnation needs to be considered a real possibility. I guess there really was no predicting tonight's outcomes no matter what I did.

But I was sort of proud of myself for just making it this far. For once, I dove head first into a bunch of new challenges and uncomfortable situations. And I survived it all with no experience in the unknown whatsoever. Suddenly, I felt a second wind of confidence pushing against my wings. In that moment, I began to believe I was going to make it out alive.

I trusted myself and thought things over. The couple didn't look sickly for their age. If I ran for their front door, they might catch me before I make it. Especially since I have the weight of their dog on my shoulders. Instead, the better plan of action was to go for the back door. I would have to ram through them.

With a hard twist, I flung their dead animal across my collar bone like a mink scarf and held the dog lengthwise in front of my face. The dog was a big, golden retriever with lots of body length. I charged forward through the center of the couple. Each end of the dead pooch clotheslined the couple. Its ass smacked hard into the wife's chin knocking her to the floor and its skull head butted with the husband knocking him unconscious. I then slammed the dog's body so hard into the backdoor, the damn thing burst right off the hinges. The impact sent a spritz of dog blood up into my face. I felt it dripping over my ear as I went flying forward out into the field of corn the couple had planted in their backyard.

I just kept running and running, using the dog to shield my face from corn stalks whipping at my head. I didn't stop sprinting till I reached a road on the other side of the field. By then, I felt like it was safe enough to take a breath.

It was a difficult journey home. I was warned it would be at the beginning of this adventure. I was hoping at some point Mike's car would pass me by. Without seeing them, I was worried I was going the wrong way. Every now and then, I'd hear sirens in the distance and think the cops were on my tail. I'm not sure if they ever really were though, they never passed me by. At several times on my trek I thought it might not be so bad to just get arrested and sleep the night off in jail. But eventually, I found my way back to The Show and my hopes returned. I knew our motel was just a half-hour walk down the road.

I made it back by sunrise. As I walked through the parking lot, I was pissed to see Mike's car parked in the lot. They must have taken a different route home. I used every last ounce of energy I had to lug the dead dog up to their motel room and pound its head on the door like a battering ram.

Being the only one to go to bed sober, I expected Mike to be awakened by my racket. But it was Raphael who answered my call instead. With an angry snarl, I shoved the dog into his arms and shouted. "There! You saw it."

"I'm sorry," said Raphael staring at the dog in confusion. "Do I, uh, know you?"

"Raphy, for fuck sake!" I growled in frustration. "I went to the strip club with y'all last night. I was right there beside you... the whole time!"

"Oh..." shrugged Raphy. "What's with the dog?"

"It's the fucking victim! I had to get it for you guys to witness!"

"Oh right... because SHOUT died," Raphy nodded, he was finally beginning to remember. "Mike told you to do this, didn't he?"

I nodded slowly, my neck aching with each subtle movement. It was nice to have the weight off of it, but my face was left drooping and defeated

"It's five in the morning," said Raphael checking his watch. "Say now, how long do you have till your interview?"

"four hours." I said softly, forcing the words from my dry, scratchy throat.

Raphael nodded. "Go change. And shower. Meet me back here, asap. Let me, please, buy you some breakfast... we need to talk."

I did as instructed. I couldn't really hurry, though. I just didn't have the energy. I had to sit in the shower cause my legs hurt so bad. I was worried if I tried to stand they'd slip out from under me on the cheap linoleum.

At the point, I realized I wouldn't be getting sleep before my interview. I moved on and started banking on Plan B: caffeine.

Raphy got behind the wheel of Mike's car. I joined him up front. Raphy turned to me as he turned the ignition and asked if there was anywhere I'd like to go in particular. I didn't really care. Anything with some coffee was appreciated.

We went with McDonald's since the Sheetz was closed for maintenance. I ordered a couple McMuffins along with my drink and sat down across from Raphy. He was nice enough to pay for my meal. He tried to smile a couple times while glaring at me, but he couldn't coax me into joining him. My night was surely nowhere near as fun as his own.

"Mike was our DD last night, but he's not our leader. I fear he may have given you that impression," explained Raphael. "He had no place telling you to fill-in for SHOUT. That was my call. And... I was too drunk to protect you. I'm sorry."

"Did... did I even help, then? Or was it all just a prank."

"No-no. You... you helped. It just wasn't supposed to be your responsibility. Mike just... well he claims he hates sinners, but really... he hates all mortals. Especially the ones he thinks are cute."

"Boonie and Steve were all for it, too."

"yeah well... Steven's a big suck-up. And Boonie's just a mean drunk."

"Jesus Christ... you know it might just have been satisfying if I were putting a real craz-o in the confines of Hell. But the couple I saw. They were just putting down a dog. It was missing tufts of fur and even some teeth. I think it was just sick."

Raphael shrugged. "Sometimes it's like the Sheetz shooter. Sometimes it's more like what you witnessed. They're all acts of wrath. That's a cardinal sin."

"It was a mercy killing!" I argued.

"That's an oxymoron. Like a 'just war'. Or a 'self-righteous suicide'. Intentions can't change a sin into a virtue. The rules are set in stone."

"But the rules are... bullshit. I mean what about those two gentlemen, huh?" I pointed to two early birds eating their breakfast not too far from where we were seated. These obese men were holding hands and smiling as they enjoyed a well-deserved breakfast of 75 McNuggets each. Behind them were a crew of observers watching them with deadly serious glances. They looked like vultures stalking an injured animal. "What does that crew cover?" I asked.

"Them?" Raphy looked closely at the observers' faces. "Pretty sure that's GOUT."

"Oh come on," I groaned. "How are you gonna' be friends with Mike and then be okay with those folks going to Hell for the same thing?"

Raphael rolled his eyes. "The G is for gluttony... not gay."

I lifted my palm to my face and sighed heavily. "I don't know if either really seems all that worth punishing... tell me. Will I at least stop seeing you guys, eventually? I'm sick of knowing whose getting judged."

"No. Once you become aware. We stick out forever."

"Are there more like me? Who've become aware?"

Raphael shook his head. "There's much more SHOUTs, ROUTs, and GENOUTs than there are SCOUTs. Most of us don't party hard on the job because we're witnessing real atrocities and we have to get up close and personal with psychopaths to do it. So, no, there's not a lot of opportunities besides SCOUT for mortals to really join in any fun. You came across a chance encounter. You're very much alone."

"God, but there's just so many of you! What about those guys?" I said, pointing at a crew right outside the restaurant. Their eyes had been pointed on me and Raphy since we started eating. "The fuck are those ones staring at?"

"That's definitely OOUT. They're basically internal affairs officers. They're following us around just in case I kill you. But don't worry, it's not set in stone. Observers are harder to predict than mortals. I, personally, don't think it's necessary to kill you. I don't want to be a sinner myself. And there's other ways to keep you quiet after all that you've witnessed. How about a reward?" Raphy pulled out a tablet from a satchel he had draped around his shoulder. Using a stylus, he started typing my name onto the screen. "Is this spelled correctly?"

I nodded with a suspicious look.

"Strippers are just a job, you know?" said Raphy.

"Yes, *I* know," I replied snidely. "*You're* the ones filing them to eternal damnation."

Raphy nodded. "That's my point. Mortals sin so carelessly in the pursuit of their occupation. Sometimes a sin is... just a job. It happens most to the ambitious ones... like you. If you're seeking a position at the top of society, I don't think you realize yet how much you'll sacrifice to hold onto that position. One day we're going to be watching you from your window when you don't think twice about ordering some waste to get thrown into the ocean... or outsource some child labor... or replace half your staff with touch screens and robots. You know, just the little things businessmen do every day. Well I just entered your name on a very exclusive listserv. And if your name ever comes up on someone's day planner, they'll miss your appointment on purpose. And whatever sin you commit goes unseen."

I lowered my head. I grabbed my food and tossed it all back into the bag it came in.

"It's a good reward, contingent upon your discretion... Do you understand that?"

I crinkled up the top of my bag, sealing in my food. I shoved it under my arm and jumped out my seat. "Why the fuck is it so easy to go to Hell?" I growled.

Raphael grabbed my arm before I could run away. I turned around to face him. His face changed to something serious. It reminded me of the kind of jaded glance Mike was stuck with. He stood up beside me and leaned in close to my ear. "Cause Heaven is sweet. And God won't share."

Pizza Crow IX

I got my old job back, which wasn't easy in this economy. I had to show them my protruding rib cage to get them to feel some pity on me. I can afford pizza again, but I'll tell you what, the work is still as shitty as it ever was. I still dream of ditching the corporate ladder for another good get-rich-quick scheme. I don't know why I want to do that to myself. I guess some of us are just addicted to opportunism.

I noticed I've been friendlier to birds, lately. I feed the pigeons in the park. I give bread to the ducks. I made a bird feeder outside my home. I'm not sure if it's the guilt I feel for killing off that poor crow or it's something more sinister.

Maybe I want to find another magic bird. Maybe I want to find another writing machine. Maybe I hope that one of these ducks trades me for this baguette with a haiku written on a napkin. But I doubt I'll ever be so lucky ever again.

I've spent a lot of time wondering where the crow's gifts came from. I'd tried to follow him on several occasions. I wanted to shake down whatever author was responsible for the pages and tell him to mature up! Write something not so god damn unusual for a change! But the crow flies high and fast, and there was never a chance I could keep up.

The furthest I'd ever chased the bird led me deep into the woods of central Illinois. But as I chased further and further into the dark, I noticed the world around me stopped making any sense. The air smelled like pasta boiling and the trees were growing bigger and bigger. Soon the sky itself began to shout obscenities down at me, and the stars appeared as mushrooms. I heard wild animals coming at me from all directions and the dirt began to feel like warm tar beneath my feet. The world itself became as surreal as the stories themselves until I could no longer press onward in fear that I too would become a pile of nonsense.

So then maybe that's it. Maybe the stories were forged in this nonsensical neck of the woods and so that's why the stories could never be anything more than abstract. The world from which these pages came from was a shapeless, formless blob. I shouldn't expect the material to diverge from its source. Instead, the wise thing to do is find a mundane story where mundane stories all come from. Mundane places.

So I found a dude at a coffee shop with a square jaw and a beanie. I offered to be his agent and push his political fiction to new heights he never thought possible. His book, Bania Theory, is a currently a best seller. And I'm finally rolling in dough.

Boring. Cheeseless. Sauceless. Pepperoni-and-Mushroomless. Plain-Jane, dough

Subscribe to OddFiction.com for more amazing stories from the same author.

Follow us on Twitter: https://twitter.com/FictionOdd

Facebook: https://www.facebook.com/Odd-Fiction-241902600032534/

Instagram: https://www.instagram.com/oddfiction528/

And, most importantly, leave a review on Amazon and Goodreads, especially if you want more books like this.

And while you're at it, shoot me an email and tell me just about anything in the world: oddfiction528@gmail.com.